Dedication

To Julie, my lovely wife, without whom I would be dust in the wind.

To Marc, for teaching me the way of the samurai author.

To Wilbur, for friendship from the finest fiction writer in the history of man.

To all of my teachers, who patiently armored me with knowledge.

To Kilik, for pulling me across the river.

And to you—the reader—without whom this book is nothing.

Chapter 1

*T*oday we become merciless gods.

These five words would change Antonio Pessoa's life forever.

He chanted the mantra in his mind as he surveyed the crowded lower level of the Cherry Creek Mall, gazing down from the level above. Sunlight poured through glass ceiling panels onto shoppers as they flowed around him like a living river.

His heart hammered over tranquil music wafting from a nearby shop. He lifted his hands from the railing, noting sweaty handprints left in the chrome. Would they be found later?

Of course not. Thousands of people touch these railings every day.

Detesting his fear, he smudged the prints with his forearm and dried his palms on his jeans.

We will create a new reality.

The power of Beeman's words calmed him. He pushed away his hesitation. It was time to break free. Time to become a god.

His eyes settled on a girl on the level below. His breath caught in his chest as she looked up and locked eyes with him. She was plain, heavy, and her stringy hair seemed pasted to her skull. He grinned awkwardly, repulsed by her splotchy complexion and the blank expression on her face. She looked away and kept walking.

Another reject.

But would she remember his face?

Stop! Thinking fearful thoughts causes fear.

Okay, then. But the more time he spent just standing around, the more likely it was that he would lose his nerve. He needed to find the right person and get it over with. He'd been trolling the mall for hours. Beeman would be getting impatient, which made Antonio feel—

He turned to the sound of rich feminine laughter behind him.

Two young women in white shorts strolled by. He pivoted to watch them pass. Tan, sculpted legs ending in wedge sandals thumped on the tile, an alluring rhythm to their walk. One blonde, one brunette, both pretty. Early twenties. They had the hair, the clothes, the *look*. Expensive purses and shopping bags dangled from their arms.

Pampered women leading pampered lives.

When they were a dozen feet away, he fell into step behind them.

As he matched their pace, he studied them more carefully, admiring them, stoking his imagination and igniting an inner fire that burned away his anxiety. A completely different kind of energy flowed through him now. It felt good.

Either would be perfect, but *both*?

Would it be possible?

Antonio felt the Primal Ecstasy pulsing through him, just as Beeman had predicted, and he was certain Beeman would approve; he would admire the audacity. Taking *both* women would exercise Antonio's appetites, strengthening him proportionately. The shopping bags told him they'd been here in the mall for some time. It was just past four p.m., and he figured they'd be leaving before too long.

If they split up, he'd stick with the brunette. If they headed together to one car, he would—with Beeman's approval—take both women.

At that moment, unseen and unknown, the future of every other pretty young woman happening to be in the mall that day was restored, and only Antonio knew it. He controlled so many destinies at once, simply by making this choice.

Now he was thinking like a god.

He faded back into the flow of shoppers to follow from a safe distance and texted Beeman to expect precise directions soon.

shopping done choice made expect directions soon

Beeman texted back:

Ready, at west ramp.

Now they needed some luck. It would help if the girls had parked in the west lot, as Beeman was already there. It could take him too long to circle around to the east lot if the girls moved quickly. They'd need a few minutes away from prying eyes once the action commenced, and Beeman's SUV would have to be in place before Antonio made his move.

Antonio texted again:

sites on pair of perfect ones! probly same car, get both?

He waited for a reply. Then his phone buzzed in his hand again.

Interesting. See how it plays out.

Antonio smiled and kept pace with this new prey. They seemed to be heading to the second-level exit onto the west lot, which was perfect.

• • •

Much later, Christie Jensen would agonize over the irony. She'd marveled at Jackie Dawson's skill at the art of drawing male attention, and for this, she would later curse her own naïveté. But for now, it was just a fun summer Denver afternoon shared by best friends savoring their last few weeks together before Christie left for Dartmouth to start work on her master's degree in chemical engineering.

"What do you mean, 'When I grow up'?" Jackie's laughter was infectious. "All I know is, we're going to San Diego for the weekend. That's as far ahead as I can think." Shaking her shoulders, Jackie sent ripples to her chest while tossing her lustrous brown hair over her shoulder, her signature move. "Hotel Del. I'll really make him forget about the dent."

Christie smiled and shook her head, wondering what it would be like to live Jackie's life. No school, work or career anxiety; just rich men and eventual marriage. And maybe a baby or two. If only life could be so simple. Life, liberty and the pursuit of happiness through sex with sugar daddies.

"What are you smiling about, CJ?"

"Nothing," Christie said. "You should tell him, before he sees it."

"I know, right? Like, get it behind me. But how do I tell him? Couldn't we, like, make something up? I mean, this sucks big time." Jackie sighed. "How pissed will he be?"

"Don't know, Jax. But he's under your spell, that's for sure."

"You think?" Jackie smiled. "Two-way street. And I don't care what my fosters say. Fuck them—wait, you know I don't mean that."

"I know."

"It's just—the pressure of the whole thing wears me down."

Jackie's biological parents had passed away when she was ten. Foster parents had raised her through her teens, living in a run-down apartment in Lakewood. Her current romance was with Robert Sand, an African American man, which her foster parents did not seem to mind. What made it an outright travesty for them was that at fifty-six, Sand was more than twice Jackie's age. Christie knew Jackie loved her foster parents and burned at the thought of disappointing them, but her feelings for Robert were strong—at least for now—and Sand was *hot*. Christie remembered how Jackie had first described him. *Tight as a bowstring, gentle as a puppy, a face like Denzel; a bit of gray and a ton of green, hot as black embers and warm as the sun.*

Christie's upbringing had been much different than Jackie's. Her father was one of the most successful trial lawyers in the country. He owned several homes and two jets. She'd grown up wanting for nothing.

"That's the price you pay to do your own thing," Christie said. "But the pressure comes from you, Jax. They worry, but they don't judge."

Jackie had moved out of her foster parents' apartment when she was nineteen to attend Denver University. Living on financial aid and student loans, she'd moved in with Christie, sharing an apartment for two years before dropping out to wait tables in an upscale steakhouse owned by a former NFL quarterback. There she'd met Robert, a regular customer who usually came in later in the evening when things were slower. Flirting turned into conversations, which led to meeting for coffee, dinner dates, and when things got serious, Jackie moved in with him.

With Robert, Jackie finally had a taste of an affluent lifestyle, but she swore that his money wasn't what held their relationship together. Christie believed her. She was happy for them, but she wondered if the floor would drop out, leaving Jackie once again adrift.

"Let's get out of here," Christie said. "Get it over with."

"Be with me while I tell him?" Jackie asked. "Have dinner with us?"

Christie moaned. "Bribing me with food?"

They pushed through the exit doors to the parking garage.

• • •

Antonio followed them onto the dimly lit third level of the west parking lot, whispering into his phone. "Coming out. West lot. Deck Three. Same door I came in. I'm right behind them."

There was no response.

He worked some saliva into his mouth. "I'm ready. I can do this.

We might be able to take them right here, snatch and go, like you said. Or we can follow them. Your call. But I don't see anybody around."

Beeman did not respond.

"Where are you?" Antonio asked.

After a few more seconds of silence, Beeman's voice crawled into his ear, "Look to your left."

Thirty yards away, Beeman softly revved the engine of their rented SUV.

Antonio nodded, slipped the phone into his pocket and kept walking.

•   •   •

Behind the wheel, Beeman shifted his attention to Antonio as he picked up his pace to close on the women, absorbing the whole scene as if through a microscope, studying how predatory life-forms learn to consume prey.

Beeman did not know that he was, himself, being observed, nor that his watchers were themselves under the scrutiny of others.

•   •   •

Thirty yards farther down, on the other side of the parking aisle, a sniper in the back of a dark van keyed his throat mike. He aimed the scope of his short-barrel Heckler & Koch PSG1 semiautomatic sniper rifle through one-way optical film that concealed a firing aperture in the van's armored side panel. His call sign was Skunk Two. He was a GS-12 federal employee, formerly a Hostage Rescue Team assaulter, now assigned to the elite Special Surveillance Group of the JTTF, or Joint Terrorism Task Force. He was part of the so-called Skunk Team, an elite SSG unit tasked with tracking and direct action in the containment of terror cells and foreign espionage on domestic soil. Their legal charter was murky, as they were essentially paramilitary operators functioning contrary to at least the spirit of *posse comitatus*, a statutory limitation constraining federal military operations other than training on US soil.

"Skunk Two has glass on the Wallies."

Wallies was FBI jargon, based on *Wha-lee*, Korean slang for a security officer—North Korean agents in this case, three of whom were seated in a small black BMW with darkened windows. They covertly watched Beeman—whom the FBI had assigned the code name *Farmer*—as he inched quietly forward in a rented Buick SUV, creeping closer to the two women he and Pessoa—code name *Dirt Worm*—were tracking.

"Roger, Skunk Two."

Against protocol, Skunk Two shifted his scope. "Farmer and Dirt Worm are converging on civilians with hostile intent."

"Skunk Two, text intercepts confirm imminent Code Silver." The commander spoke from a mobile command post out on the street, informing the SSG team to expect a kidnapping or hostage situation. "Do not intervene. The Code Silver is *not* our mission. We have bigger fish."

Skunk Two gripped the stock of his rifle and laid his finger gently on the trigger. "Christ, guys. Are we really going to let this play out?"

"Skunk Two, you are ten-twelve," came Skunk One's terse reply in his earpiece, meaning *hold position, take no action pending further orders.* "Long game, eyes on the prize."

The SSG team's mission brief stated the *only* subjects of interest were the North Koreans. Skunk Two should not have moved his scope away from the BMW. Too much was at stake, and it had taken too much work—and luck—to get this close to the Wallies, who might make a move on Beeman under the watchful eyes of the JTTF and the National Security Agency, or NSA.

Everyone on the SSG team was supposed to operate under specific rules of engagement, which specified that collateral damage was acceptable, particularly if it were the result of purely domestic crimes, such as assault. The women were potential casualty statistics, nothing more. The high-value prizes were the Wallies and Beeman himself. If they could roll up the North Korean, or DPRK spy ring, the intelligence harvest could help keep Kim Jong-un—known at Foggy Bottom as The Young'un—behind his fence a little while longer.

Skunk Two could only engage a target if the Wallies were to spot and assault the SSG surveillance team or make a grab for Beeman, who carried in his head information too valuable and dangerous for them to allow to fall into enemy hands.

"Roger." Skunk Two lifted his finger from the trigger and sighed deeply as he refocused his scope on the BMW. This was the overarching tactical plan. National security took priority. He would simply observe unless ordered to engage.

But Christ, it did suck. He had a daughter of his own.

Chapter 2

As the girls approached a gleaming green Jaguar XKE Roadster, Antonio could just make out what they were saying. Slowing his pace, he watched them carefully. The brunette started to get in on the driver's side but seemed to change her mind. She stepped around to the passenger side and set her shopping bag on the cement behind the car. The blonde did the same and bent down to run her hand across the fender.

Antonio noticed a dent just above the right-rear wheel well.

The brunette groaned. "What's another ding? The whole car has to be repainted, right?"

"I don't know," the blonde responded, feeling the damage with her fingers.

"Ouch!" Antonio said, startling the girls as he spoke from behind them. "What happened?"

The girls stood and turned to face him. "Oh, I was backing out of a parking spot," explained the brunette, "and this old dude bumped us. Didn't see him coming. Actually, he was the one who didn't see me coming. I was backing out to get lined up better."

Antonio shrugged and kept smiling. "Happens all the time." He couldn't believe how this was landing in his lap. Now he had to play it cool, not try too hard, roll with it and project confidence. He choked down his fear, and an idea came to him.

Beeman was right. The magic will blossom.

"Shame! Such a nice car. Vintage. What year?"

The brunette turned to touch the dent. "It's a '67. Think they can fix it?"

Antonio knew right then how it was going to work. "They? Hell, *I* can fix it, right here and now, if you want. Paint's fine—you just need a special tool."

A dark green SUV pulled to a stop behind the Jaguar. At the wheel a kindly looking older man smiled gave a casual wave.

"That's my dad. Tools are in the car. You got a few minutes?"

"You can really fix that?" The brunette asked.

"Sure. Twenty minutes, tops. You'll never know it was there. I'll show you how and explain it before I touch anything." He held out his hand. "Jimmy Rivers," he said, nodding toward the SUV. "I work in my dad's body shop. Should I give it a shot? Do it for free."

"What's the name of the shop?" The blonde asked.

"Dad's Body Shop," Antonio laughed. "That's my dad, Sam Rivers."

The blonde looked uncertain, but the brunette shook his hand. "I'm Jackie and this is Christie, and yeah, that'd be great!"

"How do you do it?" Christie asked, shifting her purse from one arm to the other so that she too could shake hands. "Don't you have to take stuff apart to get in behind the dent?"

"Well, that's the easy part," Antonio said. Stepping to the SUV, he lifted the back hatch and unzipped a canvas bag. "We go in through the trunk. The magic is in the equipment." Antonio lowered his voice slightly. "This is a trade secret. If it got out, we'd be out of business; these tools are so easy to use. See?"

The girls stepped closer, better to hear and see the special tools.

Antonio turned to face them with what appeared to be two garage door openers, one in each hand.

"No, no! Jackie—" Christie started, recognizing the devices.

Antonio fired the Tasers at point-blank range, sending pairs of small darts into the belly of each girl, first one and then the other.

Snap! Snap!

Five seconds later the girls lay prone at Antonio's feet, jerking and twitching as more than sixty thousand volts coursed through their bodies. He quickly bundled handfuls of the thin wire that fed current to the darts, stuffing the expended units back into the canvas bag. Then he zipped the bag shut and tossed it into the rear compartment. The rear seats were folded forward to make extra room.

Beeman sprang from the car and lifted Christie into the back of the Buick.

As Antonio lifted Jackie in his arms, he was surprised by how light she was. He could feel the weight and shape of her; the shimmering silky feel of her skin electrified him. He set her down in the back of the SUV. Before Antonio expected it, the girls were moaning, beginning to come around.

"Hush," Beeman hissed, pointing an aerosol can in their faces and spraying until they went still, and for several more seconds for good measure. He pulled a blanket over them, holding his breath and stepping back to remain clear of the vapor.

Antonio snatched up the shopping bags and purses, tossed them in with the girls and duffle bag and slammed the hatch. "Let's move," he said, looking furtively about for witnesses. Seeing nothing, they climbed into the SUV and pulled away, Beeman gently spiraling around the many corners to reach the ground-level exit.

"Why so slow?" Antonio asked breathlessly.

"Why draw attention?" Beeman responded.

"Think we were seen?"

"No, but we'll know soon enough. Once we make it to the storage shed and switch cars, we should be fine. They should stay out long enough to get them into my trunk. Then we hit the road, but remember to ditch their cell phones, or we'll lead the cops straight to us."

"God, you're right! I almost forgot about that." Antonio slapped the dashboard as they turned out of the drive and into the street. The sunlight seemed incredibly bright as they merged into the flow of traffic.

"Five hours, and we'll be at the cabin," Beeman announced.

Chapter 3

Christie's eyes fluttered as she fought to reach the surface. She swam as hard as she could through hot volcanic lava. Something very important was waiting at the surface. She had to reach it. But she was running out of breath.

A blazing red light flared in her mind and then vanished. After a time, it returned again, but only briefly. Would it guide her to the surface like a beacon? She needed to reach the surface, where she could breathe, but currents were throwing her about. With great effort, she pried her eyelids open. A blossoming flare of red light chased away the darkness.

Then total darkness once again. And extreme heat. A familiar sound, almost like waves breaking on a beach.

Where was she?

Her mind slowly began to clear, but she couldn't breathe properly. *Oh, my God!*

There was something in her mouth!

She tried to reach for her face, to clear away whatever was blocking her mouth. Her face tingled with panic when she realized her arms would not respond. Where were her hands?

Her breath came through her nose in short, urgent sniffs. She tried to turn over, to straighten out her legs, but something was holding her in place.

She felt movement and vibration.

Another realization: the red light was a *brake light*.

She was bound and gagged—hogtied—in the trunk of a moving car!

She couldn't get enough air.

Her chest heaved as she struggled against whatever was binding her wrists and legs behind her. She tried to scream but gave only a muffled squeal that pushed more mucous into her already clogged nasal passages, making it even more difficult to get any air. Fueled by adrenaline, her body's demand for oxygen was rapidly exceeding what she could sip in the hot, dank and confined trunk. She gagged again and again on whatever was in her mouth and feared she might drown in her own vomit. Her terror grew to be overwhelming.

Having reached its apex, her awareness now declined rapidly.

The red light flashed briefly, and when it vanished, she went with it, sinking into merciful oblivion. Her last conscious thought was that someone was lying next to her in the darkness.

• • •

"I never could have done this alone," Antonio said as they descended from the western side of the Eisenhower Tunnel toward Silverthorne, driving with the flow of weekend traffic on I-70.

Beeman gazed out the window, a faint smile on his lips. "Actually, you could," he said softly. "On your own, eventually, you would have evolved this far. You proved that today."

"But you know the path."

"History teaches us the path," Beeman intoned in the hypnotic drone Antonio found so comforting, "For thousands of years, men have risen to positions of greatness by rejecting the bondage of conventionality. Thomas Jefferson took liberties as he saw fit with the slaves on his plantation before becoming a great American president. Alexander conquered the known world—using cruelty, ruthlessness and cunning—as did Genghis Khan. They chose to lead through domination, taking whatever they wanted and cultivating their own power as they tightened their grips on all who came into their worlds. Ruthless men who never held themselves back."

Beeman's voice grew even more electric. The power he radiated comforted Antonio.

"Their appetites were legendary. Think how fulfilled they were, wielding supreme power. Venting their ruthlessness, like a panther or a lion. This *is* nature's way. Those men rose to greatness because *they obeyed their primal nature.* They allowed great power to flow through them and bent the world to their will."

"Today we become gods," Antonio recited, "by choice and without mercy."

Beeman nodded. "Exactly."

Antonio heaved a great sigh. "I'll be glad when we're there. I could really use a drink."

"We'll take our time getting settled in," Beeman said with a relaxed smile. "No point in rushing into things when we're too tired to enjoy. A good night's rest is what we need."

"You're right." Antonio was emotionally and physically drained. His inner doubts and demons were coming back, even though Beeman was right beside him. The power of Beeman's words was not enough to hold him together, and his hands were beginning to shake.

"Care for a breath strip?" Beeman offered.

"Sure. Thanks." Antonio dropped the minty sheet onto his tongue.

Within a couple of minutes, he was feeling so much better.

Chapter 4

The golden sea welcomed the sun as it dipped into the shimmering waters of the Pacific Ocean. From a hilltop high above the beach, two men on horseback gazed in silence as the bright bands of the western sky dissolved, growing deeper and darker, until the first stars began to appear. A hundred feet below, the surf crashed against the rocks of the southern California coast.

Mark Jensen shifted comfortably in his saddle, savoring the cool ocean breeze. He could practically feel the joy that emanated from the younger man beside him. *I could sit here like this for hours*, he thought, but after a while he said, "Better head back. We don't want to be late." He twisted the reins in his palm and twitched his heel lightly against his horse's ribs, guiding the animal back to the path that would take them home. Twenty minutes later as they crested a small butte, he could see his ranch-style home nested in the darkening plateau below. The trail widened on a broad sloping field, cutting diagonally down to the house and stables.

Rob Davis spurred his mount to come abreast of Jensen now that the path was wide enough. He cleared his throat and shifted in his saddle.

"This is kind of hard to say," he said. "I'm only an employee, and I'm new to the practice, but you've done so much for me. I just want to say thank you."

"For this ride?"

"More than that," Rob said. "The mentoring. For teaching me how to be a trial lawyer."

Jensen nodded. "You're a quick study."

Rob had won his first jury verdict the day before, landing $3.6 million for a boy who'd been badly burned when a defective propane stove had exploded in his face. To celebrate his victory, a firm dinner would begin in ninety minutes or so, at Roscoe's, an upscale Newport Beach restaurant a few miles north of Jensen's ranch.

Rob continued. "Here I am, riding horseback with Mark Jensen. Like we're old cronies, and I'm only two years out. It isn't lost on me how—"

"Oh, I see," Jensen said with a chuckle. "You're riding with a figure from history. Jesus, I've never felt so old."

"That's not what I meant. Shit—forget I said anything."

"Okay. Forgotten. Now, what were you saying?"

"Can't remember."

Jensen grinned. Among the younger associates working at Jensen, Marshall & Minard, Rob Davis was his favorite. His real name was Robin Davis, but he hated being called Robin, and Jensen didn't want his sidekick to be named Robin because he didn't want to be called Batman. So Rob it was.

Jensen chuckled. The million-dollar contingency fee the young associate had generated certainly didn't hurt his standing, but it wasn't the primary reason Jensen liked him—nor was it the hero-worship routine. Rob had class, whatever that meant, and a certain charisma that complimented his rugged looks. When he was a little older and wiser, he would have the world at his feet.

"We're all really proud of you, Rob," Jensen told him. "You're off to a hell of a start."

Rob flashed a thousand-watt smile. "Guess I did alright, huh?"

"I reckon you did." Jensen leaned over and clapped Davis on the shoulder, remembering how he'd felt at that stage in his own career. "Let's get on down the trail, pilgrim," he said in a poor imitation of the Duke, giving his horse a gentle prod with the heel of his boot. The animal was eager to reach the barn and broke into a brisk trot.

Within a few minutes they reached the ranch house. "There's Mrs. Jensen," Davis said, gesturing as he dismounted. "I thought she and Amy were supposed to meet us at the restaurant."

Jensen followed his gaze. "That's what I thought," he said.

As they drew closer, Jensen could read on his wife's face that something was seriously wrong. Still in her jeans, she hadn't dressed for dinner. Her arms were crossed tightly in front of her chest. As she turned to say something through the open doorway behind her, two uniformed police officers stepped onto the porch.

Jensen was instantly on guard. He had a deep-seated mistrust of police—a product of working in the criminal justice system for many years. He no longer actively handled criminal cases, but the lessons he'd learned had been hard ones he couldn't easily forget.

Was one of his civil clients in trouble? Were they going to serve him with a subpoena? Or was it something worse?

"Officers," Jensen said, reaching the porch. "What's going on?"

One of the cops glanced at a notepad. "Are you Mark Stader Jensen? Father of Christine Ann Jensen?"

Oh, dear Lord in heaven. Jensen gripped the reins tightly and swallowed.

"Yes. What's going on?"

"And may I ask who this gentleman is?"

"This is my associate, Rob Davis. Is Christie okay? What's this about?"

"I'm Officer Cisneros and this is Officer Nakayama, Irvine PD. We need to speak with you and your wife, sir."

Jensen was growing more worried by the second. "What's this about? Has something happened?"

"It might be better if we could go inside," Nakayama said, glancing conspicuously at Davis, "so we can talk privately."

Jensen dismounted and handed his reins to Davis. "Rob, would you mind taking the horses to the barn? Mike will see to them after that. Feel free to grab a shower and head over. I'll text you when I know if we're going to make it. Don't hold things up for us. I'm sure everybody's hungry."

"Sure." Davis dismounted, took the reins from Jensen's hand and led both horses away.

Jensen gestured for the policemen to follow him inside, guiding them to a cavernous sitting room adorned with Navajo rugs and pottery, wood carvings and other Native American artifacts.

"Okay, officers. What's going on?"

"Mr. Jensen," Cisneros began, "As I've explained to your wife, the Denver Police Department contacted us. They're investigating a complaint from someone who claims to be living with a friend of your daughter." The officer consulted his pad again. "Do you know Jaqueline Rosalie Dawson?"

Jensen felt a touch of relief. So this wasn't about Christie. What was it with cops and the incessant need to use middle names always?

"Yes, officer, we've met Ms. Dawson" said Janet. "Has something happened to her?"

Rather than answering, Cisneros asked, "Do you know Robert Sand?"

Janet answered, "We've never met him, but Christie's mentioned him."

Cisneros nodded and then consulted his pad once more. "Yes. An older man. We know virtually nothing about him, other than he appears to be affluent and claims to be retired. He filed a missing persons report with DPD—the Denver police. He claims Dawson moved in with him recently and is now a missing person. He reported that she and your daughter took his car to go shopping at two in the afternoon, and never returned. Dawson doesn't answer her cell. Apparently, they told Sand they were going to a mall not far from his home and would be back in time to go out for dinner. When they hadn't returned by midnight, the DPD sent a cruiser to troll the parking garages. They found Sand's car there, unlocked, with the key in the door."

Cisneros looked up from his pad. "Do you know where your daughter is now?"

Jensen looked at his watch. It was 9:45 in Denver. This didn't make sense. "Midnight? What time were they supposed to be back?"

"By eighteen hundred at the latest," Nakayama answered. "Yesterday, that is."

"They've been missing more than twenty-four hours?"

"According to Sand."

"Have they checked *Christie's* apartment?"

"Yes. No response to their knock. They didn't enter the unit."

"Have they checked with Jackie's foster parents?"

Nakayama nodded. "Scott and Anne Dawson. They haven't spoken to Jaqueline or Christine for several days."

"Have they checked to see if Christie's car is parked at her apartment? She drives a red Toyota Highlander."

"Her vehicle is still parked in front of Sand's house," Cisneros said. "You obviously have a lot of useful information and ideas. Will you and your wife come to the station and give us recorded statements?"

"Hang on a second." Jensen pulled out his iPhone and tapped the screen several times, putting the call on speaker. Christie's voice mail greeting echoed through the tinny speakers. Jensen left a short message, telling her to call him.

"She has an iPhone," Jensen said, tapping the screen of his phone some more. "We can use Find My Friends to find out where she is."

"Please go ahead." Nakayama said. "Very helpful, sir. Thank you."

After a several seconds, Jensen looked up. "Not finding it," he said, glancing at Janet. Her face was ashen. He felt his own heartbeat picking up. When he'd been a young pilot in the Air Force, flying combat missions in the First Gulf War, he'd lost friends he thought were invincible, immortal. In his law practice, he'd seen families shattered by unexpected disasters. Catastrophe strikes where and when it will, he'd learned, and survivors were always slow to recognize it when it appeared, cushioned as they were by warm cocoons of faith and belief from undeniable realities, the fragility of life and the dangers of the world.

Now, at this very unexpected moment, were he and his wife next in line?

"Let's head in," Nakayama said.

"I'd like to talk to the Denver police directly," Jensen said.

"We'll arrange that," Cisneros replied.

Chapter 5

The ancient Super Otter clawed the air as it lumbered ever upward, eleven thousand feet above the Arizona desert. At this altitude the air was mercifully cool; the desert below baked in the late afternoon sun. An endless quilted patchwork of agricultural land spread beneath them from horizon to horizon, scarred and torn by roads and irrigation canals. To the southeast, rocky spires erupted sharply from the desert—otherworldly remnants of the volcanic age.

A pocket of turbulence rocked the high-winged jump-ship as it turned, confining its climb within a block of airspace west of the town of Eloy, Arizona. Two Pratt & Whitney PT-6 turboprop engines churned out more than a thousand horsepower, so most of the plane's twenty-three jumpers had foam earplugs stuffed in their ears to soften the grinding roar within the cramped cabin.

Roady Kenehan sat on the floor at the rear of the plane, next to a clear plexiglass door. His long hair was braided and tucked down the back of his jumpsuit, and his week-old beard was beginning to darken and fill out. He glanced at the altimeter strapped to his leg strap —another thousand feet to go.

Jump-run in about two minutes.

He pulled his visor down, tugged his chin strap snug, checked that his visor was snapped and then zipped his jump suit all the way up to his throat.

The plane made one more turn and leveled off.

Kenehan rocked forward onto his knees and extended his hand, winding his gloved fingers with three other jumpers, pumping slowly *down* then *up* then *down* again before snapping the communal fist apart in silent rehearsal of the rhythm of their exit count, the way they would signal one another for a perfect simultaneous departure from the door of the airplane.

This ritual complete, he turned and slid the door upward on its teflon tracks. A fierce, cold wind swirled through the cabin. He would exit from the "front float" position, so he'd be the first to climb out into the slipstream.

A light beside the door changed from red to yellow.

Slow is smooth. Smooth is fast.

The light turned green. He leaned out to check the aircraft's position, feeling the wind pressing against his helmet. The runway was directly below, nearly three miles down. They were in perfect position for a windless day.

Time to go.

He reached up with his right hand, grabbing a steel bar above the door outside the fuselage. Pivoting his left shoulder into the slipstream, he climbed out, fighting the wind, perched by the toe of one running shoe on the bottom edge of the floor. He side-hopped to his left, toward the front of the plane, to make room in the door for two more jumpers to climb out. The last member of the four-way team squatted just inside the door, gripping Roady's arm and the chest strap of the man beside him, who made eye contact all around—a signal that all were ready to launch.

The center jumper raised his chin, dipped it, and the four men dropped away from the plane as one, in perfect unison. Kenehan turned in the air so that his feet pointed skyward, facing "down the hill," locking eyes with the man opposite him.

The four skydivers released and repeatedly gripped each other, released their grips, turned and re-gripped, forming pattern after pattern, like flying square-dancers. In the skydiving world, this was called "turning points." Each separate formation was a point. Kenehan counted nineteen before his helmet-mounted computer chimed the twenty-second mark. He was amazed at the speed and grace of the other three men who, unlike him, were all present or former world-champion skydivers.

Point after point, they moved in unison for nearly a full minute, seemingly floating, belly to earth, backs arched, heads up and arms cupped beneath their chins in a position known as "the mantis," which only the finest skydivers can maintain and fly. All too soon, altitude-sensing units in their helmets beeped the four thousand foot warning. It was time for them to break apart their formation, track away from each other like a human starburst and then deploy their parachutes.

Flaring out of his track, Kenehan cupped his arms and torso for a second or two to slow down. Then he reached behind him, gripped a leather ball at the bottom of his parachute container, jerked it loose and released it into the wind.

It is amazing that four seconds can become an eternity of help-lessness, but that's what happens after deploying a parachute—every time.

Kenehan waited—four long seconds.

When a parachute opens, the jolt is reassuringly severe, but this time Kenehan felt only a slight tug before the earth began to spin madly beneath him.

Centrifugal force pulled his chin to his chest, and he fought to lift his head, struggling to see his canopy. What he saw made him swear in his full-face helmet: a tangled bundle of nylon cupped at one end like a funnel.

Line twist—tangled slider.

No fixing this one.

His life expectancy was now down to about ten seconds unless he did the next bit perfectly.

The horizon was spinning faster. With his left hand, he gripped a small nylon pillow protruding from his harness on his left side,

peeled it quickly from its Velcro housing and yanked it to full extension to jettison the malfunctioning main canopy.

He was tossed like a Frisbee, spinning with his back to the
ground, away from the misshapen bundle of useless nylon. It took
another two seconds for him to roll, like a cat, belly to earth in a stable arch. He pulled his reserve chute with his right hand.

His reserve exploded open, slamming him into his harness. Relief
flooded through him, making him feel giddy.

Spank me, baby!

Without losing his reserve handle or cutaway pillow, he looped
his index fingers through the steering loops of his small reserve
canopy and flew toward the landing zone, a square of grass the size of
a soccer field next to an old row of hangars. The air grew warmer as
he approached the desert floor. Thirty seconds later, he was on the
ground. Condensed water droplets appeared for a few seconds on
the still-cold nylon of his jump suit. His yellow reserve canopy dangled from his hand by loops of thin nylon cord.

He shuffled into the hangar, dropped his canopy, reserve handles
and helmet on a clean patch of carpet, and shimmied out of his harness and jump suit. Then he wandered out into the desert to find his
main canopy.

Shit. Now he was done for the day—and the trip. There wasn't
time for a repack. The vacation was over. The Group had ordered
him to report for a training exercise in Florida.

•   •   •

Kenehan worked for the Brecht Group, a private company that
supplied its worldwide clientele with corporate intelligence, private
security, global threat assessment, hostage negotiation and rescue,
and other services less well known in the private sector, but con-
tracted frequently by certain governments. The Brecht Group had
offices in Charleston, London, Rome, Paris and Munich, and a new
office had just opened in Moscow, to the great amusement of the

company's aging founder, Albert Brecht. The company's Central Operations Headquarters, or COHQ, was in Baltimore, where the , then called Information Security Services, or ISS, had first formed in 1959. Older veterans still called it ISS, though the name had changed more than twenty years ago. Out of the roughly ten companies capable of competing with it in the global arena, the Brecht Group was among the oldest and largest, certainly the most prestigious and the most expensive provider of its specialized services.

Kenehan's immediate senior was Dave Thomas, a former Secret Service agent with advanced degrees in international studies and international law. Thomas had ordered Kenehan to report to the company's enormous training facility in Florida in two days. Kenehan was sorry to end this long-overdue and all-too-brief period of downtime.

He'd recently finished a long, arduous and very dangerous assignment that had ended successfully, but violently, in the Mediterranean. For the past three months, he'd been working undercover aboard the Italian freighter *MV Cogliano* under the guise of a deckhand, infiltrating a criminal cartel known as Hydrus.

The seaborne mafia of the Mediterranean, Hydrus specialized in extortion, theft, piracy, sabotage and insurance fraud.

A coalition of insurance and shipping companies had pooled their resources to contract with the Brecht Group to achieve what international law enforcement agencies had failed to—delivering a knockout punch to Hydrus and stem the escalating financial bleeding the syndicate's criminal operations had caused.

The *MV Cogliano* had been the floating headquarters of one of Hydrus's top leaders, Don Pietro Savagnelli. Masquerading as an ordinary maritime shipping vessel carrying loads of perfectly legitimate cargo, the vessel had afforded senior Hydrus henchmen the essential cover, mobility and access to the inner workings of the modern maritime world that fostered their criminal enterprises.

Kenehan's undercover work had culminated in the vessel's seizure during a massive gun battle between the ship's crew and *Gruppo Operativo Incursori*. These Italian naval special forces were part of a branch of COMSUBIN, or *Comando Subacquei ed Incursori*—the Raiders and Divers Group of the Italian Navy. GOI commandos had stormed the *Cogliano* off the coast of Sardinia, saving Kenehan's life after he had burst-transmitted hours of covertly recorded video and audio. He'd delivered sufficient evidence to convict most of Hydrus's leaders and hopefully break the organization's back.

Kenehan had lived for months in horrible conditions below deck while working eighteen-hour daily shifts. The assignment had been all but complete when his cover had been blown. Before the GOI insertion team had scaled the side of the ship, a steward had found Kenehan rifling through documents in the captain's cabin. The steward had held him at gunpoint, calling for help on his belt-mounted radio. The ship's first officer—also a senior member of the criminal cabal—had arrived within seconds.

Bleating in Italian, Kenehan had protested his innocence.

The first officer would have none of it and had marched Kenehan at gunpoint out onto the deck, shoving him against the rail with the muzzle of a cheap Beretta jammed into the base of his skull. Facing out to sea with the man at his back, Kenehan had expected immediate execution. He'd seen it before: one round to the base of the skull and they'd shove his body over the rail and into the sea.

Switching to French, Kenehan had shouted that he was with Interpol and that several other law enforcement agents were aboard the vessel. Demanding details, the first officer had jammed the Beretta harder into the back of Kenehan's head, as if to scoop the information out of his brain by force. Then in English—which he knew the first officer did not understand—Kenehan recited part of an old American poem. While drawling the words, he'd slipped a Microtech Ultratech, a slender front-opening stiletto—and a Delta favorite—from his waistband.

"Strange things are done in the midnight sun," he'd intoned, snapping the scalpel-sharp blade into position, his hand and the knife hidden behind the rail. "By the men who moil for gold. You understand? They moil for gold. In the midnight sun. *Capiche?*"

Straining to understand this jibberish, made harder by a stiff ocean breeze, the first officer had pulled Kenehan's shoulder, turning him to stare down the barrel of the pistol. Kenehan had rammed the blade deep into the man's abdomen just above his belt, stripping the gun away from the dying man with his other hand, twisting and pulling the blade upward with all his strength. The tanto blade had glided through skin, muscle and viscera, opening a long, deep furrow in the man's belly. A fountain of bright red blood had gushed forth, soaking the officer's white uniform.

Then all hell had broken loose. Kenehan had found himself running, shooting and cursing, blood-soaked and outnumbered, with nowhere to hide. The Beretta had held fifteen rounds in a staggered clip; Kenehan had eventually brought down six more men before holing up, out of ammunition, in a winch house on the afterdeck. *Oh, Mama, I'm in fear for my life... The jig is up, the news is out, they've finally found me.*

Just then, the GOI boys had come aboard.

• • •

Now, hiking through the Arizona desert, Kenehan shook the image of the bloody carnage from his mind as he came upon his tangled main canopy. Fifty feet farther on, he found his freebag and kicker plate, tethered to its spring-loaded pilot chute. Wadding them under his sweaty arm, he headed back through the scrub to the drop zone.

By the time he reached the hangar, his jump-mates had already finished repacking their chutes and were in the process of planning another dive. They knew he was out of the game for a while, as his reserve would have to be professionally re-packed by a licensed rigger. He took his gear to the rigger's loft and left it with the man who had saved his life by packing his reserve the last time. Next, he grabbed a sandwich and a cold soda before climbing into his rented Nissan.

The inside of the car was as hot as a kiln.

He started the car, lowered the windows and waited for the air conditioning to get going as he drove slowly along the dirt road to the highway, leaving a massive plume of dust in his wake. He glanced at his watch—a Panerai the GOI boys gave him last month—the fabled timepiece of the Italian frogman. It would take him an hour to reach Phoenix. He'd grab a shower and then catch the evening flight to Orlando. Arriving a full day early would give him a chance to get a last bit of rest before the exercise commenced.

He paired his phone to the car's audio system and scrolled through his playlists, settling on "Let's Ride" by Kid Rock.

Cold air was finally blowing from the vents. He raised the windows and settled in, sipping his Diet Pepsi, enjoying the song, a SpecWar anthem from when he was Army Combat Applications Group, or CAG—formerly known as Delta. He'd served in it before transferring to the Central Intelligence Agency, the CIA's elite Special Operations Group. The boys had sometimes listened to the song before missions so they could get into the right mind-set, instead of thinking about the letters their wives would get—which his current boss called "Letters to Mama." By force of habit, he kept an eye on his rearview mirror and his speed close to the limit, but he let his mind wander as he cruised through the Arizona desert.

Chapter 6

The stench rose up and hit Antonio like a punch. The rancid odor made him gag as he lifted the trunk lid and peered into the dark space.

Beeman stood a few feet away under the yellow glare of a single bulb.

The girls were no longer dazzling.

They looked like cadavers spooned together.

Antonio couldn't tell if they were breathing. They'd been in the trunk for so long, it wouldn't surprise him if they were dead. *Am I already a murderer?* He wasn't ready for that—at least not yet. He'd shielded his mind from what he knew must come eventually.

In horrid fascination, he bent down for a closer look, holding his nose and breathing shallowly through his mouth.

Both of the young women had emptied their bladders—more than once, perhaps—and brown ooze was leaking through the brunette's white cotton shorts. That was bad enough, but she'd also puked. Had she drowned in her own vomit? The tape had somehow peeled away from her mouth, so he didn't think so. Her cheek lay in a puddle of slime that had soaked into the coarse carpet lining of the trunk. Spotting a piece of undigested food in the goo, Antonio had an overpowering urge to turn and run, to empty his own stomach somewhere in the darkness beyond Beeman's driveway.

Relief flooded through him when first one and then another pair of dull, listless eyes opened, turning eventually upward to see him. The girls gradually started to squirm against their bonds. Yet he could not bring himself to move or speak.

A peculiar tingle crept upward along his arms and shoulders as he gazed into the blonde's widening eyes. The gleam of raw terror now replaced her vacant stare. Antonio felt drawn to the blue orbs glaring silently back at his own. He felt a connection, a brief but intimate contact, a psychic electricity passing between them with a shared jolt of realization.

This was happening.

Antonio, like her, was living through something totally beyond any past experience, beyond imagination. As he stared into her eyes, they *shared* the unreal nightmare. Her eyes remained locked in the primal connection that binds predator to prey.

Antonio looked away. He had crossed a line. His life would never be the same.

He filled his lungs, and the vile odor that radiated from the open trunk assaulted him again. He stepped back into the darkened driveway and took several more deep breaths, the cool mountain air clearing his head a little.

"Are you alright?" Beeman asked softly.

The engine ticked as it cooled. A cricket chirped nearby. The sounds grew louder, or so it seemed, as Antonio realized that Beeman was staring at him intently. Shadows from the bare bulb overhead sharpened his normally soft face.

Antonio looked back at Beeman and said nothing.

A faint, cold smile formed on Beeman's small mouth. He turned and pressed the button on the wall to bring down the garage door. The harsh, intrusive squeal of metal rollers broke the stillness. Antonio stepped back into the garage, ducking under the door. Silence returned as the door closed and the motor came to a stop.

Beeman held the can of aerosolized tranquilizer against his leg as he stepped around to look into the trunk himself. Leaning in, he loomed over the tear-streaked faces that peered up at him from the darkness.

Venom poured from his mouth as he spoke.

"*Dirty* girls," he hissed, his voice laced with menace. "Is this how your parents raised you? To soil yourselves on the first date?"

Holding the can where they could see it, he continued. "We use this to control animals in our lab—dogs, monkeys and other beasts —when we take them from their cages ... for experiments. Some of them struggle, try to bite. So we use this to control them."

He handed the can to Antonio and pulled a hunting knife from a sheath hidden beneath his waistband. The beautiful, hollow-ground blade was polished to a mirror finish. He waved it back and forth hypnotically a few inches from the girls' faces before touching the needle-sharp tip with his thumb, piercing his skin. A drop of bright red blood formed quickly. He smeared it on the lips of the blonde as she clamped her eyes and mouth in terror.

The blood looked like black lipstick in the dim light.

"My word, this shade suits you," Beeman said softly. "It compliments your bloodshot eyes. I wonder how it goes with your own blood?" He pressed the flat part of his blade to her cheek.

Muffled squeals and whimpers rose from the darkness as both girls began to struggle in panic against their bonds.

"What's that?" Beeman said as though he could understand them. "You want to know more about the experiments?" Wide, wet eyes followed the polished steel of the blade as Beeman carefully repositioned the blade's sharp edge against the side of the blonde's slender neck. Her face went red, and a squeal of terror and despair trumpeted through her nose. She clamped her eyes shut again, her body shaking violently.

The brunette screamed loudly, realizing her mouth was no longer taped shut.

Beeman sheathed his knife and took the can from Antonio. Aiming carefully, he pressed the button twice, sending jets of mist into each of the terrified faces. The girls went still.

Silence returned to the garage, broken only by the ticking of the engine as it cooled and Beeman's soft chuckle.

"A frightened animal with elevated respiration ingests more of the drug."

In the confined space of the garage, the odor of the spray made Antonio's head swim. He brought his arm to his face and breathed through the crook of his bent elbow, using the fabric of his shirt as a makeshift filter.

Beeman stepped back and lowered his arm.

"Goodnight, children."

Chapter 7

Mark Jensen slouched in a heavy leather chair in the den of his home in Irvine, twenty miles north of his Newport ranch, gazing without seeing through beveled glass panes of a French door. Though his body was slack, his mind was racing.

At the conclusion of jury trials, after finishing his closing argument and handing his client's case over to the jury, Jensen often returned to his seat with a vague sense of grief. From that moment, he was powerless to do anything but wait for the verdict. Pacing empty courtrooms while juries deliberated, he replayed trials in his mind, willing the time to pass quickly.

It never did.

This was worse.

Courtrooms are fearsome places, where lives are changed and sometimes destroyed, where on occasion he could chisel out a way for ruined lives to begin rebuilding. But now that he was a civil practitioner and no longer a criminal prosecutor, his trial career no longer involved actual life-or-death stakes. There was always a list of pending cases from which to pick the next new challenge, the next battle. A fresh adventure always beckoned. The end of a case was only that—and his career marched on. By never forgetting this, he'd become fearless in the courtroom. He was neither complacent nor paralyzed by fear.

He'd learned a lot about managing fear in the Air Force, before trial tactics and dodging objections had replaced air combat tactics and dodging surface-to-air missiles.

By pinpointing what makes a case difficult and approaching that challenge as a source of pleasure—if not outright fun—he'd become *lethal* in court. A lawyer who actually enjoys kicking ass and serving people can become a veritable force of nature. The best trial lawyers in America respected Jensen for his brilliant tactical mind, his courtroom poise and presence. They envied him for his hallmark ability to remain cool under pressure—smooth, brilliant and unflappable. And always, always prepared for whatever happened.

His secret: never lose sight of the fact that trials were a *game*.

Other lawyers sometimes hated him because he often refused to take things as seriously as they did. To those practitioners, Jensen was worse than cocky—he was remorseless and unremitting. But what made it unbearable for some (including a few judges) was the fact that he rarely showed signs of stress or dread or even concern until he was in front of a jury. Some accused him of being a phony because the persona he brought into a trial before a jury was entirely different from his demeanor in conference rooms. When courtroom matters involved only the judge, as in the case of motions practice, he rarely even bothered to appear. He had gifted associates for that, which contributed to his elitist, above-it-all reputation.

No, he wasn't invincible—he merely pretended. Maybe a little too hard. He was feeling the remorse that comes to a man with much hubris when he finds himself in a situation that makes him feel terrified and helpless.

Oh, how the mighty fall.

Over the years, he'd developed a mastery of his craft, amassing great wealth along the way. Now he practiced law purely for pleasure. While he wanted for nothing, he was never bored. Money made life easy, and the challenge of his work made it interesting. His growing reputation gave him the opportunity to work on only the most fascinating, compelling and lucrative cases, winning most of them, which fueled what he thought was his mystique. He was at the pinnacle of his career. Television cameras favored his face and voice. His charisma, money and humor charmed women—though he had never been a womanizer—and people greeted him with enthusiasm most places he went. People he'd never met bragged that they knew him. They dropped his name in influential circles from Hollywood to Wall Street. He'd authored several books that sold surprisingly well, and there was no end in sight.

His way of life had him constantly skirting the edge of some cliff, some precipice. Perhaps he'd missed finding the balance between confidence and humility, between pride and self-delusion, between ambition and greed. While his cool demeanor—a signature trait of many fighter pilots—helped him to thrive in the high-stakes trial work that often eats lawyers alive, now he felt that his karma had circled back on him.

Where was the boldness, the icy calm that had been his hallmark when he'd been flying Strike Eagles over the deserts of Iraq?

Gone. Now there was more at stake than he could possibly bear to lose.

His daughter's life.

This was no game. If anything happened to Christie, he wasn't sure he could cope with life. His wife Janet would surely crumble, and he was pretty sure he would as well.

"No man is as vulnerable as a man with a daughter," he whispered.

Late last night the Irvine police had sent him home to wait for a call from the Denver cops. The passing hours had been torture. He'd fallen asleep in his chair more than once, startled awake over and over again, as though his brain was shorting out. He couldn't bring himself to crawl into bed. If he did he'd just toss about in a hell-stew of anxiety. He felt he had to be upright just so he could breathe. It was easier to try to sleep in his chair, but every time he started to drift away, horrible pictures would intrude upon him like dream-demons guarding the realm of sleep to keep him out.

Images of Christie as a toddler, stamping her feet in a rain puddle.

Holding her as a baby in his arms. A suffocating moment of agony blistered his mind as he imagined police telling him they'd found her dead. He pictured Janet hearing the news, how the agony in her features would carve his heart out of his chest.

Knock it off!

He pulled his mind back into the here and now, forcing himself to concentrate on what was real. *No more runaway imaginings*, he told himself. *All we know is that she's missing, nothing more. She could be anywhere.*

He tapped the screen of his iPhone: 3:59 a.m.

He swiped the slider and touched Christie's name on the glass, watching her picture appear beneath her number for what must have been the hundredth time, noting his battery was nearly gone.

Straight to voice mail once again.

He touched END without leaving another message and reached across his desk to plug in his phone.

Now what?

Before him sat a yellow pad on which he'd scribbled a few pages of notes during the night, recording in detail what he'd pried out of the Irvine police during his interview. None of it seemed to help.

Christie, where are you, honey?

It was appalling that she'd been missing for more than twenty-four hours before the police had seen fit to contact him. The Denver police had been about as helpful as a barbell to a drowning man. They couldn't even figure out who was in charge, it seemed, as they'd passed him from officer to officer. Strange.

What was going on in Denver?

It reeked of confusion and uncertainty—but that wasn't all.

Jensen had a nagging feeling that somehow there was more to it than just bureaucratic bumbling. He couldn't say why, but he had a gut sense of something malignant in the way the Denver police had dealt with him. An inner voice honed by years of working in the justice system told him they were keeping something from him. After a dozen fruitless calls, it seemed as if they were intentionally giving him the runaround.

What was causing this nagging sense of obstruction?

The phone was getting him nowhere, and he couldn't keep sitting like this, or he would surely lose his mind. Precious time was passing, and here he was, planted on his ass, waiting for the phone to ring. If he hadn't given up smoking years ago, he would have lit a cigarette—he was surprised by how badly he wanted one, as though the craving had never left him.

Go over the facts again.

He sat up in his chair and picked up his pad once more, reading what he'd written:

Jackie Dawson—Robert Sand—report filed.

Classic Jaguar, key in lock. west p-lot, 3rd level. Started OK. Fresh scrape on fender.

No witnesses or surveillance cameras in p-lot.

Credit cards? Cell phone? GPS?

Christie's house? Her car at Sand's? No answer at home. No entry by police.

Neighbors?

Abduction or impulse trip?

Jackie Dawson. Emergency?

Hospitals—no admissions per LE.

Transport: airlines, taxis, limos? Buses?

Interviews? Investigation reports? Witness statements?

Track cell phone destinations? Warrants?

Jensen uncapped his fountain pen and circled the name Robert Sand. He flipped back a few pages.

The Denver police had taken a missing persons report from Sand, age fifty-six, who'd claimed that Jaqueline Dawson, his much younger girlfriend, was missing.

Jackie was Christie's closest friend and former roommate. Jensen had met her a few times. Jackie was twenty-two. Pretty. "A man trap," Janet had whispered on their first meeting, with uncharacteristic crassness that had surprised Jensen.

He tapped the back of his pen lightly against a tooth. Janet was right. Jackie Dawson could probably have her pick of men her own age. And who the hell was Robert Sand? What kind of man was he? Even to Jensen's sleep-deprived mind, the obvious way to start the investigation would be a background check on the man and a thorough search of his home. If Sand wouldn't consent voluntarily, that would be a red flag.

Had the police done those two things? Why hadn't he thought to ask such rudimentary questions despite covering so many other things?

The police had mentioned several times that Sand was African American. Why did that fact seem so important to them? Was it their way of marginalizing him, to minimize the importance of the fact that Jackie and Christie were missing, to justify their lack of progress?

Jensen tried to remember all he could of what Christie had told him about Sand.

He was well-off financially and *thirty-four years* older than Jackie. The detectives had also mentioned these facts more than once. Did dating a rich older black man disqualify a young girl and her friend from enjoying the benefit of a full-court-press investigation when they went missing? Did Sand's color, age and wealth immunize the man from a search of his home? Or did it make him a suspect?

Were these officers just a bunch of racist cops looking for excuses to conserve resources by neglecting an investigation or even putting the brakes on it?

Earlier, during a short nap, Jensen dreamed that he was walking on the dark coral sand of an ancient volcanic beach; now he remembered the dream, shaking his head as the symbolic meaning of it came to him: *old black sand.*

The workings of Jensen's fatigued mind intrigued him.

He'd gotten most of his details from a Detective Uttley of the Denver Police Department. Sand's race and age preoccupied Uttley, as if those two facts were the source of all answers and possibilities. Uttley's subtle indifference offended Jensen. "Maybe they just ditched Dawson's sugar daddy," he'd speculated, causing Jensen to resent the man's cavalier dismissiveness. He scribbled absently on his pad some more.

They don't take this seriously because Christie's friend was dating an older black man with lots of dough? That couldn't be—or could it?

Fighting back the bile rising in his throat, he flipped the page on his pad.

Jackie and Christie had taken Sand's car, an old Jaguar classic, to the Cherry Creek Mall. They'd said that was where they were going, and that was where police found Sand's car. The car had started on the first try, discounting the idea that the girls had abandoned the vehicle due to mechanical trouble.

Oddly, they had not dusted the car for prints. They had performed no forensic tests of any kind on it, and Sand had driven it home. Very, very strange.

He kept reading his notes, finding more questions than answers as he proceeded through the pages.

Sand had expected the girls to be gone for no more than four hours.

They were planning to go out for dinner together. The police confirmed Sand's claim that he'd made a reservation for two at Ruth's Chris, a high-end steakhouse.

What had Christie's plans been for the evening?

At 10:15 p.m., when the girls still hadn't returned, Sand had made his first call to the police.

Why so late?

Twelve hours after that, they found Sand's car in the west lot, Deck Three.

How had it possibly taken so long to find the car when they knew where to look for it?

The key was still in the driver's door, which could indicate that the girls had been nabbed—or summoned away—while getting into the car. Also, it was mildly intriguing that no one had stolen the vintage Jaguar with the key hanging from the door.

Was the evidence just a little too convenient?

He sat ruminating at his desk as the sun came up. Bright beams of light flickered off the pond in the marble patio outside, casting dreamy streaks of color on the wall.

Exhaustion finally overcame him. He closed his burning eyes to rest them, and his head rocked back, coming to rest on the back of his chair. His last waking thought was that he would head to Denver.

His breathing grew deep as he slipped away.

Just beyond the doorway of the den, his wife Janet watched him nod off, her face lined with concern, before she turned and shuffled back up the stairs.

Chapter 8

The vodka produced a warm, relaxing glow as it crept through Antonio's bloodstream, enhancing all of his senses. The aromas: burning logs and steaks on the grill. The sounds: firewood crackling and popping in the outdoor fire-pit and the sizzle of burning fat hitting the charcoal. Visual: flashes of orange light as tongues of flame occasionally lapped the scorched edges of two thick filets, briefly outshining the fire ten feet away. Antonio's mouth watered.

He sipped his drink, ice cubes clinking in his glass. How could such simple sensations produce such pleasure? His earlier tension was gone now, leaving in its wake a deep feeling of contentment and satisfaction. He felt fantastic.

He closed his eyes, propped up his feet and savored the moment.

"Man, I needed this," he said.

"Perhaps we ought to check on them," Beeman said as he swirled his own drink.

"The girls?" Antonio asked eagerly.

"The steaks. We don't want to burn them."

With a deep sigh, Antonio said, "That *would* be a crime." He lowered his boots to the flagstone and stood, raising his glass. "Just what the doctor ordered," he murmured.

Beeman smiled, raising his own drink. "Good stuff, this."

Like Antonio, Beeman was sipping frigid Grey Goose from a bottle he kept in the freezer, but, unlike Antonio, Beeman wasn't drinking vodka laced with secobarbital, a hypnotic sedative that reduces anxiety, produces mild euphoria and causes short-term antegrade amnesia.

Antonio drained his glass and set it beside the grill. Picking up a knife and barbecue tongs, he cut into a steak.

"How do you want them?"

"Bleeding." Beeman responded.

Antonio grinned, and stepped back to avoid a jet of flame from burning fat. "Then they're ready. I'll take 'em off now. How 'bout them taters?"

"Done." Beeman went inside.

Antonio put the steaks on a plate. Beeman was waiting in the kitchen with two foil-wrapped potatoes steaming on a plate of his own.

"Trade you a steak for a potato," Beeman said.

They seated themselves at the table in the kitchen, a pair of candles burning between them, melodic jazz riffing through the cabin-style house.

Between bites, Antonio picked up a CD case and turned it over to look at the back. "Good old Ben Webster," he said. "Just one more thing you've turned me onto. Old-style jazz, cultured and sophisticated, like a fine wine."

Beeman shook a bottle of steak sauce and then stopped, staring at the bottle intently.

"What's wrong?"

Beeman picked up the remote and silenced the music. "Listen," he whispered.

The faint wail of a female voice came through the ventilation duct. Even with the music off, the sound was almost below the level of Antonio's hearing.

"You heard that over the jazz? You have ears like a bat."

The sound faded away.

With a grin that reminded Antonio of a curved razor blade, Beeman restarted the music but lowered the volume.

They ate without speaking for a while.

When he finished his steak, Antonio looked up. "This reminds me of a TV show."

"Oh?"

"Watched it as a kid. Two single, uh, bachelors ..."

Dabbing his mouth with a napkin, Beeman said, "*The Odd Couple*?"

Antonio shrugged. "Or something"

"That was a comedy about two complete idiots. We are something else entirely, my friend."

Antonio was growing muddled. "What are we then?" he asked.

"We are the wolf and the eagle."

Antonio gave a broad smile. "I've always liked the sound of that. How did you learn what you've taught me? About life, death and predators?"

Beeman finished his drink. Setting his glass down, he regarded Antonio curiously for a moment. He sighed, shrugged and then continued. "It came to me late one night at the lab, after I'd ingested a small amount of LSD."

"LSD?"

"I'd been working twenty-four hours without sleep on a very complex problem, involving a nanotechnology-based technique for gene splicing, far more advanced than CRISPR."

"Crisper? What's that?"

"A tool to make changes to DNA—genetic engineering. State of the art two years ago, but our group has developed something far more advanced. With that technology, I've developed a new microbe, unlike anything on earth. It will be my legacy."

"There will be a germ called 'Arthur Beeman'?" Antonio asked, stifling a giggle. Why did everything seem so unreal?

The ends of Beeman's slit mouth curled upward slightly. "Not exactly. I will tell you something about myself that you may never repeat to anyone. Ever. It is illegal even to speak of it."

"Considering what we've done, telling me something illegal can't be that big of a deal."

"It is," Beeman insisted. "But tomorrow you'll remember not one word of what I'm going to tell you."

"You think I'm stupid?"

"Not at all," Beeman said with a warm smile uncharacteristic for him. "I just know you're going to forget this. You'll be more focused on other things."

"Seems we've gotten to where there's no point in hiding anything from each other. Don't we already know each other's darkest secret?"

"I suppose you're right. So let me finish. I was developing a protein involved in a cellular process that permits a specific type of virus —known as a bacteriophage—to reproduce with an unstable genome, perfectly reproducing certain life-cycle anomalies."

"Holy fuck! I was afraid you might have done something like that." Antonio shook his head in mock horror. "Seriously, dude. Am I supposed to understand what you just said?"

"You recall that my work involves genetics?"

"Don't tell me—you invented an alligator that can walk on its hind legs and talk on a cell phone? The ultimate lawyer or something?" Catching Beeman's look of resigned contempt, he sighed and said, "Sorry, keep going."

Beeman frowned and looked away. "My virus can be synthesized, and it reproduces. It is a manufactured living organism that can replicate itself. It in turn reprograms a strain of bacteria present in all human lungs, making the larger organisms deadly, setting a clock within them like a ticking bomb by injecting genetic material the phage itself reproduces for distribution."

"Wow." Antonio was impressed, despite his confusion. "So you made a superbug of some kind?"

"Yes. One that alters bacterial organisms, programming them to kill a host with a life cycle of infection and later apoptosis—cell death—operating on a universal timetable."

"So, like, what? You get the little guys to die all at once, at a certain time?"

Beeman nodded with raised brow, evidently surprised that Antonio was keeping up at all, which pleased Antonio to no end.

"And we can now delay the onset of symptoms for a controlled interval to allow time for transmission of the contagion and then stage the simultaneous expiration of the antigens at a point just further out to limit or adjust the magnitude of the LIE—lethal infectious epidemic—which my microbe can introduce into a specific population."

"In simple words, please?"

"I synthesized a virus that can incubate, spread, kill and then go extinct on schedule, leaving the population of a given area decimated and defenseless, but no longer contagious. Safe for invasion, relatively speaking, assuming the rampant spread of secondary infections, such as plague, is prevented by rapid disposal of bodies, preferably by fire or lime in mass graves."

"Like a germ version of a 'nucular' bomb?"

"Not quite," Beeman said. "But a normal nuclear bomb would leave radiation, which would be the equivalent of a live virus in this analogy. But my virus ceases to be contagious and dies out after the damage is done, leaving no dangerous residual to threaten invading troops entering the battle theater after decimation of the target population. This has been the objective of my work for a decade. I finally solved all the problems, but at one time it was driving me to the breaking point."

Antonio remained silent, stifling his desire to yawn. He was getting really sleepy.

"You see, this problem pushed me to unravel the very nature of life itself. I lost my way. So on impulse I synthesized and consumed a small dose of LSD. Then my mind opened a new doorway—I learned to think like the virus. It was as if *I* had become the new organism. I was navigating mentally on an atomic plane. Knowledge presented itself to me as instinct, intuition."

"Some kind of drug-induced divine inspiration?"

"You could say that, Antonio. What I knew then was beyond words, beyond expression, even mathematically. I saw the structure of life itself in the patterns and vibrations of subatomic particles."

Beeman was whispering now. Antonio noted that the music had ended.

"I saw what life is made of," Beeman continued. "Would you like to know? This discovery affects you."

"Sure."

"Life is a question, and death is the answer. Death recycles itself. Life is made from death—it emerges between cycles of death, but without death there can be no life."

"But hey, without life, there can be no death."

"There you have it. Life is death is life."

"So the only meaning of life is death?" Antonio asked.

"More aptly put, the *essential source* of life is death. This is more than just understanding the cycle of life. I'm referring to the underlying generator of the life cycle. Life itself has certain frequencies, but I've discovered that death does as well. It is a symphony, energy folding back on itself, being conserved and never destroyed—death energy from life energy and vice versa. Within a living system, such as this whole planet or a single cell in your brain, this symphony controls *everything*. It subjects all biochemical activity to its universal subatomic harmonics. This is what prompted the evolution of all life. I came to understand that harmonic frequency at the molecular and atomic levels. Genetic manipulation alone is not sufficient. Magnetic induction at extremely high frequencies is needed to stimulate and guide the biochemistry. With what I've discovered, I found the key to the creation of a potentially unlimited number of entirely new species. I can, eventually, revise the fabric of life, rearranging the tapestry of all life on this planet."

Antonio recited one of the key mantras. "A god, by choice, and without mercy?"

Beeman nodded slowly and then pressed on. "I saw all of it, on every scale. I saw the whole system, from breaking and forming bonds in biochemical reactions in a single virus all the way up the scale—to the birth of stars and the orbits of planets, and up further still to the paths of star clusters within a spinning galaxy, to the motion of galactic bands and clusters through the universe. I understand the illusions of time, space and motion that make scientists believe in the fiction of dark matter."

"Dark matter?" Antonio was lost.

"The sluggish propagation of time in the soul of a galaxy," Beeman said with a casual wave of his hand.

"A galaxy has a soul?"

"It contains life and death, in abundance. And it has consciousness. A galaxy is one great mind, an organism so vast, so massive, it seems frozen in time, but it vibrates—*resonates*, actually—with the death harmonic in unison with all living matter, everywhere."

"Are there words to the song?"

The right question, my friend, Beeman's expression communicated. Antonio smiled.

"Yes. *Death is life is death,*" he answered with metronomic rhythm, clapping the back of one hand three times into the other palm. "I saw it all, as though I were God, or on the plane of God. I saw the fabric of life and death, the true nature of reality, which is that nothing truly exists except through death. The realizations it triggered were intoxicating; they continued, falling one to the next, like an endless row of dominoes."

Antonio had a theory of what Beeman was saying. "So when life first began, it wasn't just some fluke accident or God's hand of creation or whatever—you're saying that death is built into the universe and *it* made life spring out of nowhere because it was hungry? You're fucking with my head, dude."

"This world, where beauty and horror coexist? They *must* coexist, but there is a dominant terminal, just as there is a dominant gender in every species. In the world of electricity, there is a positive terminal and a ground. The world runs on a single motor, Antonio, and it *is* death—life-giving death. The potential of your inevitable, certain death powers the motor of your life. Creatures that kill live, and those that live, die. This universe spawns *predators*. It gave rise to sharks and men. It gave rise to the wolf and the eagle. It gave rise to *us*."

"Fucking poetic, man! And you gave birth to your magic bug? What do you call it?"

"Its designation is AR-117."

"Sounds like a rifle."

"It *is* a biological rifle, of sorts. More of a biological atom bomb, as you said. AR stands for adjustable reproduction. Viral revision 117. It has one of the most rapid growth rates of any known organism. It is designed for airborne transmission. And it is resilient, until its programmed apoptosis is triggered. I based its underlying genetic structure on microorganisms found near volcanic jets on the ocean floor."

"Leftover sea monster DNA?" Antonio giggled. "I actually think I'm following you, dude, but let me ask this—because it's so deadly, you gave it the ticking self-destruct thing, so if we ever have to use it we won't become extinct ourselves?"

"Very clever, my young Jedi."

Antonio was surprised. He was still following Beeman—sort of. Who'd ever believe it? "You made this shit so we can really use it on some country overseas and not worry about it blowing back to wipe us out? That's why it's against the law for you to talk about your work?"

Beeman nodded.

"Cool. Don't fuck with the USA. But your baby should have a sexier name."

Beeman smirked. "We gave it a code name."

"What is it?"

"Black Sunrise."

"Cool. Sounds like a drink. But I wouldn't want to try it." And on that note, Antonio stood and walked unsteadily to the refrigerator, poured another shot for himself and returned to his seat with the bottle and his glass.

He tipped the bottle to Beeman, who shook his head.

"Black Sunrise," Antonio said as he put his feet back up. "Did you pick that name because it sounds so fucking scary?"

"I gave a briefing to the Army and the State Department. I said if you expose a population to the AR-117 virus, a month later the sun would rise on a land blackened by death and decay; someone said it would be a 'black sunrise.' The name stuck. But the point is that the sun *will* rise, and the target nation is yours for the taking. Your troops march in, taking the land and all the resources of the dead nation."

"You, my friend, are one spooky son of a bitch." Antonio laughed nervously as he ran his hand through his hair. "Is there an antidote?"

Beeman frowned. "You mean a vaccine? Indeed there is—or at least there soon will be. We can choose who lives and who dies. We can inoculate particular people in advance. If Hitler had possessed this technology, there would be no Jew alive anywhere in the world today, and you, my friend, would be speaking German, along with the rest of the world."

"Heil Beeman!" Antonio sipped his new drink. "State Department, huh? They must pay you a lot."

Beeman raised his glass. "My gift to mankind."

"*Pleeeeeaaaase!*" The tinny cry came faintly through the heating duct. "*Help us!*"

Beeman gave a kindly smile. "You, my friend, are the wolf. Now it is time for us to sleep."

"Thought so," Antonio said contentedly, moving to lie down on the couch and closing his eyes.

Chapter 9

Shivering in the darkness, Christie Jensen lay on her side on a foul-smelling mattress. Her chest, belly and thighs were pressed against Jackie Dawson's back and buttocks to conserve heat; both girls were naked in the damp chill. She wanted more than anything for Jackie to stop shaking. Tremors rattled constantly through Jackie's smaller frame, punctuated from time to time by wracking sobs that periodically erupted and subsided.

Though Christie was also terribly frightened, she had never seen anyone so abjectly terrified as Jackie was now. Christie feared she would likely be forever emotionally scarred by this nightmare. Beneath her outgoing veneer, Jackie was actually pretty fragile, very sensitive, easily hurt. Surrounded by total blackness, comforting Jackie gave Christie a purpose on which to concentrate, and this kept her from shattering into a thousand tiny shards. Soothing Jackie's terror seemed easier somehow than confronting her own.

Hours ago, when Christie emerged from her delirium, waves of confusion and dizziness had overwhelmed her as the world turned several directions at once. A horrid ringing in her ears forced her to flee and hide beneath an abstract mantle in her mind. Then she'd realized it wasn't there at all and that she had created it to keep from being driven mad by the hideous reverberation echoing outward from the center of her skull. Finally it had stopped, and she'd curled into a ball and retched, seized by wave after wave of dry heaves, leaving her abdominal muscles quivering.

As the hours passed, her mind had slowly cleared. Feeling around in the darkness, she'd found Jackie beside her. Continuing to explore, she'd discerned they were on a plastic mattress inside a wire cage. She'd found a toilet and a bowl of water—nothing else.

Jackie began to sob again. Christie hugged her, soothing her, but it did little good—Jackie didn't even seem to be aware that Christie was there. Her shaking reached a violent crescendo, and it felt to Christie as if the voltage of her own terror was electrocuting her friend. Christie felt the horror radiating from her, and it became contagious, soaking its way in through her abdomen.

"It's okay, baby," she whispered. "I'm with you, Jax. I'm here, honey."

Time passed slowly, and Jackie became calmer, clearly benefitting from Christie's body heat. Her shaking ceased, then resumed, then ceased again. Her breathing became deep and steady.

Christie thought she heard something else, a faint sound coming from behind her in the darkness outside the cage. Holding her breath, she sensed someone.

Turning her head very slowly, she absorbed the blackness in her vain struggle to see, forcing herself not to cry out or even breathe. Her heart pounded behind her eyes, as though it had climbed up into her head.

What lay in the void beyond?

The sound stopped. She waited, blood rushing in her ears.

Then came a reedy whisper in the darkness—a slow rasping hiss.

"*Dirty girls.*"

Gasping for air, Christie tried to clutch Jackie closer to her, but the girl had gone as stiff as a bronze statue. Christie heard screaming, and she realized it was her own before Jackie started screaming with her.

• • •

The shrill howling made it easy for Beeman to slip away unheard. When he reached the stairway, he chuckled.

How could he make Antonio understand? Beeman would have to

keep him from spoiling this delicate process in his haste to satisfy his blunt sexual urges. In Beeman's quest to unravel the secrets he sought from the human soul, timing would be everything. He took a long time reaching the top of the stairs, relishing the operatic tribute below, biting his lower lip with pleasure as he savored the dying remnants of primal terror.

Death is life is death.

In the living room, Antonio lay on the couch in his clothes, his large, hooked nose aimed upward like a mountain peak, a stream of spittle dribbling from his open mouth.

Beeman sat across the room and stared at him.

"Patience, my friend," he whispered, quoting the greatest of all men. "Each step in a journey is a journey unto itself."

And the journey was just beginning.

Chapter 10

" Twenty minutes out."

"Thanks, Rick," said Jensen, rubbing his face as he woke from his much-needed catnap. Rick Adkins was the pilot-in-command of Jensen's business jet, a Phenom 300 that at this moment was descending at 360 knots, still a couple of miles above the Rockies. The luxurious cabin was surprisingly quiet. If he hadn't been so short on sleep, he'd have flown the plane himself. For now, he was crouching just outside the entrance of the cockpit.

"Where are we?"

"Hickey, Larks Six."

Jensen knew the routing by heart, somewhat south of a direct course into Denver. "Weather?" he asked.

Adkins turned in his seat to face Jensen. "Dodged a couple of cells. We're clear of that stuff now, and have a clean shot into Centennial. Expecting a few bumps as we start down. Nothing heavy. We'll break out over the foothills."

"What's the weather on the ground?"

"Good." Adkins checked notes he'd jotted on the small clipboard strapped to his knee. "Sky clear; visibility ten plus; wind one-five-zero at six, gusting fifteen. Landing one-seven left. Temp, twenty-six." He looked up, computing in his head. "About eighty Fahrenheit. A perfect day."

"Thanks." Jensen returned to his seat.

He and Janet would soon be meeting with the Denver police.

From his years as an assistant district attorney, he thought he had a good idea of what to expect, but he was optimistic nonetheless. At least he would be directly involved in the effort to find his daughter instead of waiting idly for a phone call.

Diagonally across the aisle, Janet was curled in her seat like a cat, staring into space, her brow furrowed, deep in thought. Leaning forward, he took her hand in his.

"It's going to be okay," he said.

"I know it." Janet sighed. "But where do you think she went?"

Jensen shook his head.

"What worries me most? The key stuck in the door of that car. You think they were abducted?"

"It's possible," Jensen answered soothingly. "But there are other equally likely possibilities. All the things we've talked about, and more we haven't thought of."

"But Christie's usually so good about returning voice messages. What other explanation is there?"

Jensen had been asking himself that same question for hours. He'd conjured up several scenarios, but none seemed convincing. The problem with cooking up scenarios was that they tended to darken as you went, leading down an unproductive road. It was somehow easier to cook up a nightmare than a harmless explanation.

"How many times have we worried ourselves sick over her?" Jensen asked with a kind smile.

"A few," Janet conceded. "But never like this, with cops knocking at the door."

"Okay. So here's what we know and what we don't know. First, we know she was last seen with a close friend, someone trustworthy. Second, sometimes Christie is impulsive. She's never been one to turn down an adventure. Third, she's leaving for grad school in three weeks. What better time for one final adventure, a last road trip or something, before starting another year of school?"

"You're making me feel better," said Janet, squeezing his hand. "Go on."

"Okay. What we *don't* know is this—and just this: where she is and why that car was there. We don't even know for sure they were the last ones to drive it. They could have lost the keys or left them in the car. Someone might have stolen the car for a joyride. There are a lot of possibilities; most are harmless. They could have met up with some friends and gone out, spent the night at a friend's, gone camping or on a road trip. Just bad timing. She might have lost her phone. Or her purse. We know she probably isn't hurt—the cops have checked every hospital in town. And as they pointed out, how could someone abduct two women from a crowded mall—even the parking garage—without anyone seeing a thing?"

It made Jensen feel dishonest to use his formidable advocacy skills to sell an idea he wasn't sure he believed in, but making Janet feel better was worth it.

"I'll be glad when we can go by her place and pound on the door ourselves," she said.

"No need," Jensen said, producing a key. "We can let ourselves in."

• • •

Denver Police Headquarters sits near the Denver Art Museum, but no two buildings could be less similar. The museum is a modern work of angles and lines reminiscent of Frank Lloyd Wright, while the police building looks like a postmodern blend of hardened bunker and medieval castle, foreboding and unfriendly, with little in the way of markings. To Jensen, the fortress of concrete slabs appeared designed to repel rioting hoards, as though the city planners expected Denver to sink into violent chaos.

Within the building, they waited for thirty minutes on a hard bench in a starkly lit waiting area before a detective came out to greet them. He wore dark green slacks, cowboy boots and a large western buckle hiding beneath his overhanging belly.

"Mr. and Mrs. Jensen?"

Jensen stood and extended his hand. "Yes, I'm Mark Jensen, and this is my wife, Janet."

Rather than shaking hands, the detective gestured toward the door from which he'd just emerged. "I'm Detective Taylor. Please come this way." They followed him down a long hallway and into a small conference room.

Once they sat down, Taylor opened a cream-colored folder. "You folks just flew in from California?"

Jensen nodded.

"Well, thanks for coming in today," Taylor said. "This case has moved around some, but now it's assigned to me."

"Thank you for taking the time to meet with us," Jensen said, noting the tightness in Taylor's voice and his lack of eye contact.

Taylor cleared his throat and placed a small digital recorder on the table. "Okay. So. This Dawson thing. Robert Sand's missing white girl."

Shocked at the unveiled racism, Jensen raised his brow. "Excuse me?"

Taylor appeared not to have heard him. "You folks mind if we record this?" Without waiting for an answer, he pressed a button on the recorder and a small red light came on.

Jensen glanced at Janet. Her face had gone slack.

"Detective," Jensen began, "We're here because—"

"Of course," Taylor cut in. "It's about *your* daughter too. Christine Jensen. Still haven't heard from her?"

"Correct. We've checked—."

"Yeah, I know. Home, cell, neighbors, but that's it?" Leaning to one side, Taylor reached into his back pocket and withdrew a metal tin of chewing tobacco. He pushed a wad into his mouth, tamping it next to his cheek. "We were hoping you could give us a few more leads. Names of friends, other contacts, employers, known hangouts."

Jensen slipped a small envelope from his jacket and placed it on the table. "We brought some photographs of Christie and Jackie together, taken this summer."

"Thanks." Taylor opened the envelope and examined the snap-shots. "Your daughter is the blonde?"

Jensen nodded.

"Pretty girl. Does she also hang out with Sand?"

This time Janet responded, her eyes sharp. "She's spending her summer break in Denver, Detective Taylor. She's working a summer internship with a medical company called Medtronic. She has just finished her bachelor's degree in chemical engineering at DU. We understand she disappeared two days ago with Jackie and that you have them both officially listed as missing."

Taylor continued looking at the snapshots.

There was a knock at the door. Taylor made no move to rise, and the door opened. A tall man stepped into the room; he wore a pressed white shirt with a dark brown tie that matched his short hair. Mark and Janet came to their feet. Reaching across the table, he shook hands with each of them, speaking softly as he introduced himself.

"Special Agent Derek Sawyer, Federal Bureau of Investigation. Sorry I'm late."

"What section are you with, Agent Sawyer?" Jensen asked, men-tally ticking off the legal jurisdictional flags potentially raised by the FBI's involvement in a local missing persons case. This was a bad sign —the first thing that came to mind was the interstate transport of kidnapping victims.

"Major Crimes. Colorado Office. We do a lot of the same stuff as Taylor and his team."

"His team?"

"I'm just here to listen," Sawyer said as he took a seat at the table. "Have a seat, everybody. Don't let me interrupt."

Returning to his chair, Jensen asked, "What triggered FBI juris-diction on this?"

"Nothing. Like I said, I'm just here to observe."

"What else can you tell us about the girls?" Taylor asked.

Jensen shrugged. "What would you like to know?"

"Do you have any guesses where they are?"

"If I did—"

Taylor nodded. "If you did, you wouldn't have come to Denver, I get it." He pointed to the recorder. "We just have to ask the question, Mr. Jensen."

"We just arrived, and we plan to check her apartment as soon as —"

Taylor interrupted. "You have a key?"

"Yes."

"And you're a lawyer?"

"Yes. A prosecutor, in my former life." The change in direction of Taylor's questions surprised Jensen. He'd expected the man to ask if he could tag along and gain access to the apartment for a consensual search.

"Used to be?"

"Now I am in private practice."

"Criminal work?"

Jensen raised his hands with his palms outward. "I don't defend criminals. Strictly civil litigation."

"Lucrative practice?" Taylor flashed a plastic smile, gazed into the file before him once more, scanning a handwritten note clipped inside. "Flush enough to make your girl a ransom target?"

Jensen shrugged. "I suppose so. Why? Has someone contacted you?"

"Not us. You?"

"No." Jensen shifted his gaze from Taylor to back to Sawyer. "Why is the FBI 'unofficially' involved in this case?"

Taylor cut in. "Tell us about Sand."

"We don't know him. I'd like an answer to my question."

"There is no answer to your question," said Sawyer, "I'm here strictly as an observer. There's nothing that would invoke FBI jurisdiction on this matter. This is Detective Taylor's case. I really don't want to interfere with his work or be a distraction. I'll leave if there's a problem with my being here."

"No problem," Jensen said. "I just want to make sure all the cards are on the table."

"Okay," Taylor said. "Back to Sand. You know anything at all about the guy or your daughter's relationship with him?"

"Only that he's an older man who's dating Christie's friend Jackie. I don't think Christie has any kind of 'relationship' with him other than a casual acquaintance. Detective, we were hoping you could tell *us* something."

Taylor nodded, stealing a sideward glance at Sawyer, who remained impassive. "Okay. Here's what we know. They ditched Sand's car with the key in the door at the Cherry Creek Mall parking lot, west deck, level three, and took off somewhere."

"How do you know they ditched it there? All you really know is that you *found* it there. And what is it that leads you to the conclusion that they 'took off' as you put it?"

"Hey, counselor, ease up," Taylor said with a gentle tone. "No sign of foul play. They'll probably turn up." Taylor closed his file on the table and stood. Sawyer rose with him, reaching for the door. "Only reason we've opened a file is because of Sand's reports."

"Reports, plural?" Jensen asked.

"Several calls. Very persistent fellow."

"Wait a minute," Jensen protested. He looked imploringly at the FBI man. "What's going on here?"

Sawyer met his gaze. "We don't have enough information to be sure of anything," he said, "They may very well have just ditched the car. When they turn up, we'll know for sure."

"Gentlemen," Jensen said in a voice that reflected three decades of court battles, "These girls are *missing*. They didn't run off. They wouldn't do that. Sand expected them back at his house *two* days ago, *with his car*. They never made it. They wouldn't just 'ditch' a car entrusted to them and wander away for days without leaving word with somebody. You can't just wait for them to 'turn up.'"

"Mr. Jensen—" Taylor started.

"Please hear me out. You've got to do more. I can see why Sand made so many calls. This is a serious case. They've *vanished*; they're *missing*, and it is *your* job to find them."

"Settle down, cowboy," Taylor said caustically. "We've already started."

"If this were *your* daughter—"

"Hey, we're not blowing this off." Taylor raised the file in his hand. "We've opened a case file. We're investigating."

"Exactly how are you investigating?" Jensen probed.

"We're following up on any leads we might come across. Taking statements."

"Any leads you might come across?" Jensen parodied. "What does that mean, exactly?"

"We've taken your statements now," Taylor countered, standing.

"Just a minute," Jensen said. "Please, sit back down."

Taylor hesitated but then resumed his seat.

"You say you've taken our statements?" Jensen said softly. "You've barely interviewed us. This is no investigation. We're getting the bum's rush—a brush-off. Not unusual in a municipal police station, I concede, particularly on a missing persons complaint no one is taking seriously. But why would the FBI Major Crimes Unit have a man sitting in if this isn't a real case? With all due respect, officers, this doesn't pass the smell test. I'm asking you to be straight with me."

Taylor and Sawyer just stared at him. Jensen waited for an answer, letting the awkward silence build pressure.

Taylor spoke first. "We've searched Sand's home. He gave his consent. First time we asked. Dawson keeps her things there. Clothes, toiletries, shoes—all in her own closet in the bedroom. She is twenty-two; he is fifty-six. Clearly a sexual relationship. Now, we've canvassed the mall. There are no video cameras in the parking lot where we found the car. No reports to mall security. We've rechecked every day. There were no signs of struggle inside or outside the car. We've dusted it for prints and found only a few; all seem to be Jackie's or Sand's or your daughter's."

"But we heard no one checked the car for fingerprints," Jensen said.

"We finally got around to it. We compared them with samples taken from various objects Sands offered for sampling. Your daughter's prints are on file, from her application for a concealed-carry permit. Sand volunteered to be printed, and we took him up on it. He's exArmy, but his prints are missing from the database. We sampled Dawson's prints from personal possessions, like hairbrushes, a purse, her personal scrapbook and other places. There have been no calls made or received on either of their cell phones since before they failed to show up at Sand's home. We're following up on phone numbers from their cell records. There have been no credit card purchases on the cards we've located. There are no known witnesses who claim to have seen either of the girls after they departed from Sand's home. We have interviewed store owners and employees at the mall."

Jensen nodded appraisingly. "Why didn't you tell us any of this sooner?," he said quietly. What else do you plan to do?"

"We'll see," Taylor said. "You know a lot about police procedure, Mr. Jensen?"

"As I said, I used to be a prosecutor."

"Any recent arguments with your daughter?"

"No," Jensen answered tiredly. "Do you consider Sand a suspect?"

"Too soon to say," Taylor dodged. "But like I said, he didn't blink when we asked to search his residence. He was actually very helpful. My read is that if he's hiding something, he's a pretty good actor."

"Have you pulled his sheet, done a background check?"

"Yup." Taylor shrugged. "Clean. No priors, no complaints. Sand was ex-Army, but his prints were missing from the database. That might be one red flag at least."

"You have him under surveillance?"

"Counselor," Sawyer cut in with a good-natured chuckle, "you know he can't disclose something like that in an ongoing investigation, even to you. Detective Taylor has already given you a more detailed and candid report than policy allows at this stage. You must understand that at this point we have essentially the same information you do. Less."

"We?"

"We'll keep you informed and ask you to do the same." Sawyer obviously wanted the meeting to end. Taylor picked up on the cue and turned off the recorder before rising from his chair.

"*Us?*" Jensen asked, probing again. "So you're officially in the loop?"

Sawyer gave Jensen a small smile, shaking his head slowly.

Taylor patted Jensen's arm. "We got your mobile number from Irvine PD. How long are you planning to stay in town?"

"Until we find my daughter."

"Okay. Let us know where you're staying. If you leave Denver, please inform me before you go."

"May we have Mr. Sand's address and telephone number?"

Taylor shook his head. "I'm afraid we can't release that information."

"He's listed," Sawyer chimed in. "Google him."

Chapter 11

Dawn brought the gift of faint light. Christie could at last make out shapes and surfaces that became clearer as the light grew stronger and the fog in her mind continued to lift. They were against a concrete wall inside a cage of three sides of chain link and steel poles, roughly ten feet by six, with a roof about six feet up from the cement floor. Her eyes traced rough timber joists above.

A basement.

She sat up, which made her head throb and brought on another wave of dizziness. The cage contained only Jackie and herself, the plastic mattress, a porcelain toilet and a roll of toilet paper on the floor next to a dog bowl. Beside her, Jackie slept on her belly, breathing deeply, her long hair matted and filthy, crusty with dried bile.

How long had they been in here? It seemed like days. She was aware of getting drugged repeatedly, and she dimly remembered a long, terrifying journey in the trunk of a car.

Where were they?

They were both still naked, but she didn't think either of them had been sexually assaulted. *At least not yet.*

She was desperately thirsty. She looked at the dog bowl. It was empty and dry. She had knocked it over during the night in the darkness.

Her lips were parched and beginning to crack. She thought of drinking out of the toilet, but she could not yet bring herself to do it.

Maybe she would change her mind later.

She saw a hose coiled on the floor outside the cage. It ran upward along the cement wall, where it was attached to a spigot. In the shadows, she saw a long table and a cabinet that looked antique. There were objects on the table, but she couldn't make out what they were.

She tried to stand, but a searing pain behind her eyes got the better of her, and she lay back down and waited for it to pass, closing her eyes. After several minutes the pain subsided, but her head still throbbed. She ticked off the possible causes in her mind: drugs, dehydration, low blood sugar. She would kill for a couple of Tylenol. She scooted furtively to the edge of the mattress.

Steel bars securely bolted the corners of the cage to the cement floor. Several steel bands welded into place secured the chain link. Her stomach tightened as she realized how solid the cage was. This was no makeshift thing—it was a permanent part of the house.

The smell raised a frightening thought. Had others been here before her? Were they still alive?

When she tried to recall what happened, her mind swam.

It was easier to focus on the present. Sitting up again with great effort, she sighed and looked down at Jackie, who twitched and moaned, curling in her sleep into a fetal position. She was dreaming, but no matter how bad her dream might be, it could never equal the nightmare of reality.

Christie would let her sleep as long as possible.

That their captors had stripped and caged them made it seem most likely that they had taken them to serve some dark cravings. The thought made her stomach hurt. She noticed the sharp curve of Jackie's hip and the size of her breasts. She looked down at her own body. She was scrawny compared to Jackie. Her skin was white; Jackie was tan. Her short hair was matted to her face. The skin of one breast was bruised and tender to the touch. It made her shudder. She wanted something, anything, to wear.

She would be grateful for just a sheet, or even a burlap sack.

And some water in the bowl.

Their captors were dehumanizing them. She considered the effort that had obviously gone into the construction of the cage, the presence of the toilet and the water, and her spirits lifted slightly. Whoever had taken them must plan to keep them alive, at least for a while. As she wondered what other preparations they had made, she realized something that made her sigh with relief—rape, torture and abuse might not be the reason they'd taken them.

They might only be after money.

Surviving this ordeal, regardless of the motives of her abductors, would require her to keep her mind sharp and her emotions under control. If she could face whatever was coming with her eyes open, she could find a way to deal with it, provided they stopped drugging her.

Her father had taught her that her mind was her only real weapon. She knew this to be true, and when she was drugged, her mind was useless. And in this situation, beauty was a liability. Christie's only advantages right now were her intelligence and her self-control.

And Jackie.

Feeling slightly guilty at the thought, Christie considered how much worse it would be if she were here in the cage alone.

Whatever happened, she would do her best to protect Jackie.

She thought of her time at SALO—Survival and Leadership Outdoors—a youth leadership school near Jackson Hole, Wyoming. Her father had sent her there during the summer between high school and college. At SALO, she'd scaled cliff walls, forded rivers, learned to build fires using only what was available in nature, spanned ravines and learned leadership skills. All the activities had challenged her, and while some parts of the course had scared the crap out of her, she'd loved every minute. Each activity had aimed to deliver one message: *you can do it.* Whatever it is, *you can do it*—if you observe, learn, plan and execute: SALO's version of the famous loop developed by the Air Force military tactician John Boyd. As a pilot in survival school, her father had learned about the OODA loop. He'd taught it to her before she'd even gone to SALO: observe, orient, decide and act.

In her mind, she could still see and hear SALO coaches drilling their messages into her and her fellow students as they'd kayaked whitewater rapids, hung from rock walls and huddled around camp-fires at night. *Use your head, control your emotions and have faith in yourself. Above all else, never quit. When you're the only friend you have, don't abandon yourself.* At SALO, she had learned the importance of fighting panic and self-doubt. The experience had been one of the most valuable gifts her dad had ever bought for her. He had drummed into her that being *able* was the most important thing, earned by a lifetime of work and effort, and rewarded by a lifetime of achievement and satisfaction.

What lessons had she learned at SALO that could help her now?

She pictured the head instructor, Peter Gundersen, a former mas-ter rock climber. A spinal tumor had paralyzed him, but he'd taught his students from a sport-modified wheelchair. What would he tell her?

Ask yourself questions.

Okay. Where are we?

She had no idea.

Well, what do I know?

I know I'm so thirsty I'm about to drink out of the toilet.

Think, Christie! What happened? What can you remember?

She pushed herself to probe the jumbled images in her memory.

The mall. She'd been at the Cherry Creek Mall with Jackie. They had been shopping.

Okay. That's a start. What else?

She remembered Jackie had been worried about a dent in Robert's car. She envisioned the car in her mind, and her stomach hurt. That was the last thing she could remember.

Go over it again.

What about the dent?

Jackie had been worried Robert would be angry. And then—

Oh, yeah. That man came up and offered to fix the dent.

She remembered he had a large, hooked nose that reminded her of an Indian chief. A heavy black mustache, which she'd guessed he cultivated to make his nose appear less pronounced. What was his name—Jimmy Waters or something? Or was it Jimmy Rivers? Yes, that was it, Jimmy Rivers. And his dad was there too, in a car. He owned Dad's Body Shop.

Then she remembered the rest.

He shot us with stun guns.

She cursed her stupidity—how mindless she had been.

She remembered waking up in the trunk of a car—that part hadn't left her. She had wet herself while screaming into her gag, nearly suffocating. She'd heard choking in the darkness. She remembered the horrible smell.

Then the older man, the sadist with the huge knife.

She'd been sure he was going to cut her throat. The memory caused her eyes to well over slightly, but she willed away her weakness. Prying out these details was like drilling through rock, as though her mind had walled them off. She guessed that the drugs were blocking her memory. She'd have to be persistent and tease out one detail after another.

Okay, Christie. Good so far. What else?

• • •

Sunlight streaming through Antonio's eyelids awakened him, warming his face, making him sweat.

He felt like shit.

He checked his watch. It was almost eleven. He'd slept on the couch in his clothes and boots. His head hurt, and his neck was very stiff. He'd been dreaming about sex, but he couldn't remember the dream. He had an erection. He was starved, thirsty and had to piss.

He could hear Beeman rattling around in the kitchen. "Good morning, sunshine. Feeling a little hung over?"

"Hung big over," Antonio mumbled as he slid his legs to the floor and rose to his feet.

Beeman handed him a mug of coffee. "You look like a man who needs a fresh start. Care for some ibuprofen?" Beeman rattled a small plastic bottle.

Antonio let Beeman shake a couple of Advil gel caps into his palm. Then he took a sip of coffee to wash them down.

• • •

Beeman watched him walk stiffly to the bathroom. He had to slow the fool down without appearing to do so. He'd control him—as he had been doing for months since meeting him—without Antonio realizing he was manipulating him. He had long since mastered the art of pulling Antonio's strings, starting on the night of their first meeting at an upscale gentlemen's club. Requiring someone like Antonio to make the present experiment possible, Beeman had trolled strip joints until he found the right subject. Then he'd spent months exploring, cultivating and controlling various recesses and impulses in Antonio's cluttered, dysfunctional mind.

Antonio's libido had been the key, of course. That, coupled with his profound self-doubt and sense of alienation.

Beeman had picked the right man.

Now, a year after their first "chance" meeting, they had come so far. He would have to control the experiment very carefully, for now there was something to lose. A year of work, a massive amount of risk, and now all the pieces were in place. He could not let all of it go to waste due to uncontrolled, undisciplined and impulsive foolishness.

His human laboratory was now equipped and provisioned, and it was time to begin—but slowly, with purpose and keen observation.

In fact, Beeman was conducting an experiment with three separate organisms, all *Homo sapiens*, who were merely large, organized colonies of cells working together as a complex system. The invisible central driving force was the same as any living system: death.

Life is death is life. Harness death to harness life and all existence.

He would have to mold each of the three organisms into its role. When Antonio killed one—or both—of the girls, it was imperative that he be completely sober, conscious and aware of the fact he was destroying another living being, so that he would *absorb* his victims and not merely murder them. Beeman's ability to study the process, and its effect upon Antonio, would depend upon elimination of transient urges—momentary flashes of passion. They must filter and distill the driving forces, leaving only the Primal Ecstasy—the deep, pervasive compulsion to live by creating death and spinning it like a spider web. It serves as a conduit for the fundamental channel that ebbs and flows like the sea—powerful enough to batter rock into fine sand—in the souls of those living organisms that chart the path of evolution.

It was equally essential that each girl, as she died, understood her role in the process. She would need to be the prey, the Eaten, and to be as aware as Antonio would be when she surrendered her existence to him, willingly or not, so that he might thrive as a predatory consumer of life and in so doing morph into something new.

"I can't believe I fucking fell asleep," Antonio groused. "We wasted a night."

Beeman smiled and waved his hand dismissively. "No rush, my friend. Anticipation is at least half of the fun."

Antonio blinked at him and gulped his coffee. "Did you do anything?"

Beeman went still, stifling his reaction. Then realizing with relief what Antonio was asking, he shook his head. "Too much to drink."

"Me too. Reminds me of a date I had once. Ruined it before I even got started. Never saw her again."

"They're ours now, Antonio. We'd be stupid to rush. Savor it. We can take our time and work into things slowly. I promise you it will be much more exquisite that way. All the work we've gone to—we need to move slowly and savor each bit."

"Yeah, I guess." Antonio looked at his watch. "Shit. Almost time for the bus. Maybe I should just call in—"

"No," Beeman smoothly cut him off. "This is your *alibi*. This is *vital to your safety and survival.*" Beeman emphasized words in a weird way that drove them like spikes into Antonio's mind, making ideas immovable and permanent, foreclosing avenues of argument but clarifying things in a way that made sense. "You *must* report for work on time. You *must* have a safety net. Remember, we're risking *life in prison.*"

Antonio stroked his mustache with a glazed expression. "Okay."

"Antonio, we've got to do this right, according to our plan, like a symphony." Beeman gripped Antonio's arm tightly, his metallic voice drilling into the younger man with characteristic force and intensity. "While you're gone, I'll stay away from them *completely*, except to feed and clean them. And look over them. They'll be ready for you when you get back. Just for you." Beeman released Antonio's arm. "Trust me."

"Okay." Antonio looked at his watch again, and Beeman knew he'd gotten through.

"Just three short days. Vary nothing in your routine."

"Okay. But how do I explain my missing car?"

"Ride your motorcycle, go to the bar in Salida as we discussed." Beeman smiled and shrugged. "Talk about your boring weekend at home. I'll spend some time in town after I drop you off at the station. Stock up on groceries and a few other things. Maybe go for a hike."

"Shouldn't we at least check on them?"

Beeman shook his head. "We can't risk you missing the bus."

"Okay," Antonio said. "But I've got to see them, just for a minute."

"Don't spoil it, Antonio," Beeman chided, his voice taking on a metallic ring of authority that made Antonio cringe. "Let me get them cleaned up and ready for you. That's all. It will be so much more exciting for you that way."

"Okay." Antonio's resolve deflated.

Beeman took him by the arm and guided him to the garage.

"You'll be back before you know it."

Chapter 12

Mark and Janet Jensen stood at the front door of Robert Sand's elegant single-story house in the heart of Bonnie Brae, one of Denver's oldest high-end neighborhoods. The home was red brick and looked like it dated from the thirties. Ancient trees formed an overhead canopy running the length of the avenue, shading impeccably manicured yards. The neighborhood exuded a sense of quiet understatement. Jensen was mildly surprised; he'd expected Sand's neighborhood to be livelier, younger somehow. But why had he? He'd known Sand was older and wealthy, so he should have reflected instead of making blind assumptions.

Guard against stereotypes, monitor your assumptions, he cautioned himself as he reached for the bell. Before he touched the button, the heavy oak door swung inward, revealing a trim and very fit African American man with splashes of gray at his temples. "I'm Robert Sand. Please, come in." Sand stood back and motioned them into his home, shaking hands. "Very glad to meet you both. Coffee and snacks in the kitchen. Let's get comfortable, so we can talk."

Following Sand into the depths of his home, Jensen's eyes swept rapidly, surveying and appraising what he could see of the dwelling. As they passed through Sand's tastefully decorated living room, Jensen noticed several framed photos on a wall above a small credenza upon which a pair of Japanese swords rested upon a lacquered rack. One of the photos depicted a group of Asian men in traditional karate uniforms, and Sand stood out as the only non-Asian. One photo depicted a group of soldiers in military uniform. Sand was the only black man. Judging by how young Sand looked in the picture, the image was at least thirty years old. So Sand was exArmy; he'd served in Japan or Okinawa, and practiced karate—or judo. The swords below the photos looked authentic, but he wasn't an expert on Japanese antiques.

They followed him through the home and reached a brightly lit and well-appointed kitchen. Motioning them to stools at a center island, Sand poured coffee. A tray of pastries beckoned.

"This is awkward," Sand said as he settled onto his stool, cradling his mug.

"Awkward?" Jensen echoed. "How so?"

Sand's soft brown eyes settled on Jensen. A sad smile formed at the corners of his mouth, but he said nothing.

"Okay," Jensen shrugged with a sigh. "Awkward it is."

Sand nodded. "You flew in from Los Angeles?"

"Yes," Jensen said. "This morning."

"You met with Taylor?"

"Taylor, yes, and an FBI man," said Jensen. "Derek Sawyer."

Sand shook his head gently. "Bet *that* was fun."

"Not really," Jensen said, holding eye contact.

"Well." Sand placed his palms on the granite before him. "Let me see if I can make this easier. First, I know what must be going through your minds. I'm a stranger; I'm the only person you know of who's connected with your daughter's disappearance, even though all I did was notify the police. Worse, I'm way too old to be dating your daughter's best friend. I know it looks bad—hell, it would look bad even if they weren't missing. Even worse under *these* circumstances. I'm not oblivious to the intrigue, for lack of a better word— of my relationship with Jackie. And my skin color doesn't help."

"Mr. Sand, we don't—"

Sand raised his palms to hold Jensen off. "It is what it is. I know the question is hanging. Just exactly who am I?"

Janet spoke. "Ordinarily none of our business."

"Ordinarily, no," Sand said soothingly. "But it *is* your business now; you have a right to know." He slid from his stool and walked over to the counter. He picked up two enlarged color photographs and handed them to Jensen.

The first was of Christie and Jackie, in jeans and sweaters, standing beside a piano in what appeared to be an upscale bar or restaurant. The setting looked familiar to Jensen, but he couldn't place it. The second photo was of Sand, seated at the piano, with Jackie and Christie behind him, beaming at the camera. Jackie's hand rested affectionately on Sand's shoulder and her other arm was wrapped around Christie.

"Taken two months ago," Sand narrated. "Jackie and I have something special—despite the differences in our age and race. Not just physical. Far more than just that. Jackie means more to me than anything in this world. She's the center of my life. Every day we spend together is a gift."

Jensen could feel the sincerity of Sand's words. He cleared his throat. "How well do you know our daughter?"

"Christie's an angel," Sand replied. "She's been to my home many times. Jackie's best friend. More like a sister. Do you know Jackie?"

"We've met her, but we don't know her well."

"I want you to know. The thing with Jackie. I tried to fight it, at least for a while," Sand said softly. "But I lost that battle."

"Why did you try to fight it, Mr. Sand?" Janet asked, surprising her husband with the question.

Sand looked at her and then shook his head. "Age gap, race gap. Appearances. My own better judgment. Don't really know. At least not now. But at the start, well, the electricity between us was palpable. I told myself it was just physical attraction, but she just ..." Sand shrugged. "You get the idea."

It wasn't hard for Jensen to see how it could have unfolded.

Sand's athletic physique was obvious beneath his slacks and golf shirt. His square chin and angular features were rugged and masculine in a movie-star way. Jensen couldn't help but picture Sand in a courtroom. He spoke in a smooth, deep baritone, and projected an image most jurors would love—as long as they harbored no racial baggage. He pictured Sand with Jackie, remembering her flirtatious nature and that she'd struck him as a walking collection of curves and ellipses that moved with a pleasing rhythm and an electric smile. She was delicate, like a flower, but full of life and mystery. *She could be the yin to Sand's yang,* Jensen thought, cringing at how that would have sounded if he'd said it out loud. He rephrased his thoughts. *The chemistry would be there. Easy to see how it could happen.*

Sand continued. "The race issue never meant anything. We always knew it could be an issue for other people, but we don't care about that part. But the *age* difference? That's a bigger issue."

"Mr. Sand," Janet offered, "Christie and I talk." She cast a sideways glance at Jensen. "Mother–daughter."

"Christie said the same," said Sand. "And the rest is none of my business."

"She disapproves. And ... she thinks it's wonderful."

Sand laughed softly. "That makes two of us."

"Christie enjoys spending time with you both," Janet continued. "We respect our daughter and her judgment. She's very selective when it comes to her friends."

Sand rested his elbows on the countertop. "The police are not as tactful."

"How so?" Jensen asked.

Sand met his eyes. "Sugar daddy ditched by young hottie—not the top of the police blotter."

"They actually said that?"

"Not in so many words. But the message came loud and clear."

"Are you a suspect?"

"I'm sure I would be if they took the investigation seriously," Sand conceded. "But they don't really seem to buy into the idea that the girls are even missing. That's the part I can't understand. They are obviously missing—not to worry you, but this is serious. The police seem to have concluded that Jackie just got bored and made for greener pastures."

"They actually said that out loud?" Jensen asked.

"Yeah, they say it—but it's like a canned line," Sand replied. "The official party line. It bothers me, because it's both silly and artificial."

"Artificial?"

"Like they don't really believe that, but they can't say so."

"Have they searched your house?"

"I actually insisted they do so. They finally took me up on it yesterday. They didn't find anything interesting to them. Took nothing but a few swabs from surfaces, some fingerprints and some hair samples. They didn't remove any objects from my home. They only fingerprinted me when I asked them why they hadn't done so, and it was like they only did it to make me happy, or at least less suspicious."

"Suspicious?"

"You bet. Suspicious. There's something really off here." Sand leaned back on his stool and folded his hands in his lap. The man's poise and quiet confidence impressed Jensen. His instinct was that Sand was an ally, but he wouldn't drop his guard just yet.

"Do you mind if I ask you a few personal questions, Mr. Sand?"

"Fire away," Sand said evenly.

"You have a criminal record of any kind?"

"No."

"Have any trouble with the law at all?"

"None," Sand replied.

"Ex-military?"

"Noticed the photos?"

Jensen nodded.

Sand chuckled. "Christie said you catch everything."

Jensen ignored the comment. "Army? Gulf War? Panama? Kosovo? Grenada?"

"Army," said Sand. "Enlisted. Various stations through Southeast Asia."

"Then what?"

"Some private contractor stuff."

"Contractor stuff?"

"Sorry," Sand said with a shrug. "You could call it private security."

Jensen nodded. "Where were you when the girls were out?"

"Napping on the couch. You?"

"I have another question, Mr. Sand," Janet interjected, breaking the cadence and irritating Jensen slightly.

"Yes?"

"Did you harm either Christie or Jackie?"

Sand looked at her evenly. "No, Mrs. Jensen. I would never do that."

She held his gaze for a long moment. "You can call me Janet," she said at length, as though signaling that she'd reached a decision about Sand. "These last two days have been terrible."

Sand nodded. "Yes, they have been that, Janet."

"So let me ask you this," Jensen said. "The day the girls went missing. Will you take me through that in detail?"

Sand relayed that Christie and Jackie had taken his car to go to the Cherry Creek Mall; he'd expected them back in a couple of hours, but they'd never returned. He'd called the police twice. At about 12:40 the following morning, he'd gotten a return call. They had found his car in the mall parking garage, one of the only remaining cars. The key was still in the driver's-side door.

"They had their purses and phones when they left. Next day, I got on the computer and sent the police a list of the charges Jackie had put on my credit card on the afternoon they went missing. Neiman Marcus," he said. "Her favorite. A few others. This proved she went inside the mall, which they seemed to doubt for no good reason."

"How long was it between your first call and when they found your car?" Jensen asked.

"About four hours," Sand said.

"What were they wearing?"

"Summer clothes," Sand said. He glanced at Janet and then looked at his hands. "Tight shorts, skimpy tops."

"What exactly did you tell the police?"

Sand relayed the conversations, and Jensen grilled him on every detail, tossing in random questions to keep the flow of ideas from becoming too predictable. It was obvious he was interrogating Sand and Sand was willing to go through it. Janet sat quietly and let her husband work. It went on like that for a quarter of an hour. Sand had called hospitals, and so had the police. He'd tried Christie's cell—her number was in his iPhone—and he'd even called the Denver Athletic Club, where Jackie and Christie often worked out together.

"Did they tell you I offered to take a lie detector test?" Sand asked.

"No." Jensen shook his head.

"I wonder if you wouldn't mind giving us a minute," Jensen said. "We'll just step outside if you don't mind."

Sand nodded. "Sure."

On the front porch, Jensen asked his wife, "What do you think?"

Janet shrugged. "Not sure. He's very charming and seems sincere. My instinct is, he's telling the truth. I don't think he harmed the girls or knows where they are—but how can we be sure?"

"Interesting he volunteered to take a polygraph," Jensen mused. "We should verify that with Taylor."

"You think he would say that if he hadn't really volunteered?"

Jensen pulled out his cell phone and dialed Taylor's number. It took a minute to get through, but the detective took his call. He quickly confirmed that Sand had indeed offered to undergo a polygraph. Other than that, nothing new.

Jensen slid his phone back into his pocket. "He volunteered a poly. They didn't doubt his veracity, so they let it go."

"So they didn't actually do the polygraph?"

"No."

"Mark, I believe him. Gut instinct only. I think we're in this together with him," Janet sighed. "And it does feel like they're stonewalling us." A tear trickled down Janet's cheek. "The police aren't going to help, are they? Are they just waiting for it to blow over?"

"Sort of feels like they're hiding something." Jensen didn't mean to say it out loud, but there it was. "Sand thinks so as well."

Janet nodded, wiping her eyes. "It is odd, isn't it, Mark?"

"Let's go back inside," Jensen said. "We'll work with him. We can probably trust him, at least up to a point."

They rejoined Sand in the kitchen.

"What's the verdict?" Sand asked bluntly.

"We've got to help each other," Jensen responded. "We've got too much to lose."

"That we do," Sand conceded gravely.

Janet asked, "Where do we go from here?"

For a few minutes, nobody spoke.

Finally, Sand looked up. "Your daughter told me you're the best lawyer in the country. Seems to me that if it was a sexual assault, a rapist would want to get *one girl* alone. So maybe there is more to it."

"Money?" Jensen replied. "We thought of that. But when do I get a ransom demand?"

"Not necessarily *your* money," cautioned Sand.

"What do you mean?" Janet asked.

"My guess would be that if ransom was the object, it may be that Jackie is the real target, and your daughter just got in the way."

"I'm afraid you've lost me," Jensen admitted.

"I don't talk about it, but I'm pretty well off myself. Actually, I've got a pretty heavy portfolio," Sand said. "A very wealthy, very famous man left a lot of that money to me. I swore I would never reveal his name. The rest I earned myself." Sand shrugged. "A little digging would uncover those assets. Also, I've made a few enemies during my life."

"Did Jackie know about your money?" Jensen asked.

Sand shook his head. "Not in numerical terms, but she knows I've got enough to own this house, a few cars, and we go shopping a lot. I buy a lot of things for Jackie. I can't help myself."

"So, if you don't mind me asking, what are we talking about?" Jensen asked.

Sand paused. "I know you're well off, Mark. I've done some checking, just out of curiosity. Christie mentioned once that you have a couple of jets and more than one home. I've read articles about you in the Wall Street Journal. So I guess you can know a little about me. My portfolio runs well into nine figures."

Hundreds of millions. More than me, Jensen mused. "Who else might know about that?"

"In the Leaky Information Age?" Sand replied. "Anybody."

"So the girls, taken together, could make for quite a ransom," Jensen concluded. "This could have been a planned abduction. And I've got another confession for you. I have kidnap and ransom coverage on my family. A fifty million dollar policy limit. It's with Chubb. They take security seriously, so I doubt that's known, but as you said, this is the age of leaky information."

"Have you notified your insurance company of this situation?"

"Not yet."

They fell into an awkward silence. Jensen helped himself to a pastry, washing it down with some black coffee.

"You're ex-Air Force?" Sand asked.

"Yes."

"Intel?"

"No," Jensen said. "Pilot."

"What did you fly?"

"Strike Eagles," Jensen said.

Sand nodded and then looked away. "When I was a younger man, with connections I don't have anymore, I would have been all over this. But those resources are no longer available."

Jensen nibbled at his croissant, thinking. "I want to bring in some professional help," he said at last.

"Private investigator?"

"I don't know. I just have an idea."

Sand shook his head slightly. "Someone in mind?"

Jensen nodded slowly, as though lost in thought. "When I was young, my dad and I played golf a few times with a man who'd been a deep-cover agent in Eastern Europe after World War II. Years after that, he founded some kind of elite private intelligence agency together with some of his CIA cronies. He'd be too old to help us now, if he's even alive, but his company was a big deal. Had more resources than some countries, which is why governments and large corporations around the world often hired them."

"Who are they?"

"I don't remember the man's name or the name of his outfit, but my father might," Jensen said. "If we're lucky."

"Lucky?"

"Dad has Alzheimer's. Half the time he can't remember what he had for breakfast. Other times he's pretty lucid. It comes and goes. You have to catch him on a good day. I can call him now, but I'd like to make that call in private."

Sand showed Jensen to his den.

As it turned out, Jensen hit his father on a good day.

After a few pleasantries, mentioning nothing about Christie going missing, Jensen moved directly to the question.

"Hey, Dad, do you remember that old intelligence officer? The one we golfed with? He said he owed you the favor of a lifetime?"

A long silence, then the reply. "Sure, son. Why do you ask?"

"Well, it's kind of a long story, Dad. A client matter; I can't really talk about it." Jensen didn't want to distress his father's fragile mind with bad news. An emotional shock could push him over the edge. "But I think I could use that man's help."

"Is anything wrong?"

"No, Dad, nothing to worry about. It's just ... something's come up in my practice that needs some really special handling, and I thought of your friend. If his company's still in business, maybe I can send some business their way."

"That important, is it, son?"

Jensen paused. "Pretty important, Dad."

"Uh huh."

Another long pause. Then the older Jensen rallied, speaking with renewed strength and timbre in his voice. "Don't bullshit me, son. If you're in trouble, give it up. Don't protect me or coddle me. Hell, I probably won't even remember it by dinnertime. So spill it."

"I can't, Dad. Confidentiality. You know. What was his name?"

"Albert Brecht." He spelled the name. "We've slipped out of touch; I don't even know if he's still breathing."

"Do you remember the name of his company?"

"Not right now. It might come to me. You could try calling Albert. He lives in Baltimore, or at least he used to. He's got to be past eighty. I might have his number here somewhere. Hold on. I'll get Myrna to help me find it in my book."

Five minutes or so ticked by. Jensen could hear his father talking to his nurse in the background. He muted the phone, stuck his head out the door and asked Janet to Google the name Albert Brecht. She pulled out her own phone and did so, and after a minute or two she looked up with wide eyes.

"Wow," she said. "A historic figure. But I'm not seeing any contact information."

Jensen's father came back on the line. "Okay, son. You got a pen ready?"

Spotting a notepad on Sand's desk, Jensen took down the number, promising to call his father to update him about Albert Brecht if he succeeded in making contact. He signed off and then punched in the number his father had given him.

A recorded voice answered with a raspy growl, sounding even older than his father. "Albert Brecht here. Leave a message. Thanks."

Jensen left a detailed message.

Chapter 13

"See you Saturday," Beeman said.

"Talk before that?" Antonio touched Beeman's shoulder. "Tonight?"

"Of course."

"Be good, dude." Antonio stroked his mustache for a moment before getting out of the car. Beeman watched as he struggled with his pack before vanishing through the mirrored glass door of the Greyhound bus station.

Holding the wheel loosely, Beeman pulled the Toyota out of the parking lot, crossed over the Yampa, then turned left onto Lincoln and parked, watching the bus station across the river. He waited for twenty minutes before a bus emerged from behind the depot and rolled away, belching a cloud of black diesel smoke. Beeman observed the station for another half hour to be sure Antonio did not emerge.

Satisfied, he made his way down Lincoln Avenue until it became Colorado Highway 40. Keeping his speed below the posted limit, his window halfway down, he was glad to be out of Denver; it was always cooler in the mountains.

He welcomed the drive, for it gave him time to think without the distraction of keeping Antonio under constant observation. The timing of the younger man's return to the city was perfect. Absence from his job as a limousine driver might draw attention and was worth avoiding, but more importantly, Antonio's time in Denver would permit Beeman time to make his own final preparations, unhampered by the younger man's impatient meddling and ignorance.

For the next three days, Antonio's mind would be spinning like a top, roiling with fantasies, fears and doubts. Anticipation and panic would be pulling him apart. Antonio would return to the stage just when Beeman was ready for him, and he would be a frenetic mess, mentally exhausted from carrying the weight of his guilt, dread, lust and confusion every waking minute. Unremitting conflicts would pry open his mind, and Beeman would fill that void with the Primal Ecstasy, programming him to become a predator, driven by his restored basic nature to kill, purely for the sake of consuming another being. He would unmask the Hidden Engine.

Once the drugs burned through Antonio's system, he would be on a ragged edge. By the time of his return on Saturday afternoon, having endured a five-hour mountain bus ride, he'd be exhausted, agitated and susceptible to suggestion, even without chemical conditioning. Beeman would then begin to titrate Antonio's drug regimen without his knowing it, affording just enough release to permit him to think clearly without artificial euphoria or masked impulses. Dose management in an unwitting subject as complex as a human was a true challenge, but Beeman was ready. In fact, he was looking forward to it.

But first, there was work to do.

Twenty minutes later, he took the turnoff for Colorado Road 24, and ten minutes after that, he rolled to a stop in the driveway of his cabin. As he pushed open the door and climbed out of the car, the hair on the back of his neck bristled, standing literally on end.

He felt eyes raking over him as if touching his skin.

He gently closed the car door and slowly turned, scanning the shadows and recesses of nearby groves of aspen and pine, his ears straining, scouring the environment for signs of human presence.

But for the soft whisper of a gentle breeze caressing gently swaying pines, there was no sound. Aspen leaves flickered in the sunlight. A squirrel darted across his driveway, vanishing into the forest.

Beeman continued to turn in place, like a human radar dish, seeing no one, hoping to ping on some anomaly in his visual field, or instinctively sense the direction from which an observer might be watching, but no bearing called out to him over any other.

As quickly as it had come, the presentiment was gone.

He exhaled.

It must have been his imagination, merely an after-echo of the fearsome paranoia he'd implanted in Antonio's mind throughout the morning, nothing more. To be safe, he might take a hike later to inspect the woods for signs of human intrusion. He left his car in the driveway, avoiding the use of the electric garage door and the noise it would generate. Unlocking the front door, he entered quietly, closing it softly behind him. He stood in the entryway in silence, his ears still attuned to the faintest sound.

Slipping out of his loafers, he padded through the living room to the kitchen.

He had his hunting knife on his belt. He unsnapped the sheath before heading down the wooden stairway to the basement. Weeks ago, he'd added dozens of galvanized deck screws and additional shims beneath the stairs, covering them with felt padding to ensure they would not creak. He crept down the stairs now in stocking feet. When he reached the basement, he quietly opened a latch on a span of particleboard coated with a thin veneer of cement to look like a slab of concrete in an unfinished basement wall. The panel angled silently open on well-oiled, industrial hinges. Beeman pulled the panel open only far enough to allow him to slip through.

It took some time for his eyes to adjust to the dim light, but he could see the tangle of arms and legs on the mattress inside on the floor of the cage. The girls were sleeping, holding one another in a way that Beeman knew would arouse Antonio.

Nestled together on the mattress, they were at peace. He wondered if they were dreaming. He bent to pick up a hose that lay coiled on the floor. Grasping the nozzle with one hand, he turned a spigot on the pipe with the other, and the hose grew stiff as it filled with water.

Like the idiot, Beeman mused.

The soft hiss of water in the plumbing did not disturb the sleeping females. Squatting next to the cage, Beeman gripped the pistol-style nozzle and took aim. His grip tightened on the handle, and a spear of ice-cold water shot into the cage, hitting the brunette in the face.

She jerked and grunted, rolling over, and began to wail.

Beeman moved the stream to his left, tracing the icy blast along the blonde's spine. She arched her back involuntarily and raised her head. He held the jet on the side of her head for a second and then returned his attention to the brunette, who was scrambling to sit up and cover her breasts with her slender arms. He shot her in the face once more, blinding her.

She rolled onto her hands and knees, whimpering incoherently.

Beeman released the handle.

Soaked skin glistened under the pale light of the bulb.

The pungent smell of wet concrete filled the room.

"Thirsty?" Beeman asked.

The brunette whimpered and whined, but the blonde just glared at him. Beeman could see a pulsing artery throbbing on the side of her neck. Her heart was racing. He could see that her lips had swollen and cracked from dehydration. Beeman fired off another short blast that caught her in the eyes. The blonde cried out and then began to sob.

Beeman whispered menacingly, "I asked you if you are thirsty."

Her chest heaving, she caught her breath. "I just want to drink."

With a less forceful jet, Beeman filled the dog bowl that lay on the floor next to the soaked mattress. "Then feel free," he said.

The blonde hesitated but then crawled across the mattress to its edge, reaching down to pick up the bowl.

"Like a dog," Beeman snapped.

She hesitated again, looking at the water. Water was survival.

This was a critical moment—the first time he had given a command.

The blonde stole a glance upward at him. At that moment, looking into the woman's reddened eyes, Beeman could read her thoughts. For an instant, the connection between them was absolute. Her hesitation intrigued him, as did the defiant look in her eye as she recovered her composure. Her eyes flashed again, and she lowered her head slowly, with control, and began to drink from the bowl.

Beeman considered the path of the experiment.

Perhaps she would be the final objective, breaking only as she died.

Or ... could he turn *her* into a killer?

He needed more data.

Chapter 14

Albert Brecht walked slowly across his study, placed his age-spotted hands on an antique liquor cabinet, looked down at them and sighed. Gazing at his gnarled, misshapen knuckles, he changed his mind and decided against alcohol—the pain of his arthritis was tolerable. He poured a glass of mineral water and then turned and rested his hip against a brass rail running the length of the ancient wooden fixture.

He allowed his mind to drift back, nearly sixty years.

A lifetime ago.

The images still lurked in his mind like unwanted houseguests, keeping to quiet spaces, but underfoot nevertheless. His recollection was vivid in some respects, murky in others. His life had been shaped by events surrounding a time when he had lingered, much more closely than even today, at the very boundary of death.

Much had come to pass since that time—Brecht's family, now running into a fourth generation below him, his influence on world history, the growth of his company, so many victories and a few bitter failures. All of this had become possible through the remarkable heroism of one man, a humble hero who thought of himself as lacking in courage, a man whose own mark on history encompassed the life of Albert Brecht and more.

Brecht was one of the last remaining fathers of the Cold War. He'd kept the secrets of kings and presidents, killed and protected spies and soldiers, shaped world politics and altered the course of history more than once. He was a living legend in the intelligence community, known in the murky world of black operations as a man of iron will who did not know the meaning of the word "fear." Yet, as he sipped his San Pellegrino, his hands trembled.

Powerful emotions and old age made it difficult to hold his glass steady.

He replayed the voice message once more.

Oh, Lord, thank you for this. Do not let me fail. This will be my last request.

He slowly keyed in the number for a private line that had once been his own.

"Thomas," answered a crisp voice over the digitally secure line immediately. "How are you, sir?"

"David." Brecht let the silence hang, signaling the gravity of this call.

"It's good to hear from you, sir. What can I do for you?"

"Dave, come to my home. At once, please. I need to speak with you."

"Of course."

• • •

An hour later, Brecht and Thomas sat facing one another on antique chairs in Brecht's study. Thomas waited patiently for Brecht to begin. The ticking of an old grandfather clock marked the passage of time while Brecht composed his thoughts.

"You know something of my background," Brecht began, gravel in his throat.

"Some," Thomas shrugged. "Not everything."

No, Brecht thought, *not everything. Not by a long shot.* "You were born in 1979, weren't you, David?"

"That's right."

"A couple of decades before you were born, I was working for the CIA—it was a young agency then. I had been active behind the Iron Curtain for some time. Moscow, mostly—deep cover. Worst place for a NOC—so much at stake. We were scrambling for information, trying to grasp the implications of the communist bloc's growing nuclear capabilities. In Eisenhower's mind, our credibility was at stake. A failure in Moscow could disrupt NATO and weaken American influence in West Germany. It was the key to the balance of power in Europe.

"I was just a boy in my mid-twenties, but I was a quick study. I spoke Russian and understood Soviet doctrine. I was a recruiter of spies, a case officer, a handler. I was ambitious—did whatever needed doing.

"During one escapade, I was shot. Nearly died. You knew that much?"

"Yes, sir. You've never elaborated. I've noticed the scar behind your ear."

"You need to know more now. This isn't senility or dementia causing me to reminisce. The reason will become clear very soon, but first I need you to endure this background tale for me."

"Of course."

"Though what I'm about to tell you happened more than half a century ago, some of this material remains classified to this day." Brecht sighed deeply, resting his voice before continuing. "I needn't go into too much operational detail. We were working on a young Soviet Army general, a rising star we thought we'd turned. You may recognize the name: Vadim Kozlov."

Thomas adjusted his wire-rimmed glasses. "Kozlov? I know that name. Oleg Kozlov's father. Double agent, wasn't he? He got people killed, including his handler, if memory serves."

Brecht shook his head with a small smile. "Nearly, but not quite."

Thomas gaped. "That was you?"

Brecht ran an unsteady hand through his thick white hair. "Kozlov wanted me to get him out, wanted asylum. Claimed they'd intercepted one of his dead drops. We'd lose him if we didn't help. He expected arrest at any moment. He promised a treasure trove of intelligence on everything from Soviet guided missile technology to the Kremlin's plans for Iran. We had an evacuation plan, and I arranged a meeting.

"It was a trap. Details are immaterial. The only relevant fact today is that I was shot—one round in the abdomen, another in the head. Left for dead in a pool of blood in a cold, dark alley in the heart of Moscow."

Thomas shook his head slowly in amazement. "How have we come this far without my knowing that?"

"I never talk about it."

"How did you make it out alive?"

"Two Brits found us and contacted the American attaché."

"Us?"

"A female agent was with me," Brecht explained. "She was killed."

"But you survived and escaped," Thomas observed. "Jesus."

"*Iisus lyubit durakov s tolstymi cherepami.*"

"Jesus favors fools with thick skulls," Thomas translated.

"And, as you know, David, I have a particularly thick skull."

Thomas smiled. "I'll keep my own counsel on that, sir."

Brecht touched the back of his head. "One slug lodged in my spleen, the other in my occipital bone. Nine millimeters, fired out of a cheap Makarov—back when parabellum ammo was less powerful than it is today. The head shot sent a shockwave through my brain that gave me a very severe concussion, and the nose of the bullet was poking into my brain. I was comatose—hardly breathing and in shock. Bleeding out. The Brits carried me to the basement of a library. I was slipping fast. The American attaché went for help.

"Now, this fellow had a big problem on his hands. There was no such thing as a secure phone line in Moscow. Radio was out of the question. Our man took a gamble and drove to the American embassy, which was *always* under surveillance."

"What other option did he have?" Thomas asked.

"One," Brecht answered. "Leaving me to die. But obviously, his gamble paid off. At the embassy, the US ambassador was entertaining a group of American surgeons who were in town for an international medical symposium."

"Spaso House," Thomas chimed in, referring to the American embassy in Moscow. "Was that Chip Bohlen?" Thomas asked.

"No, Ike had demoted him two years earlier. Never could get along with Soviet leaders. This was the year Nixon visited as veep, spoke personally with Khrushchev. Broke new ground."

"Ah." Thomas nodded. "The ambassador in those days was Llewellyn Thompson?"

"Very good. Lynn hosted plenty of socials at Spaso House during Nixon's time there, including a private dinner with some heavy brass. One night, the night of the infamous Kitchen Debate, he had Nixon, Khrushchev, the president's brother Milt—who was the head of Johns Hopkins at the time—and a few others in attendance. Of course there were some intelligence boys also in residence. After that, the Sovs gave Lynn some extra leash, so getting in and out of Spaso House was just a little bit easier. We credit Nixon for that."

"Stroke of luck," Thomas acknowledged. "Were any of the visiting docs operational?"

"No." Brecht shook his head. "Civilians all."

"Don't tell me. They asked for volunteers."

"Not exactly," Brecht said. "The situation was too sensitive to disclose to the whole group. Half a dozen surgeons were there that night. It would have been wonderful if they could have taken me to the embassy, but there was no way—too conspicuous, too cumbersome. I was dying. Time was running out. Getting me *in* would be one hell of a lot tougher than getting one of the docs *out*. Lynn had to pick one man, based only on what he had been able to learn about these fellows over cocktails."

"I take it he was a good judge of character."

"At least that night," Brecht said. *Never mind what the fool had done later in life*, he thought. But that was another story. "So they chose a man—whispered in his ear in the middle of his dinner and discretely took him upstairs to meet the Chief of Station. They shared no operational details; they told him only that his country badly needed his services and that he would be in great danger if he agreed. He was free to decline; he could simply return to the dinner table, and no one would think any less of him. He had to make a blind decision. The clock was ticking; they needed his immediate answer.

"You have to remember—this man did not have diplomatic immunity. He was not a soldier. If they caught him, the best he could hope for was a bullet of his own. At worst, torture, interrogation and a lifetime in a Soviet prison."

Thomas shook his head. "What a thing to drop in his lap."

Brecht nodded in agreement. "They asked him if he would be willing to take a great risk for his country. He accepted without hesitation."

Thomas nodded. "Good man."

"So they smuggled him out in a laundry van, drove past the library at just past midnight, stopping only for a few seconds to shove him out with the attaché, and bustled him into the basement, where I was stashed behind a boiler. He had only a few surgical tools and some drugs that he had scrounged at the embassy and stuffed into a satchel. No x-ray machine, no operating room, no trained surgical assistants. No anesthetic gas. Nothing.

"He worked for ten hours without rest, mostly by the light of a flashlight that eventually ran out of battery, and a bit of light from the boiler fire. He cut the round out of my spleen as carefully as he could and sewed my belly closed. Then he dug the bullet out of my skull and relieved the pressure on my brain with the barrel of a pen. He sutured and bandaged my scalp around a small rubber shunt. My pulse got a little stronger. I stabilized enough for them to move me to a safe house."

"What happened to the doctor?"

"Our boys drove him to his hotel in Moscow, where he rejoined his medical group, thinking it would be safer than trying to smuggle him back into the embassy. That turned out to be the wrong decision. When he entered the hotel late, on his own, the watchers took notice. I think word had gotten around that a dead American had gone missing; one who wasn't really dead."

"So they caught him?"

"They took him in for questioning, interrogated him for two days before the ambassador was able to apply enough pressure—by sheer bluster—to secure his release."

"Did they torture him?"

"He's never said, but I don't believe so."

"You've spoken to him since?"

"We golfed a few times in the years that followed."

"So he made it out?"

"The Sovs didn't hand him over to the ambassador. They just put him directly on a flight to London, without his luggage, keeping his passport. By that time, they had moved me to a safe house, and an Army medical team tended me for two weeks. When I was strong enough to move again, they smuggled me out of the country in a tanker truck with a hidden compartment. I recovered in an Army hospital in Germany."

"So now," Thomas queried, "you're having trouble? Complications from the brain injury?"

"I wouldn't bother you with that," said Brecht.

Thomas nodded, waiting silently for Brecht to continue.

"Sixty years, David. That's what he gave me."

"That's quite a debt," Thomas acknowledged.

"The doctor's name was Conrad Jensen. The second life he gave me was longer than your own so far. Conrad risked his life for me—a complete stranger—in service to his country. He didn't *sign* up, but when the nation called on him, he *stepped* up." Brecht paused to allow Thomas to consider what he'd said, and then he continued. "Dave, today I received a message from Conrad Jensen's son. Conrad's granddaughter is missing. The circumstances are troubling. The family needs my help."

Thomas gave a gentle smile. "Our new op, sir?"

Brecht nodded. "Assemble your best K&R, forensic, cyber and tac-ops people," he said, referring to specialists in kidnap and ransom, crime scene forensics, computer hackers and door-kickers. "We're going to Denver."

"Yes, sir."

"Move quickly, David. And if it's possible, bring the man who cracked Hydrus."

Chapter 15

❝ What if …" Janet Jensen's eyes welled over. "You know."

Jensen gazed at his wife, feeling her misery as his own. "No more of that," he said softly. "We're going to find her; that's all there is to it."

"But how do you know?" She wiped her eyes with a wad of tissue clutched in her fist.

Jensen hugged her gently. "I just do. And so do you."

She buried her head in his chest. The familiar touch of the wife he'd loved for more than a quarter of a century warmed him and broke his heart at the same time. "Reach out," Jensen whispered, stroking her cheek. "With your heart. Can you feel her?"

Janet gazed up into his eyes. "I know she's alive."

There was a soft knock at the bedroom door, and then it opened. It was Sand, holding Jensen's cell phone. "You left this in the kitchen," he said. "It was vibrating, so I answered it. Hope you don't mind. The man you just called, I think. He got your message."

Jensen took the phone and held it to his ear. "This is Mark Jensen."

"Albert Brecht here, Mr. Jensen." The voice was clearly that of a very old man. "You're Conrad's boy?"

"Yes, sir. Been years, but we've met. Very kind of you to call me back. Do you remember me? I joined you and Dad for golf a couple of times."

"Of course," Brecht said. "But your daughter—have you found her?"

"No. We're getting nowhere. I'm embarrassed to bother you this way. I'm hoping you might be able to give me some advice. My father spoke very highly of you. He says you are a good man to know in a pinch, and we're in a pinch."

"Your father ... is he still with us?"

"Yes. He's doing well for his age, at least most days. He's in Palm Springs. Assisted living. He doesn't know his granddaughter is missing."

After a pause, Brecht said, "Better that way, for now. I'll call him later. I'm very eager to help with your daughter. I have resources at my disposal that should prove useful."

"Mr. Brecht, you can't know how much I appreciate this."

"Fill me in, please. Big picture first, then details."

Jensen recapped what had happened during the past two days. By old habit, he paced with the phone held to his ear, speaking crisply and methodically, a veteran trial lawyer briefing a master of espionage. First he covered the facts as he knew them, and only after that did he offer his opinions, speculations and suspicions. He went on for several minutes, covering everything that had transpired from his first meetings with Irvine PD to his fresh acquaintance with Robert Sand.

Finishing, he said, "We've run out of options. Cops are stonewalling. FBI involvement with no explanation? Feels very wrong to this ex-prosecutor. We need some real professional help. We can pay—whatever you ask."

"Mr. Jensen, when we find your daughter, I *will* ask something in return, but it won't be money. For now, we must concentrate all of our thoughts on finding your daughter and returning her safely home."

Jensen blew out a long sigh. "Thank you."

"Are you still with Mr. Sand?"

"Yes. Did you speak with him?"

"Not in depth. But my team and I will need to do so. Mark, I don't want to add to your stress, but as you understand, I can't emphasize strongly enough how important it is that we act quickly."

"I know that," Jensen said. "Are you still in Baltimore? I can send my jet for you."

"Ah, most convenient. It will save time, as our aircraft are all deployed at the moment. If your pilot leaves right away, my advance team will be ready to deploy by the time he touches down. There'll be four or five of us, I think, with a little luggage and a bit of equipment. Send your plane to the Signature FBO at Baltimore-Washington Thurgood Marshall Airport. Designator is KBWI."

"Hold on just a minute, Mr. Brecht."

Jensen turned to his wife. "Call Adkins. I want him and Goodman on the ground at KBWI, Baltimore, Signature FBO, as fast as they can get there. Expect a hot turnaround with a full load back to Centennial. Five passengers with luggage. Get those people here ASAP. Call now on another phone while I'm on with Mr. Brecht."

Janet nodded sharply, relief evident on her face. "KBWI. Signature. Got it." She pulled her own phone from her handbag and stepped out of the room to make the call.

"The plane is on its way, Mr. Brecht."

"Good. We'll have the rest of the team join us tomorrow or the day after. Now some things for you. Write down every fact given to you. Note the source of each detail: who told you and when. Give the same instruction to Sand and to your wife. Don't tell anyone we're involved. Do not speak to the press, and only speak to the police if they contact you—don't call them. Don't give my name to anyone. Tell your pilots to keep very quiet about this. Keep your cell phones charged. Try to get some food and rest. Also, do *not* touch that old Jaguar. When the rest of the team arrives, we'll have a full forensic inspection. Is it in a garage?"

"Yes, protected from the elements," Jensen replied. He could hear Janet in the next room, telling the pilot to get wheels up, pronto. "The rest of your team? How are they getting here?"

"Two large motor coaches, specially equipped," Brecht answered.

"Wow," Jensen said. "You're coming in force."

"Not initially," Brecht chuckled. "But we can if we need to. We begin with a dozen or so. More than that, why, we just get in each other's way. I'll see you in a few hours."

Brecht signed off.

Slipping the phone into his pocket, Jensen smiled grimly. "I think we've just unleashed a dragon."

"A dragon," said Sand with a nod, "is exactly what we need."

Chapter 16

Deep in the Florida Everglades, Roady Kenehan squatted near the edge of a brook, balancing on the balls of his feet. He held his breath as a snake slipped past, undulating gracefully toward the water. Ringed with red bands, it was either a scarlet king or a coral. Though similar in appearance, the former was harmless, while the latter was the deadliest snake in Florida, with a neurotoxic venom that rapidly caused respiratory failure and death. The easiest way to tell them apart was the color of the head: the harmless scarlet king's was red; the dreaded coral's was black.

The snake slithering past Kenehan's right foot had a head as black as death.

Kenehan remembered a story he'd heard as a boy, of a farmer chopping wood somewhere in the southeastern US as his toddler son played nearby. The boy cried out, showing his father bite marks on his finger, and the father saw the coral snake slithering away. With only seconds to act, the man gripped his young son's tiny forearm, squeezing as tightly as he could to keep the venom from spreading, and set the boy's arm over a log. Screaming in anguish, the man chopped through the boy's arm with his axe, severing it above the wrist—saving the boy's life. People hailed the father as a hero, for had he not acted, the boy would likely have died within two minutes, but he'd been a tortured soul from that day forward.

As if sensing Kenehan's recognition, the serpent came to a stop, its great body inflating and deflating with a deep gasp. Kenehan guessed its length at five feet. It was as thick as Kenehan's wrist. The serpent's evil head shifted furtively from side to side, its tongue darting as it sensed the environment.

Kenehan fought the urge to jump away. The snake was not coiled to strike.

He considered drawing the combat knife sheathed at the small of his back, but he remembered that the blade and tip had been rounded off for use in simulated combat exercises. He wore loose-fitting black Nomex military coveralls and soft black Kevlar boots with spongy rubber soles. The thick fabric of the boots covered his ankles and might stop the coral's short fangs, but if the serpent decided to strike, it would likely be at knee height or above. The lightweight fabric of Kenehan's coveralls would not protect him from its needle-sharp fangs. He thought of the Glock 34 strapped to his right thigh, in which a dozen rounds of Simunition were staggered in the clip. Though non-lethal, the projectiles would stun or perhaps kill the snake if he could hit it at this range, which would be easy if he could get the gun out before the coral struck—but that was unlikely.

Kenehan smiled. Was he closing in on the last five minutes of his life?

Snake eyes, the song went. It was time to breathe.

His nostrils flared slightly as he slowly took in the murky scent of the Everglades, waiting for his slithering friend to decide what to do next. The snake seemed perfectly content to remain where it was. Kenehan felt the beast's diabolical patience and made it his own.

We'll wait this out together, my friend.

He glanced at the river, with the banded serpent highlighted in his peripheral vision, watching the murky water drift past. A large water spider shot across the surface in ambitious spurts, leaving miniature ripples where its feet touched fleetingly, using surface tension to stay afloat. Countless other insects buzzed unseen in the nearby thicket of woods.

The light was fading quickly. He'd been waiting for the light to recede, and in another half hour it would be time for him to move in on his own prey.

The heat of the summer Florida sun made wearing long-sleeved black clothing uncomfortable, but Kenehan's attire was perfect for operational night exercises in the Everglades, providing stealth and protection from poisonous insects and plants, if not snakes. The day was drawing to a close. He focused on his breathing—slow, deep and quiet.

Time slipped by. The light was fading.

Soundlessly, the huge coral moved again. It slipped into the water and floated away.

Later, friend.

If the snake had killed him, or if he had killed the snake, neither of them would have felt remorse—for that was the essence of nature's best killers. But Kenehan was glad things had turned out otherwise. Had he been a superstitious man, he might have considered the snake's harmless passage a sign that he carried no evil karma, that he had been forgiven for his deeds, but he was not superstitious. Kenehan believed only in planning and ability—and occasionally, very rarely, in luck.

He mouthed the plastic tube of his camelback, drinking deeply from the bladder within. The water was warm and tasted brackish from added electrolytes.

Kenehan's long brown hair was tied back, braided and tucked into his coveralls. It had grown long during his years as a Brecht operative, making some infiltration and covert operations easier because he looked less like a cop or soldier and more like a biker or surfer. He could pass as a steelworker, an artist or a drug dealer with ease. Though his long hair was a distinguishing feature that made him easier to identify, he could bleach or cut it in minutes if need be to change his appearance quickly.

The sound of insects in the woods, so loud in the Florida dusk until now, decreased slightly. A bird called from the woodlands at his back—but it was no bird.

Snipers in the trees.

Kenehan was mildly surprised. Six men were in the opposing force, or OPFOR, charged with one defensive goal: prevent Kenehan from infiltrating a guarded compound to snatch an aluminum case containing fictitious "intelligence material." The exercise aimed to train the protectors. The mysterious intel package was usually something ridiculous, such as a bottle of Dewar's, a Playboy and a bag of Cheetos.

Kenehan had expected the OPFOR to form a defensive perimeter, close and compact, but this group of trainees had decided to go on the offensive, to track him down and neutralize him. An interesting idea—but a bad one. It would disperse their forces away from the prize, making each member of the defense team easier to pick off.

• • •

Robert Partridge lay across the limb of a large tree, looking through his night vision goggles at the spot where he'd seen movement a few minutes before. He was sure the light green blur had been the Intruder. If Partridge could nail him now, the exercise would be over—just like that. Piece of cake. His team's proactive strategy, bringing the battle to the enemy, would prove out.

Time ticked by as the darkness deepened.

Thirty minutes passed since he'd seen the rustling in the tall grass at the edge of the stream, but he held his position, glued to the bough of the tree, ten feet from the ground, as though part of it. He considered keying his throat mike to alert his team, but he was seduced by the idea of neutralizing the Intruder—typically an experienced instructor—without help, and right now silence was golden.

He thumbed the safety of his AR-15 to OFF, notching the muzzle brake on the edge of a thick branch to stabilize it, his red dot optic riveted to the spot where he knew the man was still hiding.

But then, a hand clamped over his mouth and wrenched his head back before he could react. He felt the hard edge of a blade at his throat. Panic flashed through him as adrenaline splashed into his bloodstream. The weight of the man who had landed silently on his back forced the breath from him. A knee thrust into the base of his spine. He was immobilized in the crook of the tree.

A voice whispered in his ear.

"Condolences to your wife and all of your girlfriends. Now stay put. Nowhere you need to be. Just lie there and rot, like a good corpse." He felt hands reaching around in front of him, ripping his radio from his chest rig, quietly disconnecting the snap of his rifle sling.

Overwhelming frustration replaced alarm. Partridge grunted reluctantly, and the man released his grip and moved off him, dropping quietly to the ground, taking the radio and rifle with him.

• • •

Kenehan moved silently away from the base of the tree. His muscle control had allowed him to move silently up and down the opposite side of the tree like a spider. As he contemplated the best path to make his way deeper into the forest, a booming claxon echoed through the dark, followed by a metallic voice over the estate-wide PA system.

"Knock-it-off, knock-it-off. Condition white. Repeat, condition white. Exercise is terminated. Team leaders acknowledge."

Kenehan looked up and saw the man in the tree wiggling his way down the branch, preparing to lower himself down.

He keyed his throat mike. "Tomahawk acknowledges condition white." He read the name tag on Partridge's breast. "Sodbuster is with me, standing down."

"I get it," Partridge muttered, shaking his head.

"What?"

"How you got above me."

Kenehan was interested. "Yeah?"

"Channelized my attention. I underestimated. I thought I fucking *had* you. I was complacent."

Kenehan nodded. "And by being out here, you made yourself a target. You overextended, gambling that you could hit me first. Dispersal of protective forces is usually a bad idea."

"Yeah. We thought we could surprise you, neutralize the threat proactively, you know, bring the fight to the enemy—but it didn't work." Partridge turned his head to one side and stepped back, realizing something. "Tomahawk? So you're Roady Kenehan, in the flesh."

Kenehan shrugged.

As an ATV pulled up and they climbed in, Partridge smiled. "At least I was killed by the best."

• • •

Kenehan blinked in the bright light cast by the fluorescent tubes overhead, enjoying the cool, dry air conditioning of the admin building. A clerk handed him a cordless phone. Only a handful of others were within earshot, but their lack of chatter and downcast gazes made it obvious they were loitering to overhear.

"Kenehan," he said quietly into the phone.

"Thomas here. Get ready to mobilize. We're going to Denver. High-profile K&R recovery. The Old Man is coming with us. It's his op."

Alpha-Bravo himself.

The line went dead.

Going operational with Albert Brecht? Kenehan smiled as he handed the phone back to the clerk. *Shit hot.*

Chapter 17

The weathered, hand-painted awning bore the words "Blashfield's Saddlery" in faded red bounty-flyer lettering. Beeman stepped up onto the boardwalk, strode past the hardware store and entered the dimly lit tack-and-saddle shop. His rubber-soled loafers carried him quietly over aging wooden floor timbers amid deep shelves stuffed with saddles, saddlebags, ropes, spurs, stirrups, blankets, chaps, feedbags, leather vests, boots, gloves, cowboy hats, currycombs, brushes, bridles and countless other equestrian supplies.

He stopped to caress the meticulously tooled leather of a finely crafted saddle, noting its exorbitant price tag. He tried on a Stetson and hefted a coil of calf rope. It was too stiff for binding slender wrists and ankles, so he draped it back over its hook on the wall and returned the Stetson to its place on the shelf.

He made his way to the back of the store, where a long glass counter displayed a collection of hand-made bullwhips stretched out like snakes in a glass sarcophagus, bathed in fluorescent light.

Beeman had come in search of a particular kind of whip.

Rather than the safe and friendly toys sold in sex shops, he sought the cruel weapon used for centuries to dominate longhorn beasts. Inhaling the astringent scents of pine and rawhide, he carefully studied the collection: show whips, working whips, buggy whips, hand crops, hand whips, crackers and rods, but none suited his purpose.

He came upon another glass case in the back corner of the store.

A particularly exquisite lash lay coiled within, woven of tan, orange and black leather bands. It had a rawhide handle nearly two feet long. The body of the whip thickened slightly a few feet from the handle, becoming nearly an inch in diameter, then thinned gradually, tapering to an end with a six-inch thong branching into three twisted strands of thin red rawhide. A card rested in the center of the coil, proclaiming in beautiful copperplate:

TWELVE-PLAIT, SEVEN-FOOT BLACKSNAKE STOCK WHIP
KANGAROO HIDE FROM PERTH, AUSTRALIA
~~ $950 ~~

The checkered pattern of its braids made it seem alive. The bright red fall at the end reminded Beeman of a scorpion' stinger. It was beautiful.

Lifting his gaze, Beeman noticed a framed photo on the wall behind the counter, a grainy black-and-white image of a cowboy riding amid a sea of cattle. The rider had twisted in his saddle, looking over his shoulder. Above his head hovered a whip, a stylized arc floating in space, an airborne serpent preparing to strike.

Beeman thought to make an offer for the photo along with the whip, for it was a remarkable piece of art. Black lightning erupted from the cowboy's palm as an extension of his arm. With it he could reach out twice the length of his own body and deliver a thunderbolt of agony with a vicious touch. Beeman gazed down once again into the case. The tricolored bullwhip was more than a length of leather rope. In skilled hands it would be a living, predatory viper. With scientific detachment, Beeman considered the jolt of agony such a tool could inflict on human skin. The speeding rawhide tips would rend epidermis, and a fraction of a second later, sensory nerves would deliver to the brain an electrical copy of that carnage. The mind would feel millivolts of current as megawatts of force and fury.

Provided she remains conscious.

The thought of goading Antonio to use such a vicious tool on another human being was alluring. How would Antonio react to such an experience? Would he crave the sensation, or would he shrink away from the horror? Would he become addicted to the intoxicating power, or would his feeble conscience and squeamishness regain control?

He crafted sentences he knew would mesmerize the younger man. *Pick it up and try it out. It's fun to play with.* Then later, *Her mind is a canvas, waiting for your mark. Pain is your paint. The whip is your brush. Work it deftly, with the hand of a master. Express yourself fully, as you've dreamed. Take ownership. Release your longings. Impose your fury. Be a god!*

For Beeman, exotic sexual practices were no more interesting than a common cold, but the power to fundamentally alter a living being was a worthy goal. He would morph Antonio from an overgrown child, crippled by his own self-loathing, into a wanton death machine. The distant promise of an even more wondrous transformation also teased him from the horizon of his imagination. The slender blonde displayed signs of inner steel, steel they might yet forge into something marvelous. Beeman pictured her strangling Antonio with this very whip, perhaps avenging the death of her friend—

The contentment blossoming within Beeman's mind vanished abruptly. He felt a warm, tingling sensation in his cheeks and at the small of his back, just as he'd experienced at his cabin.

Glancing about, he saw that a man had appeared silently behind him.

Beeman turned to face a tall Asian man who looked to be in his thirties, dressed in loose-fitting jeans and a designer golf shirt, with sunglasses resting atop his head, buried in a tuft of black hair. The man's flat black eyes gazed unflinchingly at him, and the corners of his mouth turned slightly upward to match the half-smile on Beeman's face.

Taking a step to his left, the man pointed at the whip in the glass case. His brow raised in childlike innocence. In an intimate whisper, he asked, "A bit harsh, don't you think?"

Beeman moved to step away. The man stayed with him.

"How are your patients faring, doctor?"

"Excuse me?" Beeman looked at the man, seeing danger behind the humor in his dark eyes.

"How are your houseguests holding up?"

"What?"

"Are they still alive?"

Beeman froze for a moment and then looked past the man, his eyes scanning the store. Aside from an old woman tending a cash register at the opposite counter thirty feet away, they had the store to themselves.

"Who are you?"

The man held out his hand. "My name is Jimmy Kim, Dr. Beeman."

Beeman refused the handshake. "What do you want?"

Kim dropped his hand, and his smile vanished. "To meet a brilliant scientist."

"I see," Beeman said flatly.

What now? Arrest? Blackmail? Something else?

Kim smiled once more, sheepishly now, and asked, "Can I buy you a cup of coffee?"

Beeman sent back a mocking imitation of that furtive grin.

• • •

He followed Kim to the Starbucks a few blocks down Main Street, thinking quickly, scientifically. That he was not facing arrest narrowed the probabilities. *Blackmail?* It was possible. Someone had devised a scheme to acquire Black Sunrise.

He had developed it in the underground DataHelix labs in Colorado to be the supreme bioweapon system, consisting of an engineered virus and companion software.

Black Sunrise was a candle that lit itself.

This was the biological magic Beeman had genetically engineered. He had given the world a virulent plague with an adjustable R_0.

Pronounced "R naught," it was the reproduction number that predicts just how contagious an infectious disease will be. As an infection spreads, it reproduces itself. R_0 represents the average number of people who will catch it from one infected person. If a disease has an R_0 of 18, a contagious person will transmit the virus to an average of eighteen other people, assuming a lack of vaccination. The longer a disease takes to incapacitate or immobilize someone, and the longer the pathogen itself remains viable in the host, the greater the reproduction number. Beeman's technology could control both of those variables. He had designed it to incapacitate enemy states without running rampant beyond the geological and chronological boundaries set by strategic military doctrine.

When coupled with a cyber warfare assault, the pandemic would be even more devastating because a companion cyberattack would hobble any effort to impose quarantine by cutting communication lines, hence the Black Sunrise weapons package included cyber-warfare modules.

When deployed, Black Sunrise would spread rapidly—but only for a set interval. It would quickly flare and burn out, leaving enemy forces and infrastructures decimated and incapable of resistance, without destroying cities, with no nuclear fallout or permanently contaminated water supplies or croplands. Secondary infections could arise from heaps of decaying cadavers, but the more virulent Black Sunrise virus would be gone, and conventional biohazard precautions would protect invading forces.

Assuming an invasion would even be necessary.

It would have been a truly effective solution to ISIS, for example, if it were to have become a globally threatening caliphate with its own borders and WMDs, weapons of mass destruction.

The software and hardware was just as important as the pathogen itself, if not more so. Given the data files stored on the subterranean

DataHelix servers—isolated from any network connections—anyone with access to the technological specifications of the required genetic sequencing equipment and software platforms could cultivate and deploy the weapon.

Beeman had developed the virus; he had not designed the analytics and cyber-warfare aspects of the computing technology, though he had access to all of it.

Of all the countries that would want to possess the virus if they knew of it, potential Black Sunrise targets themselves—North Korea, Iran, Pakistan and Israel—were the nations that were most likely actually to try to obtain it. Beeman had been briefed on this scenario many times, but he'd never considered the threat as anything other than theoretical.

Though it was his first successful effort to control the fundamental machinery of life and death, AR-117 would not be Beeman's last. His research in the lab, and here in the mountains, would propel him to entirely new vistas.

Now there was an unintended and unwanted connection between his two experimental worlds.

This had been inevitable, he realized. It had only been a matter of time, though the timing could not have been worse.

Or perhaps it could not have been better.

Beeman chose to move from this universe into another, from his past into his future. It was his way of controlling reality with his mind. He glided into a new plane. His mind began to whirl, weaving solutions and braiding them together like the strands of the whip he'd been admiring. *The brutal simplicity of sheer will. New dimensions, seen and unseen, continuously evolving and changing in the quantum realm.*

They ordered coffees and seated themselves at an outdoor table.

Kim stirred his with a stick, saying nothing.

Beeman finally broke the silence. "Who are you, Mr. Kim?"

"I'm a talent scout."

Beeman waited, his mouth a thin line, his eyes as dead as Kim's. After a moment, Kim spoke again, raising his coffee.

"To the Wild West: a rugged culture—rough and tumble, where everybody does what they want."

Beeman spoke with hooded eyes. "You're an admirer of the West?"

Kim smirked. "Dude. I'm from SoCal."

"I doubt that, *dude* ... more like NorKor?"

Kim leaned forward, slipping the sleeve from his paper cup. "Take this thing, for example. A stroke of genius, this way to hold hot coffee. Cheaper than a second cup. The guy who invented it should be worth millions."

"The rewards of ingenuity," Beeman said.

Kim removed his sunglasses. "At the very least, one would think he's earned the right to do what he wants with his spare time. To pursue his interests—whatever they may be—in privacy." Kim smiled before continuing. "With financial freedom and the means to handle any travel needs that might arise suddenly. This sleeve—so simple, yet so useful. A way of safely handling something *extremely hot*. The inventor of such a thing should be rewarded ... no matter what he does in his spare time."

Kim set the sleeve on the table and lowered his cup into it. When he'd spoken the words "no matter what," Beeman had detected a trace of Asian accent: *no matta wat*. Foreign born. But the flaws in Kim's obviously rehearsed approach did not prevent Beeman from appreciating the dangers, and the possibilities, he represented.

Beeman probed. "Travel? To where?"

"Smart men with exotic hobbies need to be able to move out at the drop of a hat." Kim evaded, pressing his palms together as though praying.

"I've traveled the world," Beeman said. "Some places are better than others."

"Perhaps," Kim parried, "but it's important to have options, don't you think?"

"Options," Beeman admitted, "are always desirable."

"As opposed to not having any."

Beeman smirked. "One always has options,"

"The trick is picking the right one," Kim countered. "The safest one."

Beeman took his first sip. "To do that, Mr. Kim, one must know a host of things. Your country—"

Kim cut him off with a sharp wave of the hand. "Hey, I'm a California boy."

"Right," Beeman cooed.

He wondered what the North Koreans, assuming that was who had sent Kim on this errand, planned to do with Black Sunrise if they acquired it. Were they prepared to use it? Was an invasion of South Korea on the horizon? The entire world had been holding its breath for half a century, waiting for that to happen again.

Beeman felt the Primal Ecstasy coursing: he might now hold the power to spark a world war! It seemed so fitting. This was *his* new reality.

A merciless god.

If an invasion *was* their plan, they would need more than just a sample of the virus. To use Black Sunrise to its full tactical potential, they would need to know how to replicate it in bulk, how to deploy it properly and how to protect their own forces from the biological backlash of the retrovirus. They would need all of Beeman's knowledge and expertise, together with the essential data and cyberattack software.

Kim remained silent for a full minute before he finally spoke. "Men have different priorities. One man might pay dearly to see the sunrise. Another might take it for granted."

How clever this little man thinks he is, Beeman mused. He waited while a girl in a filthy green apron cleaned a nearby table. When she was gone, he said, "And how much, exactly, would one pay for the sunrise?"

"In addition to freedom itself?"

Beeman nodded.

"Millions."

Beeman considered the possibility of actually receiving the money against the probability of ending up in a ditch with a bullet in his head—or rotting in prison.

"Perhaps as much as fifty million?" *That is how many people I will help you kill,* he thought to himself.

Kim shook his head slightly. "Perhaps as much as five million. With freedom to pursue one's interests, in peace and privacy, in a new home."

Beeman said nothing.

Finally, Kim stood and tossed his cup into a trash bin. "Perhaps we could meet here again, the day after tomorrow? At seven a.m.? We'll have another cup of this excellent western coffee, and I'll have a gift for you."

"A gift?"

"A sign of good faith, Dr. Beeman."

Beeman nodded. "I'll be here."

"Two days, then." Kim turned to walk away and then stopped. "Go buy your whip."

Chapter 18

Beeman shaved the skin from an apple with his knife. On the wooden table before him lay two purses. His mind was rolling through dozens of possibilities, chewing on the ramifications of his meeting with Kim, working on revisions to his plan.

The knife slipped, cutting deeply into his left thumb. So intense was his concentration and so sharp was his knife that he did not immediately notice the deep slit in his flesh. Only when he saw his blood spread across the white meat of the apple did he realize he was cut. Squeezing his thumb, he smeared a wide streak of blood across the fresh surface he had peeled and took a bite.

A small smile formed on his thin lips. There was no pain, so he put the apple down, opened the cut, and the pain came. He contemplated it. *Wondrous thing, pain.* It became its own reality. He sucked the cut until it stopped bleeding.

He picked up the larger purse, poured its contents onto the table and took a seat.

A few cosmetic items, a package of birth-control pills, an empty cell phone case—the phone lay crushed at the bottom of a sewer drain in Denver—and a leather wallet, the folds of which contained credit cards, several post-it notes stuck together like a miniature notebook, and a driver's license.

Jaqueline Rosalie Dawson.

The one Antonio had nicknamed *Kitten.* How banal, his need to rename them, to strip them of their identities

Two snapshots lay among the credit cards. One was of an elderly couple who might have been the girl's parents. The other pictured an older black man, at least fifty, with gray sprouting at his temples.

Who would this be?

He pulled the photo from its plastic sleeve and looked at it more closely. The man was smiling, yet there was a glimmer of strength in his soft brown eyes. Beeman turned the snapshot over. There was writing on the reverse side.

Jax—Moments and memories—R.S.

A romantic relationship? Quite an age difference here. A wealthy man? Beeman smiled. Now the little Kitten has nothing but fear; her moments and memories would soon contain little else.

Beeman replaced the items and picked up the second purse.

It too contained a leather wallet, but one a man rather than a woman would carry. Business cards from many different people stuffed into one side, and the other held a few credit cards. After a moment of rummaging, he found the driver's license.

Christine Ann Jensen.

Antonio called her *Dove* because she was slender and graceful.

Her license said she was an organ donor.

She also had a concealed weapons permit but no gun in her purse.

Interesting.

Beeman examined other items, which included a collapsible hairbrush, a tube of lipstick, a few bills and coins, a jade heart and a folded brochure for *Cirque du Soleil*. Replacing the items, he put both purses in a drawer and then stepped into the bathroom to wrap a bandage around his thumb.

He returned to the kitchen to make sandwiches.

The first meal for the women.

It was time to begin their indoctrination.

Of course he had considered aborting this adventuresome experiment; but the idea was repulsive to him. These new developments could become *part* of the experience, and he would not allow Kim to control him or deter him. Other more profitable possibilities would emerge, he was sure.

As he puttered in the kitchen, Beeman contemplated Kim and his unseen comrades. Of course, Kim might not be what he appeared— an agent of the North Korean government—but what else could he be? An American agent? Very unlikely. A false-flag operative of some other nation? Certainly possible. A corporate contractor? Far less likely.

If North Korea were preparing an invasion of South Korea, a biological weapon would be a far more practical means of preemptively crippling the republic than a nuclear attack. That would likely result in the total destruction of both Koreas. It would thus defeat the goals of Korean unity and the liberation of North Korea from its unsustainable confinement within the prison of international sanctions imposed by UN Security Council resolutions.

Insane as it was, a biological attack on its neighbor to the south was North Korea's only option—a Hail Mary gambit: unleash a Black Sunrise plague, timed and modulated like a controlled forest-service back-burn, and wait for it to spread. Soon after the first symptoms began to appear throughout South Korea, massive casualties would occur practically all at once, producing mortality statistics beyond imagination. Without warning of any kind, a substantial segment of the South Korean population would fall ill and die in a couple of days. In the panic and chaos that would follow, South Korea, a small nation about the size of Arkansas, would be easy pickings for the massive "built-to-invade" DPRK military.

A simple tip to the press would trigger congressional investigation under the microscope of UN oversight. They would eventually trace the plague back to America's biological weapons program. America would lose international influence and face threats of retaliation from all corners of the globe. Worldwide confusion and panic would work in the North's favor, at least for a crucial period, while its conventional army—two million strong—flooded steadily over the border. In four weeks or less, the whole thing would be a *fait accompli* before America could disentangle itself from world scorn and mount a workable full-scale military response.

Kim Jung Un could even stack world opinion in his favor by simulating a small biological attack on his own people—killing starved peasants who produced almost nothing—before the much larger South Korean casualties began to mount. This would give him the pretext to cross the border in what he could claim was self-defense.

It would be like stealing candy from a baby, as long as China stood still. And it would, for it would see the Korean invasion as an opportunity to snatch back Taiwan and most of the contested islands in the South China Sea. China would reap fantastic bounty with much less sacrifice than it would require to repel the surging North Korean army, which in turn would require China to invade *both* North and South Korea. A tacit agreement of sorts would arise, a trade-off, changing the face of Asia forever. A new and eventually more stable Asian axis of power would emerge.

So, yes, the most likely scenario was that Kim was a deep-cover North Korean agent, blackmailing Beeman to hand over the key to a military coup that was the only means of survival for his desperate rogue namesake dictator. Beeman could envision the chubby little tyrant grinning like an idiot beneath his ghastly cat-as-a-hat hairnest when his emaciated, sycophantic military advisors laid the plan before him.

But it could work. A new world would follow, a new life for all— especially for Beeman—fueled by death on a massive scale, engineered by his genius.

It all fit together so beautifully.

Destruction was the motor that drove creation.

Kim was right: Beeman needed better resources and more personal freedom. Human test subjects were vital to his continued path of discovery. North Korea would afford him an unlimited supply.

Beeman spread butter evenly on four slices of bread and continued musing.

The makeup of life at the molecular level mirrored the most basic mechanics of consciousness. The impulse to survive possessed by a tiny viral particle was a function of the arrangement of atoms within its DNA, and its ability to reproduce was a function of its physical structure and its environment.

What differentiated chemical compounds from living material? Shift certain atoms, and a viral organism loses its impetus to continue as an organism, becoming merely inert matter.

Why?

Beeman had never admitted to his colleagues that his understanding of the structure of viral genetics was more intuitive than analytical. The mathematics of biochemistry played a major role in his accomplishments, but Beeman had begun to form an innate sense of how the building blocks of life operate, which transcended the mathematics of computational chemistry.

He found molecular virology fascinating because viruses were the most elemental form of life. Chemistry was dull; viral engineering was the path through which one learned to become a god. By studying viruses, one could observe the distinction between chemistry and life most closely. Survival for a virus meant only one thing: *reproduction*. On the other hand, a human's will to live fluctuated in response to the perceived worth of continued existence. Viruses reversed the food chain: smaller and simpler organisms fed upon larger and more complex ones. The laws of chemistry and physics are the same for all organisms, but the natural outcome of where those forces lead is exactly opposite for a virus than for any other organism—except humans. Humans were not the only life-forms to destroy themselves systematically, but they, like viruses, virulently infiltrated their environment and worked steadily to destroy it.

Through sheer luck, Beeman had been able to observe human beings as they experienced death and near-death, and he had seen the same process he could actually detect when studying the behavior of genetically engineered particles. Beeman sought the common denominator that bound these processes, one ingrained into the very structure of reality.

For centuries the question of how life animated matter had captured the imaginations of religious leaders, storytellers and physicians.

Beeman sought to know, not for preserving life, but rather to understand the mechanism by which life abandons its hold on matter.

Beyond anger, fear and hunger, what was the genesis of the urge to kill? Or the urge to die? Conventional psychology provided no answers, but studying the interface between life and matter had shed some light upon the nature of life itself.

It was the nature of life to trade in the currency of death.

A key ingredient of this mechanism existed in the frustrated libidos of Antonio and men like him, in their inability to act out their impulses freely—ironically the same sexual urges that propagate the human species. This inability drove their behavior in some ways and stunted it in others.

The death-sex urge and survival-sex urge were two sides of the same coin, but the death-sex urge was the more powerful force, leading to rape, pillage, conquest, war, organized armies, weapons, fortresses, catapults, rockets, atom bombs and supercharged human advancement, while the survival-sex urge led only to babies, famine and disease.

Antonio's unrequited lust was the tool Beeman would redirect to make him crave torture and killing. The war Antonio was fighting with his conscience would end, and Antonio would be reborn as a new and much more powerful being—a walking, talking version of Black Sunrise, and just as sure to self-destruct eventually.

But he had to prepare the bait, to serve as the irresistible lure necessary to draw the sloppy fool across those lines his parents and other childhood programmers had scored into his mind.

As Beeman arranged the sliced meats, cheeses and bread for sandwiches, he turned his thoughts to how he would handle the meeting in two days with Kim, before he picked Antonio up at the bus station.

He pulled out his phone and did a quick bit of Google research. The North Korean Worker's Party ran several separate intelligence agencies. Most of the organizational branches were concerned with undermining the South Korean government and preparing for massive attacks upon the US forces stationed there. A group called the Research Department for External Intelligence, or RDEI, was responsible for gathering intelligence in the US, answering to the Central Committee of the Worker's Party. There was also something called the Reconnaissance Bureau of the General Staff Department and another arm called the State Security Department. An administrative maze.

Would Kim really pay him millions and leave his criminal acts undisclosed if Beeman were to give him samples of the virus and the data needed to reproduce and deploy it? It was easy to envision that Kim would simply kill him to keep him quiet, unless, of course, they wished him to defect and continue his research. In that case, they might allow him to live in luxury, as Kim had hinted, while guiding further bioweapons research for his new host nation. There would be many benefits, and a few downsides, to a new life in North Korea. First among the downsides was the lack of state-of-the-art computing and gene-splicing technology. Beeman could help with that, provided he received sufficient resources of other kinds, including money and logistical support.

So should he offer to defect? It seemed so, but what was he missing?

Beeman had no doubt that if he did not at least appear willing to cooperate with Kim, they would kill him, for the DPRK could not risk having their plans and activities on US soil discovered.

The sandwiches were ready.

Beeman placed each on a paper plate adorned with a handful of potato chips and a few slices of pickle.

Loving touches.

He needed more information and the time to work it all out.

He would hold Kim at bay with talk of the logistical difficulties of removing the virus and the data from the lab, which would give him at least a little time to make *other* preparations. Kim would push him, but Beeman knew he was the essential ingredient of the plan. It was very, very unlikely they had any other means of acquiring Black Sunrise, so he had a much greater degree of bargaining power than Kim would want him to recognize.

Beeman should be able to prevent Kim from interfering with his plans here at the cabin, at least for several more days. He would demand that as part of the non-negotiable price in return for his full cooperation and defection.

It will be a delicate balancing act, he thought with a smile, as he balanced a can of cola on each plate, making his way carefully down the stairs to the basement.

Chapter 19

Christie's slim body stiffened when she heard the sound of someone coming.

Jackie heard it too and slid back against the rear wall of the cage, pulling her knees up to her chest and crossing her ankles to shield as much of her body as possible from view.

Christie rose unsteadily to her feet, fighting a wave of dizziness, and stepped to the front of the cage. She wanted to be comfortable with her nakedness, knowing that whoever was coming would feed on fear.

Her movement woke Jackie, who sat up. "What are we doing here?" she asked, her brown eyes wide with fear. "Are we going to die?"

"Quiet, baby," Christie whispered. "Someone's coming."

•   •   •

Sliding the hidden panel slowly open with his elbow, Beeman entered the concealed room, setting the plates and soda cans on a table.

"Good afternoon, ladies. I'm terribly sorry to disturb you, but I thought you might like to have something for lunch."

Both girls stared at him in silence, breathing heavily, from either fear or relief at the prospect of eating. Probably both.

For the past two days, they'd been drinking out of the toilet's tank, surviving without food, shivering fiercely in the night with cold mountain air pouring in from somewhere. Burning energy without replenishing it, they had lost weight and were what Antonio would call "model slim." Both were weak; Kitten was lethargic.

Yet Dove stood upright and gazed at him defiantly.

"What? Not hungry?" Beeman shrugged. "Then I'll take these away." As he started for the door, the brunette whimpered. He stopped but did not turn to face them.

"Please," said the blonde. "Please, we are starving."

Beeman very slowly turned to face her.

Her fingers clutched the wire fence, as if to tear the material apart. She was definitely the bolder and more self-assured of the two. She would be the last to break, and almost certainly the most useful in the long run. Watching them carefully, Beeman savored the possibilities.

He would use Antonio to break Kitten, and when she was broken and obedient beyond all doubt or hesitation, he would goad Antonio into killing her. After all, Kitten would never make the journey from prey to predator, would she? Could he then use her death to manipulate the older girl and make *her* into a weapon? Perhaps one to kill Antonio?

And then to kill herself?

Delicious, reprogramming life and death. It was what he had been born to do. Cruelty was nothing more than a way for man to free himself.

Approaching the cage once again, Beeman smiled. "I'm so glad," he said. "I would hate to see these go to waste. It's nice to be appreciated. To see that the little things I do aren't taken for granted."

When it was clear that he was waiting for a reply, Kitten spoke. "What do we have to do so you will give us the food?"

Beeman smiled broadly, sliding the table on which he'd placed the food closer to the cage. "Stand up, Kitten. Come here."

Whimpering, Jackie stood and did so, covering her chest with her arms, though Beeman never looked anywhere except into her eyes. He raised each plate, still balancing the sodas precariously.

"Look at this food, Kitten. Which one would you like?"

"I don't—" She stopped herself. "Whichever one you want to give me?"

Beeman set the plates on the short wooden table along the wall outside the cage. He dug into his pocket and withdrew the key to the padlock. As he removed it and raised the horseshoe-shaped latch, it reminded him of the gate he'd left unlocked when he was in third grade, causing a vicious Rottweiler he'd been taunting for days to maul Pamela Clark to death. He'd watched the hideously gratifying spectacle from the safety of his perch high in a tree.

"Kitten, *you* may come out." His voice remained soft and soothing. The brunette bent down to step out through the small door, never taking her eyes off Beeman. As she was stepping through, Dove reached out and put her hand furtively on the younger girl's shoulder.

"Be careful, Jax."

In a flash, Beeman slipped his knife from its sheath and slashed Dove's right forearm. The blonde hissed and cried out, quickly pulling her arm back. Blood poured freely from the laceration. Beeman was surprised by how gratifying it felt to slice human skin. He'd performed ghastly experiments on animals, with no feeling of pleasure or regret, in the course of his lab work, but cutting *human* flesh was another thing entirely.

He hadn't expected that.

Kitten turned involuntarily, crying out at the sight of the knife and Beeman's startling speed. With his free hand, he took a fistful of her hair and yanked her the rest of the way out of the cage. She stumbled and fell to her hands and knees. Beeman quickly shut the door, and replaced the padlock, snapping it shut with a crescent frown twisting his thin lips.

Dove clutched her arm to her chest. Blood seeped from between her fingers and trickled in deep red lines over her belly and down her pale thighs. A loud groan pealed from her throat.

She looked at the man who'd cut her, in shock and disbelief.

He dragged Kitten away by her hair, leaving the sandwiches on the table.

As Beeman left, he heard Dove start to cry, and once she started, she couldn't stop. He stood just out of sight of the cage, listening and savoring the melodic tones of her sobbing.

What fun!

Chapter 20

Christie whimpered as she rocked back and forth, sitting on edge of the toilet. She watched the blood run copiously from between her fingers as she pressed her hand tightly over the deep cut, cradling her forearm against her abdomen.

She was afraid to lift her hand from the cut, fearful of how deep it might be. Her arm felt like it was on fire. The shock of what had happened, combined with the terrifying sight of so much of her own blood, led her to fear that the blade had filleted her arm to the bone.

She opened and closed her right fist, relieved that there was no loss of function or feeling in her fingers. That meant the slash had not severed her tendons. She guessed there was no serious damage to nerves or muscle, but she couldn't be sure.

She hoped she was right, but she would have to look.

She forced herself to peel back her hand and look at the gash.

Pivoting on the edge of the seat, she raised the porcelain lid from the toilet tank and set it on the cement floor. She scooped handfuls of water onto the cut. The water made the laceration burn. Tears poured down her cheeks.

The cut was deep but did not appear to have reached muscle. She could get by without stitches, but there would definitely be a scar. Blood was still pouring freely from it, but the water made it easier to inspect. It was nearly four inches long. While she could see the cross-section of her skin along the wall of it, it was not deep enough to reach muscle or any major blood vessels.

The sharp pain gradually turned into a deep throbbing that radiated up her arm. She replayed in her mind the instant the knife had flashed unexpectedly into her skin, feeling more like a sledgehammer than a blade.

One of the keys to functioning under extreme pressure, she'd learned at SALO, was to accept reality while keeping it separate from fears and imaginings. Plans, goals and tactics were far more useful than visualized worst-case scenarios. Even though they felt real, thoughts and feelings were not reality. They were just reactions; indeed, you had to experience them without criticism or condemnation but never confuse them with reality. Unlike useless feelings, her ability to control her viewpoint, direct her attention and actions could influence future reality. She had to remain calm, view her reactions dispassionately, accept them and let them pass.

There was no one in the room now. She was hurt, but not badly. Her cut was clean. She covered it by wrapping her arm with toilet paper.

But it was so hard.

No, she thought, *not hard. Easy.*

There was nothing she had to do. Nothing at all. Just let the terrible feelings bore through her and depart. The key was not to push the fear and sadness away but to be present in the moment, aware of everything, clinging to nothing.

Dad, thank you for SALO.

She focused on her breathing while she finished washing the cut and flushed the toilet to evacuate the bloody water. Then she replaced the heavy porcelain lid. As she did so, it slipped from her wet hands and banged against the tank. A chip of white porcelain, roughly the size of her finger, landed by her foot.

She picked it up. One edge was literally razor sharp. The opposite side was flat and smooth. She held it, pinched between her thumb and middle finger, the flat back surface pressed against her index finger, and made a cutting motion in the air.

Now she too could lash out suddenly.

She saw that the missing part of the lid was visible when it was back in place on the tank, so she turned it around and put it back down. The broken part was now hidden from the view of someone outside the cage.

She stared at the ceramic fragment. Running her finger lightly over the sharp edge, she realized she could use it to cut away some of the mattress to make a bandage. Of course, if she did so, the man would know she had found a cutting tool and take it from her. So she tucked the precious sliver beneath a corner of the mattress and lay down, curling into a ball with her back to the wall, as had become her habit.

She thought of the cut on her arm and how it would feel to grip the ceramic sliver tightly, lash out and slit that old fucker's throat.

Could she do it? Could she cut him?

Was she quick enough? Did she have the courage?

She had never hurt anyone on purpose, but then again, she'd never had a good reason to do so—until now.

What was happening to Jackie?

She quieted her breathing and listened for any sound that might provide some clue as to what was going on upstairs, but there was only silence.

Time crept past with excruciating slowness.

What was going on upstairs?

She wished she could hear something. The silence was unbearable, but when it was later broken, Christie would give anything not to hear.

•   •   •

The man dragged Jackie up the stairs by her hair. Her mind had become like jelly, but a voice from deep inside of her said that this was the price she would pay for how she had used natural attributes to control men. As a young teen, she'd learned to watch men for signs of approval. She'd learned that they could be manipulated and controlled by the way she moved her body, how she locked eyes, how she controlled her voice, how she kept track of what was important to them. She'd learned what made men tick.

All for a single purpose. To find love and acceptance—and she'd come so close with Robert. She'd found her place in life. She'd made a future for herself with a man she could love forever. But now, there was no future, no happy ending. She knew she would die here, and perhaps in the next few minutes. She might never see Robert again —a thought which tore her soul from her chest. She knew that her death would tear him apart; she longed for a way to soften his pain and to ease her terror.

At least let it be quick.

As they neared the top, he jerked her head closer to him and spoke into her ear. "Resist me in any way, any way at all, and your friend downstairs dies in agony."

When they reached the kitchen, he released her. She stumbled, trembling, but did not struggle or fight.

"Sit down," he hissed, pointing to a chair at the table.

She obeyed, her eyes on the knife in his hand. As he returned it to its leather scabbard, she relaxed slightly, taking a small sip of air.

When the man spoke, his voice remained silky with menace. "It's much too nice a day to be sitting around inside. Why don't we get some fresh air?"

Jackie's head was swimming. What sick things did this crazy old fucker have in mind for her? Was he going to parade her about naked for his neighbors to see? If so, maybe they would call the police.

The man held open the screen door and motioned for her to step out onto a wooden patio deck. She complied. He followed her out and pointed at a plastic chair on the patio. "Hey, would you be a sweetheart," he said as though he were addressing a close friend, "and carry that chair for me?"

Numbed by fear, Jackie picked up the plastic chair and followed the man around the side of the cabin to the backyard. She moved awkwardly, blinking in the bright light, not sure how many days it had been since she'd seen the sky. Three? Four? It seemed like months.

Following his silent gestures, she carried the chair around the corner, noting that there was nothing in any direction but a dense forest of pines.

Where were they?

Pointing to the ground beside a window well, the man said, "Put the chair down *right there.*"

Jackie lowered the chair, its legs crunching in the brittle dead pine needles that poked her soles painfully. The mountain breeze and sun were warm on her bare skin, but she shivered, cold with dread.

The man turned the chair to face the wall of the cabin, just in front of the window well.

"Have a seat. Make yourself comfortable."

She obeyed, noticing a large spider creeping along the mortar between the wooden logs of the cabin wall.

"Who are you?"

"I am God, Kitten," he replied. "You do understand that, don't you?"

She hesitated but then answered, "Yes, sir."

"Then say it."

"You are God." She began to cry softly. Why had he faced the chair so that she was looking at the wall?

"Again."

"You—you are ..." She couldn't finish.

"You doubt me, don't you?"

"No! No, I don't doubt ... don't doubt ..."

He put his hand on the handle of his knife. "Then say it, *and believe it,* or die. I will know if you're lying to me. If you are being insincere, saying what I want to hear, I'll know. I'll be able to tell whether you believe what you are saying."

She considered this, and she knew he was ready to end her life.

That made him God, at least from her point of view, didn't it? Yes. She knew that it was true. For her, right now, he really was God. After a moment, she said it. "You are God."

This earned her two things: a smile, and his hand came away from his knife.

God lowered himself to his hands and knees; he reached down into the window well near her feet. He lifted some items out, laying them on the ground; then he crouched next to her. She looked down at the items. There was a roll of heavy tape, some rope, a paper bag and a metal watering can with a spout like a showerhead. A pair of pliers and a few long nails.

He picked up the can. She could tell by the way he lifted it that it was full of water.

"What do you want most in this world?"

She wasn't sure what he wanted to hear her say. That what she wanted most was to obey him, serve him? Or that she was thirsty? Should she ask for water? For her freedom? She didn't know what might get her in trouble. He was impossible to predict or even understand, considering how he had cruelly slashed poor Christie. He was clearly willing to cut them. Having abducted her and Christie, he likely thought he'd eventually have to kill them both—they'd seen his face, and his companion's.

He picked up the roll of thick silver tape, obviously planning to secure her to the chair. She thought of running but decided she dare not. He might kill Christie, as he had threatened. Besides, Jackie was too frightened to move and too weak to make it far into the deep forest.

"I'm waiting for an answer," the man said as he worked the roll around and around her arms and ankles, binding her tightly to the chair. She tried to think, but her mind was like thick mud.

When he was finished with the tape, she was completely immobilized.

His work finished, God stood, tilting his head to one side with a quizzical expression. "Well?"

"I want to go home," she whimpered.

"Home? You want to go *home*?" He shook his head in disappointment. "Oh, that makes me so sad. So very, very sad."

He bent and picked up the watering can. She wondered if he would give her some to drink. He didn't. Instead, he held the can over her head and poured it on her, dousing her under a shower that poured forth from the perforated spout.

"The right answer was obvious, but your heart is *not* pure."

The water was cold on her bare skin, the breeze making it more so. It soaked her hair, trickling down her back, cascading over her shoulders and dripping from her stiff brown nipples onto her thighs. It burned her eyes, and she blinked to clear her vision.

What was that smell?

It was familiar, but it took a few seconds for her to recognize it. When she did, she thought her chest would split.

Gasoline!

She watched him toss the empty can aside and dig into the paper bag. He withdrew a butane lighter with a long metal neck—the kind used to start barbecues.

Jackie was panting like an Olympic sprinter, hyperventilating as her adrenal glands responded to the terror blossoming in her mind.

He's going to burn me alive!

"No! Oh please, God!"

Then all she could do was scream.

She did not realize that her terrified shrieking projected down the window well to drill a hole in the mind of her imprisoned friend— that she was playing her part perfectly in God's macabre play.

• • •

Beeman had never actually *intended* to burn the girl but only to traumatize her, secure her absolute obedience, so that the next phase of the process could unfold smoothly upon Antonio's arrival. He'd only intended put her into a state of total, unthinking obedience so that her conditioning could continue.

But now, as she sat before him, squealing in terror, dripping with Amoco Ultimate Premium Unleaded, he was compelled to squeeze the trigger on the lighter, imagining what it would be like. *Push the plastic safety lever forward, snap the trigger, touch off a blaze and jump back to watch the blistering, bubbling skin, hair ablaze, eyelids peeled back by the scorching flames.* He visualized her thrashing, then twitching, then going still as the fire cooked her, screams fading slowly to silence.

His chest heaved. He pushed the safety lever forward with his thumb. His finger tightened on the trigger switch. He brought the lighter up and touched the end to her gasoline-soaked hair.

Her screaming grew even louder, until her voice grew hoarse. Then she began to make a croaking noise, coughing and sputtering incoherently.

Do it!

No. That would ruin the plan.

But wasn't it ruined already? Hadn't Kim changed everything? Was this the closest he would come to looking the dragon in the eye? Balancing on the razor edge that separated life from death, the urge to immolate this child was so powerful it was intoxicating, irresistible.

He felt his finger pulling the trigger back, hearing the audible *click*.

The lighter did not ignite. These damn things never did on the first try.

The little bitch's head tipped forward as she fainted.

With a deep sigh, Beeman tossed the lighter aside.

Then he chuckled.

He should have videotaped this.

Chapter 21

First Dave Thomas and then Albert Brecht climbed into the plane, raising eyebrows among the three junior members of the team who were already aboard. Jennifer Takaki was a former DOD electronics intelligence cryptanalyst and hacker with skill in financial tracking, photoreconnaissance analysis and logistics. Marcus Ortega was a forensic technician who had been a crime scene investigator with the FBI for several years. And Paul Boyer was an expert in criminal profiling who had also been with the FBI.

When the last two men climbed into the cabin, Takaki raised an eyebrow: *both the director of operations and the Old Man himself?* A lot of clout. Then Roady Kenehan climbed aboard, adding even more to the intrigue. Kenehan was a nearly mythical figure within the closed, secretive world of covert ops, where rumors were forbidden but had a nasty way of creeping about. This was clearly a hot assignment. Receiving it had to be a good sign, career-wise.

While the pilots worked through the preflight checklist and taxied for takeoff, Thomas gestured for the team to don the headsets clipped to the bulkhead beside each of the seats. He then gave them a concise summary of their objective: the safe recovery of two young adult females believed abducted from a shopping mall in Denver, Colorado. The present whereabouts of the abductees was unknown. There had been no ransom demand. State and federal investigations were supposedly underway but appeared to have stalled for unclear reasons. The missing subjects included a college student and a former waitress.

Curious. Location and recovery of missing persons on US soil was not a typical assignment for the Brecht Group. Usually state or federal law enforcement handled kidnappings, primarily because few private citizens could afford to pay the Brecht Group's fees. Exceptions included kidnapping victims related to affluent VIPs, high-level government officials or those with some strategic value and cases where the US government needed to remain officially uninvolved.

A college student and a former waitress? Very curious indeed. Who were these girls, and to whom were they related? They sounded like Everyday Janes. What was it about them that could bring Brecht himself to the operation? The Old Man hadn't been actively involved in operations for how long?

Takaki wasn't sure, but it had been years.

During the three-hour flight, most of the passengers aboard Jensen's Phenom 300 caught a bit of sleep and then hunkered down at the run-down Ramada on the airfield at Centennial Airport.

They convened at seven the next morning in a private executive conference room at the Denver Jet Center, where they downed a catered breakfast with plenty of coffee.

Now, all the team members sat around a large conference table. Their clients soon joined them: Mark and Janet Jensen and Robert Sand. No one had ever heard of them.

When Mark, Janet and Robert entered the room, Brecht greeted them warmly, introducing Thomas, Takaki, Ortega and Boyer and Kenehan to them in turn, giving brief summaries of their roles and skills. Everyone wore casual attire except Brecht, who sported his customary bespoke suit with a striped tie.

Brecht nodded to Thomas to signal that he was ready to begin.

• • •

Jensen was a little surprised by Brecht's quaint appearance but impressed with his demeanor. *He has the manner of a commanding general,* he mused.

Brecht began to speak, slowly and with deliberation, his deep baritone voice conveying purpose and authority that Jensen found comforting in light of the man's age. "We are here," Brecht said, "to find and retrieve two young ladies who have vanished without explanation. We believe they were abducted. Missing now for four days. You'll receive dossiers and photographs in a moment.

"With us this morning are Mark and Janet Jensen, the parents of Christine Anne Jensen, age twenty-six, the older of the two missing women." Brecht gestured across the table. "This gentleman is Robert Sand, the last known person to have seen the girls before they went missing. They departed from his home in his car for a shopping excursion. Mr. Sand resides with the other missing woman, Jaqueline Rosalie Dawson, age twenty-two." Brecht cleared his throat. "They are romantically involved. The women did not return as expected on the evening of their disappearance. Mr. Sand filed a report with the Denver police, who have done very little on this case.

"Mr. Jensen has spoken with detectives and an FBI liaison. He is a former criminal prosecutor. He feels that details of the investigation are inconsistent with his extensive experience in similar matters. He suspects something may be going on behind the scenes to divert resources away from finding the missing women, or at the very least that the Denver police have formed a biased view of the situation due to circumstances we will get into more deeply in a moment.

"Police found Mr. Sand's car in a multilevel parking garage at the mall the girls had said they were going to. The driver's-side door was partially open, and the key was still in the outside lock."

Brecht focused his attention on Mark and Janet. "Some of you will inspect that location later this morning; others will inspect Mr. Sand's car. The rest of you will see to logistics and coordination to prepare for the arrival of the main Mobile Response Team, which consists of several more specialists coming in two of our MAO motor coaches." He turned to Mark Jensen and continued. "These special retrofitted buses serve as mobile analysis and operations bases to house team members and equipment during ongoing field operations. They should be here by midday tomorrow."

Brecht returned his attention to the rest of the team, gazing at each of them in rotation while he spoke. "There are no known videotapes of the women in the mall or the parking lot. No known witnesses saw the women after they left Mr. Sand's house.

"In a moment, the Jensens and Mr. Sand will tell us what they have learned, including what little they've been able to pick during police interviews. There isn't much. More importantly, they'll educate us about the missing women—their personalities, backgrounds, habits and contacts." Brecht paused. The team members were obviously pondering the as-yet unmentioned elephants in the room. Jensen noticed that all eyes had fallen on Sand, who calmly locked eyes with Brecht and nodded slightly, signaling Brecht to proceed into difficult but unavoidable subject matter.

"This much you already know," Brecht said, his palms turned outward toward the group. "Before we go any further, let me address your most obvious questions. First, is Mr. Sand a suspect, given he saw them last, and second, who is he? Also, why are David and I here personally to oversee what would usually be a relatively low-level assignment?"

After another pause, Brecht continued. "Let me tackle the last question first." He cleared his throat and played with the knot of his tie. "For more than forty years," he said, his deep voice dropping yet another octave, "I have served as the chairman and president of this organization. In that time, we've worked for presidents and kings, noblemen and aristocrats, despots and playboys. We have grown since our formation during the Cold War. We've taken risks; occasionally we've lost good people, and I've made no apologies for the fact that we sometimes do dirty work in a dirty business. I don't apologize because our work *is* necessary, and we have always done it well. We've known success, and, on occasion, we've suffered bitter failure."

Brecht pulled a pen from his breast pocket, holding it like a wand in his gnarled hand, using it to gesture as he spoke. "Our accomplishments have placed us in the ranks of the elite. This has been no accident. We *are* the elite of the elite. Employment in our organization is coveted. We steal the best from SOCOM, the FBI, Blackwater, Triple Canopy, SIS and SAS. We limit our ranks to the finest analysts, logisticians and paramilitary professionals, who are almost all former Tier One operators. Our standards are exacting, and our methods, techniques and resources are equal or superior to those of most governmental agencies.

"Acting extrajudicially, we have improved the world in measurable degrees, but we've never betrayed the public trust attendant to our function. Yet we *have* preserved, for the most part, our anonymity, which is our lifeblood.

"So now, it is with a mixture of regret and pride that I will very soon announce my retirement, in the hope that I will end my professional life with dignity and pride."

Brecht paused for several seconds before continuing. "Whether that comes to pass, as I hope, remains to be seen." He leaned forward, his elbows on the table, and systematically renewed his eye contact with each member of the team—his vivid blue eyes boring into each person like a pair of cold lasers.

"This is not, as some of you may assume, a run-of-the-mill, find-the-kids assignment. This is *not* a matter of negligible importance. In your time with our Group, and perhaps before that, most of you participated in operations of national or even global import. I see on your faces that you question whether this kind of case warrants what I have chosen to put into it.

"Don't make the mistake of questioning such a thing. On the contrary, this is your *final* test before I hand over the reins. This operation will define the measure of what we have built, painstakingly, for more than half a century. Do not fail me."

A few heads nodded, almost imperceptibly. Janet's eyes were brimming with tears, and she gave a sad smile. "Thank you," she said, her voice cracking. "I needed to hear that."

Brecht nodded to her. Then his aging eyes wandered from person to person. "With that question covered, we move to the next one hovering in your minds: Robert Sand." During Brecht's monologue, Jensen had seen Roady Kenehan gazing at Robert Sand. He could practically see sparks passing between the two men.

For several moments, Brecht said nothing, and it became clear that he wanted Sand to introduce himself.

Sand chuckled. "Now we're going to talk about little-old me. No sense trying to talk around this. I'm fifty-six years old, black and shacked up with a much younger white woman. I'm head over heels in love with her. I know how it looks, but that isn't how it is. Jackie is twenty-two years old. She's an adult; she makes her own decisions."

"What do you do, Mr. Sand?" Takaki asked.

"For a living, you mean?"

"Yes, sir."

"I'm retired."

"May I ask from what?"

Sand turned his soft brown eyes downward. After a moment, he said, "Got your radar all lit up, don't I?"

"Well, I'm just curious."

"So am I," Kenehan said.

Sand smiled. "Just as I'm curious about you, Mr. Kenehan, but I think we can read each other."

Thomas interjected, "Mr. Sand, we've done background checks. As you might guess, we have access to some restricted databases. We've got your Army record. We've got your credit records and much of your financial information. But most of your adult life is an empty page. For about twenty years, you were off the grid, and during that time you made a *lot* of money. We're still digging, but you could save us some time. Your background, we need."

Sand sighed. "After I left the Army, I was a private contractor."

"Your service jacket indicates you suffered a gunshot wound when stationed in Japan, inflicted by a member of your platoon; then you left the service. A Japanese dignitary took you under his wing somehow. The Japanese government listed him as a 'national treasure.' A special lineage, a descendent of royalty or something?"

"Master Konuma."

"And?"

Sand stared off into space, into the past. "I was trying to protect him from my drunken fellow soldiers, in a bar. It was a servicemen's bar; it catered to GIs like us. Why he would risk walking into a place like that, at a time like that, I still have no idea. The GIs preferred to discourage the locals from coming, which wasn't much of a problem, given how xenophobic the Japanese can be.

"Master Konuma walked in wearing a traditional Japanese ceremonial kimono. His niece worked there; he just came to visit her. The GIs started up on him. He was too old for that, I thought. But those men were drunk and didn't take any kindlier to my skin than they did his. So when I shoved my nose into it, I took a .45 to the belly for my trouble.

"He worked it out with those boys and saw to it that I received immediate medical attention. You see, he was one of the last remaining samurai masters, a descendent of a royal line. He had some heavy political clout. After my release from the hospital, he took me in, arranged for me to receive an honorable discharge—which was looking like it was going to be a problem because those boys cooked up a story that *I* had assaulted *them*."

"And some of them were severely injured." Thomas added. "You said he 'worked it out with them.' The record indicates that six young infantrymen, who had all been through basic training and a few of which had seen combat, were throttled within an inch of their lives. They blamed it on you, but two witnesses reported that you were shot before any of the fighting started. Konuma was a martial arts expert; he disarmed and incapacitated the man with the pistol and then decommissioned the rest. Or so it says."

"So what happened next?" Kenehan asked. "You convalesced in his house?"

"Something like that."

Kenehan blinked twice. "And then he *trained* you."

"Something like that."

"Then you fell off the grid and made millions."

"Something like that."

"Working for whom?"

"I moved around a lot."

"*Wakarimasen*," Kenehan said in Japanese. *I don't understand.*

"*Nihongo hanase-mas-ka?*" Sand replied. *You speak Japanese?*

"*Osukoshi.*" *A little.*

"*Hai. Yoi dess.*" *Yes. Good.*

"*Anata-wa ronin ka?*" *You were a mercenary?*

"The ronin died out with the samurai," Sand replied in English.

"A private operator?"

"Takes one to know one. When I was your age, I was you—but I never had hair quite that long."

"So ... black ops for hire?"

"Black ops? Jesus, fellas. Give a black guy a break."

Sand's humor fell flat until Brecht chuckled. The mood in the room lightened notably until Brecht's face went slack; he appeared startled by a revelation. "Oh," he said, "You worked for *him*, didn't you?"

"Him who?"

"Former US president. Texas oil baron; that's what they called him, 'The Baron.' Rumor has it that after leaving office, he spent years making amends for sins the world will never know. You were his Army of One."

"I don't know what you're talking about."

Brecht gave a Mona Lisa smile. "Rest assured, we respect confidentiality. We have what we need. I'll obtain the rest on my own."

Chapter 22

"It seems fitting, sir, that such a mind would produce such a weapon," said Jimmy Kim into his encrypted cell phone.

"Indeed," replied Young Wan Li, known in the US as David Young. "Your assessment: Can we assume that merely a combination of enticements and threats can control such insanity? Or will we require stronger measures?"

Kim had spent a great deal of time pondering that very question. He was not sure enough yet to stake his credibility on an answer. Young was one of the few men Kim truly feared. The man could be mercurial and ruthless. He had cut unsuccessful subordinates off at the knees. He demanded results, and he had a tendency to think in terms of brute force. Kim, on the other hand, thought himself as more of a strategist. Yet believing oneself to be superior to a senior officer was nothing short of blasphemy in the North Korean intelligence services, and it could lead to the kind of slip that could result in elimination. Young saw things in black-and-white terms with little room for finesse or subtlety. Torture, threats and drugs were sometimes the fastest and surest way to ensure compliance, but it was necessary that Beeman be functional. The scientist would have to be able to make it into and out of the secure DataHelix lab under the watchful eyes of trained security, with video, biotelemetry sensors and possible toxicology screening.

"I don't know, sir. For a moment we were sure the scientist was going to immolate the girl—burn her alive for his pleasure. You could see it on his face. This man has a true lust for suffering and death. He is a psychopath. We thought—"

Kim's senior cut him off. "Yes, yes, you already told me how you *felt*, which is of no value at all to me. You are not answering my question. My time is valuable."

Chastised, Kim said, "Deeply sorry, sir."

"Have you nothing more to add?"

Kim cringed at his superior's recriminating tone. "Sir, this man is quite obviously deranged, but he is also brilliant, extremely observant, manipulative and inherently unpredictable. We must be *very* cautious."

"You've studied him for months, observed him, interacted with him, measured his reactions. You are presumably trained in such matters."

Before Kim could formulate his response, Young added, "Much rests on this mission. Our Supreme Leader requires strategic options to accompany his nuclear inventory, which is a potent threat but not usable as an offensive weapon. He has entrusted us to bring him the Black Sunrise weapon system. This is a great honor, and you must not fail or allow anyone to discover you. The lives of all of your families depend upon success. Need I repeat this?"

"No, sir, but it would be improper to give assurances in which I lack confidence. We must assume Beeman *will* surprise us and be ready for anything he does. It could be a grave error to become reliant on incorrect predictions. We learned much from our year of surveillance over him, but this chance to speak with him added new information."

Young grunted his grudging agreement.

"When I spoke with him," Kim continued, "his eyes revealed nothing. It was like talking to a stone idol; one could see what one wished but only as the product of imagination. This man does not reveal his true feelings—assuming he has any. He had to have been shocked to discover we know his crimes, but he showed no signs of distress not portrayed intentionally, as deception. No nervous mannerisms. He is a skilled actor with superb self-control—a man who has been concealing himself from the world all of his life and has now become a master at doing so. Confronted with a shocking revelation, with the possibility of prison or worse, his brow did not dampen, his hands did not tremble, his eyes were placid, his blinking remained infrequent and his awareness of his surroundings remained acute."

"The unshakability of a zealot?"

"I think not, sir. He is no patriot, and he has no traceable ideology. He's a killer, a criminal and an intellectual twisted into one."

"Then why has he labored with such frenzy to craft such a weapon for his country?"

"Not for the sake of his country. For him it is not a matter of nationalism, patriotism or ideology."

Young sighed in exasperation. "Then what is it?"

"For the sake of the weapon itself. It is his progeny. He has labored for the love of death. For the joy of creating it. In my opinion, he is in love with death. He developed the weapon so that someone would use it."

"Who does he hate?" Young asked.

"I doubt he hates anyone. Or perhaps he hates everyone. I think he values all people, but only for their capacity to die. I doubt he cares who uses it, upon whom or why. So long as his brainchild causes massive casualties, it will *fulfill* him. He's given birth to this living weapon, and he wants to see it mature to achieve its purpose."

"So you believe you do understand him?"

"Yes, sir, but only to a degree."

"Then I return to my original question: *How do* we *control him?*" Young's voice had risen to the point where he was practically yelling.

"Our best enticement is not to try to play on his fears. The typical reasons for treason—ideology, ego, religion, profit or revenge—do not motivate him. I believe he *does* have an ego, but it is not what compels him to act."

"Then what does, Kim?"

"I believe we can entice him by giving him the belief that his weapon, his death-fixation and his destiny can only reach fruition through service to our supreme leader. He must see his useful contributions to our excellent comrade's grand plan as integral to his own sense of destiny. We can only do this if we convince him that we plan to invade the South and that his bioweapon will be the first wave of the attack. If he believes this to be true, he'll join the party willingly, I think."

"You can't be serious."

"Sir, I believe this to be the most powerful motivation we can offer him; of course, we may dangle the other customary punishments and rewards. He could become a true asset, and he may yet improve on his invention."

"And he could decide to start a war before we're ready. He certainly has the means."

"Just so," Kim conceded. "We must do more than blackmail him. We must *recruit* him. Completely."

"What you suggest carries vastly greater risk than our original mission objectives: obtain the virus and technical data, kill him and return home."

"Recruiting him will be more effective for three reasons. First, this virus is unlike any pathogen. To master the strategic application of this weapon, we will require his expertise. Second, if we set him up with the equipment and resources he needs, he might improve on the weapon or develop something even more useful."

Kim paused.

"And your third reason?" Young probed.

Kim cleared his throat. "If the supreme leader chooses to unleash the American plague on an enemy nation, it could be very useful for there to be an alternative explanation for the epidemic. Beeman could become a scapegoat to draw blame away from us. This could make a huge difference in how the world responds, whether we face nuclear retaliation or not. A rogue, known to have stolen the weapon he developed. A provably unstable criminal—a kidnapper. Such a credible alternative explanation of how the plague occurred could infuse enough doubt in the world court of public opinion to make the difference between our nation's survival and its destruction. This one choice could change the course of history."

Silence.

Kim began to wonder whether his superior had hung up on him. He'd clearly overstepped his place. Daring to think above his pay grade carried the potential to advance his career or to lead to his destruction, but he placed his nation's safety above his own, for his lifelong indoctrination in the philosophy of Juche had programmed him to do so.

Finally, the coin landed, and Kim knew he was golden.

"Your thinking may be sound. I will consider this, Kim."

"Yes, sir." The relief Kim felt was so overpowering he felt lightheaded.

"Provide more definitive answers quickly. Make no changes to the original plan without approval. Your first priority is to obtain the virus and the technology of its production and deployment. Recruiting this man could be a bonus, but it would also make our mission more cumbersome, operating so deeply inside America. Until we have the weapon, Beeman is a threat, an enemy we cannot kill. He is our only path to what the supreme leader sent us for."

"I understand."

The connection ended.

Kim slipped the encrypted cell phone back into his pocket.

He had long ago resigned himself to the likelihood that the government could torture his parents, sister and brother to death as retribution for any error he could make. His steady success in the Ministry of Intelligence had landed him with missions that were simply too complex and dangerous to allow continuous perfect performance to be a realistic expectation.

Fatalistic acceptance of the inevitable was entrenched in the minds and hearts of DPRK covert action specialists. Training them to accept their own deaths aimed to give them courage. The threat of loved ones being hideously maimed and killed was the tether that held agents to their posts after setting them free in the Western world. Rarely were operatives loosed beyond the North Korean borders who did not have close family ties at home.

Those espionage professionals allowed to operate for extended periods in Western nations often received reminders of the consequences of betrayal or disobedience during return visits to their homeland. Kim had to watch a missing agent's family members undergo extreme tortures; it had later come to light that the agent had committed suicide instead of returning home. Suffering and death in a North Korean re-education camp was beyond the imagination of most Westerners. In these camps, they slowly cooked prisoners alive, subjected them to systematic amputation of digits and limbs or disfiguring surgery without anesthetic and forced them to cannibalize other prisoners.

To maintain some semblance of sanity, Kim had tried to grind all affection for his family out of his soul and program himself to forget they even existed. He never spoke *of* them, and during the past ten years, he had not once spoken *to* them. Ever. If asked about his family, he would shrug. "Useless fools," was all he would say.

But when Young had overtly reminded him of the threat, he knew he was very close to the precipice. All it would take to condemn Kim and his family to hell and extinction would be a single text message from that man.

He had to keep cool, as the American slang went, and remain steady in thought and deed. He'd never counted on luck or fortune. His intellect and training were his strengths, and he was very good at what he did, so long as he remained detached and in control.

Always in control.

The secret to controlling himself was to focus utterly and exclusively on the mission.

Fear was a distraction.

Error was the product of distraction.

Death was the product of error.

And thus, fear would bring death.

Tomorrow, he would be very careful and very observant, so he could answer Young's questions without risking a wrong guess. He would find a way to make the American demon reveal something of his inner essence.

Chapter 23

Roady Kenehan looked at the two files handed to him. Each member of the team had received identical copies. They were all engrossed in absorbing their contents.

He started with the file on Jaqueline Dawson. The expected photo was there on the left, opposite a single page listing vital statistics and other summary data.

The photo was a professional one, taken in a studio. The label affixed to the bottom-right corner of the photo showed the estimated date, from about a year ago.

The girl was more than just pretty; she was a knockout. She had long, wavy brown hair, a heart-shaped face, full lips and huge dark eyes. Her skin was perfect, as were the teeth showing through her dazzling smile. In her eyes, Kenehan thought he detected a mixture of teasing mirth and a touch of sadness. Kenehan sensed from the photo that she was a girl who had developed a mastery when it came to using her visual appeal, one who could radiate her beauty like a shield or a weapon. Kenehan could see how Sand, or any man for that matter, could fall prey to such a woman.

If she sets her sights on you, down you go.

The Group's personnel dossiers usually had at least two or three photos, and often more, so he lifted the head shot to check for other pictures. The next image depicted her in a slender black evening gown standing beside Robert Sand. Her low-cut dress revealed her very well-endowed figure. *Definitely stunning—she'd draw predators everywhere she went.* Beneath that photo were copies of her driver's license, birth certificate and other records.

Kenehan looked up, glancing surreptitiously at Sand so that he could mentally pair them.

Sand was already looking directly at him, expecting the scrutiny.

Kenehan nodded back, his mouth set.

Rather than commencing his detailed study of the remaining contents of Dawson's file, Roady picked up and opened the second file.

The photo mesmerized Kenehan.

Christine Jensen was older and more mature, and from her picture, she appeared more self-possessed but was not as overtly glamorous as Dawson.

But.

Something in the image reached out and grabbed onto Roady, catching him off-guard. She had a slender face, with a tapered chin and a high forehead. Her half-smile was subtle but more genuine than Dawson's, at least in this photograph. Unlike Dawson's professional head shot, this picture was obviously the product of a portable camera or cell phone—but a good one. The image was crisp and clear.

It was her eyes.

They conveyed something special, something alive. The jade eyes emanated a piercing intelligence, but there was something else. From the warmth of her expression, Roady guessed someone she greatly liked—or loved—took the photo. Her dad, maybe? Jackie Dawson? A boyfriend?

Kenehan pondered the photo and his reaction to it, trying to find a word for the quality it captured. Vulnerability? No, not at all. Openness? Maybe.

The photo was much more descriptive than the photos of the Dawson girl. She had not posed for it, so it captured her personality more candidly. It seemed fitting to Roady that her dossier contained this photo.

The dossier depicted a young woman who was full of life and joy. The kind of woman who made spreading happiness and sharing the excitement of challenge a personal signature. The more he read, the more real she became. The sheets below contained printouts of various social media posts and pictures. Dawson's file had not contained such things; Kenehan wondered why not.

It's a picture of a pretty girl whom I've never met before. So what's with the pull? Something I'm ginning up to get myself motivated? Or is it that I've met her parents and seen the fear in her mother's eyes?

There was no second photo, so he lowered the bottom edge slowly and continued to study the image, noting the shape of her ears and the way the corners of her mouth formed small dimples. Her eyes radiated guileless confidence. He imagined she would be steady under pressure, just as her father appeared to be. Kenehan recalled Mark Jensen mentioning her outdoor survival training and how much she had gotten out of it.

She's just a subject, he reminded himself scoldingly. *Remain objective.*

Kenehan glanced at Jensen. *The man has a lot to be proud of. A lot to lose. He must be going out of his mind with this.* He judged that Jensen was fairly fit and tan for a guy with a desk job. He had the kind of personality that said he realized there was more to life than just arguing cases in court and making money. *Different from a lot of high-dollar lawyers.* Jensen had less of the vainly affluent air of superiority he'd seen in other men of similar professional stature, of whom Roady had encountered many. *Girl comes from good stock,* Kenehan assayed. He felt a powerful sense of remorse as he contemplated what might have become of these two beautiful women who vanished during the process of getting into a car after a day of shopping.

The worst-case scenario was obvious.

In spite of the Old Man's pep talk, he had to be realistic. But there was clearly money behind both of these girls. He could hope it was a kidnapping for ransom and that they were still alive. The undeniable possibility that some degenerate beast may have taken them for his twisted pleasure made him queasy. The world was full of sick bastards who were willing to ruin other people's lives for their own gratification. The thought of finding the girls in the possession of such a person was repellent and attractive at the same time. He would love to rescue these women and just maybe have the chance to—

Stow that for later. Get to work.

He dug into the files now, memorizing them.

• • •

An hour later, the group split up to head for their various assigned destinations. Sand rode with Mark and Janet in their rental, on the way to the mall where police had found his car.

Brecht, Thomas and Ortega followed Sand's car in a minivan rented from Hertz, into which they had loaded four Pelican cases containing various items of crime scene equipment, communications gear and other electronics. Takaki and Boyer had gone to arrange lodging and a place to berth the mobile command coaches that would hit Denver tomorrow.

"What a bunch," Sand said, breaking a silence that had lasted for twenty minutes as Jensen negotiated his way northward along the lockstep crawl of I-25. Sitting behind Mark in the rear seat, Janet nodded in agreement.

"What do you think of them?" she asked.

"Quite a mix," Sand observed with a wry smile. "Little of this, little of that. The lady is supposedly an expert in computer intel. The Old Man, as they call him, and his protégé, Thomas, are a couple of top-end spooks. NSA types—or CIA. Seen their kind before. I'm guessing Brecht was in the OSS, or Office of Strategic Services, in his youth. The other two, the former FBI spooks, are harder to read, but I can tell you a couple of things about that long-haired boy."

"Yeah?" Jensen was interested. He had come to respect Sand.

"First, that boy is lethal. He moves like a cat. I suspect he could snap your neck in a half second and not even blink. Did you notice the scars on his forearms? The calluses on his knuckles? The steel in his eyes? He's trained with a blade, his fists and his mind. I'd like to know more about him."

"Robert, what was all that about back there? Were you in their line of work? And did you really work for President—" Janet started.

Sand turned in his seat to look back at her. "I'll tell you the story sometime, but not just now. Well, we wanted horsepower, didn't we? I think we got it. Bus-loads of private operators driven by a boss with something to prove and the experience to get it done."

Jensen was beginning to think that with Sand on board, they may have picked up even more horsepower than just what Brecht had brought to town. "What's the second thing?"

"I think he fell for your little girl just looking at her picture."

Chapter 24

"Working at Starbucks beats sitting in class all day, doesn't it?" Beeman asked. "You've never regretted dropping out?"

"You can say that again." The barista smiled. "How did you know?"

Beeman picked up two cups of coffee and returned to his table. He glanced at his watch. Eight-fifteen. Kim was late, which surprised him. The town of Steamboat Springs was not large enough to have traffic problems, and Kim had struck Beeman as a man far too disciplined to be late accidentally. So Beeman concluded that either Kim was making him wait for psychological reasons, in which case he should arrive soon, or the meeting was off because someone had compromised Kim and his team.

Nothing to do but wait and plan.

Beeman's intuition had always worked that way. He'd always believed in the power of deductive reasoning, but his greatest mental feats had generally sprung from his intuition, his innate awareness of things that were invisible.

He assumed he was under surveillance even as he sat there, so he decided he'd already waited too long. He was giving up too much.

He made an exaggerated show of looking at his watch and stood to leave.

A block away, he saw Kim leaning nonchalantly against Beeman's parked Toyota, smoking a cigarette. This fit the pattern Beeman was building in his mind. Kim was creative, taking small risks to project the image that he was always one step ahead of Beeman, that he would always turn out to be the one in charge, so Beeman had better get used to it.

Beeman smiled.

In the dozen paces remaining, he formulated his response.

"Oh, there you are! What a relief. I thought I'd made a mistake. I went to the coffee shop and waited for you there."

"We do not wish to draw too much attention to our acquaintance, Arthur."

Beeman, who preferred using his surname, very nearly corrected Kim. Realizing that this would be out of character for the role he'd chosen to play, he stopped himself.

"Call me Artie. I hate Arthur. Or you can call me Dr. Beeman if you like, Jimmy." He gave a small smile.

Kim smirked in return. "Let's go for a ride."

Beeman got in the car and started the engine, reaching across to unlock the passenger-side door. Kim slid in and pulled his door shut. As the car pulled away, Kim unrolled the window on his side of the car. The morning mountain air was still cool.

Beeman kept one eye on the rearview mirror. Kim would have a preplanned destination; likely a place without witnesses and limited escape routes, one that would compromise Beeman's immediate physical safety. He glanced to his right and saw that Kim was adjusting his own side-view mirror. Kim was also interested in determining whether anyone was following them, which meant that his own people might not be the only observers Beeman had to worry about.

Within two blocks they came to a red light in the middle of town. Beeman stopped the car and looked at Kim. "Where to?"

Kim looked at his watch. "We have plenty of time. Mr. Pessoa's bus won't arrive for another three hours, so why don't we just head on down the road toward Craig and talk while you drive? I'll have you back in town in plenty of time to drop me off and pick him up."

Beeman was not surprised Kim knew Antonio's name and bus schedule.

He'd assumed North Korean intelligence would have had him

and the young fool under observation for quite some time; an operation of this magnitude would have taken a great deal of resources and planning. There were likely electronic listening devices in the cabin and perhaps even hidden video cameras as well. Antonio was probably under surveillance of his own at this moment. There might even be an agent with him on the bus. Probably another Asian. Beeman doubted they had made contact with Antonio, who was obviously too skittish to trust under the additional pressure that would cause.

"It must be hard," Beeman said.

"What's that, Artie?"

"Running a spy operation in a nation where you stand out so."

"You've got that racial thing going again."

"Who, me? Aren't you planning to wipe out all of us?"

"See, that's what I'm talking about. 'Make America Great Again' has turned into 'Make America Hate Again.' Despite the sculpted rhetoric of the liberal media, a massive silent majority in America laps up the sauce of xenophobic hatred, of petulant isolationism. They thrive on the sweet adrenal rush that comes from fantasizing about taking out all enemies, foreign *and* domestic. So hardworking Asians like me always draw suspicion."

"Did they make you memorize that?"

Kim laughed.

Beeman felt contentment settle into his chest. "Global war is coming."

"And it might rain this afternoon. Just drive the car."

Ten minutes later when they were on a winding two-lane highway, Kim spoke again. "You strike me as a dangerous man, Artie," he said casually, tossing his cigarette out the window.

Beeman shrugged and said nothing. The silence hung in the car for a time. Beeman enjoyed it, knowing that Kim expected some sort of response from which he could more closely gauge Beeman's personality and predict how he would respond to various manipulation tactics. After a while, Beeman noticed that Kim's gaze was riveted to the side-view mirror.

Beeman had become distracted and had failed to notice that a car had come up behind them. It was a police car, the state patrol. No sooner did Beeman realize this than the lights atop the patrol car began to flash.

"Pull over slowly, right over there, and listen to me," Kim said sharply. "You were not speeding, so this could be a serious problem. Whatever happens, make no trouble. Do nothing other than what the officer tells you. Comply with every command he gives. Make no argument. If he tries to arrest either or both of us, we go peacefully. My people will handle it from there. Do you understand?"

As he pulled the Toyota to a stop on the shoulder of the road, Beeman shot a sideward glance at Kim and nodded.

Could this be a ruse Kim had orchestrated?

Could the police have tracked the girls to Beeman?

Had Antonio cracked or slipped up, leading the police to Beeman? That had always been a major risk.

Death is life is death, thought Beeman. Only time will tell.

Beeman's hunting knife was strapped to his calf beneath his baggy trousers. His age and appearance would possibly buy him time to kill the officer, and perhaps Kim as well, and make a dash for safety. He watched the patrol car in his mirror. He reached across and opened the glove box, removing the registration and proof of insurance; then he pulled his wallet from his back pocket and took out his license.

Two minutes passed.

Beeman put down his window and placed his hands on the wheel with his license visible for the approaching officer.

"Step out of the car, sir," the cop barked. Bending down to see Kim, the patrolman added, "You too, sir. Step out of the car."

"Certainly, officer." Kim opened his door and stepped out, and the cop moved two paces backward so that Beeman could step out as well. As he did so, the patrolman took him by the elbow and guided him to the other side of the car, away from the road.

"License and registration," said the trooper.

Beeman handed them over and waited while the officer returned with them to his cruiser to run them against outstanding warrants. Five minutes later, the officer returned and handed back the license and registration.

"What do you suppose I stopped you for?"

The possibilities are endless, Beeman thought. *Kidnapping. Conspiracy. National security issues. Failing to signal. Helping to orchestrate World War III. Treason. Lack of social skills. Poor taste in friends.*

"Was I speeding?" Beeman asked, offering the only offense he had not committed.

The officer shook his head resolutely. "Nah. You weren't speeding, sir." He continued to stare at each of them in turn, his eyes moving back and forth like a spectator at a tennis tournament. "You don't even know, do you? You don't even realize what you did. You weren't even thinking."

Now the officer nodded, as if the lesson were sinking in. It seemed vaguely comical to Beeman. This had to be something completely out of the blue. But what was it? If he were to arrest them for capital crimes, the officer would not have undertaken to do it on his own.

"Your goddamn cigarette!" The officer stabbed the air in front of Kim's face with his finger. "The driest summer we've had in a hundred years, fires burning in six places, millions in suppression costs, hundreds of thousands of acres of forestland gone—just like *that*." The officer snapped his fingers to punctuate what he was saying. "And folks, you just tossed a lit cigarette butt from the car without even thinking about what you could start. Jesus, what does it take to get you people to turn your heads on?"

"Officer, I'm glad you pulled us over. I don't even smoke," Beeman said obsequiously, "and I have lectured this idiot about how he makes the rest of us into victims with his filthy, stinking, antisocial habit, but he keeps not listening. So thank you. Now he's hearing it from more than just me." He shook his head in disgust at Kim and then softened his tone somewhat, turning back to the patrolman. "You going to take him in? Should I follow you?"

The officer started cooling off. He shook his head. "Naw, but I'm thinking of writing *you* a citation. The fine would be over one thousand dollars. As the operator of the vehicle, you are responsible for unsafe conduct on the part of your passengers. You realize that? You were driving, so you are legally responsible for any objects thrown from your car. That's the law." He turned his face to Kim. "How would you feel if he got a big ticket for *your* carelessness? Would that be fair?"

Kim shook his head forcefully. "That would be awful, sir. I don't know what to say. I'm really sorry. He's been right all along, and I've been an ass. You're right, officer. I didn't even think about what I was doing, but you can bet—I will in the future."

The cop seemed placated. "I'll tell you what. We'll just let it go with a warning this time. But if something like this happens again, I *will* write a ticket, and I'll take you both in. Swear to God. Remember this: you start a fire—you're looking at prison time. You got that?"

"Most definitely, officer. Read you five by five," Kim assured him.

"You in the Army, son?"

"No, sir. Marines."

"Well, I was Army. And we had a saying: You can always tell a marine. But you just can't tell him much. Semper Fi, son. Get your head out of your ass and your ass on the road."

Kim chuckled politely. "Yes, sir."

"Alright, boys. On your way." With this, the uniformed man turned on his heel and stomped back to his patrol car. As Beeman stood watching, the officer sat behind the wheel. He reached down and pulled a microphone to his lips, making a radio call; then he started the car and pulled onto the highway to turn the car around to head back toward town.

After a few seconds, Kim shook his head and got back into the car. When Beeman joined him in the vehicle, he smiled. "That was impressive, Artie. Indeed. You have a mind for espionage."

A handy segue, mused Beeman. "Not really," he retorted with a snort. "I really just don't like smokers."

"But you appear to have no aversion to fire," Kim said softly.

This confirmed Beeman's suspicions. He was under total surveillance. They had seen his little session with Kitten.

"Nothing like an outdoor barbecue," he quipped as he pulled back onto the highway. A mile or so down the road, Kim shifted in his seat to face Beeman.

"Of your ruthlessness I have little doubt."

"I'm not ruthless. I just like to ..." Beeman had been about to say "experiment," but he changed his course mid-sentence. "... to entertain myself."

"And yet I wonder why you would be so careless with your freedom. If you had touched off that lighter, you'd surely be in custody now. And all of that screaming. The risks you take are unreasonable. You jeopardized my goals, not to mention your own life. You must be more discrete. I must insist that you keep this situation with your women under control, do a better job of staying below the radar."

"*I* strike *you* as careless? You're the one who tossed a lit cigarette from the car in plain view of the highway patrol." As soon as he said the words, something troubled him. How had he failed to see the cruiser?

"Do not be snide," Kim said, "you are simply reckless."

"Well, I guess you have a point there—you got me."

Beeman took his hands from the wheel and pressed the accelerator to the floor, folding his arms in front of his chest. The car began to speed up. Within a few seconds, it was traveling ninety miles per hour and drifting into the opposite lane.

Beeman never saw the blow that rendered him unconscious.

Chapter 25

"This is where the car was parked—this slot, here where this Subaru is." Sand pointed to the space where a battered gray Subaru now sat. With them were Mark, Janet, Kenehan, Marcus Ortega and Robert Partridge, who had arrived that morning on a Delta flight from Miami. They were standing on the third level of the west parking garage at the Cherry Creek Mall. It was a few minutes before eleven, and the mall was busy.

"I'd like to scan the surface with UV and maybe try some electro-static film," Ortega said, his hands on his hips. "But I doubt we'll get anything useful."

Partridge addressed Kenehan. "Would you like me to move that car?"

"Yeah, thanks. Put it over there."

Partridge stepped over to the van and dug out some gear. From his left hand dangled several rings of keys strung together on a loop of wire cable. Within a minute, Partridge had the car door open and the engine running. He backed the Subaru out of the spot and moved it to a vacant stall a few spaces down; then he shut off the engine and got out, relocking the door.

"Owner will never notice."

Kenehan nodded. "Nice work."

Jensen was impressed. It was obvious that this kind of thing was completely normal for these people. Sand's word nailed it: *horsepower*.

As if reading his thoughts, Janet said, "They obviously know what they're doing."

During his days as a prosecutor, Jensen had frequently accompanied the police at scene inspections; part of his job had been to supervise, to ensure no one violated the law in any way that might lead to the suppression of evidence. Surgical care was necessary to keep the guilty from going free. A procedural fowl-up could lead to the release of a dangerous criminal, whose constitutional rights took precedence over obtaining a conviction. But finding his daughter was a priority that eclipsed any due process issues—particularly given the very real possibility that there might be no "legal" process for the abductors when they found Christie and Jackie. If abductors had taken his little girl, they would take others, and should be stopped.

Thinking like a father, not a lawyer.

Attitude adjustment, Sand had called it.

Jensen had come to think of the perpetrators in the plural. It made more sense than a single assailant, for whom a dual abduction would likely be impossible. It had also occurred to him that the logistics of the abduction would be demanding enough that the assailants must have prepared it in advance. This was not the result of some drunken maniac's snap decision to snatch a pretty girl. No, a coordinated, planned and skillfully executed action involving more than one participant was the only plausible likelihood he could envision. That suggested a ransom demand might be forthcoming. If a thrill-killing or mere sexual assault was the motive, there would probably have been signs of struggle.

During the meeting at the airport that morning, as the group migrated out of the conference room, he'd told Brecht and Thomas of this theory. Thomas had played devil's advocate. "Why discount the idea of a lone attacker threatening the girls with a gun to make them get in a car or van and just driving away?" he'd asked.

"You'd have to know Christie," Jensen had replied. "She'd run, scream or fight back. She would know it was her only chance. Even at gunpoint she'd never get in a car willingly, especially with a friend to help her make a ruckus."

When Jensen had asked Brecht whether he would use his political clout to spur the police into action, Thomas had answered for Brecht. "We tend to do better without interference from local authorities," he'd explained. "They get underfoot."

Jensen continued to observe the team.

Kenehan scrutinized the reinforced concrete above, looking for video cameras. Jensen had done the same thing during his first visit here two days earlier.

He'd found none, which surprised him; in this day and age cameras were everywhere. This had to be the only upscale commercial parking lot in the city with no cameras. A good risk manager or insurance specialist should have spotted that and pushed to have a video security system installed, with a live feed to a security room or booth somewhere. Cameras conspicuously placed can deter criminal assaults.

The plaintiff lawyer in Jensen reared its head. *Cheap, cost-cutting bean counters. When we find Christie, I'm going to sue these fuckers blind, just for therapy. Tear them a new one. She'll be home safe, and she'll own this mall.*

Ortega unpacked an ultraviolet lamp that looked like an oversize flashlight and knelt at the edge of the parking space, switching on the black light. Under the ultraviolet rays, spots of oil glowed fluorescent yellow. Jensen knew that motor oil would phosphoresce under UV, and he wondered what else might do so. Electrostatic film might produce readable footprints, and luminol spray might make blood products or other biological oxidants light up under the black light, but seeing it required a fairly dark environment. Ortega used a large and expensive digital camera to take dozens of photos from a variety of locations, concentrating primarily on the area near where the driver's-side door of the Jaguar would have been.

These tests were long shots given how much time had passed.

Kenehan crouched beside Partridge, examining the rough concrete surface under the ultraviolet light. He instructed Partridge to direct the beam back to a missed spot. Out came the electrostatic film, rollers and spray, along with another special camera and a small box on a tripod, which Jensen recognized.

"Lidar?" Jensen asked.

"Right." Ortega answered. "We're making a high-res digital point cloud to go with our imagery. I'm afraid there's not much here to work with, Mr. Jensen," he added, shaking his head. "No security cameras, no fresh bodily fluids, no abrasion marks in the concrete, no readable footprints, no unusual marks on the concrete. Just normal petrochemical and tire residue. We'll swab for surface chemistry."

"What kinds of chemicals are you looking for?" Janet asked.

"Anything you wouldn't expect to leak out of cars," Jensen answered.

"Correct," Ortega confirmed.

"We use some of this technology occasionally in my civil practice," Jensen explained to Janet. "Plant explosions, train wrecks, air crashes. We used to use a Total Station to survey a scene one point at a time. Lidar is miles above that. We've even used lidar with airborne drones."

"Cool," Ortega said. "Didn't know lawyers had that kind of tech."

"We contract with experts, forensic investigators and engineers. But they're nothing compared to you guys." *And they don't hotwire cars or snap people's necks,* Jensen mused.

What had his father done to earn the loyalty of a man like Albert Brecht?

• • •

Kenehan stepped to the nearby half-wall of the parking garage and surveyed the landscape below. A thick forest of old trees spread a considerable distance from the mall property. He scanned the canopy of vegetation, noting the brick-and-shingle structures that occasionally emerged above the growth. Each rooftop represented a family home. The view was beautiful. He saw it as a reminder of what he was here to do: see that which is obscured.

It was a big world, full of predators, and much of it was hidden. Yet here they were, charged with the task of working a miracle, staving off the tragedy of unbearable loss, of lives ended and others ruined forever. To protect the goodness of family love and keep the harshness of reality at bay for these people.

He thought of Louis Armstrong's beautiful, aching melody: *The colors of the rainbow, so pretty in the sky.* How did the rest go? *I see friends shaking hands, saying how do you do? They're really saying I love you. Hear babies crying, I watch them grow. They learn much more than I'll ever know. And I think to myself, what a wonderful world.*

Except it wasn't. The world was a jungle, filled with predators, haters, evil men doing evil deeds—including himself.

And out there somewhere were two beautiful girls, just two more victims, statistics so minute they were negligible, barely worthy of police attention—victims who did not merit an all-points-bulletin, a dragnet or a national alert.

Assuming they were alive.

What were the odds?

One step at a time.

When things seem hopeless, you focus on the task before you, and perform that one thing with focus, zeal and vigilance; when you finish that task, you start on the next. Then the next. Never lose sight of your goal, and never let thoughts of failure take root, or they'll take over, and then you're done.

Failure is not an option, Brecht had said.

For just a moment, Roady felt like he could see through Mark Jensen's eyes.

His daughter. What could be more precious?

Roady had never had children nor been married, but in officer candidate school, he'd had a glimpse of what it must be like to be a parent. One day the command master sergeant had issued a call for volunteers, for those who would give up their one and only day of leave for the week to donate time to underprivileged kids so they could go to a circus. He'd volunteered without thinking.

What a mistake that had been.

On the Saturday in question, he'd ridden the bus with the other volunteers to the parking lot where single mothers dropped off their children, leaving them in the hands of officer candidates in uniform for a day of fun.

They had assigned Kenehan two young girls—sisters—ages ten and six.

They'd ridden the bus for an hour, while he'd awkwardly tried to make small talk with them. The older one had surprised him with her world-wise demeanor, her unexpected maturity, the by-product of growing up in poverty without a father, facing the harshness of the world without protection. She was ten, going on forty.

He'd bought them cotton candy, listened to them squeal at the acrobatic feats of the trapeze artists, the skills of jugglers, the massive elephants and fierce tigers. He'd bought them souvenirs, more cotton candy, Cokes—anything they wanted. The hours had slipped past with cruel speed.

They had stolen his heart.

All too soon they'd boarded the bus again, headed back to the lot where the girls' mother would be waiting with the other parents. During the ride back, a bee had landed on the younger girl's arm. Instead of flicking it away, she'd looked up at Roady with eyes the size of saucers.

"Bug!" she'd proclaimed, giggling.

Roady's heart had fallen out of his chest, and he'd never felt so fulfilled.

When the bus had pulled to a stop in the parking lot, mothers had approached furtively out of the darkness to collect their kids. When almost all the other mothers had gathered their litters and departed, his girls' mom had showed up with an apologetic look on her face.

"Sorry I'm late," she had said. "The car wouldn't start."

"It's okay," Roady had said, holding the younger girl's hand. He then knelt down to meet her at eye level. "I told you Mommy would be here. It's time for you to go home now."

"Okay," she'd said, her eyes pouring tears. The resigned tone of her voice had torn his intestines out and dumped them on the gravel of the parking lot. He'd thought he would die. The pain had been—

Oh, Jesus, what was I thinking?

And then he had done the unthinkable.

He simply had shaken the mother's hand and climbed onto the bus with the rest of the officer candidates, riding in silence back to the base.

And that night, he had tossed in his bunk and cried, for the first time in years.

I just left them ...

Failure is not an option, the Old Man had proclaimed.

Albert Brecht. God of Risk. Kingmaker. Beater of odds.

Roady took a deep breath and glanced for a moment over his shoulder at Janet. She was talking softly to her husband, and she stole a glance back at him. He met her eyes briefly and then turned his gaze back to the southwest. He could see through her barely controlled façade, how she fought to make herself strong, holding her fears at bay—one second at a time.

A remarkable woman, he thought. *Christie comes from good stock.*

Looking out across the leafy plaza for a while longer, an idea came to him. A possibility worth pursuing. "Partridge, Ortega, come over here for a minute."

Partridge arrived at his side. Ortega finished sealing the swabs he'd collected into glass tubes and packed them in protective styrofoam within his Pelican case; then he stepped up as well.

The others sidled closer to listen in.

"Roady?" Ortega queried.

"What do you see, guys?"

A moment passed before Partridge answered. "Trees, grass, street-lights, river." After a few more seconds, he added, "Rooftops ... and those apartment buildings. *Aahhh.*" His head nodded slowly. "High-end condos, management companies. Security. Video surveillance?"

"Definitely worth a try." Kenehan gave Partridge's shoulder a comradely slap. "Let's visit the unit managers of those high-rise con-dos. They'll have offices on prem. Those houses over there look ex-pensive, and they sit near a busy street, so they may have security cameras as well. If we get more than one video angle, maybe we can run 'em through the BEAST and bring out a face, a license plate, or some other clue. Canvass the area—get people on it now. Also, get me the tapes from inside the mall."

Partridge nodded. "On it. Anything else?"

Coming out of his dark place now, Kenehan paused before con-tinuing. "Have our people in Baltimore start working on the credit cards. We'll need a list of the stores where Christie and Jackie made purchases so we can run photos by sales people and see if they ob-served anything. Memories are fading as we speak, so do it fast."

"You got it," Partridge said.

"We may also be able to come up with the names of some other shoppers in the mall that afternoon who may have seen them. We'll probably have to hack that info to get it fast enough. Get Takaki on it. Find a mall guide online. We need a list of all the stores here."

"Will do."

"Good man." Roady felt better now. They were finally in motion.

He noticed a man strolling by, observing with interest. People had been walking past intermittently, stopping occasionally to gawk for the past hour, so he made nothing of the gangly guy with a dark mustache and a long, beaked nose.

Antonio had been unable to fight off the urge to visit the mall. Beeman had warned him not to come back here, but the allure was too strong.

He'd spent so many afternoons exploring this place, scoping it out, spotting bitches, planning how to take them and reporting back to Beeman. Of all the places he'd scoped out, this mall was clearly the best hunting ground. He'd started thinking of it as the Cherry Mall. It was busy and upscale, with plenty of hot chicks. Classier bitches, with money. Most importantly though, this mall had two huge, dark, enclosed parking garages amazingly free of security cameras.

He'd spent afternoons wandering the mall, mentally rehearsing how it might go down, wondering if he could really do it, working himself up with the visual stimulus of beautiful women in their revealing summer shorts and skimpy tops.

Mindless cherries, there to be picked, and devoured with gusto.

He liked to take pictures of the prettier ones as they strolled by, holding his phone in front of his face as though skimming Facebook, snapping shot after shot.

After a session of hunting and shooting, he would settle down in one of the large leather chairs scattered throughout the large central atrium, discretely checking his work. He'd gotten a thrill from taking those shots. Taking them had been a way of learning how to take ownership of a woman without her knowledge or consent. In that way it was watered-down rehearsal for the main event: taking *total* ownership *with* her knowledge. Fuck consent.

Strewn about Antonio's house were color inkjet printouts of women, cropped and enlarged to zoom in on their sweet cleavages, tender buttocks, and other private regions. He savored the invasion of their privacy. He was a modern day Peeping Tom, armed with his Galaxy phone, hunting undetected while in plain sight. Each image had a frozen candor that made them all look so important, so secretive, in the instant he'd captured them.

Captured. He loved that word, now that he had proven himself a man.

A man? No. A *god.*

Staring at the pictures, his fantasies had run wild. He would think, *I could have that one, or that one, or her ... or this one.* They just kept getting better and better, as did his skill with the cell phone camera as he practiced.

And now he had *two* of them! Live, moving, warm, afraid and helpless.

He giggled. *Nothing like a spare in case of a flat.*

Did he have the stones to give life to his fantasies? It was time to find out. He'd been dancing around this question for the three days, with the girls in the basement, taking his time, in no hurry, as Beeman wanted. God but that man was brilliant. Almost a savior, in a way.

Very soon, it would be time.

Nut-cutting time, he thought. *Or more accurately, cunt-cutting time.*

It was time to head back into the hills and taste the fruit.

He'd thought of nothing else for the past three days. Now, with a few hours to kill before his bus left, he'd decided to visit the place where he'd planned the thing, where he'd raised the courage, where he'd played it out in his mind countless times—and where he'd done it.

Where he'd evolved into a god.

For real, dude.

He'd come back to the scene of the crime to find out whether the place would look any different now that he'd crossed the line.

Before leaving the mall, Antonio took one last look at the spot where he'd caught up with the girls as they were getting into their car. He strolled toward the stall where the Jag had been parked—

what a stroke of luck that had been. The stupid bitches had actually believed him when he'd said he could fix the car on the spot.

Mindless cows, just as Beeman had predicted.

He wondered if the Jag would still be there, but he doubted it. Someone would have towed or stolen it by now.

As he approached the spot, he saw men taking pictures of the floor where the Jag had been parked.

He almost shit himself.

There were half a dozen people inspecting the scene—five men and a woman. They didn't look like police. He wanted to stop and watch, to figure out who they were, but he kept walking. He didn't want them to notice him.

He had a bus to catch.

Chapter 26

Kim reached over, gripped the wheel and carefully guided the Toyota onto the gravel shoulder of the road. Breathing hard, he yanked up the emergency brake with his other hand, then pushed the shift knob into neutral. The car came safely to a stop, clear of any traffic that might go by.

He sat for a moment, panting, scanning in every direction for cars, hikers or another state patrol. There was no one. After a few moments he began to feel calmer. "Crazy suicidal bastard," Kim said in English, wishing he could simply cut Beeman's throat and leave him.

He shoved the passenger door open and got out; then he dragged the unconscious man across the center console. He grunted with the exertion of hauling the man's dead weight across to the passenger seat. It was an awkward, limb-at-a-time, exercise. Once he had the inert form in the passenger seat, he reclined it, hoping it would appear to any observer that Beeman was merely napping. He slammed the passenger door, stepped around to the driver's side and got in behind the wheel. The engine was still idling. His eyes continued to scan the road, forward and rearward. A wave of fatigue washed over him, the aftereffect of the adrenaline burning off. He took several cleansing breaths to center himself.

He checked Beeman's pulse and breathing to ensure that the hard blow to the base of his skull had not killed him and that he would not asphyxiate due to airway obstruction. Serious neurological trauma was unlikely. He suppressed the urge to punch Beeman several more times simply for satisfaction.

The plan was still in place, which was actually quite amazing in light of all that had happened.

The great luck he'd had thus far left Kim with a feeling of awe and humility. If he'd been forced to kill the policeman, it would have greatly reduced the likelihood of mission success. If Beeman had crashed the car, they both would have likely died. If Kim's punch to the base of Beeman's skull had killed him, it would have ruined the mission.

If, if, if ... It was luck that had carried him this far.

Reliance on luck is the surest road to failure.

Stupid, tossing that cigarette butt from the car.

Stupider still to have become so distracted by Beeman that he'd lost his tactical awareness and missed seeing the police cruiser, which must have been sitting on the side of the road.

In spite of his incompetence, success was still attainable. So many risks, so many unexpected problems, yet the mission was still on track, though not because he had been particularly skilled or competent. He'd missed important warning signs, allowed his awareness to be disbursed and he'd failed to anticipate the extremity of Beeman's mercurial insanity—even though he had preached impertinently to his own commander about how unpredictable Beeman could be.

Where was his backup? Had the highway patrol also pulled them over? Several more minutes went by before a brown Taurus pulled up behind him. Kim watched Chul and Pak through the rearview mirror as they sat for a moment, talking to one another before getting out. *Curious,* Kim thought. *What are they discussing?*

Kim put down his window and extended his arm, signaling impatiently for Chul to approach. "What happened?" Chul asked as he came up to Kim's window. "The police stopped you."

"No time to explain," Kim snapped. "Follow me to the shed." He put the Toyota in gear and pulled away. The Taurus followed. Three miles on, he turned onto a dirt road that wound up a heavily forested hillside. Half a mile from the highway, he turned off the gravel road, taking a rutted, unimproved dirt track. The Taurus followed close behind.

The two sedans bucked and jumped as they picked their way, slowly and gingerly, for another half mile, scraping undercarriages on protruding rocks, wheels spinning out occasionally. Eventually they reached an abandoned shed shepherds and miners had used many decades past. Kim had discovered this decrepit shack after days of searching the wilderness near Beeman's isolated cabin to find a staging area with some shelter not visible from any nearby road or home.

Both drivers killed their engines. Chul and Pak jumped from the Taurus and trotted smartly to the driver's-side door of the Toyota.

"Carry him inside," Kim ordered as he stepped out of the car.

The two men obeyed, hoisting Beeman from his seat and carrying him to the shed. Once inside, Chul growled in his native tongue.

"It was wise of you to prepare this place."

Kim nodded and ordered Pak to fetch a bag from the car. The man returned quickly with an interrogation kit. Kim ordered him to dig out some plastic tie wraps, then secured Beeman's arms behind his back, binding his wrists together, yanking hard on the plastic end, and then bound Beeman's ankles securely together.

He sat back to survey his work. Swelling and bruising was becoming visible along Beeman's jawline. It would take some explaining on Beeman's part, assuming Kim let the scientist walk out of the shack alive, which he knew he would have to do.

Reaching into the kit, Kim withdrew a small length of surgical tubing and a zippered pouch containing two syringes and a several small vials of clear fluid labeled "insulin." None of them actually contained insulin. The lot numbers on the labels ended in the digits 01 through 04, providing an identification code allowing Kim to distinguish which contained a particular drug he might need.

He selected one ending in 02, a combination of mild barbiturates and psychedelic hallucinogens, and peeled off the foil cap. He uncapped a syringe and stabbed the needle through the rubber stopper to draw fluid into the syringe. Dose amount was important. "How much would you estimate he weighs, Chul?"

Chul grinned and looked at Pak. "Were you helping me carry him?"

Kim frowned. "This is no time for humor."

Chul's grin vanished. "Very sorry, sir. I meant no disrespect. I would say he weighs about seventy-five or eighty kilos."

Trained to think in American terms, Kim converted. *About 170 pounds.* He agreed. He drew 7 ml of fluid into the syringe. "Too much of this and he remains unconscious for hours—time we don't have. Not enough and the maniac will be able to fight off the effects and try to confuse and deceive us, forcing us to waste even more time."

The angle of Beeman's arm, tied behind him as it was, made finding a protruding vein difficult, but eventually Kim slid the needle into the scientist's cubital vein and compressed the plunger with his thumb. When he withdrew the needle, a small dribble of blood ran down Beeman's forearm.

Kim handed the syringe to Chul and untied the rubber tubing.

"Now we rouse him," said Kim. He cracked open a tubule of ammonium carbonate in solution—smelling salts—waving them beneath Beeman's nose. "If I've gotten the dose right, the compound will strip away his higher cortical functions to render his mind pliable, and the psychoactive component will stimulate his speech centers and produce anxiety, prompting him to communicate while his inhibitory systems are suppressed."

"Cardiorespiratory risk?" Pak asked.

Kim nodded. "Some, but he is healthy for his age, so we should get optimal results with a seven-milliliter dose."

•   •   •

Beeman heard himself groan, wondering what was making such a discordant and irritating sound. His skin felt as if it were crawling with fire ants. He tried to brush them off, but his arms seemed to be missing from his torso.

He opened his eyes and stared into a face hovering before him. He'd seen the face before but could not remember where or when. His head, neck and jaw throbbed. He realized he'd been unconscious.

He wondered with a strange sense of detachment where he was.

A light blinded him. The man was shining a penlight into his eyes. The light was so terribly bright—it seemed to set his retinas on fire. He watched sparkles of color swarming, as though he were outside his skull looking in with the aid of a dozen spotlights to observe a pulsing bundle of fluorescent snakes writhing within.

Beeman thought the light might burn his brain or at least give him a brain tan, and he laughed softly. *It doesn't matter, I really need to get out more. A little sunlight promotes health and vitality. I'll look younger with a nicely tanned brain. I'll have a burnished intellect.* After all, his was such a fine brain—muscular and pulsing with intelligence—but pale and gray. He smiled, or at least he tried to, but something had paralyzed his mouth. Had they frozen his face?

He chuckled. His frozen face felt so *funny*.

And the light that had become his home so many whatever ago was the cause of the humor. It was radiant humor. Light-hearted stuff.

Maybe it had burned his face off. *Funnier still!*

He tried to squint, but someone was holding his eyelids open. No squinting allowed. No squinting and definitely no smiling.

What's happening?

The light went out, leaving many blue and green globes floating in front of him. He was now having trouble remembering what had been so funny. Confusion began to permeate his thoughts—layers and layers of confusion. He felt sick to his stomach. Why did the man look familiar? He struggled to remember how he had gotten here. And where was *here*?

The last thing he remembered was ... driving, in the Toyota, with ...

Ah, yes. Kim.

Now he remembered. He'd released the wheel and floored the gas pedal.

Then nothing.

We must have crashed.

Behind him, a voice spoke in Korean, a voice deeper than Kim's.

Lowering the penlight, Kim responded in the same language. Beeman detected a note of concerned relief.

"What happened?" Beeman's voice came out as a croak. His jaw and neck ached, but he didn't think he was seriously injured. He was regaining clarity. His eyes roamed back and forth, soaking up information, absorbing his surroundings.

As his mind sharpened somewhat, he discerned that he was sitting on a dirt floor within some kind of a shed or shack, resting against a box. He'd been drugged. This explained the giddiness and confusion he felt.

The walls were close, made of rough-hewn lumber.

No, wait—they weren't close after all. They were very far away. But not that far. In fact, they were quite close after all, and getting closer. Beeman sensed that the walls were angry. Very angry, threatening him, swooping closer and backing up, threatening to crush him. Terrified now, he pulled his knees up to his chest. No, the walls were not moving. Or were they?

The drug, he realized. *It's a hallucinogen.*

Waves of fear washed over him.

He wondered whether he might cry, and then he realized he was crying.

Blades of light stabbed into the darkness of the shed from between rotting wooden planks. The light. What was it about the light? It had attacked him before, hadn't it? It had tried to climb into his skull. He forced himself to focus, just as the blades of light focused.

They were checking my pupils. They are concerned about my condition.

I am important to them, but I can't remember why. They're very dangerous. And they do not tolerate facial expressions. He had to keep that in mind. *No facial expressions! No laughing! No squinting! They are dangerous men!*

A remote part of Beeman's mind registered that he was losing his capacity for rational thought. He was slipping into a place from which he could not protect himself with his intellect. He would not be able to censor what came out of his mouth. Clarity waxed and waned, pulsing in steadily diminishing cycles.

Some kind of truth serum?

Of course. It would be ... but he couldn't remember the names of the drugs that would cause this kind of effect. For that matter, he couldn't remember his own name.

Oh, yes. *I am Beeman. Beam-Man, so they shot me in the brain with light. It is the only way to kill me.*

Or was it radiation?

"What happened?" Beeman heard himself repeat, his voice that of a stranger.

"You'll be fine," the voice of Kim said, "as long as you cooperate."

He felt his head snap backward, and he literally saw stars where the globes had been, but he felt very little pain. His eyes watered, and he tried to reach up to touch his face, but found that something sharp secured his hands behind his back.

His warm blood ran down his face and dripped from his chin onto his shirt.

He could taste it. The flavor was not entirely unpleasant.

With his head down, he chuckled softly, and then he resumed crying. They knew his secrets, didn't they? They knew that he'd been a very bad boy. They knew about Antonio, about Dove and Kitten.

They know about the virus. Yes, that was it! *They want my Black Sunrise.* A part of his mind snapped to clarity for a moment and told him to be very careful. He was in great danger now. *Oh, great danger, great danger.* A fierce battle was raging in his mind. He fought the fog that infused his thoughts, systematically ruining his analytical powers, planting pockets of insanity, breaking the links that anchored the structure of his mental networks to ... *to what?*

He cried some more, then made himself stop.

"I'm so sorry," Beeman said in a throaty whisper. "I just find this a bit ironic." A swollen, numb feeling started creeping down his chest. He turned his head to one side, and gazed at the shafts of light that cut through the dusty darkness of the shed.

"As well you might," Kim said. He was standing beside the coffin, looking down on Beeman from above.

Beeman had never realized how tall Kim really was. He might be several miles tall. How did he fit into a car? After all, hadn't he been in the car with Beeman? Was he one of those weird Orientals who could be tall or short depending on what mood he was in?

I'm hallucinating. He clamped his eyes shut for a few seconds and then opened them again.

Kim descended several thousand feet and crouched beside him. "You appreciate the irony. The captor has become the captive."

"What's the difference?" Beeman heard himself ask. He watched as Kim retrieved a pack of cigarettes from somewhere and lit one.

Beeman was smiling up at him like an expectant schoolboy. "Smoking again?" he slurred. "I thought we decided it's a bad idea."

• • •

Kim was fascinated. He would soon be able to peer directly into this most bizarre of minds. He'd memorized Beeman's dossiers: Born October 23, 1951, in Coeur d'Alene, Idaho. Witnessing the death of a schoolmate mauled to death by a vicious dog had traumatized Beeman at age ten. Beeman's father, Williston Beeman, had been an accountant employed by a mining company until his suicide by overdose of barbiturates and alcohol when Beeman was fourteen. Beeman had been the one to find his father's body. One of his schoolteachers had insisted that Beeman had talked his father into doing it.

Kim believed this was possible, if not likely.

Despite these traumas, Beeman had graduated with top grades from Coeur d'Alene High School in 1968. Soon after that, his mother had also taken her own life, leaving her car running in a closed garage shortly after Beeman had left for college.

Five years after that, he'd received a BS in chemistry from MIT, graduating *magna cum laude* in 1973. He'd earned a master's degree, also from MIT, in molecular biology in 1976, following a brief withdrawal from the academic program for reasons unknown. He'd received a PhD in molecular biology from the California Institute of Technology in 1981. His doctoral thesis was entitled *Electrostatic transport phenomena influencing transmission of airborne pathogens: aero-biological and epidemiological effects of infused negative ions.* The thesis described Beeman's laboratory studies proving that electronic means could enhance or suppress the contagiousness of certain diseases. It landed Beeman a place in the spotlight of germ warfare research.

Beeman subsequently published papers on many aspects of genetic engineering, but this much was obvious: Beeman had dedicated his professional career to researching and developing new and deadly contagious diseases.

In 2007, Beeman had gone to work for DataHelix, Inc., an extremely advanced research corporation with but a single customer: the Department of Defense. During his first seven years with the company, Beeman had worked at a small clinical research facility in Irvine. Then four years ago they'd transferred him to the ultra-secure underground research facility hidden beneath the Rocky Mountain Arsenal National Wildlife Refuge a few miles northeast of downtown Denver. The Black Sunrise project was just starting up then. Most of what Kim and his colleagues knew about the Black Sunrise virus came from the world-class DPRK cyber-warriors—the best hackers in the world, or so Kim had been led to believe.

The Black Sunrise viral weapon system was Beeman's brainchild, his ultimate achievement. The innovations and discoveries attributable to Beeman's work could revolutionize the study of medicine, yet they were locked away on air-gapped underground computers that had no connections of any kind to the outside world. They were therefore unreachable by even the most sophisticated crypto-pirates. So Beeman had come under North Korean surveillance, which had produced a startling revelation: the brilliant mind that had brought deadly new life-forms into existence spent leisure time plotting with a lowlife limo driver various means of kidnapping and torturing young women.

And that mind lay open to probing and suggestion, practically in the palm of Kim's hand.

"Do you wish to die, Artie?"

Beeman slurred in reply, his nostrils clogged with coagulated blood. "Death is inevitable."

"Do you fear pain? Or do you enjoy it?"

"Why do you ask?"

When a subject answers a question with a question, it was a sign the drugs had not fully taken effect. Kim looked at his watch. It had been twenty minutes since the injection. He would give it a while longer before considering an additional dose. "I am simply curious."

"Yes, I know you are. A very *curious* fellow." Beeman giggled softly.

"As are you," Kim whispered into Beeman's ear. "What are you curious about, Artie? What is it you wish to learn?"

After a deep sigh, Beeman intoned, "The knowledge of death."

Kim paused, now more confident of his path into Beeman's psyche.

"The knowledge of death," Kim repeated thoughtfully. He drew deeply on his cigarette. This man was truly a rarity—an absolute, utter psychopath. Kim had supervised and conducted the brutal, violent interrogations of many men and women. He'd seen human beings succumb to pain and fear. He'd watched trained soldiers beg frantically before falling into hysteria and shock.

None of the truisms of interrogation applied here; Kim knew that Beeman feared neither pain nor death. Hypnosis would not affect him; drugs sufficient to open his mind would put him completely under. He would not succumb easily.

It was not a matter of courage. It was something else—a mental sickness akin to what Kim had seen in the devoutly religious, but stronger. In Beeman's case it was not a question of having the willpower to resist the horror of interrogation but rather a willingness to experience it. Beeman simply did not care, for he would embrace whatever came. He was shielded by his own insanity.

Or so Kim thought.

What drives this man?

"I take it you would find a quick death to be a disappointment," Kim said, breaking the silence as his cigarette smoke swirled upward through the slats of light that splashed across his shirt.

"I would not find a quick death to be anything," Beeman said, his voice a childlike murmur, as though talking to himself, working out a problem. "If the act of dying is sufficiently truncated, there is nothing to experience."

"And what of pain?"

"Pain is pain. But pain does not carry knowledge."

"And what does?"

"The architect of death."

"And that is you?"

"No, not only me." Beeman's voice was monotonous and empty of emotion. "I don't know who or what it is. The creator of death, which is the creator of life. The creator of death is the source of all life."

"Is that God?" Kim asked. The man's pedantry was becoming tiresome.

"It is a mind of sorts, which resides where the predator and the victim consciously share the experience of death. That experience remains in the awareness of the creator."

Kim juggled these ideas, seeking a common thread of logic.

"And that is why you have the women?"

"That is why I have the *man*," Beeman corrected. "The women are for dying. The man is for me—to forge into a creator."

Kim sat silently for a moment, contemplating what he was learning and how it would translate into the kind of reliable knowledge Young demanded. It confirmed there was more to this man than a sadist with an unrestrained libido. Kim had traction now. A few more milliliters of serum might be appropriate.

He gestured to Chul for the kit. As he was unzipping it, Beeman spoke.

"Please, no more drugs."

Kim ignored him and worked the needle of the syringe into the vial.

Beeman shook his head. "That isn't necessary."

Kim was intrigued; he'd not expected Beeman to show any evidence of obedience, to plead or submit. The threats of prison, torture and death had no discernible effect on the man, but now he was pleading to avoid a second dose of a mere injection. Interrogation was more art than science, as he'd learned at the Beong-shik Academy outside Pyongyang, where most of the DPRK elite-echelon operatives live and train for years before being sent abroad. *What opens one mind will break another and bore yet another.*

Kim turned to Chul and Pak, snapping an order in Korean. "*Bakeseo gidalisibsio.*"

The men nodded respectfully and stepped outside.

Kim held the syringe in front of Beeman's face. "What are you saying?"

"Drugging me is not the way to get what you want."

Kim knew at that moment that he had been correct when he'd predicted that the only way to control Beeman was to use methods other than the traditional ones, such as coercion and bribery. He did not fear the drug but rather the loss of control over his faculties, which was not a practical sword to hold over his head, for without his faculties he was useless to Kim. Beeman's response fit Kim's evolving psychological model. But was Kim correct in predicting that Beeman might steal the virus and technical data, and defect voluntarily, merely to see his weapon devastate a large population? And even if he claimed he would do so, how could Kim be sure Beeman would follow through rather than engineering a clever betrayal?

Could they trust this man?

Of course not.

But what choice did they have?

• • •

Beeman felt the drug wearing off as though a hard wax that had encased his mind was now melting away. His arms and wrists were numb; he was concerned about the possibility of nerve damage if he couldn't restore blood circulation to them soon. An electric tingling rampaged throughout him, a pins-and-needles itching with unpleasant waves of apprehension and claustrophobia. He wanted desperately to stand up and move about.

The drug is metabolizing, he thought. *This will pass.*

Kim was obviously deciding whether to drug him again or even whether to kill him. His power play with the car had been stupid and had backfired badly.

There were others at DataHelix with access to the virus and the technical data whom the North Koreans could co-opt. That notion distressed him. His own death, in the abstract, did not trouble him excessively; for a long time he had harbored a desire to die, but to die *now*, when he was so close to the fruition of his plans, would be unacceptable. He was panting, and his lungs felt congested. "I want my virus unleashed," Beeman heard himself say. "And I will gladly help you do it."

"You must realize," Kim said, "that if you do help us, you will be at great risk."

"I don't care," said Beeman, shifting his weight once again.

"Are you uncomfortable?"

"Somewhat."

Kim raised the cuff of Beeman's trousers and withdrew the man's hunting knife; then he reached behind him to cut the plastic restraint. Beeman looked at his hands as Kim stepped back. They were purple, and there were deep grooves in his wrists where the tie wrap had bitten into the flesh, but there was very little bleeding. It had cut his skin in places, but the cuts were shallow. Beeman flexed his fingers slowly, looking at his watch. He checked his shirt. He expected to see large bloodstains, but there were none.

"Your discomfort will pass soon. The next hour will be unpleasant. We will leave you here with your car. Do not try to drive for a while."

"How will I contact you?"

"I have the number for the phone at your cabin, and I have your cell phone number. I will call you within two days. If I do not, get the virus and the data and fly to Buenos Aires; stay at the best hotel you can find, under your own name, and wait for us to contact you."

"Five million dollars, logistical support and a way to guarantee my future safety?"

"All of that, and much, much more, Dr. Beeman, if you serve us well."

Beeman tipped his head back. "Fine. I look forward to our next meeting."

"As do I. And one more thing."

"Yes?"

"Be very careful. Do not speed. You mustn't risk the police stopping you again. And keep Pessoa under control."

"I don't smoke, and I don't speed, Mr. Kim."

"Of course not, Dr. Beeman. You are a law-abiding citizen."

• • •

An hour later, a man dressed in a Colorado State Patrol uniform picked cigarette butts from the dirt and deposited them into a clear plastic evidence bag. He had pulled Beeman and Kim over a while ago, but he was in fact a federal agent—call sign Skunk Two. He'd lifted fingerprints and DNA from Kim's driver's license and the butts, and he and his team had scoured other forensic evidence from the shed during the past month. He had a lot to add to the database the JTTF was building on the Wallies. His team would soon know more about the three DPRK agents—and hopefully the other members of their cell—than the North Koreans knew about Beeman from hacking DataHelix servers and other less secure federal databases. They had recently detected and monitored those penetrations, which was how the JTTF, FBI and NSA had discovered that the North Koreans had Beeman under surveillance.

Lastly, Skunk Two checked the hidden microphones. Then he departed.

He had a report to make before returning to the team's concealed overwatch position. It was going to be another long, tense day.

Chapter 27

Jackie's horrific screaming outside the window well had left Christie trembling with a horrible pain in her stomach. The sound was like nothing she'd ever heard. What had happened to her to make her scream in such abject terror? Was she still alive?

She froze when she heard footsteps coming down the stairs. She saw Jackie, still naked, guided by the older man to stand outside the door to the cage. Jackie's vacant stare carried the echo of the horror she'd endured—whatever it was. Unlike Christie—covered in dirt and grime with her filthy hair pasted to her scalp—Jackie had obviously bathed, and someone had blow-dried and curled her hair. She had lipstick and eye shadow on her face, but her expression was utterly empty. Her eyes were dead.

What had Jackie been through?

Would Christie be next?

Could she survive the ordeal without permanent psychological damage?

The older man unlocked and opened the cage and ordered Jackie to step inside and kneel on the mattress. She obeyed instantly, never looking at Christie, keeping her eyes downcast.

"I'll be back for you soon, Kitten." The man's voice was a frigid whisper. "Don't let your hair or makeup become spoiled."

Christie's heart pounded. "What have you done to her?"

The man smiled. "Made her pretty, and *useful*."

Christie expected him to order her out of the cage, but instead he simply relocked the door and walked away. She heard him climbing the stairs. She knew it was only because he wanted her to; when he wished, he could approach in utter silence. She turned to Jackie and touched her on the shoulder. Jackie recoiled as if Christie had shocked her with a cattle prod, finally making eye contact with her for the first time. Her eyes were wide, and she had started hyperventilating. Soon a terrible keening whine accompanied each breath.

"Jax, honey, it's okay. It's just me, baby. Just me." Although she wanted to hug Jackie and comfort her, Christie gave her space to regain her bearings. "I'm here for you, Jax. I'll always be here for you," she said soothingly.

Jackie knee-walked around Christie and grabbed a bit of toilet paper and gently dabbed her eyes, careful not to smear her mascara.

"I can't cry!"

"Why not?" Christie asked.

"Because if I mess up my eyes, he'll take them out!"

And with that, Jackie would say no more. She started hyperventilating and sat back on her heels, staring vacantly into space. She was somewhere else. Christie thought she might pass out.

Christie tried to force herself to focus. She felt guilty for not having been the one who had to go through whatever had happened to Jackie. She had to find answers to engineer a way out of the trap. She had little to hang on to, but she couldn't let her mind wander down endless dark stairways that led only to hell. She thought of the *Saw* movies and the puzzle houses they'd inspired.

If I'm smart enough, we can get out. I can solve this puzzle.

The key was to notice everything—what had she missed?

Why did he leave me here? What is he doing with Jackie?

Of course, the man could come back at any time, but why had he chosen Jackie first? Was it because she was sexier, with bigger boobs? Christie's intuition told her there was more. That man was darkly, sickly brilliant, so nothing was what it seemed. He had designed this kidnapping for more than just sexual assault. It was a psychodrama—an exercise in mental torture.

She thought of a story her father had told her one night over dinner. He'd been extolling the importance of studying the brilliant tactics of the great lawyers who'd lived before the age of computers, copy machines or even electric typewriters. He told her about a several-hour-long argument Clarence Darrow had made in the defense of two young boys who had kidnapped and killed Charles Lindburg's toddler son.

They had called it a thrill-killing.

Killing for the thrill of it? How could something so nightmarish be a thrill?

Will they kill us for the thrill of it? Are they working their way up to murdering us? Toying with us first?

She realized that the difference between Jackie's treatment and hers might not be a matter of randomly picking one girl to start with and saving the other for later. Something about Jackie drew their attention. Of course, there were her finer looks, overt sexuality and curvaceous figure. But when Christie watched the old man's eyes, there was no hint of lust. This mysterious nightmare seemed targeted but not sexually driven—their nudity aside.

Maybe they know how much money Robert has. This may not be about me at all, especially if they don't know how much money Dad has.

She felt guilty for wondering if they'd abducted her only because she'd happened to be with Jackie at that time. Then her mind spun a completely new lot of possibilities: perhaps they only wanted to play with Jax because she wasn't the valuable ransom hostage they thought Christie to be. Maybe they thought of Jackie as the expendable toy. Maybe they had planned different fates for each of them.

Don't let your imagination run away. Consider possibilities, but don't spin nightmares. Stick to what you know and what makes sense. Try a different question. Who are these men?

It was odd how different her two kidnappers were from one another. The older man was clearly very intelligent, the younger one evidently less so. A brilliant predator and a dull-witted pervert? One was in charge; the other obeyed. One was a cat, the other a mouse— like her and Jackie in a way.

Were they all in orbit around the evil game-master?

Keep going, CJ. What else?

Pushing aside the pain in her arm, she pushed her thoughts forward. Somehow the younger man was part of the older man's grand design, just as she and Jackie were, but he was outside the cage, free to leave whenever he wanted.

Or was he?

Maybe we're holding him here somehow.

Her instincts told her all three of them were stuck in the web the older guy had spun. She doubted he was actually the younger man's father. But what was the nature of their relationship? Was the younger man just a dupe, a puppet? Someone to take advantage of? If the older man could do it, maybe she could as well. The younger man might be the weak link.

Maybe she could influence him. Along with transient lust, he had fear in his eyes. And loneliness.

•   •   •

"He says he will cooperate," Kim said into the encrypted sat phone. He sat in the passenger seat while Chul drove, following Beeman's car from a discrete distance.

"Congratulations," Young replied snidely. "What is the likelihood he actually will?"

Kim was disappointed; he'd expected his superior to acknowledge he'd reached an important milestone. Kim was not a vain man; his superiors had selected him for missions of this kind precisely because he required minimal supervision and did not need emotional stroking to continue functioning in hostile territory. Nevertheless, he felt a pronounced sense of deflation.

He decided to gamble. "I believe him, but I do not trust him.

Prisoners make choices that free men discard. When his opportuni-
ties change, his goals may change with them. But for now, I sense he
sees an opportunity and not just a threat. I believe we can tap into
that, but we are far from secure."

There was a long pause. Small hail pellets peppered the windshield
and roof of the car, making a grinding noise the phone amplified in
his ear as he strained to hear his overseer's voice.

"Your scientist is more of a risk than an intelligence asset. He is
insanely unpredictable by your own admission." Kim winced at the
accusatory tone of Young's voice. "What you now propose is that we
promise him a fortune and stand by helplessly while we wait for him
to infiltrate the facility. This could take days—even weeks. After all,
what's the alternative? We can't get into the facility; we need Beeman for that. But if he betrays us, he could be a hero. Is he toying
with us?"

The line grew silent again, and Kim waited, listening to the hammering of hailstones, watching the trees roll past, their boughs swaying in the building mountain winds. The storm had intensified. His
concentration lagged, and he realized his mind was wandering. The
stress and fatigue were taking a toll. He realized he'd ignored his superior's question.

Young moved to a new topic. "The hostages add an unnecessary
element of complexity and needless danger."

"Yes, but they give us *some* leverage and serve to keep Beeman occupied to a degree, holding him in place for now as we analyze and
adapt to what we are learning. Respectfully, sir, I consider this an advantage."

"You are mistaken. He's dangerous, and his playthings make the
situation much too volatile and far more hazardous than it needs to
be."

Kim was more than a little surprised at the turn the conversation
was taking. It was a violation of operational security to use words
like "hostage," even on an encrypted line. The NSA possessed code-

breaking supercomputers thought to be capable of intercepting even secure transmissions, and such trigger words could bring their conversations to the attention of human analysts.

What was Young thinking?

"With respect, sir, our power stems from our knowledge of his twisted urges and his compromised position. This has been our plan for some time. Understanding his aberrations, his destructive needs, will provide insight into the workings of his mind. From this we aim toward total control. It is possible we could make further use of this man. He could become a valuable asset. He has vast scientific knowledge of biological weaponry."

"Smuggle him out of the country?"

"That is what I propose."

There was a hiss on the line. Was it static, or Young exhaling in disgust?

"If we succeed, the rewards are great indeed. For all of us. The funding at your disposal should be evidence of that. But if you lose control of this situation, it will be very bad."

"Yes," Kim acknowledged. "Though it is never a gamble to do one's duty."

"Of course, Kim. For now, proceed as you propose, but be ready to kill the women and Pessoa and bring Beeman to me on a moment's notice. We have no way of knowing what he may have said in their presence, particularly after you approached him."

Before Kim could seek clarification of his decision-making authority or logistics, the connection dropped.

The mountain road rolled past like a ribbon on a reel, weaving drunkenly back and forth. Eventually, the brutal hail softened to heavy rain, and the wind subsided. Kim replayed the conversation in his mind. He realized his mission was worse than urgent: it was *desperate.* A large-scale operation was obviously in the works, and the virus was central to its success.

While the Exalted One distracted the world with his missiles, he was preparing for a surprise invasion of the South.

Time was of the essence, so a huge risk was unavoidable.

Everything rested on him, and Beeman.

Chapter 28

Antonio paced back and forth across the linoleum floor of the small convenience store that served as a drop-off point for Steamboat's municipal bus line, which he'd ridden here from the bus station to rendezvous with Beeman. The store, called Kum & Go, was a combined grocery store and gas station. The name echoed over and over in his mind like a song that wouldn't go away, accompanied by bizarre alternating visions: long-awaited erotic rampages and ruinous disasters. One moment he cultivated arousing images of shimmering, shapely female flesh; the next he pictured the police arresting and pushing him head-down into a squad car with his hands cuffed behind him. He'd recited his *Miranda* rights in his head again and again during the slow, endless bus ride up from Denver. He had been living in a hellish heaven of excitement, anticipation, self-abnegation and terror for so many days now that he couldn't remember what it felt like not to have his heart forcefully battering his chest from inside.

He looked at his watch yet again. His bus from Denver had been an hour late on arrival. He'd been waiting at the Kum & Go for nearly two hours more, so Beeman was three hours late. Antonio had repeatedly called the cabin and Beeman's cell; neither number had picked up. He'd asked the counter clerk—an elderly woman with a sloppy lipstick smile painted over her onionskin lips—if anyone had asked about the bus being late. The old bat had giggled fiendishly and shaken her head at the silliness of his question. "Hon, the bus is *always* late."

Antonio's anxiety was ratcheting upward.

It was raining hard outside. Had the weather caused Beeman trouble? What if he'd been in an accident? The thought sent an icy chill through Antonio. Police responded to accidents. The Toyota and the cabin were both registered in Beeman's name. If they'd found Beeman unconscious or dead in Antonio's car, the natural course of inquiry would lead to the cabin and the girls—who could easily identify Antonio as one of their abductors—leading in turn to years upon years in prison.

Where the fuck was Beeman?

Kum & Go, man. Come and let's go, so I can go and cum. He chuckled nervously, more of a hyena whine than a laugh. He bought a bag of Doritos and a Pepsi. *You have the right to remain silent. Anything you say can and will be used against you. You have the right to an attorney.* He shoveled chips into his mouth and washed them down with Pepsi; then he let out a great belch that caught the attention of the clown-faced biddy at the register.

He'd feel better when he was with Beeman; he always felt calmer and more confident when they were together. He didn't know why.

He thought of hitchhiking to the cabin but realized that it would be impossible; few traveled the last ten miles to the place. He just had to wait. If the police were already looking for him, they would be much more likely to find him at the cabin than at this convenience store. He was safer here.

But what if Beeman never showed?

He couldn't go back to Denver without checking on the women. If they escaped, he'd be completely fucked. That thought made him cringe, for it came dangerously close to forcing him to face the truth, which was that they would eventually have to kill the girls. Sooner or later, it would come to that, wouldn't it? He'd always known it, but he pushed the thought away, focusing only on the pleasure he would get before it came to that. Besides, Beeman would guide him through it. Beeman knew what was best.

Antonio tried to ease his sense of dread by trying to turn his thoughts back to his fantasies instead of prison.

He'd definitely start with the brunette. Her tits were so totally perfect! She had a full, sensuous mouth, with dick-sucking lips that looked like little pink pillows and an hourglass figure. Delicious hips and legs. She was small, diminutive, with a submissive aura that really turned him on. On the other hand, there was something about the taller blonde that made him feel cheesy, guilty. It was the way she looked at him, silently chiding him, as if to appeal to his chivalrous nature, urging him to come to his senses. As if to say, *you know better.*

She made him uneasy rather than horny.

What he had in mind was anything but chivalrous, so he would start with the brunette. The one he called Kitten. Breaking her to his will would be awesome. If she became his total slave, maybe he could *keep* her and not have to kill her. Now *that* was a happy thought.

He could restrain himself no more. He'd try the phone again. As he reached for his cell, a hand came down on his shoulder, and time stopped. A thousand years seemed to pass in less than a second, and the only thought in Antonio's mind during that endless epoch was that he had to piss. It had to be a cop. He'd be under arrest in seconds.

At last, his body obeyed him, and he slowly turned.

It was Beeman.

Antonio let out a long breath. "Jesus fucking Christ all fucking mighty!" It came out as a whimper. Beeman nodded reassuringly. Antonio noticed two streaks of dried blood on the front of Beeman's shirt. Beeman didn't seem to realize they were there. If he had, he'd have changed his shirt before going out in public.

Blood? What the fuck?

Noticing Antonio's eyes on his chest, Beeman looked down at his shirt and then shrugged, as though accepting some secret irony. "Nothing to worry about." He turned and strode out of the store.

Antonio followed him to the car and got in on the passenger side.

"Where the fuck have you been? Why is there blood on your shirt?"

Beeman calmly put the car in gear and pulled away from the store, turning onto the highway. Antonio did not notice the abrasions on Beeman's wrists.

"We have quite an evening ahead of us, my friend."

This did not placate Antonio. "You didn't answer my question. Why were you so late? Why do you have fucking *blood* on your shirt?"

"Don't worry. Nothing is amiss. I kept my promise. I did not start without you. I saved them for you. You will be first, as we agreed."

"Did you fight with them?"

"You might say that. They're under control. Trust me. I have the whole evening planned. You're going to find it deeply satisfying to learn who you really are."

Antonio snorted. "But what kept you so long?"

"The rain." Beeman would say no more.

Antonio's abdominal muscles were quivering. Something just wasn't right. Beeman seemed *too* calm, as if he were forcing it. Then it hit him.

"Did you take something?"

Beeman looked at him sheepishly. "You mean a drug." Antonio could hear a note of guilt in his voice. "Afraid so. Just a little something to loosen me up."

Relief crept through Antonio. "You okay to drive?"

"Of course. As I said, it was just a little something from the Orient to lower my inhibitions."

"You got any more?"

"Will you need it?"

This bruised Antonio's pride. "Maybe, but I want to be in the moment. Don't want to spoil the experience. Natural is better, right?"

Beeman gave him that deadly little grin again. "You remember the movie *Pretty Woman*? It's like that. This is going to be what you call a 'sure thing.'"

An awkward laugh escaped Antonio's throat.

Beeman chuckled with him.

•　•　•

Two hours later Antonio was sitting at the kitchen table watching
as Beeman spread out a linen tablecloth and set three places. A fat
scented candle burned in the center of the table. Soft jazz played:
"My Funny Valentine." Antonio was wearing his new sport jacket
over his tee shirt and jeans. Adrenaline surged as he heard footsteps
coming down the stairway from the bedroom on the second floor.

He heard Beeman speaking softly from just beyond the doorway.
"Open your eyes, Kitten, or this will be a blind date that never ends.
Remember my grapefruit spoon."

Sighing with relief, Antonio finished his drink and wiped his
moist palms on his jeans. From around the corner, the brunette
emerged, and Antonio's breath caught. She stood before him wearing a spotless white dress and cream-colored stiletto heels. Her hair
had been washed and styled. She wore light makeup, with lots of eye
shadow. Her lipstick was a deep rouge, enhancing the shape of her
sexy mouth.

"Jesus," Antonio whispered. "She looks good enough to eat."

"You may sit, Kitten," Beeman intoned as he followed her into the
kitchen. He had changed into a chalk-colored suit, with a dark green
bowtie and shiny loafers.

"There." Beeman pointed to the chair beside Antonio's; she would
be sitting between them in her luscious dress that would soon be
gone. Whatever happened, Antonio decided, she would keep her
nasty high heel pumps *on*.

Wordlessly, she stepped across the hardwood floor and sat demurely at the table, her chin down slightly.

Antonio's mind was spinning. How had Beeman managed to pull
this off?

Before seating himself, Beeman put a gentle hand on Antonio's shoulder. Antonio remembered how startled he had been at the Kum & Go when Beeman had done the same thing.

Beeman moved to the sink and uncorked a bottle of Woodford Reserve. "Would you care for another small shot, my friend?"

Antonio gulped to clear his throat.

"Yeah, thanks," he croaked.

Chapter 29

The Palace Arms was one of Denver's oldest and finest restaurants, located in the ancient and lavish Brown Palace hotel, built in 1892 in the heart of downtown. Moguls of industry and finance, professional sports stars and even several American presidents frequented the wedge-shaped building. The accoutrements included beautiful Napoleonic artifacts. The cuisine was impeccable and priced accordingly. The smell of lilacs and well-oiled leather drifted in the air with faint harp music and light banter.

Seated at a quiet table were Mark and Janet Jensen, Robert Sand, Dave Thomas and Albert Brecht. Brecht and the Jensens were staying in the hotel, occupying two top-floor suites sealed behind walls of opaque glass, unlike the rooms on all the lower floors, which opened to a cavernous atrium looking down on the lavishly appointed lobby. Dwight Eisenhower and his retinue had occupied these top-floor suites during the summer of 1955, when he'd endured a long period of illness. Many guests reported that it felt like sleeping in the White House. The décor was the same, as was the service. While their circumstances were not conducive to the enjoyment of luxury, the pleasant surroundings provided them a welcome respite and the illusion of normalcy.

After a long and stressful day, Mark and Janet had reluctantly agreed to Brecht's suggestion that they dine in elegance and relax briefly, so they could decompress while conversing in quiet privacy at a relatively isolated table in the far corner of the restaurant.

Brecht assured them the rest of the team was still at work.

He wore his habitual black three-piece suit. "I'm sure you must have noticed the scar by now," he said, touching the spot behind his right ear. Jensen noticed a tremor in his hand. "From a bullet," Brecht continued. "Your father dug it out of my skull in the basement of a building in Moscow. It was 1956—the year after Eisenhower stayed at this hotel. I visited him often in those days, so I have bittersweet memories of this place. Then the next year I nearly died. Your father saved my life, at great personal peril. Did he ever tell you the story?"

"No," Jensen conceded. "My father was very strict about keeping other people's medical details to himself, and I have the feeling this particular event was something they warned him not to discuss."

Brecht regarded Mark for a moment, his chin lifting slightly. "There was far more to this secret than my medical privacy. The incident was highly classified, a matter of national security. The record remains sealed to this day."

Sand said, "Cold War espionage."

Brecht canted his head, twitching his cottony eyebrows.

A waiter hovered just out of earshot, politely awaiting a signal to approach. Brecht summoned him with a toss of his hand. At length, the waiter finished describing various entrées and took their orders while his second refilled water glasses with Pellegrino from a large green bottle he stored in an ice-filled decanter on a small stand beside the table. Once the waiter and his helper were gone, Brecht muttered something about waiters and spooks.

Jensen took a small sip of single malt from a heavy crystal tumbler. "Can you tell us about it, Albert?"

Brecht nodded. "You should know what happened. It is part of *your* family history, Mark, ancient history though it is." Reaching into his jacket, Brecht withdrew a large cigar and, after rolling it between his fingers for a few silent seconds, placed it on the tablecloth before him. Jensen knew he longed to light it but would not. He told himself that after they recovered Christie and Jackie safe and alive, they would smoke a pair of Cubans together.

"Different days then," Brecht said. "No spy satellites, no cell phones. No supercomputers to crack codes. None of the gadgets we have today. We gathered our intelligence the old-fashioned way. We recruited spies, co-opting men and women with access to sensitive information. We collected the secrets we stole for our analysts from dead drops that made their way to Washington in diplomatic pouches. The analysts first decrypted some of it aboard naval vessels or in basements in London. British and American intelligence agencies worked a bit more intimately in those days—the bond forged in the war was still fresh. The practicalities of geography meant a lot more back then. The Brits were stronger than they are now. We needed them."

Janet cut in with a question. "The British are still our allies though, aren't they?"

Brecht chuckled. "Yes, certainly, Janet. But the world situation is far more complicated now. Russia is an ally one day and an enemy the next. Putin supports some of our military efforts and yet threatens us with nuclear cruise missiles that can hit any spot on the globe. We play our enemies *and* our allies as pawns."

"How so? With the fall of the Iron Curtain, Russia is becoming a democracy. The Cold War is over. We are the only true superpower, aren't we? It should be simpler, not more complicated."

Brecht picked up his cigar and rolled it absently between his crooked fingers. "The US is no longer the dominant power in the world, Janet. China and India have larger armies, and China's navy is *much* larger than any other, with technology every bit the equal of our own—if not superior. Many nations have nuclear weapons, including South Africa, Israel, India, Pakistan, North Korea and soon Iran will as well, despite the best efforts of the Mossad, MI6 and the CIA. Our golden gates are closed now. The Statue of Liberty is merely a historic artifact. We live in a very unstable world. Terrorists abound and often do not know what they are fighting for or who controls them. Bin Laden is dead; Al-Qaeda has gone out of style. ISIS is on the way out, only to be replaced by dozens of terrorist spoors.

"In the late fifties, we considered a nation a superpower if it presented a nuclear threat. Given the size and geography of our country, situated between ally nations that span an entire hemisphere, and with the strength of our military, we believed that only through strategic nuclear bombardment could anyone overcome us. We deemed a nation with that ability a superpower, not on the strength of its economy, but because it was a threat to us, and we considered ourselves a 'superpower,' a word we coined for ourselves out of pure hubris. Only a nation that could vaporize cities qualified for that title.

"Today, if we apply the definitions and thinking of that era, practically every nation is a superpower. A bearded Muslim huddling in a cave can bring down skyscrapers in the heart of New York City. Our electronic infrastructure is the life support of all commerce and communication and controls every aspect of our lives. We use the internet to turn on our lights and lock our doors, yet the World Wide Web is vulnerable to crippling attacks launched from internet cafes in Buenos Aires, the Sahara or anywhere else. Computer viruses self-replicate. A teenager with a laptop could theoretically crush our stock markets. We are vulnerable in ways we never dreamed of during the Cold War, which ironically is what spawned the same internet that now leaves us so vulnerable to cyberattack. The political fragmentation of various groups hostile to our interests makes monitoring them all and predicting their actions a nightmare. In fact— oh, listen to me. I'm sorry to prattle on so."

"Not at all, Albert," Janet said encouragingly. "Your wisdom and world knowledge is truly fascinating. And frankly, I'm thankful for the distraction."

"And to think that up until tonight I blamed all of our global upsets and human cruelties on United Airlines." Everyone chuckled politely at Sand's dry jest.

"Yes," Brecht replied, "United Airlines and every other corporation that uses or manufactures advanced technology. Who made the jets that took down the World Trade Center? Who made the world a global village? Remember the *USS Cole*? Before that happened, who would have thought untrained men in a rubber raft could cripple a US Navy destroyer? Throughout the Cold War, the media and our government portrayed the USSR as a terrible menace, a threat to the future of mankind, but our friends in the Kremlin never actually attacked us on the scale of a modern terrorist."

"Are you saying they're our friends?" Janet asked.

"In some ways they are, and in other ways they're our foes," Brecht answered. "But they've never killed our civilians on our own soil. People often say we hung at the brink of nuclear war with them for more than half a century, but we enjoyed what military analysts call 'strategic peace' that entire time. That means there were no overt military hostilities of magnitude. By the end of World War II, we saw Pearl Harbor as something that would never happen again. Yet here we sit, wondering what will happen next.

"No, Janet, we are not the only superpower. There are no superpowers anymore, at least not in the definitions we used when the word was coined. Or perhaps another way to put it would be to say everybody is a superpower these days. Now every Tom, Dick and Harry can get his hands on a piece of military hardware." Brecht winked at Jensen. "Not that an L-39 in the hands of a trial lawyer is necessarily a threat to mankind," he said, in reference to Jensen's restored Soviet jet fighter.

Jensen knew better than to be surprised. *The Old Man knows everything.* "You sound like you miss the good old days," he offered.

"Not at all, Mark. There is no time like the present. I merely submit that those were very different times."

"I was just a boy then."

"We were all children. Even me."

"But you were an adult," Janet countered, "doing a tough job behind the Iron Curtain."

"In those days we thought we were fighting for the survival of mankind, or at least the 'American way of life.'"

"And what did you do in those days?"

"I was a spy, Janet. And I recruited other spies, from the Soviet military politic." As he said this, Brecht pointed to the bright red star on the side of the green bottle of mineral water that lay planted in the ice bucket next to the table, as if the bottle were a product of the communist party rather than a town in Italy.

Janet had another question. "Did you ever have to kill anyone?"

Brecht chuckled at the abruptness of the question; then his mirth subsided, and he stared at his unlit cigar for a moment before answering. When he spoke, he gazed directly into her eyes. "Janet, you may think me a monster, but I rarely *had* to kill, at least not in self-defense or to save my own life. But kill I did."

"Why?" Janet's eyes were wide.

"Honey, I don't think—"

Brecht interrupted Jensen's protestations. "Mark, hers is a fair question. It was a long time ago. I don't mind talking about it, not to the family of Conrad Jensen."

"Albert, please forget I asked. It's just—I overstepped my bounds. It was terribly rude of me. The question just slipped out." Janet was clearly flustered.

"Not to worry," Brecht placated her. "It is a perfectly natural question. Most of it is still classified, but I can tell you that I was absolutely sure that every time I took a life, it saved more lives."

"American lives?"

"American, British *and* Russian. Possibly more."

Janet nodded, lowering her eyes. "There are many evil men in the world," she whispered.

"You see," Brecht plowed on, "we were fighting to understand a mysterious and dangerous enemy. It was much more than merely a war of ideologies, a clash of political beliefs. We were on the brink of nuclear war for generations, or so we thought at the time, and the information our espionage operations generated included not only data relating to the military capabilities and readiness of the Soviet Union. We were desperate to learn how deeply the communists had infiltrated our own political system, our government and our military. We feared a cancerous ideology that could end our way of life, our great traditions."

Janet nodded. "I read a book once that suggested our own CIA assassinated JFK because the Russians had blackmailed him to become a spy. The idea was that someone had filmed him when he was young doing something so embarrassing that he had no choice but to cooperate with the Russians to avoid a scandal that could bring down the US government. They manipulated our political system to get him into the White House, and in a way, the whole country was susceptible to blackmail. He became the ultimate mole, so we had no choice but to engineer his assassination."

Brecht picked up the ball and carried it forward. "It was exactly that kind of paranoia that led to the draconian measures of the McCarthy era as we struggled to root out communism from the fabric of American society."

"Was there any truth to that theory about JFK?"

"I thought you wanted to hear about me killing people or Mark's heroic father saving me."

Janet Jensen had been married to a trial lawyer for more than two decades. "So my question is off limits?"

"Your question about JFK?"

"Yes." Janet smiled.

"Let us table that for another time. I have a tale to tell that is much closer to home for you and your husband."

"Let's hear it," Sand prompted, smiling and gesturing with his finger, as if to reel in a fish on a rod.

At that moment the waiter reappeared, this time with two assistants, to begin serving their first course. They arranged plates and refilled glasses, then the waiter and his minions departed. For a few minutes no one spoke as they started into their dinners. No one wanted to prompt Brecht or open a new subject, so they waited patiently. After he had taken a few bites of his steak, Brecht took a gulp of mineral water and cleared his throat.

"I told Dave about this a few days ago, but you will find this interesting, and I'll add some details he doesn't know yet." Brecht said. Thomas nodded encouragingly, clearly interested to hear more about Brecht's history with Conrad Jensen.

"I learned much of what I know long after it happened. I had to piece this together with scraps from various sources because my own memory was less than complete.

"During the late fifties, I was working under non-official cover in Moscow. I was a spy with no diplomatic status. My role, as I've said, was to recruit Soviet agents. Our best prospects were often the ministerial employees at government offices and factories—people who had no power but who lived in the shadows of those who did, and who had access to sensitive information. On occasion, however, we sought to recruit the bigger fish, the people who were within the Russian Bear's inner cave.

"I'll omit the trivial details of my assignment. Suffice to say that I was betrayed, shot in the head and in the stomach, and left to die.

"Through some quirk of ballistics, I survived. One bullet lodged at the occipital lobe of my brain." He pointed to a spot behind his right ear. "The slug passed through the bone but stopped just inside my skull, doing minor damage to my brain. I was bleeding intracranially; pressure was building within my skull. The other slug ruptured my spleen, and I was also bleeding internally. I was alive but in a coma. Time wasn't on my side.

"The operation was blown, but we had to find out what had gone wrong. Had the subject I was trying to recruit shot me? Had the KGB or the GRU learned of our operations, our methods? Were others at risk of assassination? Was it time to roll up our team and exfiltrate? We had to get those answers, and I was the only one who might have them. We could have a leak, a mole, a double agent—the questions went on and on. If we had a spy in the upper echelon of our service, we had to root him out. If they kept me alive long enough, details I might provide could be important to our national security. But I was dying, in the subbasement of an ancient Russian ministry building.

"It just so happened that the best brain surgeon on earth—an American by the name of Conrad Jensen—was visiting Moscow with a diplomatic medical delegation when I was shot. They actually dragged your father from dinner with the American ambassador and spirited him away to where he performed surgery on me under the light of a bare bulb with limited surgical tools.

"Conrad got the bullets out and stabilized me. A month after that I was in a British hospital and eventually made a full recovery.

"But the real story is what happened to your father, whom the KGB detained the next day. They'd singled him out from the American delegation and taken him into custody for questioning. The KGB was putting things together very quickly.

"They took him to a small room and sat him in a chair next to a steam radiator. KGB officers stared at him in silence for hours, waiting for the tension to break him. They didn't have enough information to justify a brutal interrogation or charge him with espionage, and because he was there as a diplomat, a guest of the ambassador, they had to use some restraint. What they did to him was very psychologically distressing. The unspoken threat of torture and execution—standard punishments for espionage against the motherland or at least long-term imprisonment in a Soviet labor camp—was very real. He lived in terror for two long days. They answered none of his questions. They fed him little, let him have no sleep, and the room got hotter and hotter.

"Remember that he had not eaten or slept in twenty-four hours by the time the ordeal with the KGB *first began*. He was exhausted and had no training for that kind of thing.

"Your father never cracked. He just sat there and stared down trained KGB interrogators for more than forty hours."

Stunned, Janet blinked away tears. Jensen showed no expression. Sand shook his head slowly.

"So, what happened?" Janet asked at length.

"They eventually let him go, put him on a flight to Norway. They 'lost' his luggage and all of his belongings."

Mark chuckled. "Dad used to chide my mom about the fun she missed because she stayed home for that trip. She was pregnant with my brother, Johnny." After clearing his throat, he added, "He made the trip sound like it was nothing dramatic. He said he helped you with some kind of medical procedure, but he downplayed it. I thought maybe he stitched up a cut or something. I didn't know you'd been shot on hostile soil. Years afterward, when he mentioned your intelligence background and the work you do now, I should have pieced it together."

Brecht nodded. "Here was a civilian doctor with a wife and child and another on the way, and he risked everything to save a complete stranger in the service of his country. He could have declined without dishonor or repercussion, but he rose to the occasion and did what only a hero—" Brecht's voice faltered.

After several seconds of silence, Sand's soft baritone voice carried across the table. "I'm lucky," he said. "I get to benefit from that."

Brecht took the opportunity to move to a new subject. "Tell us more about Jackie. And if you're of a mind, tell us about yourself."

With a sad smile, Sand shrugged. "That's a tough act to follow, Albert."

"Not so. I know something of your background, sir. In your younger years, you could have been a star player on our team."

Once again, Janet would not stand for mystery. "What are you talking about, Albert?"

"Robert Sand is a very interesting man, Janet. His own history is more impressive—and I mean this quite sincerely—than my own. He has done many good and heroic deeds over the years, facing danger all the way. He's a force of nature."

"Care to fill us in?" asked Mark.

Brecht tipped his head. "I'll leave that to Mr. Sand."

"Hey," said Sand, "I'm just an old reprobate trying to find my gal, so I don't have to spend the rest of my days pining away alone watching reruns of *Sanford & Son*."

Brecht's bushy eyebrows rose a notch. At that moment, a cell phone chirped from inside his jacket. He pulled it out, tapped the glass and held it to his ear. "Brecht," he said crisply. After listening for a moment, he spoke a few words. "Well done. Where are they now? ... Alright, thanks." He ended the call and returned the phone to his jacket.

"Well?" Jensen asked.

"The rest of my team is here. We've recovered some surveillance video from the other side of the river; it's poor quality, but we're hoping to enhance it. This may give us a lead; we'll know more in the morning."

No one spoke, but all stared.

"Would anyone care for dessert?"

Still no one spoke.

"In that case, would anyone object if I were to light my cigar?"

Chapter 30

While Antonio plowed through a juicy steak, sipping eighteen-year-old Oban, Beeman went upstairs. Kitten was touching up her hair and makeup. Her hands were shaking, but she tried to work with care, doing her best to make her eyes pretty—so she could keep them.

When she finished with her mascara, she put down the brush and said simply, "I'm ready."

Beeman escorted her down the stairs and into the kitchen.

He hadn't miscalculated. Antonio's response to Kitten appearing as she did—dolled up nicely in the white dress that accentuated her figure—was exactly what Beeman expected. The shoes were a fine touch; Antonio liked women in high heel shoes.

Beeman had her dressed up like a virgin at a summer wedding to commence Antonio's journey, his crossing, in his native state: civilized, inhibited, helpless and sexually frustrated. When he completed his metamorphosis, he'd become the God of Lust and Mayhem.

Now Beeman would steer Antonio's infantile mind down a psychic spiral staircase, sinking through the strata of his troubled soul to the subbasement where his most primal impulses festered and grew, far from the sunlight, like poison fungus. Beeman would be Antonio's tour guide, showing him the way. One step would lead to another, and another, until Antonio's inner beast was free, loosed upon the world. Beeman expected Antonio eventually to devour himself; his plush fantasy life had not prepared him for the ghastly realities he would soon experience at his own hand. His conscience would ultimately circle back and ambush him.

If not, then perhaps he could call upon Dove to extinguish the misfit. Beeman trusted that his sense about that woman was right—beneath her graceful demeanor lurked an iron serpent, which if awakened might empower her to use her finely manicured nails to tear away Antonio's face.

Antonio was still filling himself with beef and booze, a look of intense pleasure on his face.

A good sign. His inhibitions are relaxed.

When he saw Kitten standing demurely before him in her sultry bride-like accoutrements, Antonio's jaw literally dropped open. His pupils dilated; a reddish shimmer began to emerge along the outer edges of his large ears, signaling an endorphin dump. His breath caught in his chest; then he began to pant.

Beeman wondered if he might hyperventilate.

At this point things departed unsettlingly from his script.

Antonio's behavior made Beeman's stomach twist. Instead of displaying the cruel, lascivious grin Beeman expected, Antonio swallowed hard and stood up, to be chivalrous, pulling out her chair for her.

"Are you hungry?"

No! Antonio was rising to the occasion in the wrong way, trying to charm the girl. Beeman had considered but discounted this possibility, believing that the danger of such a response would be greater with Dove than with Kitten, which was why he'd selected the seductive, voluptuous brunette for this first phase of the drama.

He'd thought she would strike the right chord; she was well on the way to breaking completely. She radiated submissive obedience, invoking the primitive urges that coursed through Antonio's reptilian mind.

Antonio had spent most of his adult life suffering from the cumulative frustration of women he coveted rejecting and ignoring him. A girl who had meant the world to him had spurned him as a teen, cutting him deeply; many similar failures had followed, each one deepening and widening the gaping wound. Year after year, unremitting pain, loneliness and incessant pent-up libido had eventually taken their toll and bent his mind permanently.

Or so Beeman had thought.

Antonio was not a fundamentally unattractive man—he was trim and tall with jet-black hair and square shoulders. Yes, his nose was oversized and hatchet-like, his dark eyes were too closely-set and his mustache was absurdly vain. But if he'd been convincingly able to project in the presence of beautiful women the cocky confidence he pretended to have when he was alone with Beeman, he'd likely not have suffered the burning sexual isolation Beeman had painstakingly exploited through months of control and manipulation. He had brought Antonio to a boil night after night in strip clubs and topless bars, cultivating his resentment with booze, shimmering flesh, twist-ed fantasies—and no happy endings.

He'd slipped large bills to the exotic dancers Antonio found most alluring, telling them to keep Antonio turned on but never to give him more than teasing attention. Whatever they would have charged to have gone home with Antonio, Beeman had matched and more, with instructions never to offer him relief.

The hateful whores had loved it.

So now, just when the Doberman was about to slip away from its chain, it became a gentle puppy.

Disaster.

Jackie asked, "Can I have some food?"

Before Antonio could speak, Beeman took one step closer to her and whispered very softly into her ear. "Slap him as hard as you can, right now, or this is the end for you."

She obeyed without hesitation.

The sound of her palm striking Antonio's cheek was a thunder-clap.

Chapter 31

As Janet brought the car to a stop, Jensen saw two gray motor coaches that loomed nose to tail along the edge of the parking lot at Centennial Airport. "Bigger than I expected," he said as he opened the door and stepped out of the car.

"Each one is forty-five feet long," Brecht said.

"Are they identical?"

"Only on the outside." Brecht pointed to the closest of the two behemoths. "This one is a mobile command post, packed with electronics. That one is a hospitality coach. It has a full kitchen and a dozen privacy pods—fairly comfortable to sleep in, unless you're claustrophobic. A shower and toilet. Satellite receivers on the roofs link to data centers. Lots of specialized gear on board."

Mark, Janet and Robert followed Brecht as he walked to the door of the closest bus. With no side windows, it was impossible to see into either vehicle. Someone within must have seen them coming on camera; as they approached, the door opened with a hydraulic hiss, and stairs extended.

"Weapons?" Sand asked.

Brecht gave a wry smile and gestured for them to climb aboard.

Jensen stepped up first. Along one side of the vehicle's length ran a row of workstations that reminded him of NORAD, which he'd visited in a different life as an Air Force pilot. Huge monitors lined the wall; beneath each was a molded desk holding a keyboard and trackpad and other electronic devices he didn't recognize. In front of each workstation was a comfortable chair mounted on a support strut fastened to the floor. Gleaming steel lockers lined the opposite wall.

Tinted glass made up portions of the long roof overhead, letting in some light; rows of LED spots added a pleasing amber glow. The interior hummed quietly with the sound of powerful fans.

About two-thirds of the way to the back, several technicians sat together, staring intently at one of the screens. The attractive Asian woman Jensen had met two days ago, Jennifer Takaki, swept her finger lightly across the surface of the panel, leaving bright green marks on what looked like a satellite image.

"What are they doing?" Jensen asked.

"Let's go see," Brecht replied, guiding them into the depths of the coach. Looking beyond, Jensen saw a small conference room at the rear of the bus, containing an oval table surrounded by a dozen slender chairs.

They joined Roady Kenehan and Robert Partridge, standing behind two seated people, Takaki and another man they had not met before; he sported a foot-long reddish beard below his bald cranium. The map vanished, and a detailed wire-frame diagram appeared—a wireframe rendering of a structure that rotated slowly about its vertical axis.

Jensen recognized it. "The parking garage?"

Kenehan nodded. "We're integrating our lidar scans with design plans for the parking structure. We hacked Taubman's plans out of the Municipal Planning Department's server."

"Who is Taubman?"

"The developer who built the mall. We're threading the data into a high-def geolocation matrix—the kind archeologists and cranial surgeons use, only larger—along with information from a lot of other sources."

"What do you do with that?" Jensen asked.

Before answering, Kenehan looked to Brecht for approval to proceed.

"Go ahead, Roady. Lay it out."

"We use this to make an extremely detailed point cloud, which is really just a three-dimensional database."

"A three-dimensional database?" Janet queried.

"Actually, *four* dimensions," Takaki chimed in. "Geolocation on a time axis."

"What are the other sources?" Sand asked.

Kenehan hesitated, so Brecht answered for him. "Traffic cams, security cameras, satellite data streamed from orbital platforms—American, Israeli, Chinese, Russian and Indian spy birds—giving us visible spectrum, infrared, ultraviolet and all other electromagnetic bands."

"Seriously?" Jensen asked. "You have access to all that?"

"Good to have friends in high places," Sand observed.

"Not all friends," Brecht said. "Some don't know they're sharing their ELINT with us."

"Lint?" Janet asked.

"ELINT," Kenehan said. "Electronic intelligence."

Brecht continued. "We can map many kinds of radio transmissions: digital burst signals, aircraft flight paths, cell tower emissions, microwave, sat phones; we also monitor atmospheric data, seismic activity, magnetospheric anomalies and more. We track vehicular and human targets, aircraft, watercraft and heavy machinery above and below ground. Even subs."

"I take it you didn't get this equipment from Amazon," said Sand.

Partridge smiled. "At least not *all* of it."

"That's a tremendous amount of data. How do you process it?"

"We feed it into a deep learning data mining system, DLDMS," Takaki answered. "We've just finished provisioning a virtual silo for this operation. Next, we'll kickstart the first-tier pattern recognition algorithms."

"Artificial intelligence?" Jensen asked.

Kenehan shook his head. "Not quite, but close."

"Deep learning," Janet said. "This is way over my head."

"I'll explain," Brecht said taking a deep breath. "The real power of deep machine learning is the effective unlimited memory and speed of access that computers possess. As far as we've come, computers lack true insight—even those with so-called artificial intelligence. What they do bring to the party is the ability to run millions of mathematical operations on giant data collections, keep track of all the results and then use those results to start over again with new base parameters. It's like driving down every street in America to look for a collection of things without knowing the characteristics of that collection, gathering all the information, using bits of it to make assumptions and then re-driving the journey again and again until patterns become evident that would be invisible to a human brain. Computers analyze data without observance bias, which means they don't ignore, forget or treat anything as unimportant. They track all assumptions, use them and then systematically change them, again and again, repeating the process billions of times. The power of the system is repetition and memory."

"Okay," Janet said with a shrug. "So, what do you do with the results?"

"The best use of AI is to triage information so we know where to deploy human resources best. It's that simple."

"Any hot clues yet?" Sand asked.

"Actually, yes," Kenehan said. "Videos from three security cameras installed in common areas of condo complexes on the opposite side of Cherry Creek. Low quality, but we can merge and enhance the digital data streams."

Jensen nodded. "Some of this I've seen before. We hire experts to turn two-dimensional images into three-dimensional virtual worlds using the same kind of lidar scans you guys took yesterday. We hire forensic experts who use match-moving software programs like SynthEyes, PFTrack and Boujou to turn 2D images into 3D virtual spaces called moving point clouds. They make detailed and realistic accident reconstruction animations we show in court. The trick is getting them into evidence."

"I'm impressed, Mark," Kenehan said. "What we do is based on similar principles. Our software is more advanced, with bigger computers. But you've already got the basic concepts."

"How is your technology more advanced than what Mark's experts use?" Sand asked.

Kenehan gestured for Jennifer Takaki to explain.

"Spatiotemporal data and geospatial data are not the same thing. They're both based on tracking data points as they move through well-defined volumes, but the time indices are far more precise with the former."

"Huh?" Janet blinked.

"Well, we wrote our own software to plug-fill data voids in the moving digital stream."

"Can you make that a little simpler for me?" Janet asked. "As in plain English?"

Takaki shrugged. "When we have more than one video source together with high-resolution scans of the environment shown in the videos, we can interpolate between the pixels using Fourier transforms and matrix operations—"

Thomas, who had just joined the group from the rear of the bus, took over. "The mathematical question to solve is: what physical reality created each video? Each video has many possible solutions—but with more than one video, the number of potential physical solutions that could have fathered each image narrows considerably. The system randomly generates billions of imaginary realities to try out and checks each one, frame by frame, throwing out all but those that could have fathered all the images. The software guesses and corrects with error-checking routines to solve the question. It's a highly iterative stochastic process; the algorithm statistically weights point-matched constants and renders highly detailed virtual models that we can look at and manipulate."

Sand smirked. "Yup. Exactly what I thought."

"Of course," Janet said with sarcasm in her voice. "It's *obvious*."

"Can that work with small objects at a distance, like faces?" asked Jensen.

"Sometimes," Kenehan replied, nodding enthusiastically. "That's what we're hoping for, but it's a hit-and-miss technology. If it's possible, BEAST will do it."

"Beast?" Janet asked.

"It stands for Binary Evaluation of Analogue Statistical Temporals. BEAST. Our secret sauce. The group of algorithms we run on a supercomputer handles jobs that would swamp ordinary computers."

"The Brecht Group has its own supercomputer?"

"No, we use the Summit supercomputer at Oak Ridge National Laboratory in Tennessee."

"Well, for this project, I'll cover that cost," Jensen said.

Brecht shook his head. "No need. Oak Ridge lets us use Summit without cost in exchange for access to our proprietary BEAST algorithms. They use our kernels—the 'engines' that drive our software—for everything from simulating entire galaxies to enhancing digital files for the DOD."

"How did you develop that software?" Jensen asked.

"More importantly," Janet interrupted, "how did you get the videos?"

"Same place we got the design drawings for the mall," Partridge replied.

"You hacked them," Sand observed.

"Do they show what happened?" Janet asked.

"Not as they are," Kenehan replied. "You just see black shadows."

"So what you're saying," Sand summarized, "is that you've got three indistinct videos with the parking garage in the background, which might show some of what happened if they're enhanced? My car was parked along the half-wall, so maybe you can pull out usable detail with your software?"

Brecht nodded, taking a seat and dabbing his forehead with a handkerchief.

"What is the likelihood you'll be able to extract anything useful?" Jensen asked.

After taking a deep breath and letting it out slowly, Brecht said, "Well, of course there are no guarantees, but I'd say the odds are, ah, good enough that we've started preparing for ops that may be necessary after finishing the processing. We've got a tactical helicopter inbound. It'll be here on standby in case we need it. It's bringing some additional field specialists."

"Extra muscle?" Sand queried.

"Yup," Kenehan confirmed.

"An Apache?"

"No, an older Black Hawk, refurbished and refitted," Brecht explained, his voice growing weary.

Once again, Thomas picked up the discussion. "The General Services Administration auctioned it off in 2016. We picked it up for about four hundred thousand, and put another million into it. It's quite a nice bird. It should be here in a couple of hours. It's great for aerial surveillance, tracking vehicles and carrying small tactical teams. Of course, we can land it just about anywhere."

Jensen couldn't miss how pale and tired Brecht looked. "You feeling okay, Albert?"

"Oh, I'll be fine in a minute," Brecht said with a weak smile. He withdrew a pill bottle from his pocket, tapped out a couple of small white tablets and carefully placed them under his tongue. "Once the nitro gets into my system."

Janet looked worried. "That sounds serious. Do you need to see a doctor?"

Brecht waved the question away with his hand. "No, just give me a minute. He turned to Jennifer. "How long will the enhancement process take?"

Takaki looked at her watch. "A few hours at least. Maybe a day or more. It's hard to say."

No one spoke for a while. Finally, Jensen broke the silence. "Kind of reminds me of when I was a kid. Dad used to take pictures of us with a Polaroid camera. While we waited for the pictures to develop, we couldn't stand the suspense to see how they turned out."

Chapter 32

A sliver of sunlight crept slowly along the edge of the bed and finally struck Antonio in his right eye. The piercing brightness wrenched him for a panicked instant; he thought it was the beam of a police flashlight. Then he was awake, and he knew it was morning. He rolled over to move away from the intrusive glare and tried for a few seconds to go back to sleep but could not.

Something nagged at him; then he remembered it all—the flood of images from the night before carried him away.

A wave of dizziness came over him. He felt very strange. He was having a hard time catching his breath.

The images were real. It *had* happened. He *had* done the unthinkable. The actuality of it hit him like a great stone hurled by a laughing, malevolent ogre. The stone was wrapped in a note—an unbidden thought: *this is who you are now.*

He was now officially a kidnapper *and* a rapist and was well on the way to becoming a murderer. There was no turning back.

He didn't feel like a god—at least not right now.

What had happened to him? Where had his euphoria and bloodlust gone? His newfound confidence?

He opened his eyes. His buttocks and groin muscles ached from overuse and strain. His head was pounding. How had this happened to him? How had he come to this point?

"Fucking bitch," he muttered, as he fondled himself with curiosity. He felt traumatized, as though *he* were the sexually assaulted one.

He remembered the girl slapping him; he'd snapped into an animal rage. He'd been treating her all nice and stuff, and then *bam!* She'd let him have it across the face, out of nowhere, so hard he'd almost cried. Beeman had laughed, howling like a hyena, making a sound he'd never heard from the man before, scaring him and humiliating him.

So he'd slugged the bitch hard in the stomach. She'd doubled over, dropping to her knees. He'd grabbed a fistful of her hair to hold her head still while he'd slapped her face—again and again—and then dragged her up the stairs to the bedroom. He'd thrown her around, ripping her cute little dress away like wrapping paper, cutting her skin while yanking her bra and panties off, and then shimmying out of his pants. He'd taken her, every way possible. He hadn't asked, and she hadn't consented; the fierce brutality of his assault had smothered any chance of resistance on her part. He'd just used her like a rag doll. Her tears and cries had flamed his passions, his lust and his years of pent-up frustration and anger.

He'd been more than a brute—he'd been a *monster*.

At the time, the experience had been exquisite—brutally venting his lust—but something had boiled off, and right now, in the light of day, he felt like *he* was the fucking victim.

I never thought raping someone could traumatize me.

• • •

Downstairs, Beeman spoke softly into his cell phone. The conversation was going out of control.

"I said bring your friend," Kim ordered. "He's part of this now."

"But he knows nothing of—"

Kim cut Beeman off. "We're running out of time. The longer you dawdle, the greater our danger. The next phase is critical. Needless complications can't hamper us, and unless he becomes an asset, Antonio Pessoa is a needless complication."

"An asset?" Beeman fumed. This man had no idea what he was proposing. "You plan to kill him."

"Not yet. Just bring him along with you. I'm looking forward to meeting him." The line went dead.

"Were you on the phone?"

Beeman suppressed his startled response. He hadn't heard Antonio coming down the stairs. Exhaling softly, he turned slowly and gave Antonio a warm smile while he slipped his cell into his pocket.

Antonio's face was slack and haggard; his eyes blinked rapidly. Behind the dreadful idiot's bleary fatigue, Beeman could see remorse and severe anxiety.

Beeman chuckled and then said, "You look like hell, my friend."

Antonio stared at him for a moment and then grinned sheepishly.

"We need to go into town right away," Beeman added.

"What?"

"I'll explain in the car. Hurry up."

"Wait—what? Why do we ... where are we going?"

"We'll talk on the way. We need to meet someone. We have to be there by nine o'clock. We can't be late." As he spoke, Beeman guided Antonio toward the stairs. "Please, Antonio. Grab your clothes and shoes so we can leave. We'll have breakfast in town. I'll tell you everything on the way there."

Antonio groaned and headed up the stairs.

• • •

Thirty minutes later in the passenger seat of the Toyota, Antonio rubbed his shaking hands on his jeans while Beeman drove, struggling to absorb the shock of what Beeman had just said.

"You've got to be fucking kidding, man," he whined. "I can't fucking believe there was someone watching us that day. Jesus. You and your fucking superbug."

• • •

Kim stirred his coffee and looked at his watch.

The listening devices planted in the cabin revealed that the night before had been an exciting one—at least for Antonio Pessoa. And if Kim's admittedly shaky psychological profile of Beeman was even partially accurate, he too had experienced some twisted pleasurable sensation from his success in flushing out the sadistic urges of his young friend, whom Kim now knew to be the central object of Beeman's sick psychological experiment. It was clear now that he was a man who used living organisms as tools for the destruction of other living organisms; that was his vocation and his avocation. Beeman derived a sense of godlike euphoria from controlling life and death in multiple realms simultaneously.

He was a *killeo meikeo*, a killer-maker, with microbes and with people.

He could quite possibly prove to be one of the greatest assets his nation could acquire. The Outstanding Leader was working hard to lull the world into a false sense of security because he knew that the Americans had finally elected someone crazier than he pretended to be. He must have known he could not possibly prevail in an outright nuclear exchange—the gradual economic collapse of the DPRK economy left him with no choice but to retake South Korea. His own personal survival—looking more than five years ahead—depended upon it. Or so the great general apparently conceived.

A man who could quickly bring a nation to its knees, stealthily and silently, with no casualties in the North, would be worth thousands of times more than his weight in gold. Being the man who brought such a weapon home would elevate Kim's already god-like status immensely, at home and abroad.

He glanced across the street. His men were ready and attentive, waiting in a parked car. Chul gestured, signaling that Beeman and Antonio were approaching, evidently alone. In another minute, the two appeared at the doorway of the diner. Kim waved to them.

They sat down at his table without speaking. It was plain that Pessoa was on the verge of coming unraveled. The stress, fear and guilt he was experiencing was too much for him.

Kim smiled. "Coffee, gentlemen?"

Antonio glared at Kim and said nothing.

Beeman turned to Antonio as he spoke. "This is Mr. Kim. I need to speak with him privately for a moment. Perhaps you should go and wash up."

"If you say so," Antonio said breathily. He scooted back from the table and strode toward the restroom.

"What now?" Beeman asked.

"How much have you told him?"

"Only that you love coffee," he said.

"Petulance and sarcasm, Arthur. I thought we were past that."

"He knows you want the virus and that you had us under observation when we took the women. I am trying to get him to believe that your involvement is a stroke of luck rather than a disaster."

Kim sipped his coffee before responding. "Are you succeeding?"

"His mind is in turmoil."

Beeman flagged the waitress and asked for two more coffees. He asked her to hurry, smiling kindly. "I've been up all night, and I'm just dying for some caffeine."

The waitress smiled in return and stepped away to fetch the drinks. Before she returned, Kim spoke softly. "We must keep him calm and placid—prevent him from coming apart. Have you prepared for this, Arthur?"

Beeman withdrew a plastic packet of breath strips from his pocket and held it in his hand. When the waitress deposited two more steaming mugs, he peeled one of the breath strips out of the packet and stirred it into Antonio's coffee.

Kim stared at him without expression. "As I thought," he said.

Beeman's slit-mouth grin conveyed menacing irony. "We use similar methods."

"What are you giving him?"

"Just a little something I cooked up."

A moment later, Antonio returned to his seat. "Thanks," he said as he lifted his mug to his lips. "I need this." He took several sips. "Is it flavored?"

"Probably," Beeman replied. "I'll get you some cream and sugar."

Antonio reached across to a nearby table and snagged a small metal cream dispenser. "I got it," he said as he whitened his coffee. "So what's up?"

"Mr. Pessoa, this is your lucky day," said Kim.

•   •   •

By the time they got back to the car, Antonio's mood had lifted considerably. The prospect of scoring fifty grand to help Beeman get his magic serum for Kim would be much safer than taking the girls had been.

His courage had returned.

Part of his evolution, it appeared, included becoming wealthy!

Why had he been so skittish earlier? *It just takes time to adjust when you become more powerful,* he told himself. *It just takes time.*

He decided not to tell Beeman about his visit to the kidnap site; Beeman would be furious with him for returning to the scene of the crime.

Next to him, Beeman broke the silence, reading his mind as usual. "Think of the money, Antonio. I know you have always envied my financial situation. Now you'll be just like me, in that regard at least. You'll be able to spend what you want on anything that brings you pleasure."

"You think the guy's for real?"

"What do you mean?"

"He's a spy, right?" Antonio asked.

"Yes. For a corporation—one of our competitors. They want in on our lucrative government contract."

"How do you know he's not a terrorist or something?"

"In the real world, Antonio, biological and chemical research is about *money*. Terrorists use homemade bombs, crash things or take hostages to decapitate on video. They don't pay huge sums for complex biological products."

"Really?" Antonio wanted to believe Beeman, but what did it matter? He was a kidnapper and a rapist. So what if he helped terrorists? The only thing that mattered was getting the money and staying out of jail. "Are you sure he's good for it?"

Beeman nodded confidently. "Do you have any idea what the men who discovered Rogaine made from that simple little molecule?"

"I assume it was a lot."

"Two dermatologists in Denver discovered Rogaine, so to speak. The University of Colorado was testing the chemical that makes it grow hair, minoxidil, as an antihypertensive, but it produced unwanted body hair on the cardiac patients tested."

"So?"

"They consulted a couple of dermatologists. One of them was a resident, who asked himself what would happen if they rubbed the drug onto a man's scalp. He performed a test on himself. He grew a patch of hair on his shoulder; then he tested it on a bald dentist. The rest is history."

"I suppose he's a millionaire today?"

"Well, that's just it, Antonio. The drug companies tried to steal his invention. He had to hire lawyers to get his share of the money. There was a big legal battle and then years later another big legal battle, but ultimately he made a lot of money.

"How much?"

"For the resident? Millions. For Upjohn? *Billions.*"

Antonio stole another look at Beeman as he drove. "Why don't *you* use Rogaine?"

Beeman chuckled warmly at this question. "Because I have found other ways to get women."

Antonio barked a laugh, slapping the dashboard.

"I have a question, if you don't mind me asking."

"Yes?"

"Well, I was just wondering. Have you—"

"Have I had sex with either of the girls?"

Antonio sighed. "Yeah. That's my question."

"Not yet," he said, "but let me tell you, I'm having the time of my life."

"You are? Aren't you horny? Seeing them naked and all?"

"My turn-on is different from yours, Antonio."

"You like watching other people do it, don't you?"

Beeman sighed. "Antonio, there is more to the thrill of sex than just having an orgasm. For that you could simply hire a prostitute, remember?"

"I remember. It's the power of being able to do anything you want to someone, giving nothing in return. Just taking. Freedom from limits of any kind." Thinking and talking about this was making Antonio horny again. God, he felt so much better than he had two hours ago. Beeman's words always gave him strength.

"So you think we can trust this guy?" Antonio didn't want to get his hopes up when it came to the money, or risk betrayal by some greedy commercial pirate who could just as easily take Beeman's technological achievements and then turn them in instead of paying them. But the fantasy of great wealth, well, that was pretty hard to resist, and if there was as much money available as Beeman was talking about, this really could be the start of a new life for him. He imagined what he would do if he had the cash to live the high life, to stop driving and doing other demeaning jobs just to make a living.

"I think so," Beeman said at length. "But we'll be very careful— take things one step at a time."

"Right," Antonio said as Beeman parked the car in the garage. "Makes sense. But for now, let's get back to what we were doing."

Beeman shut off the engine, and they went inside.

Antonio headed straight down the stairs.

Beeman followed, gratified at Antonio's return to the game. The drugs were invaluable—as long as no one was using them on *him*, but he was growing weary of Antonio. And Kim was right—his human experiment on this dullard was becoming inconvenient under the circumstances. If Kim decided to kill him, Beeman would not object.

He would start over with another subject when things settled down.

He trailed Antonio down the stairs, through the secret door, and into the hidden room containing the cage and its human contents.

Antonio flipped on the light. "Oh, my fucking God," he croaked.

Beeman came around the corner and looked into the cage.

The cage was empty. Its door was open and the lock lay on the floor.

Chapter 33

They waited it out at The Perfect Landing, a restaurant at Centennial Airport. Hours of time, gallons of coffee. Janet talked about Christie's childhood, but her reveries went flat, so she retreated into the current edition of *Condé Nast Traveler*, flipping the glossy pages without really reading, as private jets taxied past the restaurant's enormous picture windows. Mark felt her pain.

Finally, as the afternoon was drawing to its end, Roady Kenehan approached their table and said the words they had been waiting to hear. "We've got something."

For Mark, it was a familiar feeling, like hearing a bailiff say *we've got a verdict*. He dropped a few bills on the table and then followed Kenehan, Janet and Sand back to the motor coaches stationed on the far side of the parking lot.

Late-day heat shimmered upward from the blacktop as the group traversed the expansive parking lot. "Can you tell us anything?" Janet asked.

"Better to show you," Kenehan replied, giving her a reassuring nod. "It won't be long."

Within the cool, dark confines of the coach, Jensen could sense excitement in the air. He turned to Brecht and asked, "What are we going to be seeing?"

Brecht placed a hand on his shoulder. "The results of thirty hours of supercomputer number crunching." He turned to Takaki. "Take us through it, Jennifer."

Takaki's slender fingers swept across the surface of the oversize monitor on the wall. The blue wire-frame of the parking structure reappeared. At first, Jensen was disappointed—the three-dimensional outline of the structural components of the parking facility didn't look like much. But Takaki continued tapping virtual buttons along the side and bottom of the image, and the three security videos started playing in separate windows beside the wireframe. A few more taps triggered an interesting effect. Within each video and on the wire frame, a red hairline cube appeared. It was quickly obvious to Mark that the boxes in each of the four frames represented the same block of virtual space.

Takaki tapped the MERGE FEEDS option, and after a few seconds, the three videos glided across the screen to overlap over the wireframe. The perspective of each adjusted as they became perfectly aligned trapezoids, the red boxes on each became a single merged cube and the composite image sharpened. The view zoomed, and a composite translucent box dominated the screen.

To Mark's amazement, it was possible to make out with surprising clarity details within the cube. He could literally see into the darkness between levels that had appeared on the original videos as nothing more than horizontal black rectangles. He could clearly make out the roofs of cars, but nothing below chest level.

"This is the virtual composite BEAST created," said Takaki. "As real as it looks, it is important to remember that this is the computer's interpolated depiction of the reality that best fits the pixelated data on the videos. It has weighted the artifacts and nuances to establish mathematical confluence."

"You mean it's guessing," said Sand. "It's made up one possible world that could explain little anomalies in the videos, but there could be other realities that would do the same and which might be closer to what really happened."

Jensen was impressed. Sand seemed to work hard at keeping the sharpness of his mind concealed, but it was clear he possessed a very high IQ and a substantial amount of up-to-date technological knowledge. Many people had probably underestimated this man over the years, some of whom had likely paid dearly for that mistake.

"Sort of," Takaki hedged. "But not just a *wild guess*. Hundreds of millions of data points were available, and the system forces the interpolations to satisfy statistical validation standards, so there *is* reliable information here."

"It gets better," Kenehan added. "Keep going, Jennifer."

She touched a slider bar labeled ADVANCE RATE, and a PLAY triangle appeared beneath the bar.

Mark glanced at Janet, who seemed not to understand what was coming next. He placed his arm around her waist and pulled her close.

Brecht noticed the gesture. "This is going to be tough to watch," he said, "but we've gotten some very useful data from what is—"

"Play the motherfucker," Sand cut in. "Let's get it over with."

Takaki's beautiful face tipped upward toward Brecht, who turned his aged eyes first to Mark and then to Janet, whose face was a portrait of dread.

Janet took a deep breath, swallowed and nodded several times; then she repeated Sand's impertinent command. "Play the motherfucker."

Takaki touched the PLAY triangle.

Ten seconds passed before Jensen saw motion in the background of the image. He made out two heads, then shoulders, and recognized Christie and Jackie floating as highly detailed animations— torsos without legs floating toward the virtual camera. A lump formed in his throat, and he pulled Janet closer.

The floating torsos stopped near the roof of a car, but from the angle of the view, it was impossible to see the entire vehicle. Only the roof was visible. Then Takaki tapped a few more items, and the rest of Sand's Jaguar appeared.

"She inserted a virtual XKE—a computer model of Sand's Jaguar —at the position where it was parked," Kenehan narrated. The women were looking down at the car and appeared to be talking. Jensen could see Jackie Dawson in profile, but her face blocked Christie's. Takaki swept a finger across a small panel and the image rotated slightly so that both women's faces were at least partially visible. The imagery was strikingly realistic. Their heads turned in unison away from the virtual viewpoint.

A third head and torso appeared: that of a man.

Jensen could make out the features of his face—he had a dark mustache and dark hair. He was much taller than the girls.

"Your software can enhance to this degree?" Jensen said. "Or are facial features assumed?"

"The value of massive compositing," Takaki said. "We're lucky to have more than one video stream."

The women appeared to be conversing with the man, who stooped down for a moment and dropped out of the image entirely. A few seconds later his head and upper body reappeared. He was smiling. After a few more seconds, the man turned and moved a few paces away. The faint outline of another car glided into view. The man raised the back hatch and gestured for the women to approach.

They did so.

What had he said?

"No sound," Jensen murmured.

Brecht shook his head. "No source data."

The man with the mustache turned to face the women as they approached. Christie's gaze moved downward, but it wasn't possible to see her face at this point.

Jackie Dawson's head dropped rapidly from view, and then so did Christie's.

"Oh, sweet Jesus," Janet whimpered.

The drama continued to play out. A second figure emerged from the vehicle in the background. It was not possible to make out his features, as he had his back to the viewer. All they could see of him was the back of his head and shoulders. He was shorter than the first man.

The computer filled in the vehicle from which he emerged at this point. It was a dark gray or black SUV. The rear hatch was up. The two men dropped out of view and then reappeared, leaning away from one another. Jensen guessed from the way they moved that they were lifting the girls into the back of the SUV. The hatch was closed, and the man with the mustache climbed into the passenger seat as the older man vanished behind the SUV.

The SUV glided out of the frame. The screen went blank.

Jensen could feel a rhythmic spasm in his wife through the arm he held around her waist, and he knew she was in agony. "Oh, my God," she whispered, three times in a row. She began to sob quietly. Tears poured down her cheeks onto Mark's arm.

Brecht gave them a moment to absorb what they had seen before speaking. "

Quite a shock," he said softly, "but not entirely unexpected."

Sand cleared his throat. "Now what?"

"Please be patient with us for a few more minutes," Brecht said gently. "We have more to show you." He touched Takaki on the shoulder once more, and she tapped the screen a few more times. As she worked, Brecht continued speaking. "We were unable to read a license plate number, but we identified the make and model of the vehicle, and we got something else." On the screen, a fuzzy close-up image of the man with the mustache appeared. "This is an enlargement from the enhanced animation you just watched." As the seconds passed, the computer put red pinpoints on each of the man's pupils, at the corners of his mouth and at a dozen other facial landmarks. It connected the points with thin pink lines, marking a rough topography of his features.

"There were no security cameras in the parking structure, but there are many inside the mall," Brecht explained. "We scoured them and found some images of Jacqueline and Christine. In one of them, we see this man following them for a brief time."

Takaki brought up a single video image from a ceiling-mounted security camera inside the mall. It showed Christie and Jackie walking past shop windows. The man with the mustache followed. The computer retraced the facial recognition points on his face in this video. The words CONVERGENCE: 0.97 appeared at the bottom of the screen.

"Same guy," Kenehan said.

The girls went into a shop; the man waited several paces away from the entrance. He continued to follow them when they emerged.

More clicks, and a third image appeared. "This is the same man, and *this* video is clear enough to allow facial recognition software to match with photos on file with CDOT," Kenehan explained.

"CDOT?" Jensen asked.

"The Colorado Department of Transportation. Driver's license pictures."

The girls and the man strolled out of the security camera's view, and the enhanced close-up of the man replaced the video.

Janet sniffled, reaching into her purse for a tissue. "Should we give this to the police? Maybe they can pick him out of a mug shot book or something."

"Bring up the result," Brecht ordered.

A driver's license appeared beside the enhanced facial shot.

Jensen studied the photo in the license. It was obviously the same man. He seemed a little younger, but there was no mistaking his features. The words CONVERGENCE: 0.93 appeared at the bottom.

"This is a ninety-three percent convergence," Kenehan explained. "The computer identified this as the best match from the CDOT database. It's clearly the same man. Now we know who is."

Jensen read the name on the screen. "Antonio Pessoa."

"He is a chauffeur," Brecht said. "He drives for Denver Executive Limousines, Inc. We have his home address, his cell phone number, his blood type, his age and his shopping preferences on Amazon.

We've also dug up a lot of his employment and legal history, and we've identified his next of kin."

"His family?" Janet asked.

"We know where his parents and sister live."

Jensen took Brecht by the arm. "Do you know where he is *now?*"

"We thought we'd drop by his house," Kenehan said. "See if he's home."

"We've got to take this to the police," Janet insisted. "We can't just take the law into our own hands and barge in on this hoodlum."

Everyone stared at her.

"Or you could just kill the fucker," she said.

"There's not a chance in the world Denver PD or any of their SWAT teams are trained as well as my men," Brecht said, pointing to Kenehan and gesturing toward Partridge and his teammates in the rear conference room.

Kenehan nodded in agreement. "They have rules, procedures, red tape. Restrictions and delays and barriers we don't have to deal with. Politics, jurisdictional disputes, team briefings. Mobilizing a law enforcement squad would take hours or days. My team is ready *now.* This is what we do."

Takaki brought up a satellite view of Pessoa's home. "A rented house. The title's in the name of a Maureen Wilkins, age forty-eight. Widowed and currently residing in Park City, Utah. No known relationship to Pessoa other than that of landlord and tenant."

"Registered firearms?" Sand asked.

"None," Kenehan answered.

"Now or at any time in the past?"

Kenehan shook his head. "Neither. No indication he's had any tactical or military training. No security clearances. He's never tried for a government job, never been in a serious motor vehicle accident and never been a suspect in a major crime."

"Court records?" Jensen queried.

"One temporary restraining order from 2013. Complainant was a woman who claimed Pessoa had been stalking her. Pessoa denied it but consented to the TRO. He was *pro se*, no lawyer, and no criminal charges were involved."

"So he's a nobody," Jensen said with a shrug.

"Nobody's a nobody," Sand observed quietly. "The deadliest men in the world are nobodies. Right, Roady?"

Kenehan asked, "Who's Roady?"

"Can you locate his cell phone?" Jensen asked.

"Not presently," Brecht responded. "Last recorded position was the mall. He turned it off after taking the women, before they left the parking structure. We're still digging up his messaging history."

"Pets at the house?" Sand asked. "Dogs?"

Kenehan shrugged. "Unknown. But another great question."

"Education?"

"Two years in college. No declared major."

"Where?" Sand asked.

"Arapahoe Community College."

"That's in Denver?" Jensen asked.

"Littleton, south Denver area. He took entry-level classes in accounting."

"Does he make much money as a driver?" Janet asked.

"His tax returns say less than thirty grand. So kidnapping for ransom *could* be a motive." Kenehan cleared his throat. "But the manner of the abduction suggests it occurred on a spur-of-the-moment choice. It doesn't look like they targeted the girls individually."

"How do you know that?"

Kenehan shook his head. "We don't. Just a sense I got from the videos inside the mall and the location where it took place, which they couldn't have planned in advance. I could be wrong."

"Bank accounts?"

Takaki scrolled to a new file. "One checking account with a debit card. His credit rating is shit. Debit cards only. Lots of outstanding loans and balances in default. He has a whopping $847.39 in the one account we've found so far—Bank of the West."

Jensen rubbed his chin. It was amazing how fast they'd built a dossier on the man. "Anything in his shopping history that sheds light on—"

"He bought two Tasers from a surplus military website. Paid with PayPal backed by his debit card. Lied on the order form about his employment and his military history. Claimed to be exArmy, but we know that's not true. He ordered it in his own name. No one checked, and they shipped the Tasers."

"When?"

"About a month ago."

So that was how he had taken down the girls.

At least no one shot or stabbed them when they dropped out of the frame, Jensen told himself. *Or so I hope. Dear God, let me be right.*

"When do we leave?" Sand asked.

"Soon," Kenehan said. "First we plan and run through ops review."

"Of course," Sand said, with a rueful shake of his head. "Guess I'm getting old."

"Not as old as that Colt Commander in your waistband," Kenehan chided. "You were probably better at winging it when you worked alone, without satellite intel or comms. Different times now."

Sand reached back and touched the small of his back. "Saw that, did you?"

Kenehan shrugged. "Only a flash, when you were climbing out of the car."

Sand smiled. "An oldie but a goody. Mind if Mark and I ride along?"

"Wouldn't have it any other way."

Chapter 34

Kenehan rang Antonio Pessoa's doorbell and waited. He had his right hand tucked inside the right flap of his light cotton jacket, gripping the handle of a Wilson Combat Ultralight nine-millimeter 1911 pistol. Once his hand was on the grip, Kenehan could clear leather and start landing head shots on moving targets at up to ten yards in less than eight-tenths of a second. Ironically, his pistol was not very different from the relic Sand carried, but it was almost certainly better tuned, with a 2.5-pound trigger, a disabled grip safety and Novak fiber optic sights.

For Kenehan, a tactical knife was still a deadlier weapon than a gun in many close-quarters combat scenarios. A razor-sharp tactical blade made more gruesome wounds than pistol rounds, instantly severing arteries, veins, tendons and ligaments like butter. Knives were quieter than guns, and they never ran out of ammunition. In the hands of someone with the physical, mental and emotional capacity to slash and stab other humans with speed and precision, the only drawback of a knife was its range.

Kenehan had picked up a few tidbits from Albert Brecht about how Sand had worked with a blade, long ago. A *real* tanto, a short sword of the kind samurai in feudal Japan had once carried. Sand's old—but still restricted—file jacket said he'd opened up more than one or two bad guys with that antique weapon. He'd appeared mostly at night, seemingly out of nowhere, after climbing walls, bypassing locked doors and alarms and bringing the battle to terrible men who created problems that needed permanent solutions.

A minute passed. He rang the bell again, listening carefully.

Silence from within the house.

The only sound that came to his ears was the very faint *wop-wop-wop* from the Brecht Group's restored Black Hawk holding station ten thousand feet above. If Pessoa dashed from the house by car, the bird would be able to follow him anywhere, vectoring chase cars.

Partridge, Jensen and Sand waited in one of the two cars parked at the curb behind him. Two more Brecht field operators, Jim Evans and Chuck Sullivan, were in a second car, and two additional men waited in a third car, idling in the alley behind the house. All the operators wore voice-activated earpieces with integrated jawbone microphones. The gear would digitally encrypt and stream everything they said and heard real-time to the mobile tactical operations center, or MTOC—the lead motor coach waiting at the airport.

All the team members were trained medics; three of them carried battlefield medical pouches known as "blow-out" kits.

Before pulling to a stop along the curb in front of Pessoa's house with one car blocking his driveway, all three cars had driven past the house twice. The curtains were drawn; they could not see into the dwelling. Kenehan had twice dialed the landline registered to the house. Both calls had gone unanswered.

Jennifer Takaki had phoned Denver Executive Limousine, Pessoa's part-time employer, and asked if he was working. The dispatcher had said no and asked if someone else could be of assistance. Jennifer had answered that she was a friend, just trying to find him with some great news. The operator volunteered that she'd received two other calls that same day from people trying to find Antonio. "Must be something special," the woman had added.

"Oh, that was probably my mom," Jennifer had said, fishing. The operator clarified that both of those calls had been from men.

Now Kenehan crouched and examined the deadbolt, noting the brand name stamped into the housing. An old Schlage, easy to pick.

Taking his hand from his pistol, he reached into his pocket and withdrew a small mechanical device that looked like a toy pistol with steel pins sticking out of the barrel. In a few seconds, he had the door unlocked. Partridge, Evans and Sullivan got out of their cars and moved quickly up the walk to join him.

Sand and Jensen had reluctantly agreed to remain in Kenehan's car during the entry. Jensen had no tactical training; Sand had never trained with this team and admitted it had been a long time since he'd been operational. He understood all too well that in a house-clearing operation, a stranger with a trained team could create more danger than help. Sand and Jensen could listen to the encrypted transmissions with a handheld radio.

The four men positioned themselves in the choreographed positions used universally by hostage-rescue and counterterrorism specialists. Kenehan got down on one knee, with Partridge crouching just above and behind him. The remaining two men stood on either side of the door, ready to move into the room, weapons raised to fire on any hostile targets. All wore skin-colored latex gloves, baseball caps and lightly tinted Ray Ban shooting glasses.

"Weapons ready?" Kenehan asked.

Partridge visually confirmed this and slapped Kenehan on the shoulder. "Your count."

"Three ... two ... one." Kenehan intoned quietly. "Go, go, go!"

He shoved the door open, sweeping the barrel of his 1911 up and across in a wide arc as he shuffled quickly through the doorway, still in a deep crouch. Partridge swept his weapon over Kenehan's head in the opposite direction. The other two slipped in quickly behind him, turning and sweeping their weapons along the opposite front walls and back to the center to cover preplanned fields of fire.

The front room was unoccupied.

The men split wordlessly into two teams of two and proceeded to clear the house, room by room, moving silently, working around corners with care, clearing the angles a few degrees at a time from as far back as possible, a tactic known as "pie-ing."

"Master bedroom clear." The whispered words came to Kenehan

through his earpiece. "Master bathroom clear. Den clear." Then a few seconds later: "Guest room and guest bathroom clear."

Kenehan added his part. "Kitchen clear," he said as he finished the central portion of the house with Partridge beside him. "Back patio and yard clear." Then he cleared the half-basement that was, statistically, the most dangerous part of a one-story threat-occupied house. "Basement clear. No signs of the women."

The entire process had taken less than thirty seconds.

The interior of the house was empty and dark. The air was hot, with air conditioning either not installed or turned off. The house smelled rancid. No sounds from pets or machinery. The carpeting was worn and stained. The walls were marred with watermarks and a few holes. The only furniture in the living room was a threadbare sofa and a marred wooden coffee table on which a water pipe sat on its side beside a lighter and a baggie of weed. A flat-panel television sat on the floor, leaning against the opposite wall.

The men converged in the living room, continuing to scan vigilantly; complacency could be fatal. An image flashed unbidden through Kenehan's mind: when the armed first officer aboard the *MV Cogliano* had caught him while searching the captain's cabin. That had nearly been the end of him.

He heard Dave Thomas's voice coming into his earpiece via encrypted satcom from the MTOC.

"All clear acknowledged." Thomas intoned. "Check the attic and garage and then search everything and everywhere. Paper and electronic intel; any other evidence. Get what's there and get out. We'll leave surveillance in place."

Two minutes later, Kenehan radioed that the garage and attic were clear.

"Cars in the garage?"

"No room," Kenehan replied. "Full of boxes. Too many to go through quickly. But I don't think they're Pessoa's. They're old, marked with the house owner's name."

"Then skip those," Thomas ordered. "Concentrate on the interior."

Each man took a different room, quickly rifling through drawers, checking underneath furniture and likely hiding places, scanning for documents, computers, phones or other clues as to the girls' whereabouts.

Kenehan searched the small den, which contained an old desk and two chairs, quickly fanning through the contents of the desk's file drawer. It contained bills and other household records. He found a battered Dell laptop in the center drawer. He pulled out the machine and moved aside to allow Partridge to comb through the paper files more thoroughly than he had done.

"We've got a laptop and some files," he reported.

"Skim the paper for relevant matter," Thomas came back. "Take the laptop with you."

Partridge hesitated. "But if we do, the evidence will be—"

Sand chimed in from the car. "Just *take* the fucking thing!"

"Acknowledged." Kenehan closed the laptop without turning it on.

"Sir?"

Kenehan turned as Evans entered the room with several sheets of paper in his hand. "We found these in his nightstand along with a pile of really old porn mags."

Evans handed the papers to Kenehan. They were color printouts from an inkjet printer. Flipping through them, Kenehan guessed there were about thirty sheets. Each depicted attractive young women, most wearing tight shorts or short skirts, taken covertly in various shopping malls. All the women were young, pretty and Caucasian. None were over the age of thirty; most were teenagers.

The cropped and enlarged shots created a telephoto effect, grainy and pixilated. Clearly none of the women knew that someone was taking their pictures. The images reminded Kenehan of the familiar, vaguely voyeuristic experience common to a soldier who views the world through a sniper-scope on overwatch, putting crosshairs on subjects who did not know they were two pounds of finger-pull from death.

Many of the photos were from the Cherry Creek Mall. Most of the photos had penciled-in dates below them; they dated from the weeks leading up to the abduction.

Had Christie and Jackie been the first women Antonio Pessoa and his mysterious co-perpetrator had kidnapped, or were they merely the latest victims of serial predators? If so, how long had the pair been harvesting young women from local shopping malls?

He went back through the photos, trying to absorb a sense of the man who had taken them. Pessoa clearly spent days prowling shopping malls, capturing visual samples of potential prey. He'd learned to be a hunter of women. It had obviously entertained him to capture images of women without their knowledge or consent. Many of the photos featured close-ups of the women's chests and backsides— a tawdry collection of self-made, soft-core Peeping-Tom porn. Not erotic as much as *revealing*. This is where the man's mind lived: in the folds and tucks of women's anatomy, stolen on hot summer days to fuel the dragon of the man's obsessive fantasies.

He handed the pictures to Partridge, who looked them over and furrowed his brow in disgust. "Hunter," he said. "On some kind of sick safari."

Jensen chimed in over the channel. "What did you find?"

Kenehan chose his words with care. "Digital images of women at shopping malls, taken covertly. None of Christie or Jackie, but women of similar ages. He's been hunting in recent weeks. The shots are dated, going back to June of this year."

Kenehan remembered the headshot of Christie Jensen that had so captivated him days ago, and he replayed in his mind the image of her and Jackie dropping suddenly out the frame of the computer enhancement. He felt a powerful need to end the sick fuck who had taken these shots.

It could be significant that none of the pictures depicted Christie or Jackie. Were they merely targets of opportunity? *Maybe. Maybe not.* If he had picked them at random, that could be a very bad sign. If the abductors had taken them for money, the chances were greater they would still be alive. But if they'd snatched them on a whim for sexual abuse or a thrill killing, the likelihood that they were either already dead or on their way to another country as part of a human trafficking operation was very real. This would be hard news to deliver, especially to Janet Jensen. Maybe he would just keep his thoughts between himself and the Brecht team. No, he thought, the Jensens and Sand deserved to know.

He could see Christie Jensen through Pessoa's eyes, as she must have looked to him, strolling through the mall with her stunning companion, scantily dressed on a hot summer day, innocent and oblivious to the threat, just as Pessoa had been oblivious to the fact that she was a human being. To Pessoa, she'd been nothing more than a desirable piece of meat.

The world will be a better place when you're gone, buddy.

Partridge handed the photos back to Roady. "These are probably on the hard drive. We could find some metadata to confirm the dates written on these."

"Better yet, we may find something to help track the phone he took the photos with," Kenehan said, folding the papers into his pocket. "We'll take them along with the laptop."

A few minutes later, the team left through the front door, relocking it as they did so. One car remained behind to maintain watch over the house. Roady briefed Jensen and Sand by radio on the way back, with Thomas and the rest of the team listening in. He knew Janet was listening as well, and that his words were cutting her heart apart.

At least they knew they had the right man. This was the kind of break that could unravel the case.

Chapter 35

Beeman let the broken lock slip from his hands. Antonio flinched as it struck the floor, his eyes fluttering like a high-speed camera shutter, his thin shoulders flexing involuntarily. Beeman slowly mimicked the motion, shrugging and batting his eyes, absorbing the man's terror and confusion the way a wine aficionado savors the bouquet of an expensive vintage.

Antonio's mouth hung open, and Beeman mimicked this also, dropping his jaw, while he watched the other man intently. Copying the soulless opening and closing of the man's jaw, Beeman recalled a fleeting memory from years ago.

Standing on a street corner. A drunk speeding through a red light, broadsiding another car. A horrific, satisfying impact. Beeman's face pressed to the cracked glass, absorbing from inches away the final moments of the victim trapped within. He'd tried for days to duplicate the spastic convulsions of the mortally injured woman as she writhed in agony. Twitching, choking, blood spraying from her mouth as she tried to scream, her head lolling from side to side in a paroxysm of agony, panic and neurological shutdown.

Physical mimicry was his way of preserving the raw power of what he had seen, internalizing the primal instinctive reaction to life-threatening events, splicing to his visual record a reconstruction of how it must have felt to wrestle intimately with the terror of imminent death.

A paramedic shoving him away, depriving him of the chance to savor the moment when the woman finally succumbed and went still.

He'd fantasized for years about what it would have been like to sit beside her in the car and touch her as her connection to this world dissolved, to absorb every detail as she went finally still, becoming an object rather than a being.

What a shame it was to have missed that.

Death is life is death.

With Dove, Kitten and Antonio, he'd planned to make up for the frustration of that lost opportunity. Now months of planning were ruined.

What had happened was obvious. Kim and his men had removed the females from the cabin to contain what Kim saw as an insanely unpredictable situation that could wreck his own delicate undertaking.

At that moment, as he stood there silently but absurdly mimicking Antonio's visceral shock and confusion, Beeman realized that an interesting opportunity had presented itself. Antonio had instantly become a liability but still had some residual value. Antonio would have to suffice. He was all Beeman had, at least for now.

So, dessert without dinner—but better than nothing.

The confusion and fear painted on Antonio's face was a potent aperitif. The idiot was struggling to come to grips with how badly things had turned, trying in vain to process how suddenly his nightmares had become real. His future now opened up before him like the open jaws of a python; his moist eyes bored desperately into Beeman's, silently imploring him to provide answers, reassurance, guidance—hope of any kind.

Without me, he is less than nothing. For him, oblivion will be a promotion.

Total panic had overcome Antonio. Beeman could help him hold himself together, but the very idea sickened him. It would be better to fuel this fire and see how hot it could burn.

Beeman let a sorrowful, pathetic moan escape his narrow lips as he slowly turned away, presenting his back to Antonio.

"Oh, no," he crooned. "We're caught. Our lives are over."

He reached out and pushed the door of the cage shut, as if to seal their fate.

Antonio sank to his knees on the cold cement floor and buried his face in his shaking hands. Beeman watched as the man trembled and cried.

"Jesus, Jesus, Jesus," Antonio burbled. "We're fucked, so fucked, completely—"

"Yes," Beeman said, his voice matching the tone of Antonio's plaintive whine. "We. Are. So. Very. Fucked. Everything is out of control. You'll be *lucky* if you even make it to prison."

Beeman knew that the dissociative anxiolytic compound he'd laced Antonio's breath mints with would soon wear off; the half-life of the drug was only ninety minutes. Antonio's chemical protection would be gone, leaving his nervous system a jangling bundle of raw electricity. As the last vestiges of his chemical armor evaporated, his panic would worsen exponentially. What came next could be marvelous, but Beeman had to execute his quickly formulated plan with deft skill, lest a switch in Antonio's primitive mind might flip and cause him to rally, to try to be strong. Beeman had seen signs of that kind of mental software in Antonio—such as when he'd become chivalrous with Kitten before he'd baited him into raping her. Beeman had to remain dominant, to keep Antonio completely overwhelmed.

One can control, steer, feed and harness panic, like a wild horse.

He turned to face the young idiot rocking back and forth on his knees and grabbed a fistful of his hair. "We're *dead!*" he shouted into Antonio's ear, savoring the man's quivering. Then, more quietly, he added, "But wait! Maybe they're still in the house?"

With that, he darted for the stairs, fingering the hilt of the hunting knife on his belt as he bounded up to the kitchen. He turned and waited, planning to hobble Antonio—perhaps by slicing his hamstrings with his razor-sharp knife—before working on him more surgically. He drew the blade from its leather scabbard and held it behind his leg as Antonio came into the room, out of breath, his eyes still moist, but with a flicker of hope on his face.

"It's no use, Antonio," Beeman said hopelessly, a trace of panic added for effect, crushing the hint of hope he'd planted as quickly as he'd instilled it. "They're *gone*. They'd never just wait here for us to return. We're helpless, totally helpless. We're out of options. Nothing we can do. Those women will tell the whole story of how you abducted them." Beeman took a deep sigh, and softened his voice. "Oh, well. At least the charges against me will be minimal. But you'll go to jail for life."

"What—what do you mean?"

Beeman tightened his grip on the handle of the knife behind his leg, and allowed some strength and calmness into his voice. "You beat and raped that girl, Antonio. You punched her senseless and you *raped* her, again and again. You *tortured* her. I kept my pants on the whole time. I never touched her. Not once."

"But you were part of—"

"I have knowledge the government *must* protect, Antonio. Don't you understand? The Army would *kill* to keep what I know secret. I'm the only one who knows what I do, and I'm the only one who can do it, so I'm actually a national treasure. I can afford the best of lawyers. I can cut a sweetheart deal. In the process, I can help convict a *kidnapper* and *rapist*. Rapists get long sentences, but it doesn't matter, because in prison they only last a short time. It's the code of the cellblock: rapists get raped. Again and again. Constantly. Brutally. Savagely. They are used by the biggest, strongest and most vicious convicts—homosexual sadists. Rapists usually commit suicide within the first year of incarceration. And *you* are a rapist."

Antonio's jaw flapped silently once again. Tears trickled down his cheeks.

Beeman kept on, speaking more slowly now. "I'm an old man, Antonio. A professor. You coerced me, threatened me. You *bullied* me. My employer won't want me in prison, and neither will the government. At worst, I'll spend a short time in a special facility—assuming I can't cut a deal. But you know I can. You, on the other hand, hold no cards, none at all. You'll be the guest of honor at a human sacrifice. It'll lasts for months—before *you* pull the plug. You'll eventually hang yourself."

"We've got to run while we have the chance!" As Antonio shouted, drops of spittle hit Beeman's face.

"Run?" Beeman shrugged. "Where to? In this day and age? It's impossible. Without Kim's help, we can't just disappear. And Kim won't help *you*. You have nothing to offer—to him or to any prosecutor. You're going to be a conviction statistic—that's your only value. If you're lucky, Jimmy Kim will kill you. Or his men will. They're professional mercenaries, working for the deadliest and cruelest man on the planet. He watches children being killed for entertainment while eating his dinner. They work for him. You are a threat to them."

Antonio began to hyperventilate. He turned and walked toward the living room, teetering, as if on the verge of passing out. Beeman followed, raising his hunting knife to the level of his belt. Antonio was perfectly positioned. When he turned into the living room, Beeman would come up behind him and slash through his hamstrings. Then he'd hack away the man's hands and feet, stemming blood loss by cauterizing the stumps with a torch before performing real surgery. He'd begin cutting, slowly, torturing Antonio to death, talking to him the whole time. And listening. Listening so very carefully.

It would be delicious.

But Antonio never made it into the living room.

He stopped abruptly in the entryway, looking beyond in even deeper shock at what he saw.

Chapter 36

"It will take some time to process the data," Brecht said to Jensen. "You'll be more comfortable resting at Robert's house or your hotel. We'll call you as soon as we come up with anything."

Jensen shook his head. "If it's alright with you, we'd rather stick around. We'll keep out of your way."

"Sir?" Kenehan interjected. "Why not give Mr. Jensen a terminal and let him examine the data along with us. He's trained to examine evidence. It'll give him something useful to do."

Jensen gave Kenehan a look of gratitude, nodding and mouthing the words "thank you."

Brecht nodded. "Excellent idea, Mr. Kenehan." Thomas guided Jensen to a chair at one of the workstations. Jensen had analyzed data from many computer hard drives during his years as a commercial litigator. He was exceptional at fitting pieces together, finding connections others missed. It was one of the abilities that had made him wealthy. He began opening folders and files, working his way through the data volumes they'd mounted on his desktop.

Pessoa, they'd learned, was an odd-job man, working intermittently as a limo driver, supplementing his income with occasional construction work, hanging drywall, moving furniture, planting sod, painting houses and performing other day work. He'd stored some rudimentary floor plans on his computer, made by a bare-bones architectural program.

"I've got the digital photos Roady found," one of the technicians reported. "The mall girls. They date from the five-week period before the girls disappeared."

Jensen's mind whirled.

Kenehan took Brecht aside and told him of his belief that the lack of photos of Christie or Jackie meant their abduction had probably been a spur-of-the-moment choice, rather than a ransom kidnapping, and how that might portend a bad outcome. Brecht agreed, but they kept this thought to themselves to protect the Jensens from added stress—at least for a while.

• • •

"Who's looking at his email and word processing?" Jensen inquired.

"Him," Brecht replied, pointing to the tech opposite Jensen.

"Seems like we should cross-reference our findings, in case something that looks innocuous has meaning in relation to something else," Jensen suggested.

"We are," Kenehan assured him. "They're making entries into a database, tagging metadata and running it through an AI engine."

Jensen nodded, rubbing his eyes. Of course, they would have thought of that. Compared to these specialists, he was likely to add little of value on his own, despite his experience handling computerized evidence. Brecht was humoring him by giving him access to a terminal. To avoid duplication of effort, Jensen decided to examine the files less likely to draw the scrutiny of the technicians.

He opened the files for home remodeling projects, asking himself even as he did so how this kind of data could possibly be of help.

If Pessoa had been meticulous enough in his planning to photograph potential subjects, he must have made other plans as well; he was obviously comfortable with his computer, so it was conceivable these architectural files might yield useful data.

What kind of files would answer two questions?

"He must have had a place to keep the girls, and he had the help of at least one person," he muttered to himself. "Where? Who?"

"Exactly," Sand said.

"But why *two* victims? Why double the risk?"

"Double the pleasure, double the fun? Maybe he'd been looking for a pair of women they could take together. There might or might not be a specific reason."

Janet spoke for the first time since the raid, her voice very soft. "A specific purpose? That would support an argument that they're still alive, wouldn't it?"

"They *are* still alive." Jensen met his wife's eyes. "At least Christie is." Then he looked at Sand. "They both are."

Feeling silly, he went back to opening the architectural files, of which there were about twenty. Five minutes later, Jensen came upon a file that captured his attention. Fighting down his fear, he called out to the group. "You'd better have a look at this."

The others gathered behind him. On his screen was an image of a basement, divided into two rooms. The image depicted a smaller compartment in one of them. It bore the label "CHAIN LINK CAGE," but the label was unnecessary. The program displayed a three-dimensional cage made of chain link fencing over metal bars in an inset at the top right corner. It listed quantities and measurements at the bottom and even itemized the prices.

"That could be a dog cage, a kennel?" one of the technicians observed.

Sand turned to him, excitement on his face. "A kennel with welded-in roof and a toilet? I don't think so, son. That's a cage for human prisoners."

Silence reigned for several seconds.

"There's a box for the job address here, but it's empty," Jensen said. "We've got to find out where this work took place."

"Wait," Jennifer Takaki blurted. "I think I saw something." All eyes turned to her. "An email—something about a basement."

As she spoke, she turned to her monitor, typing and clicking with a speed that only younger people trained from birth on computers can match.

The techie generation takes charge. No more jokes about fucking millennials.

A minute later she spoke again. "Here it is!"

The group moved to hover behind her. The email read as follows:

From: eagle666@mailstore.com
To: wolf666@earthlink.net
Subject: basement party

44 Mountain Top Drive. 6pm.

"No date?" Jensen asked.

"It was scrubbed from the metadata. I don't usually see that," Takaki explained.

Janet spoke. "Wolf? Eagle? 666? What do you suppose that means?"

"Six-six-six. Biblical. Mark of the Beast," Sand filled in. "'Wolf' and 'eagle' are probably self-assigned call signs. How these assholes see themselves. Psychological profilers would have a field day with this, including the design of the cage."

Takaki raised an eyebrow. "Yeah?"

Sand added with a thin smile. "You all amaze me. Really. I know you are trained in that stuff. But to a hayseed like me, it seems clear these men are acting out a sick fantasy, filling in for a sense of inadequacy. Could be cult stuff."

"Look in Pessoa's Outlook contacts for that email address," Thomas said.

"Yes, sir," Takaki answered. A moment later, she exclaimed, "Holy shit, sir!" A window opened on her screen.

C. Arthur Beeman
DataHelix
eagle666@mailstore.com

There was no street address or phone.

"Why holy shit?" Sand asked.

"DataHelix? That sounds like a private web host," Jensen observed.

"It isn't," Brecht said softly. "It's a weapons lab. Highly advanced biological warfare research and development for the DOD. They have a massive underground lab, right here in Denver."

"You just happen to know that?" Janet asked.

Brecht shrugged. An old man who knew more than he could explain.

"Perhaps we should see whether we can find C. Arthur Beeman at the DataHelix corporation," Jensen suggested.

Takaki punched several more keys. "These files are locked. I mean *locked.* Even I can't open them, at least not without a lot more work." A hint of bruised ego.

Thomas took a seat at a separate terminal. "I'll see what else we can find about DataHelix and Mr. Beeman in other databases."

Jensen tried his own search on Spokeo. "He's in the phone book. 1120 Vine Street, Denver."

Takaki ripped her keyboard at light speed. "He also has a place at 44 Mountain Top Road, Steamboat Springs, Colorado."

She brought up satellite photos of his houses in Denver and Steamboat.

"Time to mobilize," Thomas said. "I'll alert the chopper crew."

"We ride again," Sand whispered, with a faint smile.

Chapter 37

An unseen figure came up behind Beeman and took his knife hand in a vice-like grip, skillfully stripping the weapon from him in an instant. As Antonio turned, the muffled pop of a silenced automatic echoed through the kitchen. His right shoulder fired a jet of pink mist across the wall behind him, spraying Beeman's face with blood. Antonio's body jerked, twisting, snapping him back to face Beeman once again with wide eyes before sliding to the floor in shock.

Kim stepped into view.

Beeman breathed a sigh of relief.

"Thought it was the police?" Kim asked.

"Yes." Beeman saw no point in prevarication.

"What were you going to do with the knife?"

Beeman shrugged. "You have the women?"

Kim nodded. "Time to set aside distractions. Concentrate your attention on the task at hand."

Beeman scowled. "So, I gather. What do you plan to do with them?"

"You want us to save them for you?"

Beeman smiled. "Of course."

Antonio lay groaning on the floor. Kim pointed the pistol at his forehead. "And him?"

"Him as well, if you would be so generous."

"Much easier to kill him."

"Do you really plan to honor our agreement?"

"You'll return to the city, secure the virus and the data." Kim tucked his pistol into his waistband, and Antonio resumed his labored breathing once again. "The women are my safeguard against any treason on your part. They can be your toys or witnesses for the prosecution. You'll return here with what we need, and from here we will take you and your pets to your new home."

Chapter 38

"You've got to back off. If you need to hear it from higher up, I can arrange that," said Nathan Fitch, director of the NSA to Albert Brecht.

Brecht gripped the telephone so tightly in his gnarled, aging hand that his fingers trembled. His mind was racing. New pieces of the puzzle were fluttering down around him. He was scrambling for a sense of what the picture was, how the pieces fit together. So much had happened during the last twenty-four hours. The situation was now completely fluid and morphing rapidly.

In his youth, he'd have a plan. But what now?

He was too old.

Last night, Kenehan's team had taken the Black Hawk to a pasture a few miles from Beeman's mountain cabin and approached on foot. Their night vision goggles were equipped with specialized infrared optics that could literally see through walls to see the heat signatures of occupants within buildings. Kenehan had spotted distinctive thermal tracks and disturbed vegetation on the forest floor, concluding that the cabin had very recently been under close surveillance. Kenehan's team had made entry, but the cabin was unoccupied.

On the main floor, they'd found blood on the kitchen floor consistent with a gunshot wound. No shell casings, but they'd dug a nine-millimeter slug out of the drywall—a hollow-point; they'd taken blood and tissue samples for analysis. Searching the basement, they'd found nothing of interest until Kenehan had noticed a cement panel that was out of plumb with the rest of the wall—a faux cement slab on hinges. Pushing it open, the team had discovered the chain-link cage, exactly matching the dimensions shown on Pessoa's computerized plan.

A broken padlock had lain on the floor just outside the cage door, its shank split by bolt cutters. The team had taken hundreds of photos, collected hair samples from inside the cage and swabbed blood samples from the kitchen floor for comparison with samples of the girls' DNA. The lab tests were underway now using blood analyzers aboard the second motor coach.

After a thorough search of the cabin, Kenehan and his team had retreated into the forest, scouting for the watchers whose signs they had spotted earlier. Finding no one, they'd settled into their own carefully prepared sniper hide, thirty yards farther back from the cabin than the abandoned hide they'd found, and more effectively concealed. Two of Kenehan's men would remain there, living on field rations and refilling their Nalgene water bottles from a nearby stream.

Jennifer Takaki's unsuccessful effort to locate Beeman through DataHelix had evidently tripped an alarm somewhere within the US government. Because of this, Brecht was now on the phone with his old acquaintance Nathan Fitch, who had risen through the ranks to become director of the NSA.

"Nathan," Brecht said placatingly, "we're old friends. This is a purely private matter. We're not under your chain of command, but we've always cooperated with you."

"And we've helped you boys out plenty of times," Fitch responded, his voice softening. "It's been a good relationship. But this current issue, well, it's not what it looks like. Albert, you've stepped in something—the sort of mistake you've masterfully avoided over the years."

"And the director of the NSA is calling to waive us off."

"That's about the size of it," Fitch confirmed. "We want you to stand down."

Brecht remained silent for several seconds. He needed more information, but he had to tread softly. "That hot, huh?"

Fitch snorted. "Hotter. Your boys have earned their spurs. There's goodwill here—you know that—but this is just short of an executive order. We know exactly what you're trying to do, and under different circumstances, we'd cheer you on. But what you're working on now is a small part of a much larger picture. You've strayed into *terra incognito.*"

"Here in my own backyard?"

"Domestic soil isn't your backyard, Albert. It's mine."

Brecht fumed. "You're asking a lot, but you're not giving me anything."

Now it was Fitch's turn to let silence hang, so Brecht kept on. "I have ethical and contractual obligations." He intentionally left out that the obligation was purely personal. "If you want me to disregard those, I need more than you're giving me. Lives are at stake, Nathan."

The NSA's charter was not domestic crime. If the federal government was interested in this particular kidnapping—which would depend upon whether the abductors took the girls across state lines —then by rights this call should have come from the FBI. The fact Fitch was making the pitch signaled an issue of national security was implicated.

Domestic terrorism?

Brecht now knew that, regardless of the cost or risk, he had to learn more about Arthur Beeman and Antonio Pessoa. Conrad's granddaughter was caught up in something far more ominous than a mere kidnapping. She and her friend were evidently expendable pieces on a global chessboard.

He reached up and touched the scar behind his ear, and he thought of his own precious grandchildren. He'd not have had them but for Conrad. He pictured the joy on his son's face as he'd held the first of Brecht's grandchildren in his arms, looking at Brecht with tears in his eyes as he'd taken over the mantle of fatherhood. The gleeful laughter of his grandkids opening Christmas presents echoed in his mind. He saw his granddaughter as she rode, wobbling precariously, on her first bicycle after the training wheels had come off. He saw her again, years later, gliding through a forest on horseback, looking at him with loving eyes as he rode beside her. What a magical moment! Then he thought of the darkness that had enveloped him in Moscow and how—when it lifted for a moment that was mercifully brief—he had lain in agony on a basement floor as Conrad had dug the bullets out. Another image flashed before him: the relief on his wife's face when she'd seen him for the first time after his shooting in a military hospital in Germany. She'd never left his side during his recovery. They'd argued about his return to work in espionage and intelligence. How much he had loved her! How much he missed her!

He would be with her soon.

The life Conrad had given him had been so full, so rich, and now it was nearing the end. He had his regrets—all men do—but one regret he would never bear: he would not abandon Christie Jensen. Nathan Fitch could go to hell.

He heard Fitch sigh. "Albert, you've never betrayed my trust when it comes to keeping secrets safe." The way he said it told Brecht that Fitch was about to lay an egg.

"And I won't now." Brecht waited. "What is it?" He could practically hear Fitch reminding himself that the line was secure.

"Albert, your subjects are alive. They're likely to stay that way, at least for a while. We know where they are—don't ask—and if we can get them out, we will. But believe me when I tell you that what is at stake here is much greater than two civilian lives or your contract."

"Can I tell my clients that?"

"Of course not. As far as they're concerned, you're doing your best but running into one dead end after another. Beyond your control. If we can get them out, you can claim the credit with your clients."

Brecht knew that Fitch didn't expect that to happen. "What kind of time frame are you looking at?"

Fitch hedged. "Could be a while. The girls have been in the same location since they were snatched, and it looks like they'll be there a while. They'll go through some rough times, but we don't believe there is any immediate threat to their lives."

Brecht tensed. Was Fitch lying to him? Did he really not know the cabin was empty? "Do you have them under surveillance?"

"Not directly. The situation is too delicate for direct real-time observation. If we're detected, very bad things will happen. So we monitor from a distance."

"Where are they?"

"I told you not to ask."

The fact that Fitch wouldn't disclose the location told Brecht that he didn't yet know that Brecht's team had already been there and found the place empty. This meant that he probably didn't yet know that someone in Beeman's cabin had been shot. It also meant that the situation was *not* under Fitch's control, and Fitch didn't know that yet. Fitch was bullshitting, saying his team might rescue the girls. They were as good as dead to him. Fitch likely viewed them as inconvenient witnesses—their safe extraction wouldn't even be on the bottom of the priority list.

"How rough will it be for them? Can you at least give me something to prepare my client?"

"Shouldn't be that bad," Fitch said, much too quickly. "But even if I'm wrong, you're still a patriot. If this operation goes south, the cost to the nation will make the loss of those two ladies seem like *nothing*. That I can absolutely guarantee."

"Will you keep me advised?"

"To the extent I can."

The line went dead.

Brecht leaned forward in his chair and rested his arms on the table, his mind whirling. Kenehan had been certain that *someone* in the woods had placed the cabin under surveillance—the signs they'd left in the forest were unmistakable—yet Fitch claimed *not* to have the place under direct observation and seemed not to know the cabin was empty.

It made sense that Fitch had to keep his men clear because a *hostile* force was closely observing the cabin, so Fitch had to keep Brecht's team well clear of both the watchers and the occupants of the cabin—distance was both necessary and blinding. Surely Fitch had drones in the sky above the cabin during the past twenty-four hours; how could Fitch not know that the cabin was empty?

At least now, for the first time, the malaise of the Denver police made sense; the feds had suppressed their investigation. The FBI was involved, not to help, but to make local cops stand down, to keep them from interfering with the NSA's operation. The National Secrets Act conferred power over state law enforcement agencies in all matters of national security, defined in terms more elastic than a wad of warm bubblegum.

Fitch's words rang in his ears. *If this operation goes south, the cost to the nation will make the loss of those two ladies seem like nothing,* How could they possibly have gotten caught up in something that sensitive?

Brecht's powerful strategic mind went into overdrive, churning the data to find patterns and reach tentative conclusions.

Who, other than US law enforcement, had been in the forest watching Beeman's cabin? Pessoa and Beeman had abducted two ordinary girls, likely while two separate groups of observers were watching them, one serving the interests of national security, and the other likely hostile to those interests.

Fitch was watching the watchers who were watching the kidnappers.

Who was the target of the surveillance?

Pessoa was a nobody. The girls were civilian bystanders. Beeman, on the other hand, was a strategic asset. But working with a kidnapper? Was Beeman the second figure in the background on the enhanced composite video? Who else could it have been? Fitch's people may have actually seen the kidnapping take place. If so, that they had let it play out confirmed there had to be a vital national security interest at stake—something even more important than preventing a dual kidnapping.

The scenario fit everything Fitch had said, and that Brecht already knew. Enemy operatives were watching Beeman while they were themselves under observation by FBI, NSA or DOD specialists. They'd chosen not to interfere with the abduction so that they could continue to follow Beeman's watchers, perhaps to find out who they were or whom they were working with, or to prevent an attack of some kind.

It had to be something like that, didn't it? But something felt out of place.

I'm missing something. Consider every piece.

DataHelix. A private research-and-development contractor to USAMRIID, the US Army Medical Research Institute of Infectious Diseases. Biological weapons. Beeman was a researcher, a developer of new microbial strains.

What else? Go through it again.

The split lock; the bloodstains, caused by gunfire; the heat signatures Kenehan's team had seen with infrared NVGs in the woods. Someone wanted something Beeman had, and if they succeeded in getting it, America's national security would be badly damaged.

What did Beeman have, and who wanted it? Access to a bioweapon a foreign power hoped to obtain? But how would the kidnapping fit in to such a scenario?

Was someone blackmailing Beeman with evidence he'd been culpable in a kidnapping?

It was possible if not plausible.

Was Beeman himself a sexual predator, or had someone set him up for a blackmail operation? Did it matter which? No. All that mattered was that Brecht was forming a picture of who the players were.

The NSA apparently had miscalculated and had likely already have blown their own operation.

So, reconsider the nature of Beeman's motivation.

If Beeman was actively working with a foreign power, and if blackmail was *not* the motivation for his doing so, the kidnapping could have served a different purpose than simply to set up a blackmail scheme.

Had Beeman actually been the primary perpetrator of the abduction?

A bad thought: might Beeman have wanted human subjects for testing one of his experimental bioweapons—perhaps to prove the lethality of the weapon on human subjects? Someone had relocated the girls recently. Unless Fitch had them and was keeping a lid on that fact to keep the situation from going public, the enemy operators had likely moved them. And if Fitch had them, it was highly unlikely Brecht could find them. They might have moved them to a quarantine facility. On the other hand, whoever had been observing Beeman's cabin could have taken the women, which led back to the likelihood of blackmail.

Has Beeman's bio-weapon already gotten out? Was the world facing a pandemic?

Not enough data.

To find the girls, Brecht had to find Beeman, or Pessoa. It was the only thread available. Finding Beeman could be easier than finding Pessoa, for the man was the holder of a very high security clearance and would not stray far from his established behavior patterns until he was either killed or fled the country once and for all.

What else? Keep asking questions.

If Beeman had kidnapped the women for his own purposes while under surveillance by an enemy power, that power could be blackmailing him. But how plausible was it that Beeman wanted human test subjects? And why would he be working with Pessoa?

It had to be blackmail. What seemed most likely to Brecht was that the kidnapping had been unrelated to the espionage operation, and there was a good chance Beeman hadn't even known of the operation until after he and Pessoa had taken the women. That scenario made a better fit, but Brecht knew the danger of getting married to a single hypothesis too early in an investigation, which would lead to selective vision and limited thinking.

Either way, Beeman may or may not have handed over classified biotechnology.

He could be in the wind, or dead, but something delicate was still underway—at least Fitch thought so. In Fitch's mind, the situation was still fluid, which would imply Beeman was not yet in the wind. He might return to DataHelix at least one more time to steal samples of a dangerous pathogen or classified data, or both. If he hadn't already removed samples or data from the lab, it could make sense that he hadn't been aware of the blackmail and espionage operation until *after* the kidnapping. So Beeman may be likely to return to his lab, and Fitch must be counting on it. Might Beeman also make at least one more stop at his home in Denver? Perhaps to collect a few precious belongings, records, or for the sake of appearances before returning to the lab? Perhaps to buy time to plan a way to get the classified material out of the restricted facility? How long could Beeman be absent from his work without triggering alarms?

The ramifications of that scenario made Brecht shudder. If Beeman hadn't yet delivered a dangerous weapons technology to a hostile power, the NSA was taking a grave risk by letting the situation play out.

Why would they take such a terrible chance?

To identify all the foreign operatives and roll up the entire cell, of course. It would be a major intelligence coup.

Fitch must have DataHelix under lockdown. If so, the technology is secure, and the risk is minimal. Classic Nathan Fitch. Always with a powerful secret—a perfect hole card. But would he let innocent civilians die just to catch a few more spies? Was the White

House trying to send a message? Or prepare for a war? Or justify one?

As his theory sharpened, each idea triggering the next in a row of dominoes, Brecht's mind raced. The women could be the bait that held Beeman in place, and he was the bait that held a foreign spy ring in place. The NSA—probably working with the FBI—was overseeing the operation loosely from a distance. They weren't watching the women, or even Beeman. They were, in fact, watching the watchers. Everything else was secondary.

But who was the enemy?

Who would want a state-of-the-art bioweapon?

Someone who can't develop one themselves and who has an urgent need for it because they have plans to use it in the immediate future.

A terror cell? ISIS? Hamas? Al-Qaeda? Or an enemy nation-state? Iran? North Korea? Syria? Brecht ran down a list of possibilities in his mind. Russia and China had robust bioweapon programs of their own, not to mention nuclear weapons. North Korea had nukes. That left Iran. So, the top candidates were Iran and ISIS.

The intelligence community widely believed that ISIS and similar terror cells lacked the wherewithal to pull off a major espionage operation on US soil. That left Iran. Perhaps it wanted access to a WMD it could use on Israel right away, while its nuclear efforts were still incomplete—a weapon traceable back to the US. Of course, the same could apply to Palestine, but that just didn't feel right. Palestine lacked the resources and had too much to lose; it would be risking total obliteration with such an operation. Israel herself would love to have such a weapon but would never conduct a directly hostile operation on US soil. Hell, it would be an act of war no matter who did it.

Even though North Korea has nukes, I can't rule them out. And there are probably a dozen other possible players. Even Russia. God, it could be anyone.

Speculation and assumptions are poor substitutes for facts.

He needed more, but there was no more.

He'd have to go with what he had, at least for now.

Deciding what to do is always easier with fewer options.

Brecht climbed to his feet and stepped briskly to the front of the motorcoach. All eyes turned to him. As he turned to face them, he thought of the consequences of what he was about to do. He'd worked painstakingly, for *decades* to build rapport and trust with the NSA, FBI, CIA and Defense Intelligence Agency. He was about to destroy that work with a single sentence.

For Conrad.

He turned to Thomas. "Hack the DataHelix computers," he said. "I want everything we can get on Beeman and any bi0weapon research to which he has access." Then he turned to Thomas and said, "Leave your watchers at Beeman's cabin. Bring Kenehan and Partridge back here. I want them to oversee surveillance on Beeman's house and all known entrances to DataHelix."

"Yes, sir."

He stepped over to where Mark Jensen sat paying rapt attention to him, noticing once more the resemblance between the man and his father. He placed his arthritic hand on Jensen's shoulder and looked down into the man's gray eyes for a few seconds before speaking. "Much to discuss," he intoned. "But let me start with this—we have new reason to believe that the girls are alive."

Chapter 39

The partially exposed roots of a massive rotting tree trunk covered a natural dugout covered with pine boughs stripped from younger trees, ferns and long grass, providing excellent concealment for the cave-like sinkhole in the hillside.

It was just large enough for four men and their gear.

From merely ten feet away, this sniper hide was essentially invisible. Moist soil and mulch crowning the rim did a fair job of obscuring thermal signatures. Hopefully it would prevent any land-based observer with enhanced infrared optics from spotting the humans hunkered down within.

The thin roof above consisted of pine needles and branches, leaving an unobstructed line of sight to the sky—which allowed Kenehan's Iridium 9555, an encrypted satellite phone, to produce crystal clear voice communication. In his tactical headset, Dave Thomas's voice came through as though he were speaking softly into Roady's ear.

"Tomahawk, this is Greyhound, how do you read?"

"Lima Charlie," responded Kenehan. *Loud and clear.* "How you?"

"Lima Charlie," Thomas responded. "The audience is listening, Tomahawk." *You are on speaker.* "Can you voice comm for ten?"

"Affirmative. AO is clear and we are concealed niner-two." The area near Kenehan's position was uninhabited; niner-two meant that concealment was excellent from ground level, but his team would be relatively easy to spot from above, particularly by an aircraft or drone with thermal-sensing optics. "Last active patrol: sixteen-forty Zulu." Partridge had stealthily scouted the forest around the cabin only fifteen minutes earlier, confirming that the deserted hide they'd found the night before was still abandoned. Partridge assured Kenehan he'd been careful as he scoured the grounds; after his embarrassment during training in Florida, Kenehan knew Partridge's vigilance was high. The man had something to prove.

"Tomahawk, be advised: Alpha Bravo orders you and Sodbuster to detach from your team and exfiltrate for RTB ASAP. Recent incident of interest was under hostile *and* friendly eyes. Uncle was watching. Property owner at your present position is Hotel Victor—high value—and may be off the reservation. Alpha Bravo was ordered to stand down from high up, but your second element remains in concealed overwatch."

Kenehan couldn't quite believe his ears. The tech-speak meant Beeman was a high-value subject—a person of tactical importance to national interests, under surveillance by unknown hostile agents and by US forces. So, the Brecht Group had received an order to disengage and return to base.

"What source intel?"

"Expect debriefing and further data upon your arrival. Be alert; Uncle has eyes nearby, likely skilled operators, USLE, HRT, possibly even Tier One. Most urgent you recognize Alpha Bravo has avowed his intent to stop crashing Uncle's party, so our boys who stay on station need to be invisible."

Kenehan was astounded. The cabin was under observation by federal law enforcement or possibly the US military? The Old Man had promised to withdraw from the operation? His mind churned to figure out how this could be. Were they really going to abandon the operation?

How could they face the Jensens?

Sand would go apeshit—and Kenehan wouldn't blame him.

"Whiskey Tango Foxtrot, Greyhound?" This wasn't the first time

they'd yanked Kenehan in the middle of a difficult op that was making progress. All elite soldiers have tasted the bitter disappointment
that comes from the brass calling them off at times that made no
sense; it was part of the business, even in the world of civilian contractors—but *this* was extreme FUBAR. Given the horrendous evidence he and his team had discovered in Beeman's cabin, government interference could ruin any chance of bringing the girls home
alive.

Seconds passed before Thomas responded. "Uncle sees a bigger
picture. Rest assured, Tomahawk: Alpha Bravo chooses to raise
rather than fold, but at present all visible action must confirm our
compliance with Uncle's directive to demobilize. That's it until you
RTB. Acknowledge, Tomahawk."

Kenehan took a deep, calming breath. The Old Man said raise
rather than fold. "Roger that, Greyhound. Tomahawk and Sodbuster
to exfil and RTB soonest."

"Excellent. Expand your perimeter, and you'll spot the other side
of the family. Play the part, Tomahawk. Exfiltrate with Sodbuster
and leave tracks. Wave and smile on your way out. Put them at ease.
Remainder of your team stays, dug in deep, eyes on target premises
for at least another forty-eight, heads on swivels."

"Copy. Their ROEs if engaged?" Kenehan asked for their rules of
engagement.

"If by Uncle, improvise and stay friendly. If by confirmed hostiles,
report and standby for further orders, if possible. Otherwise, use
minimum force and stay invisible. Take no incoming without returning the favor. No letters to Mama."

"Copy those instructions, Greyhound. Expect us in nine-zero
mikes."

"Your ride is spooling, Tomahawk. See you soon."

• • •

The Black Hawk, tail number N1959BG, waited in a pasture four miles away on the other side of the state highway. Kenehan briefed the team, then he and Partridge hefted their rucksacks and started jogging. They left all weapons but their concealed pistols and tactical knives with the two members of the team who remained behind. Once they were well clear of the hide, they started breaking twigs and making all sorts of racket.

They looked like hikers in a hurry to get home, which they were.

When they reached the turnoff that led from the highway to the cabin, Kenehan saw a highway patrol car parked in a shaded glen, with a single trooper at the wheel gazing intently up the road. Partridge and Kenehan approached from the other side of the cruiser and tapped on the glass.

• • •

Skunk Two jolted in his seat, startled by the rapping on his passenger side window. *Fuck, fuck, fuck!* He hadn't expected this. *Security, dumbass!*

An elite warrior never forgets to keep scanning, looking everywhere, but he'd been stupid, lulled into a false sense of security by the mountain quiet and the fact that he looked for all the world like a regular cop. Turning quickly in his seat with one hand on his holstered Smith M&P, he saw a pair of hikers smiling at him.

He touched a switch and lowered the window.

"Hi, officer," said the taller of the two. A Rockies baseball cap and a pair of Maui Jim sunglasses mostly concealed his features. His untucked tee shirt was baggy enough to cover a weapon, but he'd lifted his hands away from him with his palms facing outward to reassure the man in the cruiser that he was not a threat.

"Hello, boys. What can I do for you? You lost?"

"No, sir. We're going home."

"Yeah?"

"And we want you to know we're going home."

"Okay. Why do I need to know that?"

"Well, to inform your TOC."

"My TOC? You're talking to the Colorado State Highway Patrol." He forced a smile. "You've been watching too much TV."

"Of course, officer. But the very last thing on this earth we would want is for anyone to think that my company can't take a hint. So, if you would be kind enough to do so, we would like it very much, with great respect, sir, if you'd let the rest of your team know that we're bugging out as asked. We took the hint, and we know when we're not welcome. You'll see us overhead in a few minutes. We're out of your AO."

For a brief moment, Skunk Two was at a loss.

Then he got out of the car.

Kenehan and Partridge stepped back.

"Sir," the taller man said, keeping his hands visible. "Before things get buggy, could you just make that call? You're not blown as far as we know, but you need to be read in. We'll just stand over there until you give us a green light to be on our way."

What the hell?

"Over there, by that big rock. Stay still. Keep your hands where I can see them. If you move, I'll take you into custody. Got it?"

"Absolutely."

Skunk Two sat back down in the patrol car, keeping his eyes on these two while he keyed his secure radio.

"Skunk Actual, Skunk Two. I've got a pair of hikers who claim they are 'standing down' and that you would like to know about that. They state I need to be 'read in.' Can you clarify?"

"Roger, Skunk Two. Those are contractors, hired by the families of the mall girls. Their arrival on site was *not* expected. Their boss is former high-level US intel, very connected. The NSA ordered his team to cease and desist their current investigation. They work with us on occasion. They are cooperating. Be nice and wish them a good day."

"Detain for questioning?"

"Negative. They're good guys and no longer a factor."

"How did they find the cabin?"

"Unknown, Skunk Two. They're outbound."

"Who in hell do they work for? Triple Canopy?"

"The Brecht Group. More of a shadow outfit but usually on our side."

"Roger, Skunk Actual. I'll see them to the door."

The Brecht Group. No wonder they get kid glove treatment.

Skunk Two climbed out of the car once again.

"Alright, boys. Verified your creds. Safe trip home." He actually waved and smiled, just as ordered.

The man who'd done the talking waved back. "Have a good one." As he and his friend jogged away in the summer heat, Skunk Two noticed the long ponytail running down the larger man's back, and wondered.

• • •

Several minutes later, Kenehan and Partridge climbed aboard the converted Black Hawk and strapped in while the rotors began to turn. The Brecht Group had thoroughly soundproofed this machine, unlike a military chopper, so they could talk to one another without headphones. But Kenehan donned a pair anyway so he could communicate with the cockpit.

"We need to do an overflight," he said. "I'll give you visual vectors. Stay below a thousand feet and head northwest."

"What about—"

The only actors still on scene are people we want to see us bugging out," Kenehan interrupted. "The rest are in the wind."

"Got it." The pilot complied, leveling off five hundred feet above the treetops.

Kenehan craned his neck to see out through the front wind-screen. "There—follow that road for about a mile." A minute later he said, "Okay, reduce speed. Hover over that little jog in the road, by that cluster of trees for just a minute. Flash your landing lights and then bug out."

•   •   •

An hour later, in the cool darkness of the air-conditioned coach, Kenehan and Partridge smelled like a couple of men who had slept in the forest and run for miles without taking a shower. Jensen gaped at him in wonder as he relayed his encounter with a federal agent disguised as a state trooper. His mind was spinning with all that had happened, and it was about to get worse—he could sense it.

"So, he made the radio call and then he let us go. He's staking out Beeman's place from a couple miles out, so he missed us *and* whoever was there before us until we sat in his lap."

"Now they know who you work for," Thomas said.

"So, for effect we gave him a flyover on our way out."

"You're such a drama queen."

"You said to be conspicuous."

Thomas grinned. "Uh huh."

Kenehan didn't smile. The rest of the conversation would be a *lot* harder. Taking a seat, he asked, "So, can you fill us in on the details?"

Thomas looked to Brecht.

The gray-haired man rubbed his ghostly pale face. "An old friend by the name of Nathan Fitch called me today."

Kenehan raised a brow. "NSA?"

Brecht nodded. "Yup."

"Why did he call you, sir?"

"Because our inquiry with DataHelix triggered alarms. Their software led them straight to us."

"Is that possible?" Sand asked. "I thought you scrambled your calls."

"Some of our comm lines are transparent to high-level feds," Thomas explained. "It buys us love from above now and then when we need it."

"We're team players," Brecht added.

"Are we?" Kenehan asked defensively. "They want us to walk away. Are we going to do that, sir?"

"When they took the girls, they were under direct surveillance by federal agents."

"I got that part," Kenehan said, "Why would they let them take the girls?"

"Because of a bigger picture, they say."

"What bigger picture?"

"*Foreign* agents were also observing Beeman when he and Pessoa nabbed the women. The feds were maintaining surveillance on that team and Beeman—not the girls—and they chose to let the abduction run its course to preserve an in-progress intelligence operation because they see the foreign team as a serious threat to national security, a much higher priority."

Kenehan gave a quizzical look. "So, who are they?"

"I don't know yet," Brecht said. "But I do know now that Beeman is the top brain in America when it comes to biological weapons research." He paused to catch his breath. "Genetic engineer. Works for DataHelix, as you know. He's been under observation by that cell for a long time. I'm guessing it's a country on our enemy list."

"So rather than take down a few pawns, they're waiting, watching, until they know enough to shut down the whole group or use it for counterintelligence?" Sand ventured.

"Seems that way," Brecht said.

Sand continued speculating, carrying forward thoughts that Brecht had not yet voiced. "So, the folks our people are watching present a genuine threat to our national security. An enemy nation or terrorist organization. The stakes have to be pretty damn high to justify deliberately sitting on their asses and just watching the kidnapping of two innocent civilians."

"Great sacrifices can lead to greater victories," Thomas recited.

"Sun Tzu?" Sand asked.

"No," Thomas replied, gesturing to the old man. "Albert Brecht."

Jensen massaged the back of his neck. "Any thoughts about who the *other* bad guys are?"

"Only guesses," Brecht replied.

"It would have to be a nation-state to find and stake out Beeman, a man likely subject to heavy security protocols," Sand said. "I'd guess North Korea, maybe Iran. I doubt it would be ISIS or Al-Qaeda or Hamas or any splinter cell. A terror outfit wouldn't have the skills, intel or resources to run this kind of operation."

Brecht turned to him. "North Korea has nukes. And things are cooling off on that front."

"I realize that," Sand said. "But hear me out. Biological weapons mean a whole different kind of warfare. More insidious than nuclear warheads, deadly microbes creep into people and kill or cripple them. A single test tube can potentially cause more casualties than a billion-dollar warhead. Kim launches a nuke, he's caught red-hand-ed—pun intended—the minute the missile leaves the silo. And in return we incinerate his ass in less than an hour, with China's bless-ing, as well as that of Russia and the rest of the world. No recrimina-tions against us, no matter who his rocket hits. He's just *gone*." Sand snapped his fingers. "Right now, his situation is worse than precari-ous. He's tamped down an entire nation that is literally starving to death. He can't stop the flow of information into his country any longer. His people are waking up, more and more every day, to the fact that he is the reason they're starving and living in terror when the rest of the world is eating, watching good movies and making money. It's only a matter of time before he's overthrown. Something major has to happen for him to remain in power—to remain among the living. He knows that. He needs what South Korea has. He takes back that nation, which he and his people consider rightfully his, and his people will worship him forever. Remember, the Korean War is still technically underway. All we have is an armistice and a demilitarized zone. But that fact means more than people realize, especially in North Korea.

"So, he has to take a really tough hill, but conventional military means are doomed to fail. He has absolutely no choice. None. His back is against the wall; he *has* to take back South Korea—and soon—which is why he's pretending to play nice with us now, for the first time in more than forty years. He worked as hard as he did to build an atom bomb and strategic launch vehicles to make it harder to contemplate open warfare with him, which would only be a necessary option if he invades South Korea. Why else build a bomb? But he won't use the bomb on *that* country. He can't, for several reasons, starting with the fact that he wants that landmass as his own, in a habitable state and without vaporizing his own country with him in it.

"You've heard of a Cheshire Cat smile? Well that's what I see on that little puddin' pop face of his when they show pictures of him with world leaders on CNN. He's the cat that ate the canary, or so he thinks.

"Iranians? They are still at least trying to make a go of it on the world stage. The Israelis screwed up their nuclear program five times in a row. The cost of developing atomic war-fighting capability has gotten to be more than they want to pay. So they rattle their daggers or whatever and give us hateful glares and rhetoric and burn our flag, but what they really want is money and power, which they can't get by invading *anyone*."

No one spoke, so Sand pressed on. "What purpose is there for a biological weapon of mass destruction, other than invasion? The other nations of the world threaten us but are not immediately dangerous, at least in strategic terms. No ad-hoc terror group or caliphate has the means to plan and execute a major espionage operation on our soil. Terrorist attacks are about as far as they go. So in fact we can easily narrow down the list of possibles to one. The little Doctor Evil. The Dearest Eternal Emissary of Everything Great and Wonderful, or whatever nickname he coins for himself. With him, this all makes sense. But if you scrutinize the details, none of the other usual suspects pan out. I like Kim for this."

Everyone stared at Sand without speaking.

"Wow," said Brecht, exhaling and shaking his head.

"Wow," Jensen echoed.

"You should work for us," said Thomas.

"I can see why Jackie is attracted to you," said Janet.

"Hell, sorry for running on like that," said Sand.

"What if he's right?" Thomas asked. "Does that help us?"

"Not immediately," Brecht said, shaking his head again. He turned to Kenehan. "I sense you're sitting on some more news, Roady."

Kenehan took a deep breath and let it out.

"Well, as you know, there is almost no doubt Beeman confined the girls in his cabin. We brought back hair samples and other trace evidence to analyze for DNA. We found blood and more hair samples on the kitchen floor and a wall. The blood spatter pattern indicates a gunshot injury, so we scoped and found a bullet hole in the wall.

"I dug out the slug. The bullet was hardball, full metal jacket, little deformation, so I'm guessing it was a through-and-through flesh wound. The height and angle of the bullet's path, coupled with the relatively low amount of blood, are inconsistent with a round fired into a woman even Christie's height, unless it were a head shot, which this was not. I'm guessing the OPFOR shot Beeman or Pessoa. The latter makes more sense because Pessoa is not high-value and is likely just a nuisance to the bad guys. The cabin being empty suggests Beeman and Pessoa left along with the girls—or someone took them. We found an overnight bag with clothes and shaving gear I'm guessing is Pessoa's."

Brecht looked at Kenehan with the wisdom of the ages flickering behind his watery eyes. "That's not all, is it, son?"

Kenehan shook his head gently. "No, sir."

Brecht nodded. "Mark and Janet, would you like to wait—"

Janet cut him off, her voice like a band saw. "Spill it, Roady. We have to know."

"Okay," Kenehan sighed. "We found evidence of a violent sexual assault in the second-floor bedroom. There was a torn dress and panties on the floor and a fair amount of blood on the sheets. We also found a large whip on the floor with more blood on it, additional hairs in the leather braids and more hairs in the bed."

For nearly a minute no one spoke.

Sand finally broke the silence. "Tell us about the hair."

Kenehan shook his head. "Well, on visual examination, without the benefit of a microscope—I'm so sorry, Robert. Long and brown, with some short and black. No blonde to match what we'd found in the basement cage."

Jensen resumed breathing. So, Pessoa had violently assaulted young Jackie in the bedroom, tearing away her dress, whipping—and likely raping—the poor girl, possibly injuring her severely, or worse. He was nauseated and relieved and felt angry, guilty and overwhelmed all at once. Where had Christie been while this was happening? He looked at Sand and noted that the man's soft brown eyes had gone harder than he'd ever seen them, holding death in them.

The eyes are the mirror of the soul, and his is the soul of a killer.

Sand and Kenehan passed a silent message between them with equally lethal gazes. Kenehan nodded imperceptibly.

"There's more," Kenehan added. "Outside, behind the cabin, we found a plastic chair with duct-tape on the armrests and front legs. A sharp knife had cut the tape, based on the clean edges of the cuts. Next to that, we found a watering can half-filled with gasoline. We collected more long brown hair samples there."

Jensen's mind raced. "Do you think—"

"It was mental torment," Sand said. "They taped Jackie to the chair and threatened her with fire at the window well just outside the cage in the basement, where her screams of terror would mess with Christie's head."

"To hear Jackie screaming?' Janet asked in horror.

"That would be my guess," Sand said.

"How do you know this?"

"I've seen this before," Sand answered. "It's a fast way to break someone. Creates panic that is contagious among prisoners. The technique is most effective when interrogating a captured group of men under time pressure—the general idea is to incinerate the first man who fails to answer a question. In front of his buddies. Then pour gas on others, and *everybody* talks."

Kenehan shrugged. "Could be. But there was no sign of fire or struggle outside. The surveillance position we found was fairly close to that spot, so the enemy operatives may have seen the whole thing play out. It might be what spurred them to break in, cut the lock, take the girls away from Pessoa and shoot him."

"An awful lot of speculation," Jensen observed. "But that scenario could fit the facts. If it's true, the girls are now in the hands of an enemy infiltration team or whatever you call it. I don't know if that leaves them better off or worse."

"Hey, that spy ring is under observation by American officials," Janet offered hopefully. "So if *they* have our girls, their goal is to blackmail Beeman to hand over secrets, so they would *have* to keep the girls safe, and the government agents watching them will also keep them safe."

Kenehan stared at the floor.

"What is it, Roady?" asked Janet.

"The cabin was deserted. It looked like they *all* bugged out in a hurry. I don't think they're going back there. But our fed was still covering the road to the place. When we came upon him, he was focused toward the cabin, so I think he was waiting for someone to come *down* the hill—leaving the place—rather than going up and returning. A returning car would have come from the same direction we did, and we scared the hell out of the guy. I don't think their surveillance was tight enough. They likely don't know about—"

"I concur," Brecht said. "Fitch didn't know *you* were there until you made yourself known to his man. I doubt he knew the cabin was empty when I talked to him. It is possible he still doesn't."

"So they're in the wind," said Sand.

Kenehan glared at the Old Man. "So now what, sir?"

Takaki, who had been silent all through this, spoke up. "Maybe not."

"Yes?" Thomas prodded.

"I've been running into brick walls most of the time, but I've been whacking at firewalls and less secure—"

"Cut to it, Jennifer."

Like all millennial nerds, Takaki swallowed before speaking, adjusted her glasses and then blurted, "It's called 'Black Sunrise.'"

"What?" Thomas asked.

"He won't leave home without it." She explained what her hacking had uncovered.

Chapter 40

As casually as possible, Beeman strolled up the walk to his Denver home with a brown paper bag tucked under his arm. He'd noticed a van parked a few houses down, and now he spotted a car containing two men on the opposite side of the street. Catching a glance of the occupants, he saw that one was female and the other looked Latino.

It troubled him that they were not Asian.

But he'd foreseen this, and hopefully his preparations would prove adequate. He would be ready to depart in less than twenty-four hours with everything he needed to start his new life. If he could land in a well-feathered bed, taking his research and samples with him to thrive in Kim's country, fine. If not, he had many other contingencies available to him.

Kim's decision to take custody of the women and Antonio may have been a fortunate development, but was Kim aware of *this* surveillance?

He pushed open the door to his house, half-expecting to find someone waiting inside. Once inside, he checked each room and confirmed he was alone. No observable signs indicated that anyone had been in his home. The telltales he'd left behind appeared undisturbed—bits of thread, small strips of tape and carefully placed objects on surfaces and within drawers.

Peering through a crack in the curtains, he watched the van and the car. No one emerged from them. He stood motionless for a very long time, watching, thinking and refining his plans as the sky faded from cerulean to magenta to violet to darkness.

No one came to his door.

They must not know everything yet, he decided, otherwise they would have come to arrest him. Given his signature on a number of security clearance agreements, they would not even need a warrant. So they were just watching, gathering information. He should be safe for at least this one night, which would be all he would need. This would probably be the last night he would ever spend in this home, where he'd lived for so many years.

I'm growing old, he thought. *Time to create a new reality.*

When he left in the morning, they would follow him. He'd call Kim for help in slipping away, but not until tomorrow. He locked the door and placed his sack on the counter, extracting cartons of Vietnamese food, dishing the cold contents onto a plate. He poured a glass of good merlot and sat down to nibble, continuing to play out foreseeable actions and outcomes.

Predicting the behavior of living organisms came naturally to him, and he'd devoted a lifetime to that pursuit.

Several international treaties banned the development of new biological weapons, which is why a private company had developed Black Sunrise rather than a government agency. Now that they'd completed the research, they'd transferred all known samples of the virus for further study—as permitted under the treaties for "existing" biological agents—to the new USAMRIID molecular biology lab in Fort Detrick, Maryland.

For this reason, Beeman's watchdogs would think he had no way of obtaining the virus or detailed records of his research, which would give them a false sense of security.

That would be their downfall.

Weeks ago, he'd made it out of the DataHelix lab with three sealed vials and a data chip. He'd used a time-honored way of concealing them on his person, unpleasant though it had been. One of the vials and the chip were now tied inside a condom taped behind a toilet in the filthy men's room of a nearby antique store, which had no security cameras. DataHelix had very strict stock controls, but Beeman controlled those records.

A second vial was stored in a safe beneath the floor of his uncle's gas station in Farmington, New Mexico. Even his uncle didn't know about the safe.

The third vial was set for timed release in a location where it would claim more lives than all the nuclear detonations in history, unless he chose to deactivate the device. No one knew about that ticking bomb; depending on how things went with Kim, he might share that information.

Or perhaps not.

Kim and his leaders might prefer to release the pathogen on schedule. The thought made Beeman smile; he could become a national hero in his new nation-state.

Beeman took great pride in his foresight.

His meal finished, he sat silently in his kitchen for two more hours, stilling his mind, bringing his great brain to a dormant, nearly trancelike state. He closed his eyes and banished all computational thought. He could hear the old clock ticking in the living room as he floated in endless blackness until he was completely at peace.

Around midnight, he stripped out of his clothes, took a shower and slipped into his bed. Sleep came quickly.

• • •

Beeman's house was in the middle of a long block of old homes. Slithering through bushes and crawling behind trash cans for a couple of hours, Kenehan learned that it was under surveillance by four separate vehicles: two on the street and two more in the alley behind the house. Each vehicle contained at least two men, possibly more. Unlike Kenehan, the men in the vehicles did not appear to be using night vision scopes.

Dressed in loose-fitting black jeans and a black knit pullover, Kenehan was nearly invisible in the darkness. To evade detection from the alley, he started at one end of the block and scaled a series of neighboring backyard fences, one after another, until he reached Beeman's backyard. The process took another twenty minutes. He used a CO2-powered dart to silence a dog in one yard before it could bark and then scaled a fence to traverse that backyard, stopping only long enough to withdraw the dart from the animal's neck. The hound would be out for thirty minutes or so.

Once in Beeman's backyard, he crept about outside the house for a few minutes, inspecting window frames and finding an alarm system. It was a standard ADT system. Using his throat mike, he signaled Greyhound to use their hack of Beeman's landline to swap-and-blanket the alarm link, isolating it from central telephone switching systems without triggering the automatic cut-line backup alarm. When this was done, Kenehan found Beeman's unprotected fuse box and turned off power to the house. Then he cut the landline where it led into the side of the home, near the garage.

Crouching in a window well along the rear of the house, Kenehan withdrew a glass cutter from his fanny pack.

Fucking window wells. A recurring theme.

While he cut an eight-inch circle in the glass and reached in to unlatch and slide the window open, he thought of a girl trapped in a basement, listening to screams coming through a window well such as this.

Beeman had wanted horror to come through a window well.

Have it your way, motherfucker. What comes around goes around.

He shimmied through and dropped silently to the basement floor.

Once inside, he opened his fanny pack again and withdrew a small instrument that scanned for listening devices. Finding one in the basement, he carefully examined and deactivated it. He was familiar with the type—the unit used the old GSM 06.10 digital encryption protocol—good for transmitting voice signals but poor with background noise. Thank God for small favors. There would be more of these.

He pocketed the device and moved softly up the stairs.

As he worked his way silently and carefully though the dark dwelling, he discovered at least five more listening devices were on the main floor of the home. It would not be practical to deactivate all of them. The basement was clear now, so that was where he'd have his chat with the scientist.

As Beeman had done hours earlier, Kenehan peered between the curtains to check the car and van that remained parked on Beeman's street.

• • •

Beeman was startled awake by a hand clamping roughly over his mouth.

Out of the corner of his eye, he saw a blur in the darkness; then something like a sledgehammer slammed into his solar plexus, knocking the wind out of him completely. Bile rose in his throat, and he retched. He tried to curl up into a fetal position, but strong hands pressed him flat and rolled him onto his belly. He swallowed his own vomit.

Everything occurred with remarkable speed. In his shock, he could not process what was happening. He tried to reach for his knife, but his arms were locked behind him. A knee drove into the small of his back, pinning him to the bed. In seconds, something that felt like piano wire had bound his wrists, much more painfully than what Kim had done. The hand that covered his mouth came away, as strips of heavy tape took its place.

The hands quickly stretched more tape over his eyes and forced him into a sitting position. He was nearly nude, having slept in his underwear. A picture of Dove and Kitten, writhing in the trunk of Antonio's car, flashed in his mind. He wondered how many men were in the room.

My turn now.

He heard a soft click. Something sharp bit into the side of his throat. Iron fingers dug into the nerves at the back of his neck, sending daggers of pain into his skull.

He felt lips brush his cheek. A deathly whisper purred in his ear. "Sound is death."

Beeman tried to nod, but pain paralyzed his muscles. Dizziness and nausea rocked him. He was pulled to his feet and guided blindly to his basement with a knife at his throat.

Chapter 41

Gripping Beeman by the throat, Kenehan pushed him against a concrete wall. He tore the tape from Beeman's mouth and pressed the tip of his knife into the older man's carotid artery, just below his left ear, hard enough to cause pain but not puncture the artery.

"Where are the women?"

Not the Koreans after all, Beeman thought.

"What women?"

• • •

Kenehan moved the knife down to the scientist's testicles and jabbed him there, hard enough to draw blood.

"Don't test me, Dr. Beeman."

"Of course not," Beeman rasped. "You would fail." With that, Beeman tried to headbutt Kenehan, who deftly dodged the maneuver. Kenehan released his grip on Beeman's arm and allowed focused rage to race down from his brain to meet coiled, twisting power racing up from his thighs and hips, which rotated rapidly, like a spring released. Catching the momentum, his shoulder, elbow and finally his fist funneled devastating force into Beeman's ribcage.

For good measure, he repeated the move, hammering the same spot.

Beeman grunted and dropped to his knees, gasping for breath, a trickle of blood running down his thighs. Then he fell onto his side and vomited.

Fuck, that felt good.

Too good.

Beeman was useless dead—at least for now.

Kenehan coiled his fingers once more around Beeman's esophagus, lifting the man to a standing position and pinioning him against the wall. His other hand remained knotted into a tight fist. An image flashed briefly though his mind. He saw the photo of Christie Jensen that had enchanted him so.

The girl had her mother's eyes.

Kenehan drove a third blow into the same spot, even more forceful than the first two. He heard at least a couple of ribs crack.

Beeman fought to breathe.

Kenehan fought the urge to pummel the man slowly to death.

"Care to try again?"

Beeman was covered in perspiration, shaking hard. "Yes," he gasped.

"Well?"

"I don't know. They were taken from us."

Based upon what he had seen at the cabin, Kenehan believed him. He'd anticipated this. The problem now was how to frame the next question. To display too much ignorance would cost him a psychological edge. It was the first tenet of battlefield interrogation. Beeman had to believe that Kenehan knew more than he really did, and that he would detect and punish lies. Ruthlessly.

"I know *that*. That wasn't my question."

"Kim has them. He didn't tell me where."

Kim. Maybe Sand was right about the North Koreans.

"What are you going to do?"

Beeman hesitated. "What ... what do you mean?"

Kenehan drove his knee into Beeman's groin once more, holding him against the wall so he wouldn't collapse. Then he leaned forward and whispered intimately into Beeman's ear, just above the cut he'd made a moment ago with his Microtech. "Listen to me, doctor. I shave with this knife. You have two balls, ten fingers, two eyes, two ears, ten toes and lots of other things I would like to amputate. I have a portable torch in my pocket to cauterize the stumps. I can have you *begging* for death in less than five minutes. Keep fucking with me, because I guarantee I'll really enjoy what happens if you do."

"Who are you?" Beeman choked.

Kenehan pressed the tip of his Microtech into Beeman's crotch once more. "Last chance," he growled. "Then I cut off everything, slice out your tongue, sever your Achilles tendons and hamstrings and leave you here on the floor. If you live, you'll be lame, blind, mute, disfigured and fucked for life. I learned how to do this in the mountains of Afghanistan. God, just talking about it is turning me on." On a flash of instinct, he took a terrible chance. "It doesn't matter. Antonio got away. We know where he is. We'll get what we need from him." Then, to bolster the bluff, he added, "His gunshot wound was only superficial, but it slowed him down. He's holed up in the Rabbit Ears Motel in Steamboat. Get down on your knees."

Beeman stiffened with surprise. Kenehan knew he'd scored a great hit.

"I'm going to give them the virus."

Just what the Old Man thought. "Obviously," Kenehan said, as though Beeman were trifling with him. He pushed Beeman to his knees. "I know that much. When and where?"

"I don't know yet. We had a place arranged, but—"

"You've seen the cars outside your house, haven't you?" Kenehan pressed.

"Yes."

"The people watching you are government agents," Kenehan replied, softening his voice. "I'm not with them. We only want the women."

"We?"

"You're in deep trouble, way over your head, my friend. If you co-operate, we can help you out of this mess." Kenehan slid a small switch on his comm unit. "Greyhound, Tomahawk. Do you copy?"

There was no response. The unit wasn't working, likely because they were deep in Beeman's basement. Or the unit had malfunctioned. *Everything breaks, but only at the worst possible time.*

"You're with the FBI?"

"You're not listening, Einstein," Kenehan said. "You took the wrong girls. I'm with a group of private contractors. We do quiet jobs for powerful people, and we *never* fail. What you do with your —" What was the code name Jennifer had found? "—Black Sunrise, is *not* important to us, not in the least. But we will kill as many people as we have to—starting with you—to get those girls back."

Blinded by the tape over his eyes, Beeman spoke into the darkness. "Wait. My home is under surveillance. How could you get in here without being seen?"

"What matters is that I did, baby doll, and I can get you out the same way. We'll help you if you help us."

"And if I refuse, you'll kill me now? Then you'd never find Kim and the women. Antonio doesn't have any idea where he is. I know how to contact him."

Find Kim? So, not Kim the ruler, but someone on domestic soil, possibly nearby. A North Korean operator. Sand's theory seemed to be correct. Whoever he was, Kim had the women, so he had to find him, and *fast*, or the girls would be the first of many casualties if their theory was right.

Despite his bluff about Pessoa, Beeman was Kenehan's only key.

Beeman writhed some more, but Kenehan could tell this was not a normal man. He had an amazing tolerance for pain. He'd seen this before, in Kuwait, Afghanistan, Syria and North Africa, predominantly in religious zealots, other times in highly trained operators taken prisoner and shipped to Guantanamo. They learned to live *inside* the pain, to love it in a way, to endure it.

But they all broke—eventually—unless they died first.

Kenehan knelt and grabbed Beeman's ankle, pinning him in a scissor leg lock to keep him still. He ran the blade slowly back and forth between Beeman's toes, sawing gently but firmly at the webbed flesh there, where there were many sensitive nerve endings. Beeman struggled mightily but did not cry out. He was strong for his age and size, but Kenehan was stronger. He dug a second furrow between two more toes, and then a third. Then he pried Beeman's legs apart, sliced off his underwear and slowly made a long cut just behind Beeman's scrotum, not deep enough to require sutures. The invasive nature of pain at that spot was enough to unhinge just about any man.

Beeman's breathing grew frantic, and he began to grunt.

"Listen to me, you crafty little fucker. Balls are optional now that you're my *bitch*." Intimate vulgarity was a potent way to signal there were no barriers, no rules. Just total horror, domination and humiliation. "You think you're special because you embrace pain and death. That's only because you don't know them well enough. Tonight you'll find out how fickle pain and death are. No one can befriend them, tame them or endure them. Not you, not anybody. This will be a crash course, with a pass-fail test at the end. We're not in a hurry."

This was false, but Kenehan had to exhibit the single most powerful traits of any interrogator who uses torture: patience and a passion for sadism. The victim had to believe that the torment was both unbearable and *endless*. It would only get worse, and there was only one way out. Beeman would know that, of course, but the knowledge and any edge it gave the man would evaporate in the searing heat of physical agony that marched across and through every part of his body.

Kenehan dug more furrows between the toes of Beeman's other foot. The technique was effective because it produced extreme pain and a disproportionate sense of panic in the subject, but the cuts were minor and would stop hurting within a day or so. He'd walk with an odd gait for a brief time, but then he'd be completely normal. The cuts on his perineal and scrotal regions were the same.

Neosporin would ease the pain and stave off infection. In hind-sight, Beeman would wonder why he'd fallen apart under such min-imal injury. The pain of the cuts would blend with the images of am-putations Kenehan threatened.

Beeman writhed and finally began to whine.

Kenehan tore the tape from his eyes. Beeman was blinking rapid-ly, trying to see Kenehan clearly, but the basement was much too dark, though Kenehan's compact night vision goggles made it bright as day. "I'm going to start cutting away parts of your body. You're go-ing to love it, tough guy. So am I! You know, I'm really very much better than you are at this business of torture and control, and now you're on the *receiving end,* which makes all the difference, sugar plum." He pulled on Beeman's right eyelid and poked it with the point of his blade.

"Alright! Alright! What do you—"

Kenehan touched the tip of the blade to the skin inside the lid. "When. And. Where?"

"I don't know, really. But I have a phone number."

"You on board with me now, bud?"

"Yes! Yes! I am ... Yes. I'll do whatever you want."

Bullshit, Kenehan thought. *But it was a start.*

"When we're out of here, you'll arrange a meeting place."

"And then what? They'll kill me when they find out about you."

"You play ball, we'll protect you. But only if you make yourself valuable. We get what we want, and you go free, possibly with all your God-given parts still attached. You go with Kim—or some-where else—we don't give a fuck. We just want the women."

"You'll kill Kim."

"Only if we have to, to get the women." *And you too, if I have a say in things.*

"You'll let us leave the country once you have the women?" The smell of fear and bile was disgusting. Sweat covered Beeman's trem-bling body. Kenehan knew that the man was on the verge of going into shock; he'd have to ease up or he'd have an unconscious prisoner on his hands, which didn't fit his plan at all.

"I found you without even trying. You can escape from the government, but you can never escape from my people; not even in North Korea." He felt Beeman's body tense, which could mean that Kenehan had scored another hit psychologically. "If the women are harmed, you are a dead man, along with Kim and his team. From now on, *you* are the girls' guardian fucking angel. Got it?"

Beeman nodded, his cheek on the slick, slimy floor. "I just want to live."

• • •

The vicious man cut the tie wraps from Beeman's wrists and clicked on a small red light. Beeman blinked, not surprised at what he saw. The long hair. The knife. The hollow eyes looking down at him told him the man had killed before and would do so again. Beeman was fascinated.

"They need your expertise," the man said.

"I think so," Beeman replied.

"Then you'll be safe. Your friends have bigger fish to fry. They'll want to get you and your technology out of the country. They won't want the women getting in the way. Your job is to make sure they don't start thinking it's more expedient to kill them. If they do, you're completely fucked. This can still be a win for both of us."

Beeman thought quickly. This was the missing piece he had been hoping for. The man was wrong about one thing though. Once he was in the hands of the Koreans, he would need insurance to keep him alive. Fortunately, he already had it in place. He had the power to bring North Korea—and possibly the world—to oblivion even if they killed him tomorrow, simply by letting the device he had planted count down to the preordained date and time, a few short weeks from now. This would release the virus on American soil, and millions would die. The US, knowing North Korea had been pursuing the virus, would do what she did best and retaliate. She might launch a massive retaliatory nuclear strike. The regime of Kim Jong-un would be finished forever.

"I will do as you ask," Beeman said. "Please don't hurt me any-more."

The man helped Beeman to his feet. Beeman knew the man could sense he was lying. It didn't matter. There was a lot to do, and time was running out.

Chapter 42

While Beeman had been throwing up on his basement floor, Christie Jensen was more than a thousand miles away doing the same thing.

She was seasick.

She leaned over the rail at the edge of the deck, staring down into the black water below, and heaved. Nothing came out. There was nothing left in her stomach. She wiped her brow with the gauze-bandaged back of her forearm. She looked for the horizon through the ocean haze. It was better to keep her eyes focused on things at a distance. Dawn was coming, and she could finally make out the line where sea met sky. The storm had passed. The boat was rolling less now.

She heard a man behind her.

"Feeling any better?"

She turned to face him. His Asian skin looked very dark in the dim light from the wheelhouse. The corners of his mouth curved upward slightly. He held a cup in his hands.

"I've brought you some tea." He handed her the cup. It was warm. She took a sip, welcoming the flavor. It was mint. A little bitter. Maybe it would settle her stomach. "And I have a patch for sea sickness. Here, stick it behind your ear."

"What is it?"

"Scopolamine. Anti-nausea medicine."

"Thank you," she said, peeling off the back of the patch and sticking it behind her ear. "I'm still feeling a little shaky. What's your name?"

"Call me Tom."

Christie managed a smile. "What's going to happen, Tom?"

The man looked past her to the sea. "We're just off the California coast. Los Angeles is that way. The weather is clearing," he said. "We'll be heading to port soon."

Christie's heart soared. "Will we be allowed—"

The man cut her off with a shake of his head. "We will be picking up some people who want to talk to you."

"What about?" Christie asked.

The man shrugged. "Your experience."

"What about it? I want to go home."

"Sorry. They need information about your ordeal."

"I'll tell you anything you want. Then will you take us home?"

"You're safe now."

"Why won't you people tell me who you are?"

"Don't worry. You'll be home soon." The man's expression never changed, as if painted onto his face. It was creepy, like talking to a robot. He touched her hand and then turned and walked away, disappearing through a hatch.

This boat is just another cage, she thought, but it was an improvement over her last one. She was clothed and fed. She slept in a bed. Someone had tended to the deep cut on her arm—twelve stitches, topical anesthetic, bandages, Tylenol. Everyone was very polite, but they treated her and Jackie with an ominous clinical detachment. Who were these men? Why were they all Asian? She believed them to be Korean, but she wasn't sure. She thought she might recognize the language, but so far, they'd only spoken English around her.

What did they want?

Why were they on a boat? It didn't make sense. If they'd rescued Jackie and her, why hadn't they been taken to a hospital or a police station? Were the men who had come to their aid some kind of undercover police? Could they be part of some kind of all-Oriental task force, like the army had formed in World War II?

Christie doubted it. A sense of dread ran through her, but she was strangely grateful as she sipped her tea, grateful to be alive, to be away from the horrible basement. She didn't think these men were on the same side as the two who had kidnapped them, but the possibility of some kind of human trafficking kept crossing her mind. Asians on a boat, willing to use violence—what else could it be?

She thought of the loud report of the gunshot she'd heard after the Oriental men had come down into the basement and cut the lock off the cage with a bolt cutter. They hadn't been interested in her or Jackie's nudity, but the horrible welts and bruises on Jackie's face, neck and back concerned them. They'd checked Jackie's pupils, pulse and blood pressure, and they'd given Christie a soothing ointment to rub gently over Jackie's battered skin, along with some ill-fitting clothes for each of them to wear.

The mint tea was helping. Her nausea was fading, and she was feeling slightly drowsy. When land became visible, Tom returned and escorted Christie down a steep set of stairs and back to the small compartment in which she and Jackie had slept.

"Did you put something in my tea?"

"Why do you ask?"

"I'm feeling a little drowsy."

"It's the scopolamine. You can sleep if you'd like, but it won't knock you out. Would you like something to read?"

"Yes, please."

They reached the door to her cabin. Jackie was still inside, preferring to remain in the dark. She didn't like to be on deck—it made her feel anxious and exposed, as though she'd developed a case of agoraphobia. Christie was very worried about how the trauma Jackie had endured would affect her in the long run. It might psychologically scar her for life.

Tom unlocked the door to the compartment. After he guided Christie through, she asked for some more mint tea.

"Of course. Please remain in here until we return to sea." He left the cabin and pulled the door shut behind him.

When he was gone, Christie tried the door. It was locked from the outside.

She sat in the compartment's only chair rather than climbing up onto her bunk.

Lying on her side on the lower bunk, Jackie looked up, her large brown eyes watering. "Aren't you scared, Christie?" Jackie's voice quivered.

Like Christie, Jackie was dressed in baggy jeans and a white over-sized tee shirt. She had oversized sandals on her feet.

Still on the verge of losing it, Christie thought. *Poor Jackie. I don't blame her.* "It'll be okay, Jax. I think we're safe." Christie had been strong until now, and she would find a way to get her best friend through this.

It still made her feel better to have someone other than herself to worry about.

Last night, thinking it might be good for Jackie to talk, Christie had asked her about what had happened when the men had taken her upstairs two nights ago. The plan had backfired—Jackie had started sobbing, babbling incoherently, and before she could do anything to make her calm, Christie had become dizzy and sick with the motion of the boat. She knew what had probably happened—their captors had violated Jackie in every way imaginable.

"Oh, God, what're they gonna do to us?" Jackie rose to unsteady feet and began to pace softly around the compartment, walking on her toes, moving furtively, not touching anything, as if someone else she didn't want to wake were in the room. Her breath came in short gasps. She had balled her hands into fists and pressed them into her ribcage.

"They said there's more going on than we know about, so they'll have to keep in a secret place until they've caught everybody. Our parents know we're safe."

Jackie sat down and then stood up again. "Do you believe that?"

Christie didn't, not really, but she had to keep Jackie's attitude positive for the sake of her sanity. Hope would hold her together. "Why would they lie?"

"Do you think they're, like, the FBI or something?"

"I don't know," Christie admitted. "Maybe."

"Where are we?"

"Somewhere off the California coast. We're going back to port for a short stop and then back out to sea for a little while. They don't want us going ashore yet. They said we'll be safer on this boat. Some other people are coming aboard; they want to interview us about what happened."

"Who?"

"I don't know."

"How long till we get to shore?"

"I'm not sure. They said we're pretty close."

At that moment, the door opened abruptly.

What Christie saw in the doorway made time stop.

One of the Asians roughly shoved a man into the room. He wore no shirt, and his arm was in a sling. His shoulder was heavily bandaged. He stumbled and fell to the floor at Christie's feet, groaning in pain.

It can't be! Christie thought, jumping to her feet. It was *him.* The fucker with the mustache.

Jackie slid down the wall, shaking and crying. "Oh, no! Oh, my God! No, no, no!"

Christie stood frozen for a moment, her mind reeling.

The man in the doorway pulled the door shut. Christie heard the latch slide into place.

Antonio rolled onto his back and looked up at her. His feral eyes glistened with recognition and surprise. He looked to Christie like he was high on something. "Oh, look what they've given me," he murmured, barely coherent. "I didn't recognize you with your clothes on. Let the good times roll, baby."

Before she could think, Christie raised her foot and stomped hard on his face with the heel of her flimsy shoe. She felt something turn squishy under her foot. A sickening groan bubbled up from his smashed mouth, disgusting her.

Waves of irresistible rage poured through her.

She raised her leg and did it again.

And again, and again, over and over, grunting with exertion.

Christie would later try to tell herself she hadn't known what she was doing. But she did. She knew exactly what she was doing. Blood spattered her legs and spread across the floor. The man went still; then he twitched for a while and went still again—very still, with eyelids half open but no one home, the center of his face turned to pulp.

She knew she'd just killed another person.

Deliberately. Stomped. A man. To death.

Her life would never be the same now, no matter how they came out of this.

Jackie began to cry.

Chapter 43

Jensen paced the aisle that ran down the center of the motor coach. He'd been up all night. Cumulative lack of sleep was making him foggy.

"Why not have a seat?" asked Partridge, who sat watching Jensen going back and forth. "No sense wearing yourself out."

"Sorry. I must be driving you nuts." Jensen took a seat. "Sneaking past an FBI surveillance team and getting Beeman out right from under their noses? Seems like an awful risk. Seems impossible, actually. What if they catch him?"

Partridge shook his head. "No way."

"How can you be sure? He's overdue calling in."

"Roady Kenehan?" Partridge shook his head. "How much do you know about him?"

"Not much. I know he's highly trained, and I wouldn't want him on my bad side, but that's about it."

Partridge lowered his voice. "He's on the short list of heavy lifters. Our best operator."

Despite Partridge's muted tone, Sand had overheard. "Where exactly *did* he get his training?"

"I only know bits and pieces. Like most of us, he was in the Special Forces. Roady was a legend in the mountains of Afghanistan. Speaks a bunch of languages, knows volumes about law enforcement procedures, scuba, skydiving, high-performance driving. He has a master's in international relations. He's pretty good with computers. He's the real deal, a one-man task force, a total professional. Heard he went through some really hard times a few years ago, but I don't know any more than that."

"Has he ever been married?" Janet asked.

"Don't know." Partridge shrugged. "I've been hearing about him for years, but I've only actually known him a couple of weeks."

Brecht approached. "We've got more information," he said. He held an iPad in his gnarled hand. "We've finally penetrated one of the DataHelix servers. What we found was startling. We're still analyzing it."

Jensen was fully awake now. "What did you find?"

"We already knew that DataHelix contracts with the DOD to perform biological research. Now we know what program Beeman runs. As Jennifer said, the project's code name is Black Sunrise."

"Sounds ominous," Jensen observed. "What is it?"

"As you know, Beeman is a molecular virologist."

Janet tipped her head. "Go on."

"A research scientist," Thomas responded. "He's a genetic engineer. He specializes in designing new viral weapons of mass destruction. We've got his *curriculum vitae* and some other background information that's troubling." Thomas turned to Brecht, signaling that he was yielding to him to say the rest.

Brecht looked at the iPad screen, swiping at it slowly with his thumb. "He's had an illustrious career as a researcher. He worked at the CDC and American Type Culture before joining DataHelix."

Jensen nodded. "I've heard of American Type Culture, but I don't remember much about them."

"A research company in Rockville. A biological clearinghouse for research institutions, they ship various microbial cultures to research and manufacturing facilities in about sixty countries."

"What does Beeman do at DataHelix?"

"First, let me say that the facility has a dual-use permit for a hollow fiber bioreactor," Brecht replied. "From what we can tell, they only use it for one thing."

"Well, that sounds bad," said Sand. "What the hell is it?"

"DataHelix manufactures bulk quantities of viral pathogens, something generally prohibited by international treaty, but there are exceptions for research that has peacetime applications. The work started out as cancer research but turned into banned bioweapons development. The Army was interested, so they let the technicalities slide—no obvious oversight and no enforcement of the treaty restrictions.

"Ah," Sand nodded. "They turned a blind eye, while watching carefully."

"Sounds like our government," Jensen said. "They only see what they want to."

"What do we want with weapons like that?" Janet asked. "We have nuclear missiles. Why make new diseases?"

"Biological weapons have certain advantages, both tactically and psychologically," said Brecht. "For one thing, some strains have the potential for lethal mayhem that exceeds even nuclear weapons. Also, they can be easier to deploy, particularly since electromagnetic pulses from nuclear strikes cripples military infrastructure."

"Poisoning the well is easier than splitting the atom," Sand observed.

"True that," Thomas said. "Biological warfare is a whole new kind of global nightmare."

Janet asked, "What are biological weapons actually used for?"

Brecht turned his crystal blue eyes to the ceiling. "Attrition warfare, strikes against massed troops, breaking down enemy infrastructures, crippling their economies and denigrating the psychological morale of target countries. Deterrent to chemical, nuclear or biological first strikes by hostile nation states. Some of the research is purely for scientific knowledge, but the deployment scenarios are generally destructive and militarily offensive rather than defensive."

"How can we justify creating new life-forms that are so dangerous?" Janet asked, shaking her head ruefully.

"Is a virus a true life-form?" Mark asked.

"Does it matter?" Sand asked.

"All good questions," Brecht said. "The wars America has fought so far, as terrible as they have been, are *nothing* compared to what could happen if we face another global conflict. If we went to war with China, for instance, and Russia took sides against us, not to mention Iran and other Muslim states, we would need *massively* lethal weapons—but preferably not ones that would destroy the entire planet."

Thomas chimed in. "Viral weapons are the only way to decimate another superpower without the guarantee of triggering a global nuclear winter, which would wipe out all living things on this planet larger than a soccer ball. The project Beeman has been developing is aimed at finding a virus more deadly than anything on earth, but a controllable one—something that will burn itself out in a set period of time so that we don't destroy all life, including ourselves."

Jensen had a nagging feeling in the pit of his stomach. "Just how dangerous is the Black Sunrise virus?"

Thomas fielded this question as well. "We're still studying the data we've harvested. We do know that it's a level 4 organism—the deadliest kind."

"Space suits in the lab, and all that?" asked Sand.

"Yes—but more than that. It looks like a real beauty."

"A beauty?" Jensen asked. "What do you mean?"

"Modern nuclear weapons render huge areas uninhabitable for decades," Thomas explained. "Set off a few, and pretty soon they all get launched—man ceases to live on this planet. Chemical weapons break down and dissipate relatively quickly. Biological weapons don't, because they are contagious and self-replenish each time they infect a new host. Viral agents make better weapons than bacteria because they spread more easily, are much harder to kill and don't respond to antibiotics. Plus, they're a lot tougher to filter with gas masks because they're so small. The problem is that the really lethal ones kill off hosts—carriers—before they can spread very far. The contagious incubation phase of most lethal pathogens is short—typically measured in hours or a few days at the very most. Viruses like Ebola and Lassa take their victims down before they can disseminate very widely. But this baby is specially designed."

"To do what?" Jensen asked.

"To be especially virulent—easily spread—for an extended period before it activates and starts killing its hosts. And it has a self-limiting feature as well."

"I'm still confused," Janet said. "What does all of that mean?"

"Well, if a virus or bacteria kills too quickly, it burns itself out. Victims become immobile, quarantined and then either die or recover. The number of people one person can infect varies inversely with the speed at which the virus kills or incapacitates that person. On the other hand, if a virus kills too slowly it can spread *too* far and eventually work its way back to the original population or in some other way overshoot the desired level of destruction."

"Okay, so what else?" Sand asked. "There's more, isn't there?"

"We think we may have found the document that was discovered by whatever foreign agency has Beeman under surveillance. It was an attachment to an email that should not have been on the server where we—or anyone else with advanced cyberwarfare skills—could find it. It is a draft of a letter to a high-ranking general who works at USAMRIID. The metadata suggests an analyst who worked for Beeman forwarded or copied the document to an unsecured storage location. Her name was Barbara Scheffield; she's now deceased. It dates from three years ago, and other items we've found confirm that what it describes exists and that DataHelix is in a position to produce a lot of it." Brecht handed his iPad to Thomas. "Put this on the screen so everyone can read it."

Thomas complied. The email appeared on the large high-definition monitors, and Thomas scrolled past the header to the body of the text:

General Hanson:

You have requested a short, plain-language summary of the research project we now refer to as Black Sunrise. As you know, this research developed from the use of viral vectors to deliver genetic modifications in connection with cancer research, which did not produce clinically viable results. I picked up the pieces of this technology and saw it had military potential; for the past six years, I have been refining it to weaponize it. The Black Sunrise virus is genetically engineered to carry two so-called "timers," both of which are adjustable within certain limits.

It is relatively stable in containment or storage at room temperature. DataHelix refers to this dormant stage as "phase 1."

When it enters human bodies, the virus starts metabolizing certain human proteins, which triggers a mutation process in the genetic structure. This is phase 2. During this stage, all viral offspring from that point on will bear the same genetic mutation, which proceeds on a uniform time-based reference regardless of the ages of the offspring particles. Persons infected by contact with an infected carrier all carry the virus at the same stage of metamorphosis from person to person regardless of when the virus infected them individually.

As the virus spreads, no symptoms are evident in carriers for up to six weeks. The size of the exposed population grows at an exponential rate while the metamorphosis continues to advance. As mentioned above, the metamorphic status of all particles are progressing on the same "master clock" set in motion when the virus first infected the original generation of carriers.

At a predetermined time, ideally between a week and a month later, depending upon the adjustments made to a key segment of viral DNA before deployment, the genetic metamorphosis reaches a point where the metabolic processes change. This produces and sheds lethal neurotoxins that essentially shut down the human respiratory system. At this stage, no known treatment can avert the death of the hosts, who begin to experience difficulty breathing; over the course of the next 48 to 72 hours hosts asphyxiate, practically in unison. Infected populations—ranging in size from tens of thousands to millions—simultaneously fall ill and expire.

The virus remains contagious, but the infected population abruptly becomes immobile, so the spread of the virus slows considerably. Shortly thereafter, the second "timer" activates, and the metamorphosis progresses to phase 4, where the virus breaks down and becomes inert. Until then, the target cities or nations are not yet safe for an invading force or replacement population without the use of level 4 bio-containment equipment. But soon after the mutation of the strain reaches phase 4 (apoptosis), the infected regions are free of the pathogen and generally without much remaining population.

This will decimate the war-fighting capacity and social infrastructures of the target areas. The only significant biological hazards at this point are those associated with decaying cadavers, but the CDC has established that the widespread belief that corpses pose a major health risk is largely unfounded. Bodies are very unlikely to cause outbreaks of diseases such as typhoid fever, cholera or plague. But they may transmit gastroenteritis or food poisoning syndrome for survivors if they contaminate streams, wells or other water sources. These problems are relatively minor and manageable with standard level 1 biohazard protocols.

As alluded to above, the rate and timing of these mutations are adjustable with changes to the nucleus with a highly advanced gene splicer we developed specifically for this purpose. Given sufficient information about population migration patterns, it is theoretically possible to predict the range and spread of the disease, and to fine-tune the results by modifying the key DNA sequences. This provides the ability to deliver a precisely curtailed epidemic.

Deployment of multiple strains in aerosol form at carefully selected locations of high population density, which we refer to as target deployment nodes, or TDNs, will produce hemmed extermination zones. This will cripple specific populations with acceptable levels of unintended collateral casualties and no physical damage to structures, crops or water supplies.

Small quantities of the virus are capable of infecting large groups upon triggering the exposure in large and crowded indoor spaces, such as airports, entertainment venues, refugee facilities, churches and similar locations. We are working to ascertain the smallest number of particles one must inhale or ingest to ensure a persistent infection, but we know this number is very small due to the robust nature of the virus during phase 2. Inhalation, skin contact (particularly ocular and nasal mucosa), gastric ingestion and bodily fluid transfer will all result in infection, though we have performed no specific human clinical tests to date.

We have extensively tested respiratory exposure in primates, and one human subject was inadvertently exposed during that process to an extremely small (trace) amount of the virus. Her medical course precisely tracked mathematical predictions for the modulated strain to which she was exposed. In her case, symptoms emerged 33 days after infection, and death occurred on day 34, despite immediate quarantine and intensive medical intervention that included respiratory support, hyperbaric therapy and heavy use of steroids and conventional antiviral compounds.

Thomas stopped scrolling and turned to face the group. "This is a long email. It goes on to discuss funding, research paths and a request for Army support and authorization for further research."

"If Beeman was right," Sand observed, "this is a strategic game-changer."

"Agreed," Brecht confirmed. "The perfect biological weapon."

"Is there a vaccine or antidote?" Jensen asked.

"We don't know yet," Brecht responded.

Sand rubbed his chin and stared at the floor. "Let me guess," he said, "the infected human victim was Barbara Scheffield."

Thomas nodded. "How did you know?"

Sand looked up, a wry expression on his face. "Methinks it wasn't an accident."

Jensen drummed his fingers on the table. "So Beeman was under surveillance when he took our girls, and now they're likely blackmailing him to get this weapon. If the North Koreans have a major espionage force on US soil and are hot on the trail of this stuff, I can see how the government would view it. The lives of a couple of civilians would be of trivial importance. If they don't root out the whole network, it'll be like removing only part of a cancerous tumor. The problem will come back. This could threaten the entire world. So, of course, they don't care about our girls."

"Mark!" Janet said with scorn in her voice. "How can you say such a thing?"

"Janet," Brecht said, "Fitch *must* find out how deeply the enemy network has infiltrated us. Our intelligence services are still scrambling to avoid another nine-eleven. An organized enemy cell that could present a credible threat of this magnitude is a national security emergency. If Robert is right about North Korea, millions of lives are at risk. Rooting out the whole network and learning their plans, means and methods could be the *only* way to avoid a global disaster."

Jensen couldn't shake what was bothering him. "Beeman is pathologically insane," he said. "If he has some of that virus ..."

"Unlikely," Thomas assured him. "The safety protocols at Data-Helix are more than tight—they're nearly failsafe."

"I hope you're right," Jensen muttered. "Jesus. The spreading dangers of technology have reached a whole new level."

There was a disruption at the front of the bus, and a newly arrived technician made his way quickly back to them with a cell phone in his hand. "Sorry to interrupt, sir."

"It's fine," Brecht assured him. "This is Duane Gubler, folks. What've you got?"

"Kenehan just reported in, sir. It took a while, but he made it in and out. His tactical comm unit malfunctioned. He called on his encrypted cell. He has Beeman with him. He says they have to keep moving."

"Where to?"

"He doesn't know yet. Beeman has agreed to cooperate with him, but Kenehan doesn't trust him. They plan to meet a North Korean operative named Jimmy Kim, who Beeman says is the only one who knows where the women are. He says Beeman has something with him that he might be able to trade for the girls."

Jensen sat up straight. "*What?*"

Gubler nodded. "A glass tube containing some kind of liquid and a computer chip with secret information stored on it."

For several seconds no one spoke. Then Sand palmed his face and shook his head. "Genie's out of the bottle, folks."

"Do we know the girls are alive? Are they safe?" Janet asked.

"Kenehan thinks so, but he says we need to be in a position to intervene by force on short notice. He'll contact us as soon as he has more information. But sir, there is something else." Gubler held up the cell phone.

"Is Roady still on?"

"No, sir. It's Nathan Fitch. I have him on mute. He wants to speak with you."

Chapter 44

Standing in the morning sun outside a Target store not far from Centennial Airport, Kenehan watched as Beeman tapped numbers into a disposable cell phone. He raised the device to his ear while gazing into Kenehan's eyes and touching his finger to his lips to signal silence.

"Put him on speaker," Kenehan whispered.

Beeman shook his head. "He'll know from the background noise that he's on speaker and that someone is listening. He'll hang up, I guarantee you."

Kenehan stepped closer. "Hold the phone out a bit so I can hear."

Beeman complied. Kenehan heard the ringtone, then a man's voice.

"Yes?"

"It's me," Beeman said. "We need to move our meeting. My house was under surveillance, but I've eluded whoever it was. No one's followed me. I presume they weren't with you."

"Not with us," Kim said. "And?"

"What you want—I have it with me."

A few seconds passed before the man on the other end responded.

"Eight o'clock tonight. Colorado Boulevard and Mexico. Southwest corner. If we don't show, you call this number again at this time tomorrow. If you don't show, you're a dead man. Look for a white Lexus SUV. Be ready to jump in and go. Have it with you."

"Where will we be going?"

The line went dead.

Beeman lowered the phone. "That was Kim. If I don't get in that car alone and with what they want, they'll kill me. You too, if they see you. You know what will happen to your women in that event."

"How many of them are there?"

"At least three, likely more."

"Stand right here," Kenehan ordered. "Stay off the phone." He stepped several paces away and pulled out his own cell phone, cursing the fact that his encrypted tactical headset had been damaged during his scuffle with Beeman. Kenehan had no doubt that the NSA would pick up his cell phone and that they could break its relatively weaker encryption app, but that would hopefully take a few days or at least a few hours.

"Tomahawk?" Kenehan recognized the voice of Dave Thomas.

"Affirm. S's theory is probably right. The meet is on. Nexus triple-slipper." 2000 hours, or 8:00 p.m. "He jumps in and they drive away. It's somewhere near Interstate 25." Using the most cryptic phrases possible, he filled Thomas in on the fact that Beeman and the girls were as good as dead if Beeman did not deliver the live virus into the hands of the North Koreans. He had no clear code to provide the exact rendezvous location without risking FBI intervention that could get the girls killed.

"We copy, Tomahawk. Uncle's pubes are caught in his zipper. They just realized they lost your boy. They also lost track of his new friends. They call those guys the Wallies; not sure why. It was a slip. They accused us. Dad pled ignorance. They might believe the Wallies took him away. But they're watching *us* now. Your passenger can't go to his office. It is under surveillance."

"How'd they leave it?"

"Shaky truce. Hard feelings all around. They're panicking. Dad offered our help. They want to keep us at arm's length, but not burn the relationship. They might need it later. This call is going to be decoded soon, you know."

Shit. The team couldn't give him much support.

"This bug," he whispered. "Short version."

"Real bad, Tomahawk. Worse than a nuke. Whatever happens, you can't let him give it over. The next owner will unwrap that present without waiting for Christmas. Uncle doesn't think he's got it, but if he says he does, the question remains open. Assume his stuff is real. Where is it?"

"He's keeping it where the sun doesn't shine, in case he's frisked. Should I just bring him?" Kenehan said. "He's a loose cannon."

"Stand by," Thomas said.

Nearly a minute passed; then Brecht's voice came over the line.

"Son, you've got conflicting mission objectives."

"I know that, sir. What are your orders?"

Another long pause.

"Your boy slips the leash tonight; we lose on both fronts. Very bad. We bring your man in now, we secure the bigger threat, but the girls are gone—forever. Tomahawk, you're the one on the ground. I might or might not be able to get more men to you. So, here's the question. Can we keep *everyone* safe? Or should we cash in our chips now? We can't afford to miss on this."

They want me *to decide?*

"What does the lawyer think?" Kenehan asked, stalling for time.

"He's standing right here. I'll put him on."

Oh, for fuck's sake.

Mark Jensen's voice came on. "Hey."

"I've got a question for you."

"I imagine you do."

"Do you understand the stakes?"

"Better than you," Jensen replied, his voice dead.

"Well, it comes down to this ... do we risk the world for her?"

A long pause, then Jensen answered Kenehan's question.

"Are two lives worth millions of others? Of course not. Unless it's *your* daughter. Then she's worth *the whole fucking world five times over*." Kenehan heard Jensen groan. "Oh, Jesus, this really sucks."

"Yes, it does, sir."

"We don't even have time to think, do we?"

Kenehan didn't answer right away. His guts were in knots.

Then crazy shit came out of his mouth, surprising him. "What's her favorite saying?"

"What?"

"Does she have a favorite saying? Something she lives by?"

"Yes," Jensen said at last.

"You remember it?"

"Uh, yeah." Jensen's voice caught. He cleared his throat. "It goes something like this: 'Do noble things, not dream them all day long, and make life, death and that vast forever one grand, sweet song.'"

More silence, as neither man said a word.

"Do noble things."

"Yeah. Do noble things."

This time the line was silent for a very long time until Jensen spoke again. "She wouldn't want us to take this risk for her."

"I realize that, sir. I feel like I already know her."

Brecht came back on the line.

"There's your answer, son," he said grimly, as though he were reading a death sentence—which he was. "Bring the package in now. We'll turn it over to Uncle."

"I understand what you're saying sir." Kenehan stared at the Rocky Mountains for a few seconds before continuing. "But I have a question."

"Go ahead."

"The lawyer's dad dug a bullet out of your brain?"

"He did. At great risk to himself, behind the Iron Curtain."

More silence.

"Fuck it," Kenehan muttered.

"What was that, Tomahawk?"

"I said *fuck it*, sir. I'm going."

Kenehan heard a lot of background noise, which faded eventually. He knew what it was. People were cheering in the background.

Eventually, it subsided.

Now Brecht's voice broke. "Keep us advised, Tomahawk."

"Always."

"And son?"

"Sir?"

"Don't fuck up."

Chapter 45

" I found some of Beeman's psych records," Takaki said. "I'm transferring them to your screen now."

On the large central screen, the documents lined up in layers. Each page bore the same red stamp in the top right corner:

Classified: Most Secret
Subject: Charles A. Beeman, PhD
Senior Research Lead
Aerobiological Pathogen Division
DataHelix, Inc.

"Pretty odd stuff," she muttered as she scrolled through the pages. "We definitely have a real whack-job on our hands." She closed all but one file and began reading for details, nudging her trackpad with her fingers. "Arthur Beeman is a dangerous man," she said, sweeping her black hair over her shoulder. "His psych record is disturbing. He's a loose cannon, but DataHelix can't afford to fire him. He's indispensable to their research. They coddled him, put him in therapy for a while. Evidently they decided to bury the problem to avoid jeopardizing their DOD contract."

"What makes him so important and dangerous?" Jensen asked.

"He has unique genius when it comes to genetic engineering. They afforded him special privileges. DataHelix tolerated some really aberrant behavior to harness those abilities. The man is brilliant but likely psychotic."

"What 'aberrant behavior' are you talking about?"

"Torturing lab animals," she replied. "Chimps, mostly, and some dogs."

"What was he doing?" Sand asked. "Was it part of the viral research?"

"No," Takaki said. "Not part of the research. He was *torturing* the animals. He dissected them while they were still alive." She shook her head. "No anesthetic. That kind of thing is banned by every scientific convention."

"Uh huh," Sand said. "Sounds like Jeffrey Dahmer."

"The company, DataHelix, made him undergo his therapy in-house. It took their psychiatrist a long time to get him to open up, even a little. The therapist called him 'recalcitrant.' When he finally started talking, he told the therapist things that worried everybody. They put an end to his therapy because they didn't want this stuff documented, and stored the records in an encrypted file. It took the Sierra supercomputer to decrypt them." Takaki zoomed a page on the virtual desktop. "Read this paragraph here," she said.

> Today pt willing to discuss motivation for abusing lab animals. Described 2 events that shaped his perceptions, likely inspired his pathological behavior. One occurred in early childhood; the other took place approximately 24 months ago. Pt described role in causing the death of a female elementary school classmate, whom he resented. She and pt walked same route home from school, past home w/ vicious K9 in fenced yard. Pt unlatched gate and climbed tree. When classmate approached, pt threw bottle at fence to make noise. K9 rushed to front yard, escaped through open gate and attacked classmate. She was 11 yrs old. Pt's affect while describing this event indicates pleasure. Pt watched from safety of tree. Dog owner intervened, destroying K9 with shotgun but not before it fatally mauled classmate. Pt states his feelings about this event are pride in his own ingenuity, empowerment at having "engineered a single solution to two problems," (the death of the classmate and the K9) and having "touch[ed] upon the ultimate force that drives the universe," which he relates to his research through associations

remaining to be explored in therapy.

"Even as a child," Jennifer commented, "he was more than just antisocial." She brought a second document into view with another highlighted passage. "This is from a session the following week," she said. "It describes much more recent behavior."

> Approx 2 yrs ago pt witnessed nocturnal assault in park. Violent youth whom pt says was "acting out natural instincts" shoved a woman to the ground. Pt approached and prodded assailant to continue beating the victim. Assailant "went crazy when encouraged," kicking the victim repeatedly about her head and torso. When the assailant departed, pt remained w/ victim, made effort to converse w/ her until ambulance arrived, some time later. Pt described victim's eye "hanging from its socket." This was second time he'd seen injuries of this kind. Pt was "annoyed" by arrival of ambulance, which he stated had become "a recurring problem." Pt's meaning unclear; pt declined to elaborate.

Thomas commented, "A variant of Munchausen syndrome may be at work here, with Beeman conjuring up graphic and shocking events to elicit a reaction from the therapist and draw his attention. Whether or not these events are real, a profound underlying psychosis is likely present."

Jensen read the passage a second time, trying to develop a sense of the man.

This is the monster who took away my little girl.

Sand expanded aloud on Jensen's unspoken thought. "Let me be sure I've got this straight," he said. "This is the same man who at this moment is running around with a test tube up his ass that could kill millions. We helped him get away from the FBI so he can make a deal with the most depraved and desperate leader on earth. And we have only one man watching over him. Have I accurately summarized the situation?"

No one responded.

Sand bowed his head. "Lord," he said, "watch over thy sheep and thy lambs. And particularly watch over him who is known among men as Roady Kenehan."

Chapter 46

Kenehan guided Beeman by the arm to the driver's door and pulled it open. "You drive." He walked around to the passenger side and slid into the car.

"Keys?"

Kenehan handed them over.

"Where are we going?"

"The pickup site. Drive by it a few times."

Beeman started the car and pulled onto Arapahoe Road. Kenehan knew Denver. The route to the meeting place was simple. Jump onto I-25, north to Colorado Boulevard exit and then one block north on the street. Traffic was light. It took ten minutes.

"There," Beeman pointed to the other side of the street. "That corner."

Kenehan turned in his seat as they drove past. He could see why they had chosen this site. Once Beeman was in the car, they'd have six different routes available to them within the first two-tenths a mile. They could go north or south on the interstate or take any of the four major surface streets heading in opposite cardinal directions of the compass. Spotting a following vehicle would be easy if it were too close.

"Turn around and come back at it from the north."

Beeman complied. They drove past the spot and continued south on Colorado Boulevard, crossing over the highway; then Kenehan ordered him to turn around again.

"Deciding where to put your spotters," Beeman ventured.

Kenehan nodded. Of course, there would be no others, but Beeman didn't need to know that. The remaining Brecht personnel were all in one location now, and that spot was under surveillance. They could not risk guiding the feds to the pickup site. Kenehan would completely lose control of the situation, and with it any chance of finding the girls while they were still alive.

"I need something to eat," Beeman groused.

"Pull into that parking lot."

"I've agreed to work with you, but I'm not eating at McDonald's. It's not my kind of place."

"Fine," Kenehan conceded, looking down the block. "We'll go to that Black-Eyed Pea, ahead on the right."

With a groan of pain, holding a hand to his ribs, Beeman turned, parked and got out of the car; then he waited for Kenehan to escort him to the entrance. When Kenehan came around to his side of the car, Beeman handed him the keys without him asking.

Trying to build my trust, Kenehan thought. *Playing me.*

But if the game was called "building trust," it was time for Kenehan to reciprocate. At Beeman's house, Kenehan had checked his pockets and taken his hunting knife. Then he'd slipped what looked like a credit card—but was in fact a GPS location tracker—into Beeman's fat wallet before removing the blindfold and handing over his trousers. Thomas could monitor the whereabouts of the card by satellite.

After the hostess seated them and a waitress brought them water, Kenehan reached under the back of his shirt, tugged Beeman's still-sheathed hunting knife from his waistband and handed it across beneath the table.

Beeman's face remained expressionless as he took it. "Why are you giving this to me?"

"You'll actually be less suspicious if you have it with you."

"How do you know I won't use it on you?"

Kenehan gave him a grim smile. "Because I'm your guardian angel."

"How is that?"

"You don't know what you're walking into. You may need us to get you out."

"Once you have the women."

"Only then."

"Why help me?"

"Because you're going to earn it."

"I may or may not—need you to get me out, that is."

"You have no idea, do you?"

"Point taken."

"We'll have you under surveillance. Hopefully you'll get some freedom of movement along the way to wherever you're going. If we see you with your watch on your right wrist, we'll take that as a sign that it's time to breach and engage, get the girls out. If they're not in direct jeopardy, move your watch to your left wrist and go where we can see you. If you need us to pull *you* out, put it in your pocket. Make sure both arms are visible. If you're in a car, put your head or hands against the glass if you can. Head means girls in danger, hands means you want out with them."

"My watch," Beeman's voice carried an odd sadness. "Do you have it?"

Kenehan handed it across the table.

As Beeman strapped it on, he said, "Once you attack, my options will be limited."

Kenehan shook his head. "We don't plan to unless we have no choice. We want to get them out by stealth, so we need you to give us an opening from inside. If things go to hell, you'll have to make a snap decision. You need to be ready."

"What do you mean?"

"If you stay with those boys, that's it. Once we have the women, we're gone for good. No more chance of a rescue. If you decide you want out of there, you're on your own once we're gone." Kenehan hoped Beeman was buying this.

"You aren't worried about them getting their hands on my project?"

Regardless of what else might happen, Kenehan would *never* let the virus fall into the hands of the North Koreans. Beeman would only cooperate if he thought he could escape, so he had to believe that the girls were in fact Kenehan's only priority. "My people have only one interest," Kenehan said with a shrug. "We don't care about your scientific secret. Give them whatever you want. They'll never dare use it on America. We'd nuke them into oblivion."

He nodded in agreement.

"Now," Kenehan said, changing the subject. "Tell me what you did to them—I want to know everything."

"While we had them? Nothing. We hadn't gotten that far."

"What were you planning to do?"

Beeman held back on his answer as a waitress arrived with their plates. She asked them if they needed refills on their drinks. Both men shook their heads impatiently. She asked them if there was anything else they needed. They said no. She said she would check back in a few minutes. She took her time moving away from the table.

"The waitress finds you attractive," Beeman said.

"Answer my question."

Beeman nodded and shoveled a forkful of food into his mouth, washing it down with a long pull from his iced tea. He dabbed his mouth with his napkin before speaking.

"My associate was going to torture, rape and kill them."

"Just for fun, huh?"

"There was more to it than that."

"And ransom was never a part of it?"

"Not at all."

"Did you know who they were?"

"We learned their names, but that was all. The other man chose them at random."

"Antonio Pessoa."

"Yes."

"You knew nothing about them? Or their families?"

"Nothing. Do you want to tell me?"

"No."

"How did you find us?"

"Surveillance video."

Beeman tipped his head back, looking thoughtfully down his nose at Kenehan. "Which family hired you?"

"Who do you think?"

"You obviously work for the Jensen family."

"What makes you say that?"

"She comes from better stock than the Dawson girl. Who would unleash a private army for that one?"

Kenehan chewed his food. *You have no idea, asshole.*

"The ironic thing," Beeman continued, "is that Pessoa almost decided not to take those two. He started out looking for only one woman."

"If you had taken some other women, you'd be spending the rest of your life in jail. I wouldn't be here to help you. The government would still have you under surveillance. Once things passed a certain point, they'd arrest you. The irony is, with us involved you'll probably walk away. Picking those girls was the luckiest thing you ever did. Ironic, isn't it?"

"A different tune than you sang last night."

• • •

During the next seven hours, most of which they spent in the car driving aimlessly, Kenehan traded updates with Thomas a few more times. They had traced the name *Wallie* to the Korean term for intelligence officer, confirming Sand's theory.

Thomas told him Brecht had promised Fitch that the Group was standing down, preparing to demobilize and return home to Florida, and that the Jensens would be going back to California in their private jet. To make the story convincing, Jensen had called the Denver Jet Center and had them tow his plane to the ramp while his pilots remained on standby in their hotel. One of the coaches pulled away and headed east on Interstate 70. They returned two of the team's rental cars. Three other cars went separate ways. The Black Hawk took off and repositioned to a general aviation ramp at Denver International Airport, where it was still close enough to be useful.

The team's dispersal hopefully would tax the FBI's surveillance resources enough to allow Kenehan and his team to interdict without unwanted law enforcement on their asses.

Throughout the afternoon, Partridge and Sand spoke for hours in muted tones while Jennifer comforted Janet. Jensen paced. Brecht napped on a fold-down sofa in the rear of the coach.

• • •

Kenehan looked at his watch. "Eight minutes to go," he said into his phone, watching Beeman from his car, parked in a lot on the opposite side of the boulevard.

"GPS tracking is active," Thomas responded. "Is Doctor Evil standing a few feet south of a bus stop?"

"Confirmed."

"Where are his hands?"

"Loose at his sides."

"We've got a clear marker on him."

The minutes ticked by. At exactly eight o'clock, a white Lexus pulled slowly to the side of the road, blocking Kenehan's view.

When it pulled away, Beeman was gone.

"They've got him," Kenehan said, putting the car into gear. "Two Asians with Beeman in the car. White Lexus. They're turning onto the interstate."

"We see it. They're heading north on I-25."

Kenehan let several cars pass in front of him before he took the on-ramp. He'd lost sight of the Lexus, but that made for a safer tail.

"Visual contact lost," he said.

"They are coming up on University," Thomas replied.

"Taking the exit?"

"Negative. Stay on the highway."

Kenehan followed them from a mile behind as they drove past the bright lights and skyscrapers of downtown Denver. They exited onto US Highway 36 and then onto US Highway 287. When he came to an intersection, Kenehan asked for an update. There was no reply. He repeated his request.

"Stand by, Tomahawk."

Kenehan's pulse jumped. "Have you lost them?"

"No. Stand by," Thomas repeated.

Kenehan pressed the phone tightly to his ear. He could make out voices in the background but not what they were saying. Several long seconds passed before Thomas spoke again.

"Tomahawk," Thomas said urgently, "break off. Return to Centennial."

Kenehan was perplexed. "Say again, Greyhound?"

"They're headed for another airport. Could be airborne in a matter of minutes. Get back here! Meet us at the Jet Center. Come in through the south gate. Gate code is 1776. Park on the ramp. You'll have to follow them in the air. Only chance."

Things were spinning out of control. "Greyhound, they have the package. This is no time to be gambling on hunches. I should intercept—"

"Negative, Tomahawk. No time for discussion. You can't make your move until you actually have eyes on the girls. We're spread too thin here. You're about to lose them. We need you airborne, pronto."

Thomas was right. If they had a plane waiting, ready to take off, he might not be able to intercept them at all. The Black Hawk couldn't keep up with a fast private plane, particularly if it were a light jet. It didn't have the range or the airspeed to justify the risk. They would need Jensen's fast mover. Even if he could get to the men in the Lexus before they boarded, it was too soon to send up a warning flare. If they were planning to fly Beeman to a hideout where they were holding the girls, and he made his move now, his chances of success were poor. They would likely see him coming, and they outnumbered him. On top of that, they could signal their colleagues to flee—if only by failing to arrive on time.

In that case, they would likely kill and dump Christie and Jackie.

"They're pulling onto the ramp at Jefferson County Airport as we speak."

"Are Jensen's pilots ready to go?"

"On their way to us now," Thomas responded. "The jet is fueled and ready."

"Taking the exit," Kenehan said. He would use the overpass to double back the way he had come. "Pedal to the metal."

"Don't get pulled over. We'd have to send Sodbuster alone. Better for you to be there when the party starts."

Chapter 47

As it turned out, Kenehan wasn't the one who got pulled over.

Jensen paced the Denver Jet Center lobby with his phone pressed to his ear. "Anything?" he asked.

"These dickheads are taking their time," Adkins said.

"How fast were you going?"

"The speed limit. Maybe a couple over. No more. We were specifically trying to avoid something like this."

"What exactly did the cop say?"

"He said be patient. There's an issue with our rental agreement, some kind of computer flag, so he hasn't been able to treat it as if it were registration on the vehicle. He said it's just red tape, but his hands are tied. Procedure."

Jensen didn't think so, but who knew?

Thomas approached him with an iPad. "You were right," he said. "The GPS chip collocates with a blip on FlightAware." FlightAware was a web service that provided real-time tracking of all flights with instrument flight rules—IFR transponder codes. "The flight plan lists VNY as their destination."

"That's Van Nuys."

"The plane is an old Beech, a King Air C90."

"Time en route?"

Thomas looked at the iPad. "Three-oh-five at flight level two-four-zero, direct. No remarks. Three aboard."

"Fuel?" Jensen asked.

"Fuel on board is booked as four and thirty. Plenty for IFR reserve or to divert to another destination that could be some distance from Van Nuys. But I doubt they'll deviate from the flight plan; they don't want to draw attention. Last thing they need is a fighter escort." He tapped the iPad screen. "So if they *do* divert, they'll amend their flight plan en route, and we should know about it immediately."

"Rick?" Jensen said into the phone.

"I heard all of that," Adkins replied.

"What are we showing as the estimated time en route for Van Nuys?"

"Stand by ... The Phenom can do it in about two and twenty. Forty-five minutes faster. You blast off right now, you can be on the ground at least fifteen minutes before they land."

Jensen heard voices at the entrance. Kenehan had arrived and was walking toward him, flanked by Partridge, Sand, Thomas and Brecht.

"Gotta go," Jensen said, slipping the phone into his pocket.

"Ready when you are," Kenehan said. "Pilots in the plane?"

"No pilots," Thomas said. "Cop pulled them over. He's making them cool their heels. It'll be *at least* another twenty minutes before they can get here, even if the cop turns them loose this minute, which I doubt is going to happen."

Partridge clamped his eyes shut and tipped his head backward in frustration. "God fucking damnit!"

"Wonder if it was a real cop, or an FBI spook," Kenehan said.

"It's okay," Jensen said. "Let's go."

"You can fly?" Partridge asked.

"No, but the plane can," Jensen said out of habit—an old, stale joke. "Went to a school called USAF."

Thomas and Partridge stepped a few paces away and hoisted nylon bags with shoulder straps. Partridge had two and handed one to Kenehan.

"Just the three of you?" Janet asked in a worried tone.

"No ma'am," Sand answered. "Four." He lifted two nylon cases of his own. One was a canvas satchel; the other looked like a carrying case for a disassembled pool cue, only it was curved.

Brecht, Thomas and Janet walked them to the plane, which waited on the ramp with its door open.

• • •

When Jensen slipped into the cockpit of an airplane, he became a different man. Gone was the bold legal strategist, the performer, the negotiator. He reverted to his earlier days as a professional fighter pilot as if he'd never had any other career or interest. He was a master aviator who had flown combat missions in Iraq.

Working his way carefully through a laminated checklist, Jensen threw switch after switch. Indicator lights and computer screens came alive on the instrument panel.

Kenehan sat at Jensen's right in the copilot's seat. A soft hissing came through their headsets as the avionics powered up. Jensen started the engines one at a time. A satisfying whine reverberated faintly through the soundproofed bulkheads. He turned in his seat, craning his neck to peer back into the cabin. Partridge sat with a cell phone pressed to his ear, with Sand diagonally opposite him. Their bags lay in a pile on the floor. He gestured for them to don the headsets clipped to the bulkheads beside their seats.

Kenehan's voice came over the intercom. "How do you hear?"

"Fine. Any change in their flight plan, course, speed or altitude?"

Kenehan looked at the iPad. "Negative."

"I've forgotten. Does FlightAware update computed ETAs or just show what they filed?"

"It does both."

"Hang on a sec." Jensen listened to the automatic terminal information service—ATIS—and called Centennial Ground, indicating he was ready to file an IFR flight plan.

The ground controller responded. "Three Mike Juliet, contact clearance delivery on one-two-six-point-three to file that plan. Back to me with ATIS when you're ready to taxi."

Jensen cursed himself for getting in a hurry. He switched to clearance delivery and radioed in his flight plan, reciting the necessary information in the required order from memory. Then he switched back and got clearance to taxi. He remembered to call ground from the hold line before switching to tower frequency—a procedural anomaly at Centennial Airport.

That's it, buddy, he told himself. *One step at a time. Make haste slowly.*

Once cleared for takeoff, he turned the plane's hawkish nose to point down the runway and shoved both throttles forward. The electronic flight control system spooled the beautiful Pratt & Whitney turbofans to takeoff power. In seconds he was at rotation speed, and he pulled back gently on the ram-horn yoke. When the gear and flaps retracted, the jet soared skyward like a homebound angel.

The plane had onboard Wi-Fi, so Kenehan could monitor the other plane with the iPad during the flight.

"What's our margin now?" Jensen asked.

"Twenty-one minutes," Kenehan replied. "But we'll lose time when we hit the jet stream over the Western Slope and Utah. They'll be lower than us, right? So their headwind will be less over the mountains?"

Jensen shook his head. "No, we'll be three miles higher than them, for better fuel and maximum true airspeed, and our headwinds up there will be worse than theirs all the way, but we've factored that into our cruise time, and theirs. So just keep me updated." Jensen's eyes swept back and forth as he scanned the displays on the instrument panel. After leveling off at forty-two thousand feet, he adjusted the throttles to maximum cruise speed.

The bogey that would lead him to his daughter was more than a hundred miles ahead, but they would pass over it in less than two hours. Aboard it was the most terrifying biological agent known to man, bound for delivery to the most dangerous dictator on earth.

When it landed, Jensen and his friends would be waiting.

With guns.

It was as if all the years from law school up to now had been edited from his book, and he was back in the Air Force, flying a vital tactical mission. If he weren't so terrified, he'd be in heaven.

It felt good to think like a predator instead of a victim.

We're coming, Christie. Hang on.

Chapter 48

Robert Sand gazed out the window and watched the blanket of glittering lights that was Las Vegas pass far below. He recognized the Strip, and a couple of hotels, including the Luxor, with its famous pyramid-tip spotlight.

He was thinking about what had happened to Jackie.

He knotted his fist and looked at his knuckles. They had once looked like heavy rawhide. He'd practiced on the *makiwara* board for hours at a time back then, toughening his hands and his mind. He'd practiced judo, karate, aikido and other Japanese martial arts for eight hours a day under the tutelage of a famous Japanese master.

Then he'd gone to work for the Baron.

Now his calluses were gone. His midsection was a bit thicker, his hair thinner and his eyesight much less acute. He'd been sedentary far too long, living the easy life. He remembered when he'd promised himself this would never happen again, years earlier, when he'd returned to Japan to hone his skills.

He thought of those earlier years as the "olden times."

When he'd been a special kind of warrior.

A samurai.

The Baron's ebony ninja, his angel of death.

The missions had been righteous, the results gratifying. He'd felt at peace, even while he was at war with some of the deadliest and most evil men in the world.

When the Baron had died, Sand's life as a professional warrior had ended.

He'd inherited a massive sum. The Baron's last will and testament had contained a cryptic notation in the codicil leaving him this vast wealth: *Reward for jobs well done, with no thanks from an ungrateful nation—but with deepest gratitude from a man with the wrong blood on his hands.*

In the years to follow, he'd lived alone for a time in a New York row home at 19 West 73rd Street, losing himself on warm afternoons, taking long strolls through Central Park and Times Square. He'd visited the Museum of Modern Art, the Guggenheim and the World Trade Center before madmen took it down—and Ground Zero afterward. He'd been just another member of the human hive, flowing along wear-polished sidewalks, steering clear—most of the time—of muggers and thugs. A wanderer. A man with no future, only a past, and he'd felt more lost with each passing year. He'd kept himself in decent physical condition, running his customary five miles each day, doing push-ups and yoga and Pilates and working out at the dojo with other Japanese traditionalists. He'd practiced Zen, cultivated his inner peace and sense of no-self, polishing his mind into a mirror, but he'd been the wrong kind of empty.

Without wars to fight, lacking purpose, he'd decided to pick up stakes and start a new life. He'd moved to Colorado. The flow of his destiny had rounded a bend. He'd discovered a love of the mountains, learned to ski, and become an avid backpacker. He'd donated time and money to various causes dedicated to troubled young boys, to help them reach adulthood with intact values and skills, to make something of themselves.

Then a crack had formed in the crystalline purity of his mental cultivation, and all he thought he knew about himself and the world had turned inside out.

Jackie.

What had become of her? Could he heal her? Give her enough love to repair her emotional, physical and spiritual wounds?

He knew it was possible. After a fellow soldier had shot him, he'd received nurture, love, respect and time to heal. Eventually his Ja-

panese brothers had invited him to join them in their brutally difficult training, which had given him a path. It had enabled him to recover from deep physical and psychic wounds of his own, allowing
him to grow into something better than he had been.

A samurai.

But women were different.

• • •

Jensen's flying skill impressed Kenehan, sitting in the right seat of
the cockpit beside him. The trial lawyer was as good as any professional pilot. He was focused, calm and confident on the radio.

But Kenehan was deeply troubled.

The more he thought about it, the more he realized how fucked
up this cobbled-together plan was. He played out possible scenarios
in his mind. Assuming they timed their arrival correctly, they would
have time to get out of the plane and into a rental car Jennifer had
arranged, which was, even now, on the ramp at Signature Flight
Support.

He'd considered an assault at the airport, but that would be
ridiculous and would nullify the point of this hasty pursuit.

The working theory was simple: quickly transfer to a car waiting
on the ramp, wait for Beeman's plane to land, follow Beeman and his
handlers when they landed, and observe their base of operations (a
motel room, a house, a warehouse—what would it be?). Hope the
girls were inside and still breathing, plan a two-man HRT assault
and rescue the girls before Beeman could hand anything over to the
North Koreans. Rely on improvisation, speed, violence of action and
superior tactical skills to overcome problems encountered along the
way.

Simple? The odds were *horrible.*

Kenehan didn't even know how many opposing agents they
would face, how well trained or armed they were, or where they were
holed up. It would be Partridge and himself. The two made an effec-

tive team, but just the two of them wouldn't be enough.

There was Sand, of course. Old, but obviously experienced. The man showed no fear. Could Kenehan rely on him in a firefight? Sand had brought his own weapons, which Roady had hoped was a good sign until he found out the weapons were an old Colt Commander and an ancient tanto short sword.

To each his own. Beggars can't be choosers. Improvise, adapt, overcome. Use whatever you have.

And here was the tricky part: they had to keep at least some of the Wallies alive long enough for interrogation by the FBI, to avoid utterly wrecking Fitch's goals of rooting out North Korean espionage operations in the US and unraveling whatever plan existed to deploy the Black Sunrise virus.

Fucked up didn't even scratch the surface.

He turned to Jensen and asked if he knew how to shoot a pistol.

"They gave us a crash course in shooting before deploying us to the Gulf," Jensen answered. "A long time ago. I'm comfortable with a pistol, but the only gun I ever fired in combat was a twenty-millimeter cannon built into a jet fighter. But Roady, know this: what I lack in skill, I make up for in motivation."

• • •

"We'll give you laxatives when we land," Kim said.

"Then you'll have the virus and the chip. But you'll still need me if you want to use them," Beeman replied.

"This we know, Arthur. We're your new best friends. You have nothing to fear. Your female friends will be waiting for you when we get to where we are going. Your new life will be fabulous. You will want for nothing."

"You don't have Pessoa?"

"Let's just say Mr. Pessoa won't be joining us," Kim said cryptically. Beeman considered that the man who had spirited him out of his house had been telling the truth when he'd said Antonio had gotten away.

"Where do we go when we land?" Beeman asked.

"To sea," Kim replied.

"You have a boat?"

"Yes."

"Can it cross an ocean?"

"Easily."

"Are we going to North Korea?"

"Not immediately, but eventually."

"Where do we go first?"

Kim smiled and said, "You'll see."

• • •

"We're passing them now." Kenehan held the iPad up for Jensen. "This is them, right here."

"Okay, let's see if they're on TCAS." He pushed a few buttons on the multi-function display, and several dots and arrows appeared on the moving map, showing the traffic collision avoidance system. "That's them right there. You can probably see their navigation lights just below and to the right." Jensen banked the jet for a moment. "Over there—I've got them. Do you see that?"

Kenehan leaned forward in his seat to see down past the edge of the windscreen. He saw faint blinking lights far below. "Got 'em." He thought of Beeman, sitting in that aircraft. How surprised he'd be if he looked up and saw them flying high above, at a much higher speed, and knew who was aboard.

He wondered for the hundredth time where they would go when they landed.

• • •

"Three Mike Juliet, descend at pilot's discretion to one-two thousand; contact Los Angeles approach on one-two-niner-point-two."

Jensen repeated the instructions and switched to the assigned frequency.

"November five six three Mike Juliet, Los Angeles approach, expect vectors to visual, Van Nuys runway two-eight. Confirm you have ATIS information Yankee."

Jensen glanced down at the iPad in Kenehan's lap and said, "Uh-oh."

"What?" Kenehan asked. "Did they change course?"

"Worse—they amended their flight plan. They aren't landing in Van Nuys. They're landing at Oxnard. It's a much smaller airport. That will make them easier to follow, but we don't have a car waiting there."

Kenehan saw they'd updated their flight plan to show "OXR" as the new destination.

Jensen contacted Approach Control and asked to change his own destination, receiving an amended clearance.

"Three Mike Juliet, fly heading two-seven-five, descend and maintain six thousand feet. Clear for the visual approach Oxnard runway one-seven. Contact Oxnard tower now."

Jensen keyed the mic button. "Two-seven-five, six thousand. Over to Oxnard. Three Mike Juliet out."

"It looks like we'll beat them in by about fifteen minutes," Kenehan said. "Not much time to find a ride."

Sand's voice came over the intercom from the cabin in the back. "Why not call an Uber? Commandeer the motherfucker. Pay off the driver. I've got lots of cash back here."

This man was full of surprises. Was there a better idea? "Summon it now," Kenehan said. "We'll be on the ground in about five minutes."

"Six and a half," Jensen said. "And we'll taxi to park in front of the small terminal building just north of the tower. Text the driver that's where we'll be and that we're in a hurry."

"Will do," Sand said. "Meanwhile, be ready to immobilize the driver and disable interior cameras,"

"On it," Partridge responded. He pulled a Taser from his pack and tucked it under his shirttail. Then he drew a collapsible baton from his pack and tucked it into the load-carrying loops on the outside.

Jensen reduced power, lowered the flaps and the gear and turned on the landing lights. "Seat belts, everybody," he said. "We're about to touch down."

A minute later, the Phenom rolled out and slowed to taxi speed. Jensen turned the jet to taxi back to the terminal building. As soon as they stopped, Partridge had the door open and climbed down the air-stair to the tarmac, followed by Sand and Kenehan.

Jensen remained in the cockpit to monitor the tower and ground control frequencies, so he could hear where Beeman's plane would taxi and park.

Sand groused that the Uber was only five minutes away but didn't appear to be moving even though the driver had accepted the ride request.

A teenage boy ran up to Kenehan with a clipboard in his hand. Panting, he asked, "Are you the men from the movie studio?"

Movie studio?

"That's us," Kenehan answered. "You got a car?"

"You're taking mine—we didn't have time for a rental car. Wait here! I'll be right back, Mr. Hemsworth. You look just like your brothers!"

The boy turned and sprinted off.

What the fuck?

Partridge made a call and learned that Thomas had seen the last-minute diversion on FlightAware and conjured up a quick scheme to provide them with ready transportation.

"You wouldn't believe what people will do for a chance to be in a movie," Thomas said over the phone speaker. "Be convincing. Treat Mr. Hemsworth in the manner to which he has grown accustomed—he's a big deal in Hollywood, you know. Mention the boy's screen test; tell him we'll schedule it the day after tomorrow."

Sand chuckled. "Should I cancel the Uber?"

• • •

The King Air radioed ten minutes later that it was on final approach. Jensen heard the call. He waited impatiently. When the turboprop sailed past in the middle of its landing flare, Jensen could hear the props through the open door of his jet.

A few minutes later, the King Air taxied up and stopped beside the Phenom.

As the propellers spooled down, the door came open, and an Asian man climbed down, followed by C. Arthur Beeman, PhD. Kenehan locked eyes with him for an instant and then looked away. Beeman had to have recognized him but didn't react in any visible way; he merely checked the time on his watch; it was on his left wrist. *No immediate danger.*

I hope that's a good sign, Kenehan thought.

But his stomach told him otherwise. It just didn't feel right.

Beeman and three other Asian men sauntered into the terminal building. Kenehan heard one of them say they would wait inside for their ride.

The boy pulled his Subaru Outback to a stop near the jet, jumped out, raised the tailgate and began to lift the bags into the cargo space.

Come on and grab your guns—let's ride.

Roady and the rest climbed in. "The keys are in it, Mr. Hemsworth. See you in a couple of days. Don't forget my screen test, sir."

"I won't. What's your name again?"

"Timmy Schaefer, Mr. Hemsworth."

"You know, you remind me of Billy Idol, Timmy. Do you know who that is?"

"No sir. Is that good?"

"Better than good."

Kenehan started the car, pulled out through the automatic gate and then waited alongside the terminal building for Beeman and his companions to drive past. Fifteen minutes later, as expected, Beeman and his three escorts drove out through the gate in an ancient green Mercury Marquis. Kenehan followed as discretely as possible as they pulled out of the parking lot and turned right onto West 5th Street, which ran parallel to the airport.

From the back seat, Partridge said, "Back off a little, Roady. Give them some space. We've got Beeman's GPS tracker. I can see it on my phone. We won't lose them."

Chapter 49

"I'm okay with it, CJ," Jackie murmured. She was lying on her bunk with her arm up over her eyes so she wouldn't have to look at Antonio's corpse or the pool of blood beginning to dry around his head. "In fact, I think it's just about the most wonderful horrible thing I've ever seen." She gave a slightly unhinged giggle and pointed blindly at the floor with the arm that wasn't covering her eyes. "Whatever else happens, at least we have that going for us." Another deranged chuckle.

She's been through too much, Christie thought. *And so have I.*

Seated atop a small crate, Christie stared with a mixture of horror and contempt at Antonio's body and the blood-soaked shoe on her right foot. Her brain felt like a stone someone had thrown into a deep lake, quickly sinking to the bottom and settling in mud and silt where it would remain forever.

When you kill another person, part of you dies as well.

What kind of permanent damage would *she* have to live with? She'd worried about long-term emotional scars Jackie might suffer, but that concern had been a Band-Aid that kept her attention from her own concerns. Until now. Standing up slowly, she bent over Antonio's inert form and looked at what had been his face. It was a caved-in Halloween mask now.

This was meant to be.

Where had that thought come from? It was almost as if the voice of a complete stranger had entered her mind uninvited. Meant to be? What did that mean? How could it have been? Had she been born under a cursed star, destined to become a murderer?

Wait. That wasn't murder—it was self-defense.

Except it wasn't.

The man had been lying on the ground, defenseless and injured. He'd posed no immediate threat to her, or Jackie. She had simply lifted her flimsy canvas sneaker and driven her heel into the bridge of his nose, his chin, his mouth, his forehead, again and again until she ran out of steam. She'd meant to deprive him of life. She had, quite simply, murdered the man.

Bullshit. His presence in this room was threat enough.

He'd raped and tortured Jackie. He'd have done it again, and he'd have done the same to her eventually. He was strong, injured or not.

Christie sat back down on the crate with a deep sigh.

"CJ? Honey?"

"Yeah, Jax."

"Thank you. Thank you. Thank—thank—thank—God, I love you, CJ," Jackie said. She began to cry as she did, softly at first and then much harder.

Christie stepped over Antonio's body and sat on the edge of Jackie's bunk, stroking her hair, soothing her.

It's nice to be appreciated, said the voice in her head.

She knew she'd lost a part of herself—forever.

And found another. A part she never knew she had.

Eventually Jackie drifted off to sleep.

Much later, the cabin door opened, and Tom stepped in. He looked at Antonio's still form on the floor and then at Christie, who signaled him to be quiet.

"She's sleeping," Christie whispered.

Tom laughed softly and then stepped back out and pulled the cabin door shut.

He returned a few minutes later with another sailor, who helped him drag Antonio out through to the passageway. They left the door open, and Christie heard Tom say, "We need help getting him up the stairs."

"What do we do with him?"

"Out to sea. He goes over the side."

So much for her naïve idea that these men were affiliated with law enforcement.

Be prepared, said the voice in her head. *You may have to do it again.*

That voice really scared her. But it comforted her at the same time.

She felt the vibration of the ship change. It felt like they were turning. They must be getting ready to dock. She stood silently for several minutes, listening, and feeling the motion of the ship. After a time, she was fairly certain the boat had docked.

It surprised her that the cabin door was still open. She stepped through, pulling it almost closed behind her but leaving it open just a sliver so it would not lock.

She made her way to the stairs. The trail of blood ran up them. She followed it to the deck, surprised to find it had grown dark outside. The only light came from the bulbs in wire cages along the bulkhead. She could see the blood trail, growing thinner, leading to the very same spot along the railing where she'd been seasick.

• • •

They were parked beside Ventura Harbor.

Kenehan, Partridge, Jensen and Sand watched from Timmy Schaefer's awful Subaru as two Asians escorted Beeman across a boarding ramp onto a huge cabin cruiser that had seen better days.

Kenehan relayed the location, name and registration number of the vessel to Thomas. Ventura Harbor was the perfect place for the North Koreans to stage an exfiltration. Yachts, cabin cruisers and small freighters of similar girth trolled in and out of the harbor and its adjoining marina every day.

"Time to call in the feds," Thomas said. "If the girls are alive, they're likely on that boat. Beeman, the girls and the Koreans are all in one place, with the virus. We can have an FBI SWAT team there in less than an hour."

As he listened to these words, Kenehan watched in horror as the deckhands started untying lines bound to cleats on the deck.

"We don't have that kind of time, Greyhound. They're prepping to cast off. We've got to move in the next five minutes."

"Negative, Tomahawk. If they go to sea, the Coast Guard will intercept."

"Greyhound. This is our gig. We own this."

Brecht's voice came on. "You're the boots on the ground, Tomahawk."

"We're going in hot in five."

"Leave your comm open. We'll have backup and medical help there soon."

"By the time they get here, this will be over one way or another. Tell them to bring a chopper, in case the boat makes it to open water."

"Roger, Tomahawk. Good hunting."

Are you fucking kidding me? Another gunfight on a boat?

Kenehan turned to face Jensen in the back seat. Beside him, Sand was slipping his Colt beneath his waistband.

"They're—"

"I heard," Jensen said. "Give me a gun, goddamn it!"

Kenehan nodded to Partridge, who pulled a Glock 19 from his pack and handed it to Jensen. It comforted Kenehan that Jensen press-checked the weapon, noted that the chamber was empty and then extracted the magazine to verify the load. Then the lawyer slammed the mag back into the well and racked the slide. He tucked the pistol into his pants as he'd seen Sand do.

Sand was now unzipping the case containing his Japanese short sword. He pulled it out and slid the scabbard under his belt, whispering, "The sword is the soul ..." The weapon wasn't that large—Kenehan had seen large combat knives almost as long—but it exuded a venerable lethality that was ancient, undeniable. The way Sand's hands caressed the weapon told Kenehan it was more than just a tool. It was a lover; this was obviously an old and timeworn affair. The black-and-white diamond pattern of the elongated two-hand grip reminded him of the snake he'd come across in training two weeks ago in the Florida Everglades.

Had that been an omen pointing to this moment?

Sand's eyes were not visible in the darkness of the car, but the set of his mouth and the steadiness of his movements spoke to Roady of a warrior who had been waiting for a long time to get back to doing what he was born to do.

Partridge checked his own Glock. Then he distributed a handful of tie wraps to Kenehan. "Prisoners," he said. "Hopefully we'll be taking some."

Tonight we fight or die.

He pulled his Wilson from its leather holster on his right hip, screwing a short suppressor onto the threaded barrel. He had three spare magazines in pouches on his left hip. Four more in his back pockets. His Microtec knife—a tiny automated version of Sand's tanto—was clipped in his right pants pocket. In his left pocket, he had a SureFire tactical light. He adjusted the comm unit at his throat.

"Okay," he said. "When I get out of the car, I'm going to walk up the gangplank like I own the boat. You follow at a distance but not too far back. I'll neutralize those two guys as quietly as possible and wait for you there. When you join up with me, we'll split into two groups—Jensen, you're with me—and work our way through the ship. Try to avoid lethal force, but—"

Partridge finished for him. "No letters to Mama."

Kenehan had spent enough time aboard oceangoing vessels to know when a ship was preparing for hasty disembarkation. The activity on deck signaled departure was imminent. They were rushing to complete final preparations to cast off. They'd be heading out to sea in a few minutes.

He banished thoughts of the *Cogliano* from his mind.

Here and now, baby. This fight is this fight, and no other fight is this fight.

Two more deckhands joined the first two, so Kenehan would have to deal with *four* men rather than two. Fortunately, none of them held weapons in their hands, but Kenehan could not tell what was under their shirts. He'd have to assume they were armed and knew how to fight. If the DPRK had dispatched these men for a job of this magnitude, they were likely special forces, and they didn't look malnourished.

A deckhand started untying the lines secured to cleats on the gangplank, preparing to release them. A harbor hand was walking toward the ship to assist in retracting the gangplank.

Show time, baby.

He drew his Wilson and held it behind his right thigh as he strode purposefully up the ramp. As soon as he did so, one of the deckhands produced an AK-74 from nowhere and pointed it at him.

Training took over.

Front sight. Squeeze, squeeze.

Two shots to the chest, and the man dropped like a sack full of hammers. His rifle clattered when it hit the deck. Five thousand rounds a week for a nearly a year will give you that ability. He dropped to one knee and fired three more times, hitting each of the remaining men in the chest. Two dropped immediately; the last remained standing, clutching at his chest with a look of terror on his face. Kenehan gave him a Jeff Cooper failure drill—following the two rounds to the man's chest with one to his head—and the man dropped out of the fight.

Pressing the release button behind the trigger, Kenehan dropped his depleted magazine, speed-reloaded and kept moving up the gangplank. He stopped to pick up the AK and a spare magazine for it from beneath the dead man's belt; then he signaled with his hand for the rest of his team to join him.

• • •

Christie heard the gunshots and froze.

What was going on? It was like the moment in the cabin when she'd heard the sound of the Asians shooting Asshole. When she and Jackie had been "rescued."

Another rescue? This time for real?

She had to get to the side of the boat where she could see the dock, to get some idea of what was happening. She thought of diving over the side—but she couldn't leave Jackie. She crept quietly along the deck.

She heard voices behind her, so she sprinted for the stern, her head down, her arms pumping, her legs jacking her forward.

As she came to the corner, she saw a man gunned down by someone shooting from behind him. She turned back and sprinted toward the bow of the ship. She flew up a ladder and rolled onto the foredeck.

• • •

"I'll go forward. You two go aft," Kenehan said.

Partridge led Sand to the back of the boat, signaling him to stop as they reached the afterdeck. Just as he did so, he felt something hard pressing into his kidney. "Drop your gun and get down on your belly," said a heavily accented voice behind him.

Fuck, not again!

This was worse than what had happened during training. Someone had caught him unaware once again. Partridge felt giddy with failure and resignation. What was wrong with him? He froze for a moment, considering his options. Dizziness rocked him.

He had no choice. He'd have to comply.

Just then he heard a sound that made him think of a comedian he'd loved as a young man, famous for smashing watermelons with a wooden mallet. *Schwook. Thud.* Then a voice whispered in his ear. "Keep going."

Partridge turned and saw Sand. At his feet was the headless body of a sailor.

He turned back to look toward the stern of the ship, raising his gun once more and continuing to move toward the stern. One man came around the corner, and he dropped that one with a single shot to the chest.

Then everything went forever black for Partridge as a bullet from behind him tore away the top of his skull.

• • •

Kenehan crept softly toward the ladder that led up to the flying bridge. He moved slowly, doing his best to "pie" corners—edging around them with his pistol gripped in both hands in front of him, his arms outstretched, so he'd have an early shot at anyone waiting around the corners. It slowed him down, but it was the *only* way to move around a corner in a gunfight.

He heard gunfire behind him. He turned and dropped to one knee, his pistol and his eyes tracking as a single unit.

Looking down the length of the deck, he watched in horror as a man came out from behind a storage locker and put a gun to Partridge's back. Then Sand appeared behind that man—who knew where from—and like the samurai he was, he beheaded the man with a single stroke.

Rock on, Sandman.

Just as Partridge started moving again, another man came from the front of the ship behind Kenehan and fired a few rounds from another AK. One of the rounds sliced the air near Kenehan's ear, continuing on its journey to pulp Partridge's brain.

Kenehan watched Sodbuster fall.

Oh. Letter to Mama.

I'll say a prayer for you, to make it through to the other side.

Then Sand was gone again.

Turning on one knee once again, Kenehan flattened all the way to the deck and fired two rounds with his own AK. The man who had killed Partridge staggered backward, fell against the railing and then dropped to the deck.

Kenehan gave him a security round to the head and kept moving.

• • •

From the bridge of the ship, Beeman heard gunfire and knew instantly what was happening.

The killing would be random, he realized, and he knew that if he showed himself in the wrong place at the wrong time, a bullet would end his life.

Death did not frighten Beeman, but he didn't want to die this way. He looked at the two men standing with him, as if for guidance, and one of them barked a command: "Remain here! Under no circumstances do you leave the bridge."

Both men disappeared through the hatch closest to the pier. The sound of intermittent gunfire continued. Beeman moved toward a hatch on the opposite side of the bridge—the one facing the ocean —and stepped through it.

He looked over the railing at the water below. It was quite a drop, but he could do it. The pain in his ribs was just bearable. As quickly as he could with his bruised ribs, he climbed over, took a deep breath and let go.

• • •

Jensen caught up to Kenehan and watched in horror as he fired a finishing round into the head of the man who had killed Partridge. When he'd been in the Air Force, his kind of killing was done at a distance, from his fighter-jet.

With even greater horror, he watched another man with an assault rifle lean over the railing of the deck above and aim at Roady. Yet another man rounded the corner with a pistol, also aiming at Roady. They would fire on him at the same time, and they'd appeared so unexpectedly, he hadn't seen either one of them.

Jensen's arm came up fast, and he started squeezing the trigger while he pressed Roady back against the bulkhead with his free hand. The man with the handgun went down fast, just as a curtain of bullets rained onto the deck where they had been standing an instant ago.

When the fusillade subsided, Kenehan jumped out, aiming quickly upward, and fired two careful rounds. Then he flattened his back against the wall once again, beside Jensen. He turned quickly and hammered a pair of rounds into the man Jensen had just sprayed bullets into. Kenehan flattened against the bulkhead again, dropped the magazine into his left hand to check it, shook his head and pulled the spare from his back pocket. He quickly switched out the magazines, jamming the new one into the well, hammering it home and then slapping the bolt into battery with the butt of his left hand.

It took about three seconds.

Jensen had never seen anything like it.

And Jesus, I just killed that man. He was dead before Roady hit him.

Jensen had killed from the cockpit with missiles and cannon but never up close.

Kenehan turned to face him. "Fucking awesome, dude," he said. "Go into battle with you anytime. Let's go get the girls."

The two men climbed a ladder and found themselves on the foredeck.

• • •

Topping the ladder on the opposite side of the foredeck, Christie looked up when she caught movement in her peripheral vision. She couldn't believe what she saw: her father, with a gun in his hand and blood on his shirt, looking back down the opposite side of the ship as gunfire echoed and the sound of rounds skimming the deck near his feet followed a split second later.

Ding! Ding! Ding!

She tried to call out, but her voice caught in her throat.

Beside her father appeared a younger man with a combat rifle and long hair tied back, also looking back down the ship. The man looked deadly. He met her eyes, opening his mouth as if to speak, and then turned his head again. His rifle came up fast and then locked steady, pointing down the opposite side of the boat from which she'd come. Four deafening reports sounded, and flame spit from the barrel of his rifle. Then he darted out of her field of view.

Her dad remained behind.

Tears streamed from her eyes. *Thank God!*

She was alone on the foredeck with her father.

She forced her voice to work: "*DADDY!*"

Jensen jammed his gun into his waistband and ran to her.

They came crashing together, both crying, kissing; their tears mixed as they turned slowly in space, crushing each other with love. "Oh, my baby, my baby!" Jensen crooned into her ear, stroking the back of her head. "We're going home now." He kissed her forehead, her cheeks, everywhere on her face, while he cried.

She couldn't let go of her daddy. She would never let go of her daddy.

Until she saw yet another man, an Asian, coming up the ladder she'd just climbed, with a pistol in his hand. In what almost seemed like slow motion, she watched as he paused at the top of the ladder and raised the gun, pointing it at her father's back.

She stepped in front of him to protect him—at least from the first shot or two.

The man with the gun grunted as a long, curved blade darted out of his chest and then vanished, then the man fell from the sight.

Christie was too stunned to process what had just happened.

Then Robert's head appeared, and he climbed up onto the fore-deck, holding his special sword in his hand. The blade was dripping bright red blood. He approached, cleaned his blade with the hem of his shirt, sheathed his weapon and said softly, "CJ, honey, can you take me to my baby?"

• • •

Jackie was sure she was going to die. She'd clamped her hands over her ears and screwed her eyes tightly shut. She rocked back and forth on her bunk, crying. Why wouldn't the horrible noise stop? Oh, God, she knew she was living her last seconds. Soon someone would come and kill her. She was sure of it. The fear was unbearable.

So bad, so bad.

She prayed. "God, please save me!" She said the prayer aloud, over and over, knowing there would never be an answer. Her time had come. This was the end, and she was terrified. Then she jumped in even greater horror as she felt a hand on her shoulder. She forced herself to open her eyes. It took everything she had. She looked up and saw a silhouette of a man outlined by the light from the deck behind the open door of the compartment.

"Please don't hurt me!" she cried.

The man who had touched her dropped to his knees and took both of her shoulders gently in his large hands.

"No one will ever hurt you again, Jaqueline Dawson. I swear it."

Her mind stopped. Time stopped.

Then she understood.

"Robert?"

"You're safe now, baby," Sand said softly. "Everything is going to be okay. You're going home."

"Are the bad men dead?"

"Yes," said Christie, who appeared in the doorway. "Or at least a lot of them are. We need to get out of here, Jax. Let's go."

• • •

Kim lay dying on the deck, knowing he had failed and only had a few minutes left to live. He thought of his village in North Korea. He saw his mother and father. They seemed to be telling him something. *Protect your sister*, they were saying. Tears blurred his vision. He had not been able to relay the information he'd obtained—he could not prevent disaster. Beeman's automated device would release the deadly virus in America, and as a result the US would reduce his nation to ashes.

When he first boarded the vessel, Beeman had handed him the condom containing the vial and computer chip, telling him he'd installed an insurance policy. He'd planted a self-arming viral "bomb" that would go off in a few weeks. He'd told him when and where, as a show of good faith.

"You can find it and disarm it or let it go off as you wish," Beeman had said. "It gives you another option." Kim had been horrified, knowing that if the device released the virus on US soil after the FBI had learned of Beeman's betrayal of his nation, they would blame North Korea for the massive casualties they would suffer. They would surely unleash nuclear hell on his homeland. His family would all perish, as would his entire nation.

He had to avert the madman's plan, but he was slipping fast.

Kim was the only one who knew where Beeman had planted the device and when it would go off. Another half hour, and Kim could have had time to radio the information. But just as they'd been ready to cast off—after being docked for less than thirty minutes—the unexpected assault on their vessel had commenced. The FBI must have deployed one of their legendary counter-terror tactical units to attack the ship. The entire North Korean intelligence apparatus in the US was aboard this ship as far as Kim knew.

Disaster.

Kim's last thoughts were that he should have learned how to pray. *The entire world will burn,* he thought, as numbness began to climb up from his legs to his torso. An odd humming filled his ears and resolved into the sound of his mother's voice. *Protect your sister.*

He took no comfort from the fact he would not be there to experience his country's end, but he knew he should. Death was not welcome, but it had come nonetheless. His precious little sister—for whose safety he had feared for years—was a DRPK hostage to ensure his fidelity while he operated in Western countries. She would also die, executed as retribution for his failure or reduced to ashes in America's retributive strike.

He could do nothing to prevent it.

Both of his parents were calling out to him now, but their voices competed with the sound of distant sirens drawing nearer, drowning them out in his mind.

His vision cleared briefly. Faces looming above him replaced the image of his parents. Western faces. They held guns to his head, as if death was not sitting in his chest already.

A voice came to him as though from a great distance.

"Where is Beeman?"

Blood erupted from Kim's mouth as he tried to speak. He coughed several times and managed to utter five final words.

"Crew ... nine ... ball ... virus ... smoke."

Kim's long-dead mother and father actually took his hands. He reached out, begging for forgiveness.

Chapter 50

The blazing red lights were everywhere. The pier and adjacent lot were flooded with police cruisers, ambulances, fire trucks and two—no, make that three, no, *four*—SWAT vans from which men poured in full tactical regalia. Coroner's meat wagons, and, at last, a pair of helicopters touched down. Other choppers circled overhead, lighting up the harbor as if it were high noon with their airborne spotlights.

Kenehan keyed his throat mike. "Greyhound, this is Tomahawk."

"Go ahead, Tomahawk. The audience is listening," Thomas replied.

"Good news and bad. Sodbuster is KIA. Professor is in the wind." He stopped talking. Let the worst news sink in before bringing the good.

Brecht's voice was terse. "Continue, Tomahawk."

"We have secured the virus and data."

Brecht's raspy voice chimed in. "Jesus, boy. Am I going to have to kick your ass? Get on with it!"

"Christie Jensen and Jackie Dawson are alive and well. They are unhurt. Mark is with them now."

Kenehan did not expect an immediate reply, and he did not get one. After a moment, he continued. "Uncle isn't giving us a lot of love, but no handcuffs yet. Can you run some interference?"

"Status of the Wallies?" Thomas asked.

"No known prisoners," Kenehan said. "No choice. They severely outnumbered us. There may or may not be survivors. These were NorKor special forces, Tier One. The only people on this boat who didn't shoot at us were the girls. All return fire was in self-defense. There may be actionable intel on board; Uncle will be scouring this shitcan for weeks."

"The professor—elaborate, Tomahawk." said Thomas.

"Whereabouts unknown. But I watched him board this vessel."

"In hiding?"

"Could be, but I doubt it. I think he squirted. Over the side."

There was a long pause Kenehan did not expect. Then Thomas came on the line. "Tomahawk, be advised, Uncle is about to take you into custody. Go easy. Do not resist. This is procedure."

Kenehan saw four SWAT team members approaching him with their rifles raised. "I see them coming, Greyhound. This is fucked."

"Have faith, son," Brecht said. "I'm calling the president now."

"Hands where we can see them!" the SWAT lead yelled.

Kenehan dropped the AK that had been dangling loose at his side and raised his hands. Men in black combat fatigues and M4 rifles quickly surrounded him. His main goal right now was to avoid taking friendly fire. Bodies everywhere, nobody read in, all hoping to get home tonight or even become heroes.

Late to the party, but full of adrenaline.

"I'm not a threat," Kenehan said, raising his hands slowly. "I'm on your side."

"Down on your knees, goddammit! Lace your fingers behind your head."

Kenehan complied.

The SWAT leader keyed his own throat mike. "Skunk Actual, Skunk Two. We've got another operator," he said. Then he turned to one of the men closest to him. "Cuff him, pat him down and put him in the van."

The soldier obeyed, ratcheting the cuffs around Kenehan's right wrist then pulling his arms down and locking them together behind his back. He pulled Kenehan to his feet, lifting his Wilson from its holster without bothering to check the cuff-key pocket in his tactical trousers.

What was with these people?

"You let me go last time, Skunk Two."

The SWAT leader pulled a tactical flashlight and shone it in Kenehan's face, blinding him. "You," he said.

"Me," Kenehan said.

"I know who you are."

"I doubt it," Kenehan parried.

"Stand up."

Kenehan rocked back onto his toes and rose to a standing position. He moved his right foot back to keep his balance, ready to deliver a fast kick to the man if there was some whip-ass on his mind.

"I know you," Skunk Two repeated.

"You said that."

"How did you get here so fast?"

"I could ask you the same thing."

"You had to show off with your private Black Hawk." Skunk Two chuckled. "Even then, I thought it might be you."

"How's that?"

"I was in the First, Mosul, in sixteen and seventeen."

"Nineveh," Kenehan said.

Skunk Two nodded. "We were late to that party. Like tonight."

"You came right on time," Kenehan said. "Then and now."

"You're *Tomahawk*."

Kenehan said nothing.

"What's it like?"

"What do you mean?"

"Working for the Old Man?"

"It has its ups and downs. Now and then my own people cuff me."

Skunk Two's eyes shimmered. "It's okay, Tomahawk. Take 'em off."

Kenehan had the cuffs off in a few seconds. "Thanks, Skunk Two. Been a rough night. We lost one of our own. A former Ranger. Treat him with respect."

Skunk Two lowered his gaze; then he looked up again. "Point him out."

Kenehan guided the team to where Sodbuster had fallen. "That's him."

"We'll take care of him."

"Thanks. And Skunk?"

"Yeah?"

"The old black man?"

"Who?"

"The elderly African American gentleman you have in custody. He's with us. A good guy."

"We have no such detainee. He might have gone down, or over the side."

I'll catch up with you later, samurai.

Skunk Two's eyes glazed over, focusing at a distance. Kenehan knew he was receiving information though his earpiece. He nodded several times and then said, "Acknowledged. We'll bring him down." He looked at Kenehan and said, "You've got friends in high places, Tomahawk. Let's go."

"Do me one favor."

"What is it?"

"Take care of those girls as if they were princesses."

Skunk Two's eyes grew cloudy. He held very still.

"What's wrong?"

"I was there," he said, lowering his eyes. "When it happened. I was under orders." He looked up, his face open, hoping for forgiveness that would never come, for he would never forgive himself. Kenehan looked into the man's eyes and saw waves of unspeakable pain.

Chain of command can suck. He said nothing.

Skunk Two touched Kenehan's shoulder. "Thanks from me, Tomahawk. I mean it. Those girls are royalty, and we'll treat them as such. I guarantee it. They're with Mr. Jensen, over there." He pointed to one of the ambulances below. Near them, Kenehan saw Robert Sand tending to Jackie along with a paramedic.

Skunk Two told his man to give Kenehan back his gun. The man complied.

"Nice piece."

"Thanks," Kenehan said, holstering his Wilson beneath his shirt.

"Let's head down, Tomahawk. People want to talk to you."

Kenehan followed the men down the ramp to the asphalt where the official vehicles were waiting.

Chapter 51

A troupe of military intelligence and law enforcement muckety-mucks debriefed Christie over a three-day period in Jensen's living room in Irvine. Every day, representatives from various planets of the intelligence and law enforcement galaxies took turns squeezing details from her. They'd set a video camera on a tripod, and Christie would sit in her father's favorite chair answering their questions.

Most of the questions related to Beeman: did he talk about the North Koreans? Did he mention a virus, a biological weapon? Did she ever hear the phrase "Black Sunrise?" Did she have the feeling he was working with the men on the boat? Where were they going to take her? Did Beeman seem unhinged?

"What kind of question is that?" she asked. "Of course he was unhinged."

"In what way?"

"Are you kidding me?"

At Brecht's request, they permitted Kenehan and Thomas to observe. They sat with Christie and her father between sessions. To her surprise, the questioning didn't turn to Antonio until the third day.

"The other man. Did you know him? Had you ever seen him before?"

"No."

And that was it. No accusations, no explanations, no questions or remarks about how he had died. At the next break, she asked her father, "Do they know?"

"Know what?" Jensen asked.

She looked in turn at her father, Thomas and Kenehan. She kept her eyes on Roady because she could not look at her father to say what came next.

"I killed that man. I stomped his face in, and he died. I did it on purpose." She thought she saw surprise on Kenehan's face, but only for an instant.

Once the words were out, she looked at her father to gauge his reaction.

"I killed a man myself, getting to you," he said. "It's something we will both have to learn to live with."

Kenehan remained silent.

•   •   •

Christie slept in her childhood bed, with her parents just down the hall, but nightmares plagued her sleep. On the second night, just as she was falling asleep, she awoke with a jolt, her heart racing, sure she heard whispering in her ear.

Dirty girls.

She threw back her covers and prowled the house. She went into the kitchen to make herself some warm milk. As she was tapping on the microwave, her father came in, wearing his robe and slippers.

"Can't sleep?" he asked.

"I'll be okay."

"What are you making?"

"Warm milk," she replied. "Want some?"

"Sure."

They sat at the table together, sipping in silence for a while. Christie stared at her glass.

"Daddy?"

"Yes?"

"I saw you with that gun. You were fighting along with the other man. Bullets were flying everywhere. The dead people—did you and Roady kill them all? I mean other than the one Robert stabbed."

"Robert killed two of them. I killed one. Another member of the team shot some of them as well."

"Why haven't I met him?"

"He died, baby."

"Oh, no." Her eyes filled with tears. "What was his name?"

"Partridge. They called him Sodbuster."

"So many dead people," Christie said, her voice imbued with sadness. "How many were there?"

"Thirteen."

"Thirteen people died on that boat that night? Counting the one I killed?"

"Yes."

"The people you were with when you came on the boat—you hired them? They weren't police?"

"No. They work for a private agency. Mr. Brecht runs it. He's a friend of Granddad's. In fact, Granddad saved his life many years ago, during the Cold War."

"I like Mr. Brecht. He's very nice."

"He likes you too, Christie."

"How could you be so brave, Daddy?"

"Brave?" Jensen gave a grim smile. "No, Christie." He tipped his head, looking into her eyes. "Brave is the one thing I was *not*. I was lucky. If you want to see a really brave man, look at Roady Kenehan. He saved both of our lives."

"What kind of a guy is he?"

Jensen pondered the question. "He's hard to describe."

"Did you spend a lot of time with him?"

"Yes."

"Do you like him?"

"Yes. Very much."

"What does he do when he's not—"

"Rescuing damsels in distress?"

She smiled. "Yes. When he's not rescuing damsels in distress."

"I don't know. All I really know is that he works for Mr. Brecht. He was a soldier in the Army. He's very highly trained."

"He's a professional killer?"

"No, Christie. He's what they call a field operative—sort of a hired investigator with combat training."

"He has really long hair for a soldier."

"He works as a private contractor, sometimes undercover, in disguise. His long hair helps with that."

"He's really fit."

"That he is." Jensen wondered if she'd noticed that whenever Roady gazed at her, he looked like a puppy.

"I'm glad he's sitting in with us. I'll be glad when this debriefing thing is over. I've told them everything I know. And I don't like everything I say being recorded. What are you smiling about, Daddy?"

"Nothing, baby. I'm just glad to have you home."

"It was a hard thing to go through. I think I'm going to be okay, but I'm really worried about Jackie."

• • •

During the next few days, Christie and Robert visited Jackie at the hospital. The first few days with her were dark and difficult. At first, she would not talk about what had happened. Her doctor strictly limited access to her by the officials wanting to question her, warning that it could cause irreparable harm to force her to confront her experiences before she was ready.

Christie and Robert sat with her in her room for hours on end, sometimes taking her on long walks around the hospital grounds. Other times they would just watch television together. A hospital psychiatrist by the name of Dr. White stopped by Jackie's room each day and spent an hour alone with her. The stern-looking woman suggested that Jackie begin a regimen of antidepressants and benzodiazepines. Jackie refused.

One afternoon, Dr. White took Sand and Christie aside and asked them to help, to intervene on her behalf.

"What do you want us to do?" Christie asked.

"Encourage Jackie to cooperate. It's for her own good."

"Let's go talk to her together," Sand said.

The three of them stepped into Jackie's room.

"Honey," Sand said. "Doctor White tells me you don't want to take the pills she's prescribed. Can we talk about that?"

Jackie shrugged. "Sure. Whatever."

"Now, Doctor White here is trying to help you, honey." Sand flashed a brilliant smile at the psychiatrist before continuing. "But don't let yourself get confused about this. No matter what, don't let anybody talk you into taking psych drugs. You've made the right decision, and I want you to know that we're with you on this. We'll work through this together."

Dr. White glared at Sand.

"You'll get better, Jackie. It *will* take time. But these poisons the shrinks hand out will never do you any good. They'll just make you stupid and quiet—prevent you from healing. People will think you're better because you'll have a dreamy look on your face, but your brain will have just that much more crap to deal with."

Dr. White snatched up her clipboard and stomped furiously from the room.

Jackie smiled for the first time.

Over the coming days, with constant support from Christie and Robert, Jackie started to brighten up.

"I want to get out of here," Jackie said one morning as she toyed with one of the flowers Sand had arranged at her bedside. "I want to be with you. Do you still want me?"

Sand's eyes grew moist. "More than ever, baby."

• • •

Janet invited Robert and Jackie to spend some time on Jensen's ranch. There would be space for long hikes and even longer horse-back rides within sight of the beach. "It's the perfect place for minds and hearts to mend," Janet told them.

After a few days, they settled into a comfortable routine. Jackie and Robert spent a lot of time outdoors. At first, Christie spent most of her time with her parents. Janet called a few of Christie's high-school friends, who dropped by to see her. Most of the visits lifted her spirits.

But then, one day, Brad Miller came calling.

He'd been a high-school sweetheart for a few weeks during Christie's junior year, but the relationship ended badly when Brad had asked her to marry him and Christie decided it was time to break it off. The Jensen family called him "The Terminator" because he was impervious to pain and never, ever gave up. For a period of several weeks, he'd called every day after school. Janet's mother would always tell Brad that Christie didn't want to speak to him, but he would call again the next day, refusing to get the message. It had taken a stern warning from Mark Jensen to end the calls.

Now, feeling awkward, Christie met Brad on the front porch.

"Just thought I'd drop by," he said. "I was worried about you."

"I'm fine," she said coolly.

"I heard a little bit about what you went through."

"Well, that's over now."

Brad plucked a weed from between the posts of the porch rail and stuck it in his mouth.

Christie wrinkled her nose. *He thinks he's James Dean.*

"I just thought that maybe you needed some support," he said.

How could she get rid of him? His neediness was like a loathsome disease. A chill ran up her spine as she pictured him growing older. Sporting a mustache. Living in a fantasy world. Kidnapping a woman to take out all the frustration of rejection he had accumulat-ed over the years.

She shuddered, pushing the image from her mind.

"Cold?" he asked, as he moved closer to put his arm around her. Repelled, Christie started to duck under his arm, and he stopped when Janet appeared at the sliding glass door and announced that Christie had another visitor.

Thank God. "Who is it, Mom?" Christie asked cheerfully.

Instead of answering, Janet slid the screen aside, and in a stage whisper clearly meant for Brad's ears, she said, "Go on out. I'm sure she'll be more than a little glad to see you."

Roady Kenehan stepped onto the porch. He held a gift-wrapped box in his hand. He was a foot taller than Brad.

"I'm sorry if I'm interrupting anything," he said. "I can come back later."

She went to his side and put her arm around his narrow waist. "Not a chance," she said. "I thought you'd never come."

Mom, please tell me you gave him the lowdown on Brad.

As if reading her mind, Kenehan gave Brad a look that said, *Why don't you just head on home now?* Christie knew he could crush Brad without a second thought. From the look on the younger man's face, Brad got the message.

Amazing, Christie thought. *Animal magnetism.*

"Guess I'll be leaving," said Brad in a dejected voice.

"Guess so," Janet said. "Thanks for coming by."

Chapter 52

Perched on the railing, Christie smiled at Kenehan. "Thank you for coming to my rescue once more."

"Rescue?"

"From Brad. He practically stalked me during my senior year in high school. He asked me to marry him, and when I said no he dropped out. I haven't seen him in five years. He hasn't changed a bit. One of my friends told him what happened." She shook her head. "I guess he thought I'd be vulnerable now, and he'd have a chance to win me over."

She cringed as she said it. It made her sound conceited.

Kenehan noticed her expression. "I think your mom scared him off. Sounds like a creep."

"I've met worse." She winced again. "Open mouth, insert foot," she said.

Kenehan smiled. "Do I make you nervous?"

"Not at all."

"Why?" he asked.

Did he just ignore her answer? He could read her. "It's like being in a room with a panther," she said.

"Do I bring back bad memories?"

"No. What I meant was ..." She trailed off and just smiled at him. He smiled back. She realized it was the first time she'd seen him do so, and she liked it.

Rescuer or not, he really was a very good-looking guy.

"Aren't you going to open your present?"

Christie grinned and shrugged in surrender, grateful for the distraction. Kenehan handed her the package, wrapped in gold-and-blue paper. There was no bow, but it had a card taped to the top. She opened the card and read aloud.

"Do noble things, not dream them all day long: and make life, death and that vast forever one grand, sweet song." She looked up. "Wow. Believe it or not, that's my favorite saying. It's by Charles Kingsley. Did you know that?"

"As a matter of fact, I did."

She tore away the paper and opened the box inside, pulling out a small porcelain seraph. "My God, it's beautiful," she cooed, turning it in her hand.

"It's your guardian angel," he said softly.

"No ... it's just a symbol. *You* are my guardian angel."

Kenehan shook his head. "It just seems that way."

"My father told me you work for Mr. Brecht."

"I work for the company he started, yes."

"The Brecht Group," she said. "My father says they're more powerful than the CIA and the FBI combined. He said Mr. Brecht felt he owed an old debt to our family."

"Half a century ago, your grandfather saved the Old Man's life."

"How?"

"It's quite a story, but I'll let your father or your grandfather tell it to you."

She set the angel on the table and turned the card in her hands. "It seems you know a lot about my family, Mr. Kenehan."

"Your parents have become close friends of mine."

"I'll say. They think you walk on water."

"I do," Kenehan said with a smile. "Every time it rains. The streets get wet."

"And you're a comedian to boot."

"I just like to see you smile."

She stood and walked over to him. "I'm glad you came. If you want to see me smile," she said, taking his hand, "there's something you have to do for me."

"What's that?"

"Stay for dinner."

"I don't want to intrude," he said.

Jensen slid the screen open and stepped onto the porch. He'd been eavesdropping. "If I have to slash your tires to make sure you stick around, I will." He held a cold can of beer in each hand. He passed one to Kenehan and one to his daughter. "It's a long walk back to the city."

"Then it's settled," Christie said with a twinkle in her eye. She looked at her watch. "We still have some time before dinner. Do you like horses, Mr. Kenehan?"

"If you don't start calling me Roady, I *will* walk home. And yes, I love horses."

"Then save your beer for when we get back. Riding will make you thirsty. Follow me." She skipped down the steps and set out for the corral. They saddled a pair of mares and set out on the trail that led to the ocean.

When they reached the cliff top that overlooked the beach far below, Kenehan stopped his horse, and Christie did the same.

"You never answered the question I asked back at the house," Kenehan said. "Do I bring back memories of the nightmare?"

Christie shook her head with a sigh. "You remind me the nightmare's end."

By the time Roady and the Jensen family sat down for dinner, Christie couldn't take her eyes off Roady. She knew it was probably a clinical infatuation or some kind of post-traumatic fixation with a hero figure—but she didn't care.

• • •

Over dinner, Janet asked Kenehan about his plans for the next few days.

"Well," he answered, "Actually, I have some time off coming, but I haven't decided how I'm going to spend it."

Christie lowered her fork and beamed at him. "Why don't you come with me to Denver?"

Jensen cleared his throat.

"Dad, Jackie and Robert are going home tomorrow. I was planning to go with them. I've got to get back there eventually—to clear out my apartment before school starts. I've got to be in Dartmouth in five weeks. Roady has some time off, so he could come along. Is that okay with you?"

"We still haven't heard whether Roady actually wants to go with you," Janet interjected. Jensen rubbed his face.

Kenehan toyed with his food for a moment, considering the offer. "How would you folks feel about that?" he asked softly.

Jensen met his eyes, giving him an arch look usually reserved for witnesses just before he eviscerated them on cross-examination. "The four of you? I'll have Adkins take you in the Phenom."

Chapter 53

"Jimmy Kim's real name was Jueng Soon-jae," Fitch said. "He was second-in-command of the North Korean contingent in the US. It was a small cell, operating off the ship. The North Korean Ministry of Defense denies it's a state-run operation. The head of the cell died in the gun battle. We've found some papers and other odds and ends, but other than your man's capture of the vial and chip, the intel we've picked up is not great. They were being careful, in case someone seized the ship."

Brecht gazed at the image of Fitch on his monitor. "I doubt they'll ask for the ship's return."

"Agreed. But they want the survivors back."

"The three who were in the engine room during the assault?"

"Yes."

"Have you interrogated them?"

"Before we get to that, Albert, it's time for total truth between us. How much do you already know?"

"We accessed DataHelix's servers; we know about Black Sunrise; we found an email from Beeman to General Harris describing the program, which we assume DPRK hackers also found. Nothing more."

"So you know how bad this can get?"

Brecht nodded. "We know how bad it could have gotten if we hadn't recovered the virus and data chip."

"Albert, at least two vials are still missing."

The words hit Brecht like a fist. In the wake of Kenehan's successful recovery of the material from the North Korean ship, it seemed the mission had been successful. Disaster averted. Brecht's meddling in national security forgiven by the DOD, FBI and NSA. But now the crisis was just beginning.

"What?" Brecht cleared his throat. "How do you know this?"

Nathan Fitch's face darkened on the video monitor. "I found out thirty minutes ago. General Harris called to tell me. USAMRIID cross-checked its physical inventory against original DataHelix paper lab records and found the discrepancy. DataHelix claims it didn't know about the missing vials, which is plausible, in that they didn't do the verification cross-check. Beeman altered the computerized files, but they had already scanned and sent the paper records to Maryland before he smuggled out the samples."

"Are we sure Beeman took the missing vials?"

Fitch shrugged. "He took the others."

"We have to assume—"

"Right." Fitch interrupted. He paused before continuing. "We have a national emergency on our hands." Fitch sat forward and glanced down at something below the field of the camera's view. "The branching domino theory. Release a single vial of the aerosolized virus in a poorly ventilated area and infect a hundred people. Depending upon how many social contacts occur in each chain of contamination, the casualties at the end of phase 3 would be in the order of a million souls."

"Beeman's gift to mankind."

"The missing strain mutates to phase 3 approximately four weeks after exposure of the first-generation carriers. And there is enough in those last two vials to infect *several* hundred people in a large, poorly ventilated area—a church, theater or commercial airliner."

Brecht rubbed his face. "Such destructive power, contained in a tube the size of a pencil stub."

"And Beeman is still out there with *two* of them still in his possession."

"He's completely insane."

"Yes," Fitch acknowledged.

"Am I correct in assuming we have no way of knowing whether he has already released the virus? Whether infected carriers are already spreading it? For all we know, it could be 'marching' as we speak," Brecht said, referring to the phase of genetic mutation during which the virus spreads without causing symptoms.

"There's a test for exposure. The CDC is conducting randomized tests in California and Colorado. Results should start coming in within a day or two, but we doubt they'll be reliable. It's hard to guess whom to test in a heavily populated area."

"Is there a vaccine?"

Fitch sighed. "They developed one, but it's not available in significant quantities. Never tested on humans. It'll take months to produce enough to make a difference, and even if we *could* vaccinate the general population, we'd be foolish to try until we're sure there is a need. If we announce this to the public, we'll have a global panic on our hands. If this gets out, Albert, the sociopolitical result will be cataclysmic, even if *no one* is infected. Markets will crash. War could be inevitable—particularly with North Korea and perhaps even China—and millions would die. Maybe tens of millions, or more."

"We simply have to find Beeman. We could—"

"There's more," Fitch cut in. "Now to the interrogation of the three prisoners. They know Beeman is a scientist who developed a biological weapon. One of them believes he overheard a conversation between Beeman and Jueng in which Beeman said something about planting a timed-release mechanism somewhere as 'insurance,' but that is all he heard."

"Why would Beeman do that?"

"We don't know. There may not even be a reason. Maybe Jueng put him up to it, as the first wave of an attack on America. Or maybe Beeman wanted something to hold over the North Koreans."

"Could Beeman still be headed there?"

"North Korea?" Fitch shook his head. "Doubtful. We believe all of his contacts are dead or in custody. We don't think he has any way to communicate with them. We're sniffing for ELINT from the airwaves, but so far nothing."

"What are we doing with the Kim regime?"

"The State Department is pushing hard on Pyongyang, but as expected, they're denying everything. We're warning them that if they go near him or the virus, we'll retaliate militarily. We raised the DEFCON level this morning, so they know we're serious. The president will be talking to the Young-un this afternoon. The public doesn't know it yet, but right now Beeman is the most wanted man in the world." Fitch sighed, removed his glasses and rubbed the bridge of his nose. "My guess is that Beeman is still in this country."

Brecht spoke softly. "I'm very sorry about this, Nathan."

Nathan surprised Brecht with what he said next. "I'll be candid, Albert—you've earned it. We were more in the dark than I let on. Before you got involved, we didn't know Beeman had already smuggled out the vials and data. We didn't know about the Korean ship. If he'd made it onto that ship without you there ... if you hadn't tracked Beeman, the odds are fair that North Korea would have gotten Beeman *and* the technology. Now there is at least some doubt."

"What would Kim Jong-un do with the virus?"

"His economy is in tatters. His people are starving and on edge of revolt. The alert status of their military is at an all-time high. We keep saying it, but it's true: the Kim regime is beyond desperate. We learned from one of the prisoners that they were on a strict timetable."

"What about Jueng's last words?"

"Our linguistics and crypto people are working on it. We've run the words through our computers in every language. So far, nothing."

Brecht knew that when it came to codes, Fitch had the Brecht Group outdone. The NSA supercomputers were larger than Sierra or Titan and could cross-reference vast volumes of compiled data instantaneously, searching all forms of printed literature, intercepted electronic messages and recorded conversations. If the code-breakers at NSA couldn't solve the riddle, it wasn't solvable. Brecht recited the words: "Crew, ball, nine, virus, smoke."

"Assuming your man's memory is accurate."

"Kenehan and Jensen both agree those were the words."

"We think Kim was trying to tell us about Beeman's device when he died," Fitch said.

"Why would he want us to know about it?"

"Isn't it obvious? To avert war. He knew what will happen if that thing goes off on our soil."

"Have the interrogations given you anything else you can share?"

"We've used potent drugs on the survivors, but North Korean intelligence is highly compartmentalized. We've picked up some good background information, and we'll get more in the months to come, but of the missing vials they have no knowledge. None of them know anything specific about Beeman's so-called insurance policy."

Brecht considered Fitch's words for several seconds before he spoke. "I have to ask: if the feds had mounted the raid, would they have done anything differently?"

Fitch grunted. "Differently? Hell, yes. This isn't what I'll say if I'm subpoenaed to a congressional hearing mind you, but we would have gotten there *after* the ship left the harbor, assuming we even found out about the ship, which is unlikely. Then we probably would have sunk it in deep water—we had a destroyer patrolling nearby, but we wouldn't have tried to board her. Those girls would be dead now."

"Why?"

Fitch's voice took on a note of cynicism. "We wanted to cauterize the situation. Don't forget, at that point we didn't know about the other two vials. You scored intel we wouldn't have gotten on our own. Without your involvement, we'd know nothing about the possibility of an automated release of the virus."

Brecht smiled sadly. "But Beeman would be dead." He was

stunned and flattered by Fitch's concessions, but the news that Beeman was still free with samples of the virus depressed him greatly.
Had the operation gone differently, it would have been the perfect
way to end his career.

But time had run out—this had been his final play.

"What can I do to help?" Brecht asked.

"I've given this information to you as a courtesy, but you've had
your Hail Mary pass. Your official directions are to stay off the case.
We'll handle it from here."

"Very well," said Brecht.

"But if you hear anything ..."

Brecht chuckled softly. "You'll be the first to know."

Chapter 54

"Fantastic," Christie said, closing her eyes. "I'm still high! I think I may be hooked."

Kenehan shut off the engine. "A skydive will do that for you. After my first jump, I felt that way for days. I couldn't wait to get back in the air."

"That's what they mean when they say 'skies call,' isn't it?"

Kenehan smiled. "The shortest skydiving poem: 'Man small, why fall? Skies call, that's all.'"

"Hmmm." Christie nodded. "I get it."

The afternoon was growing late. Kenehan had driven Christie to a small airport outside Longmont, Colorado and arranged for her to make a tandem skydive with him. Some of the staff there knew him. The skydiving world is small and tightly knit. Strapped to an instructor with whom she shared a parachute, she'd experienced her first taste of free fall. Diving out of the airplane a second later, Kenehan had tracked down and gently docked with her, planting a kiss at 120 miles-per-hour, then he'd done a back flip before tracking away to pull his chute.

Being with her made him want to show off.

"Come on," she said, clutching the thumb drive with the video of her skydive. "Let's go inside."

When they reached the elevator, Kenehan hesitated. He hadn't been inside her apartment since before her rescue. He'd searched it while she was missing, but she didn't know that.

"Don't be shy," she said, brushing a lock of blonde hair behind her ear as she smiled at him. "Come on up." They rode the elevator together to the seventh floor.

When they reached her door, Christie scooped up a newspaper. "Looks like I'm finally getting the *Denver Post* again," she said, tucking it under her arm and unlocking the door. "The manager put my subscription on hold. They really piled up while ... while I was gone." She unlocked the door and pushed it open with her foot. "Come on in." She dropped the paper, her keys and the thumb drive on the counter as Kenehan shut the door behind him.

"I feel like some herbal tea. Would you like some?" she asked.

"That would be great."

"Or you could have a beer."

Alcohol right now would be a really, really dumb idea.

"Tea sounds better," he said.

A few minutes later, they were sitting at her kitchen table, sipping from steaming mugs. "Chamomile?" Kenehan asked.

"It has a very relaxing effect."

Kenehan said nothing. He just stared into his cup.

"Anything wrong?" she asked. "You seem preoccupied."

Kenehan shook his head. "Sorry."

"Wondering if you should be here? In my apartment?"

"Yes."

"Well, don't worry about it. You're not breaking any laws."

Kenehan struggled to find the words that would help her understand his hesitation. "It's just that—"

"I know. You're wondering if you should maintain your professional detachment."

He grinned. "Not quite. I gave up on that idea a long time ago."

"Then what is it?"

"I'm just thinking. I shouldn't—"

She leaned across, reached behind his head and untied the leather strip that bound his long hair. "That's right. You shouldn't be thinking. So stop doing it. It's bad for your brain." She kissed him slowly and lightly on the mouth; then, cupping the back of his head with her palm, she pulled him closer and kissed him much harder. Her lips parted.

Kenehan's mind was reeling. His body felt like overcooked pasta—except in one place, where he was moving more toward *al dente*.

Eventually she pulled away—only long enough to utter four breathless words. "Take me to bed."

A great writer once said that some things demand to be done.

• • •

"Now, tell me what you were thinking so hard about," Christie said with an impish grin, her head propped on her elbow.

Kenehan brushed his fingertips along the curve of her hip, savoring the smooth vibrancy of her skin. "You were right—I *was* thinking too much."

She said, "I understand. You have a code."

He just looked at her, saying nothing.

"You're a warrior. You've killed people, and you'll do it again. You have to live with what you've done, with who you are. So you rely upon your moral compass to keep you from getting lost. Your professionalism. It's what keeps you sane. It's your anchor."

"Your dad tell you that?"

She shook her head. "It's obvious," she said. "But sometimes it can hold you back."

"What do you mean?"

"I know you want to be with me," she explained, "But you're afraid to be with me."

"Oh, I see."

"It's because you think you're taking advantage of some unfair psychological leverage. I've been through a nightmare; my life was at risk—and you saved me. So you know that makes me vulnerable, and you don't want to exploit that. Like a doctor whose ethics prevent him from sleeping with his patients."

"Am I that transparent?"

"To me you are."

"So what do we do about it?"

"Acknowledge it and move past it," she said. "So we don't miss out on something special."

"How do I know that's in your best interest?"

"You would rather I be with someone who would never worry about what's in my best interest?"

Kenehan rolled onto his back and closed his eyes. "That's part of the syndrome," he said. "The identification of a rescuer as an ultimate benefactor, a spiritual ally, a soul mate that fate delivered. Only it's just an emotional reaction."

"The Old Man teach you that?" she asked.

"Touché."

"Let me ask you something—something serious."

He rolled back onto his side, facing her again. "Go ahead."

"When did *I* start having an unfair psychological advantage over *you*?"

Kenehan laughed. Being with Christie made him feel like a man who had been trekking across an endless burning desert with a hundred pounds of gear, who finally found an oasis—green, verdant and cool, with water and shade. He'd been alone for so long he'd forgotten what this kind of experience was like. It wasn't just the fact he'd had sex for the first time in over two years. He hadn't felt this way for as long as he could remember.

"Well?" Christie persisted.

"It'll sound silly," he said.

"Try me."

"When I first saw your picture. My first day on the case."

Christie sat up in the bed. "What?"

"We saw head shots of you and Jackie in our first briefing."

"And you didn't fall for Jax?" Christie asked. "Usually she's the one who—"

"No. It was *you*. The minute I saw your photo. I knew that no matter what it took, we had to get you back safely."

"And *now* you're suddenly worried about moving too fast?"

"A little."

She pointed to a scar on his shoulder. "What's that from?" she asked.

"I was in the Army. Got shot."

"Did it hurt?"

"Not at the time," he replied, "but afterward."

"Was that the first time?"

"No," he said. "It was the second time."

"Where was the first?"

"Afghanistan."

"I mean where on your body?" She pulled down the sheet.

Kenehan pointed to a star-shaped scar on his side.

"Any others?"

"No."

"And the men who shot you?"

"Let's talk about something else."

Christie shook her head. "Roady, you know I killed Antonio Pessoa."

"I'm sorry that had to happen," he said.

"But that's just it," Christie pressed. "You understand. It *had* to happen."

"I do," he said.

"So, I'm like you—and you're like me. We're both killers now. You're just more experienced and better at it."

Kenehan stared into her eyes. He rolled onto his back again and pulled her on top of him. She straddled him eagerly.

He couldn't remember ever feeling so alive and so lost at the same time.

I'm out of control.

Much later, when Christie was staring at the ceiling, Roady said, "Now you're the one who looks preoccupied."

"I was trying to solve the riddle."

"You mean the man on the boat? His last words?"

"Yeah," she said. "I'll never forget them. It's very important, isn't it?"

"A lot of lives could be at stake."

"What do they think it means? The NSA, the FBI, your people?"

"They don't know."

"I thought they knew everything."

• • •

The sun was setting. Kenehan had fallen asleep. Christie lay beside him in her darkening room, marveling at the sinuous, sculpted form of his body, spoiled only by the smattering of scars on his arms and torso. There were signs of more injuries than just the two bullet wounds. He'd been cut, possibly hit by shrapnel, and it looked like he'd been burned in a few spots. She wondered what stories lurked behind each of the scars on his beautiful body, idly stroking the scar on her own forearm from Beeman's hunting knife.

Making love had made her thirsty. As quietly as she could, she slipped from the bed and pulled her robe from the closet.

Kenehan stirred.

"Sorry," she said, snugging the robe around her. "Did I wake you?"

"I've got an idea," he said.

"What's that?"

"Let me take you out for dinner. Somewhere nice."

"I like that idea," she said.

"Can I use your shower?"

"I'd rather you did."

When she heard the water start, she opened the paper, realizing it was the first time she'd seen one in more than a month. After the

390   B R E T T   G O D F R E Y

raid on the boat, she and Jackie had been in the papers for a while, but she'd avoided reading those articles.

When she did read the paper, Christie preferred to read the society pages. Her eyes scanned the columns, taking comfort in non-threatening prattle about charity events, style, fashion, theater, music and food. It was mindless stuff, but it was comforting to take refuge in an imaginary world that was safe, where the biggest issues resolved around what kind of designer evening gown the mayor's wife was wearing.

She spotted an article about a gala ball that would take place that night in Denver—apparently one of the city's most noteworthy social events.

It had an odd name, a Cajun title in honor of the fact that alumni of Louisiana State University were hosting the event. It was a fundraiser, a masquerade ball. Something nagged at her as she read, so she returned to the top. What was the name of the event?

When she found it, her hands trembled.

She read the article again. One particular paragraph caught her attention:

> The Krewe De Colorado annual fundraiser for the Denver Children's Home raises nearly $500,000 each year for this worthy organization. Auction prizes include a sunset champagne flight over the Rockies, box tickets to the Avalanche playoffs and other exciting items. Bidding ends with the announcement of winners at 9:00 p.m., but the ball runs till midnight with a live Cajun band and refreshments.

Christie grabbed a pencil from her nightstand and circled three items:

Krewe. Ball and *9:00 p.m.*

The only words that were missing were *virus* and *smoke*.

But she wouldn't expect to see those words here.

Krewe—ball—nine—virus—smoke. If there's even a chance I'm right ... Oh, my God, we've got to do something!

She glanced at the clock by her bed, a shock-flash ran through her when she saw how late it was. Nearly eight. The ball had started hours ago. Clutching the paper, she ran into the bathroom, where Kenehan was drying off with a towel.

Chapter 55

"No time to argue," Christie warned.

"I said go back inside!" Kenehan said sternly, holding the door of the elevator open for her to step out.

"And I said there's no time to argue," she insisted, swatting his hand away from the door so that it could close. "Now let's get moving." She pressed the button for the lobby.

Kenehan shook his head as the elevator started down.

"This could be dangerous. You're waiting in the car."

"Lives are at stake. You need my help."

They sprinted through the lobby to the parking lot.

"Take my car. It's closer," Christie said, pointing to a small black Mercedes coupe her father had given her. "And it's faster than your rental." She handed him the key fob. "You drive."

• • •

Weaving in and out of traffic, the compact Mercedes blasted up Speer Boulevard. Steering with one hand, Kenehan pulled out his cell phone and handed it to her.

"Dial a number for me."

Christie released her death grip on the door handle. "Car's got a built-in speakerphone," she said. "Give me the number."

Kenehan recited the digits, and Christie punched them into a keypad on the console.

"David Thomas," answered the metallic voice on the first ring.

"Greyhound, Tomahawk. Non-secure comm," Kenehan said. "We've got a Code One."

"Sitrep?"

Kenehan lowered his voice. "Thumper cracked the code. Masquerade ball in downtown Denver. Ball as in dance. Called the Krewe De Colorado something. K-R-E-W-E. Charity fundraiser. Big prize auction at nine tonight. Large indoor crowd. She's here with me in the car. We're headed there now. ETA five minutes. She'll give you're the address."

Christie turned on the dome light and fumbled with the crumpled article she'd torn from the paper. "It's at the Denver Center for the Performing Arts, in the Seawell Grand Ballroom. I've been there before. I know exactly where it is." She recited the address loudly enough to be audible over the tortured squeal of tires. Kenehan expertly snapped the wheel, swerving between two slow-moving cars, stabbing the brakes briefly; then he gunned the turbocharged engine, shooting down the median at ninety miles per hour.

"K-R-E-W-E ... crew?" The voice came over the speaker. "Are you sure it's pronounced that way?" Thomas asked, a note of urgency in his voice.

"It's Cajun," Christie said. "LSU alumni run it. There'll be hundreds of people there." She reiterated what Kenehan had said in more detail. "They have an auction to raise money for charity. They announce the winners at nine sharp, with everyone gathered in one place. Perfect for spreading the virus to a large number of people in a confined space. Krewe. Ball. Nine. As in nine p.m. Oh, fuck!"

"Krewe, ball, nine, virus, smoke," Kenehan shouted. "If she's right —and the thing's set to release at nine o'clock, we've got only twenty minutes or so to get there and find it."

"Tomahawk, stand down. Do not enter that building. We'll send a hazmat team to evacuate. They'll find it if it's there. This thing could kill you both."

"No time, no choice," Kenehan barked. "Almost there. Seconds could make the difference. *Smoke* and *virus*, Dave. This could be the end of the world." Kenehan hit the brakes again, grateful for the car's nimble handling.

Red lights flashed behind them. A police cruiser was trying to pull them over.

"Look for a smoke machine. You said this was a ball?" Thomas asked.

"A costume ball," Christie chimed in. "Maybe they have a smoke-effect generator set up."

"You're going to have to move fast. If you haven't found it by eight-fifty-five, I want your asses out of there."

The police car behind them turned on its siren.

"Try to get the cops off my ass," Kenehan said, flooring the accelerator as he rounded a corner. "We'll call you when we have a chance."

"It's right there," Christie pointed. "Stop over by that pole, and we'll run the rest of the way."

"Put your hands on the dash," Kenehan ordered.

She did as he told her. "Why?"

"When we stop, the cops are going to be on top of us. I don't want them getting edgy and doing something stupid. If we run from the car, they might fire on us. I have to deal with them fast." He brought the car to a stop along the side of the boulevard, stabbed the button to lower his window and placed his hands back on the wheel where they would be in plain sight.

Within seconds, a uniformed officer approached the car with his automatic in one hand and a flashlight in the other.

"Sir, step out of the car."

"Yes, officer. I'm stepping out now."

The light shone in his eyes. The officer didn't ask for Kenehan's license. "Turn around and place your hands on the roof of the car."

"Yes, sir."

Kenehan turned and put his hands on the car, spreading his feet as he knew the cop would demand. "Check my identification, officer. Back pocket, right side. CIA. Matter of national security. Literally life and death, sir. Seconds matter. Let us go, and come with us."

"First things first," said the cop, keeping his distance and raising his gun slightly. "Reach slowly into your pocket and pull it out for me."

Kenehan stood upright and withdrew his wallet. There was no CIA identification card, but he had to put the officer at ease by degrees so he could get closer to the man. They were wasting valuable seconds. He pulled out his driver's license and held it out for the officer, who holstered his weapon to take the card.

As the officer reached out to take his license, Kenehan grabbed his wrist, yanking him forward with sudden force, then stopping the man's momentum with the back of his opposite arm across the officer's throat, pulling him to the side, tripping him with his leg. *Pencak silat*—an Indonesian martial art. In a single smooth motion, he drove the officer to the ground. Kenehan landed with a knee in the man's chest and one hand at his throat, tripping the retention lever on the holster and pulling his gun free.

"Now listen to me," Kenehan said. "More lives are at stake than you can count. We're going up to the Seawell Ballroom to try to find a biological weapon. Hazmat teams are on their way. Get back into your car and call for backup."

Keeping the man's pistol trained on the downed officer, Kenehan scanned behind him for his partner, but saw no one. The officer patrolled solo. Kenehan picked up his license and flicked it onto his chest. "There's my license. Have your dispatcher call your SWAT team leader and ask for a level 4 biological containment team. Give them my name and tell them where we are going. The main ballroom. Seawell, it's called. You got that?"

The cop nodded as Kenehan rose to his feet.

"Then get in your car and stay there. If you try to slow us down, I'll shoot you dead. Make your call now. Understand?"

The cop nodded again, climbing to his feet as well.

Kenehan picked up the officer's flashlight. "I'll give you back your gun and light later. Now get moving."

As the officer headed back to his patrol car, Kenehan ran up the flights of concrete steps to the entrance of the main ballroom.

Only when he reached the door did he realize Christie was still with him.

The dance floor of the massive Seawell Ballroom was awash with color. Tuxedos and gowns capped with garish masks and feathers gyrated to the sound of live jazz. A ten-foot-tall clown teetered above the crowd on stilts, his conical wizard's hat nearly scraping the ceiling. Upon the stage at the far end of the capacious hall, a jazz band played loudly, and a woman sang in low, smoky notes.

Christie darted ahead of Kenehan, pushing through the crowd toward the stage. She stepped up onto the platform, waving her arms and shouting something lost in the din. No one seemed to take notice of her until she snatched the singer's microphone from her hand. As if someone had pulled a plug, the band stopped playing.

"Ladies and gentlemen!" Christie shouted into the microphone, "I must have your attention." The din of the crowd diminished quickly. "Please! I have something very important to tell you!"

After several seconds, the buzz of the crowd faded and went silent.

"Thank you," she said, softening her voice. "I'm very sorry for the inconvenience, but we've had a small fire in the kitchen. We've extinguished the fire. You're perfectly safe, but we really need you to make an orderly exit from the building as quickly as possible. Please remain calm but leave the building immediately. Police will be waiting for you outside with further instructions."

As he slipped the police officer's automatic into his waistband under his shirt, Kenehan admired Christie's presence of mind. Without causing a panic, she'd infused the crowd with sufficient reason to clear the room. People herded toward the doors at the opposite end of the ballroom.

"Thank you for your cooperation, ladies and gentlemen. Please don't worry about your belongings. It's a beautiful night outside. This should only take a few minutes—then we'll have you all back in. It's important to let the fire department confirm the building is safe, so please get moving now."

As Christie droned into the microphone, encouraging the crowd's rapid exit, Kenehan scanned the ceiling.

His heart sank when he saw the intricate rolls of molding impregnated with thousands of tiny built-in lights and dozens of recessed panels for larger spotlights. The intricate array of lights and fixtures merged into a visually complicated inverted landscape.

And then he saw it.

A smoke detector lay at an odd angle along one of the undulating rolls of paneling that formed the ceiling. He craned his neck to look for others like it, but there were none. Normally no one would notice it, but if you were looking for something irregular, it stood out like a sore thumb, as though someone had slapped it onto the ceiling as an afterthought.

Virus. Smoke.

An idea struck Kenehan.

"You there," Kenehan called out at the top of his lungs. The clown "giant" was preparing to climb down from his stilts, having rolled his freakishly long pantlegs up to his human knees, revealing the metal of the stilts. Kenehan waved his arms.

"Yes, you. On the stilts. Over here. I need you to help me."

The clown shook his head. "I've got to get out of here."

"No—it's alright. I'm with the fire department. I need you to pull down this smoke detector for me. It may have been a false alarm. We need to check this thing out."

With a shrug of his shoulders, the man lumbered to the center of the room, looming over Kenehan, who pointed at the smoke detector. The clown reached up, but he could not quite grasp it, even on stilts. His hand fell a foot short by mere inches.

Kenehan pulled two chairs together. "Can you step up if I hold them?"

The clown looked down and nodded with a demonic smile, the paint on his face making him look like an apparition from hell.

He stepped up, first onto one chair, then the other. As his hand closed around the smoke detector and he began to pull it free, he lost his balance and teetered backward. Kenehan reached for one of the stilts to hold him upright, but it was too late. The clown toppled backward. Like a tall pine felled by a lumberjack, he swayed farther and farther away from the base that held him aloft before crashing down with a terrible crunch onto a table, accompanied by the sound of shattering glass and splintering wood.

The smoke detector fell from his hand and rolled across the floor, coming to a stop under another table. On his hands and knees, Kenehan crawled to it. He saw a red light blinking on the base. It was odd that the light was on the underside—on a normal smoke detector, the light would be on the outer shell so it could visibly confirm the unit was operating. As he watched, the speed of the blinking increased.

So did his pulse.

He looked at his watch. Four minutes until nine.

He crawled out from under the table and stood beneath a halogen spotlight. The plastic of the casing looked melted around the edges of the small red light, as if someone had poked the hole with a soldering iron. There was no label on the unit. Double-stick foam pads on the base had fastened it to the ceiling. No wires emerged from it to connect it to anything else. There was no way anyone would use a battery-operated smoke detector in a commercial facility such as this.

He knew for sure he had found Beeman's device. On the top of the unit, vents in the plastic that would normally allow air to flow into the machine for testing would spew aerosol when the device triggered.

One-way tamperproof screws held the unit together. He thought of smashing the case to get to the circuitry inside. But he realized he might break the container within and cause the release of the virus, particularly if it were in a glass vial like the one Beeman had given to the North Koreans.

It may have already detonated.

Christie appeared at his side. In her hands, she held a carton of plastic trash bags. "Found these in the kitchen." She started yanking bag after bag from the box.

Kenehan slipped the smoke detector into a bag. He twisted the top and then put it into another bag, twisting that closed as well. Christie continued feeding him trash bags. He stuffed the growing blob of plastic into one after another, working frantically until two men in white environmental suits appeared at his side.

By now his package looked like a giant black beach ball.

He handed it to one of the spacesuit-clad men; then he took Christie by the arm, and they ran out of the building.

When he next looked at his watch, it was 9:03.

•   •   •

More men in hazmat suits guided Kenehan to a large silver-panel truck with the words "Mobile Isolation Unit" stenciled on the side.

He climbed in, taking a seat on a bench next to Christie. He put his arm around her. The injured clown lay on the bench on the opposite side of the space. He looked up in pain.

The men slammed the door shut, and the truck pulled away.

Chapter 56

Deep within the DataHelix facility several stories below ground, Jensen paced the hallway outside Lab 7. The harsh neon light made his grave features resemble an Inca carving. Janet glanced up at him as he strode past, too distraught to speak.

His mind was whirling. He could not accept the notion that after all that had passed, he might *still* lose his daughter to that bastard Arthur Beeman.

He imagined what Christie would go through if she tested positive for exposure to the Black Sunrise virus. They would quarantine her; she'd endure a six-week nightmare, waiting for a horrible death unless the experimental vaccine proved effective.

They had never tested it on human subjects.

The door to the lab opened. An elderly woman emerged wearing a white lab coat. Jensen stopped in his tracks and glared at her, waiting for her to speak.

"Hello, I'm doctor Tanya Murphy. Please, come in," she said.

Mark and Janet stepped into what appeared to be an anteroom. A large laboratory filled with gleaming steel equipment loomed beyond a glass wall at the opposite end of the massive room. The unpleasant neon glare enhanced the sterile, artificial sense of unreality that crept into Jensen's pores.

"The virus hasn't infected them," Dr. Murphy said without preamble.

Jensen's legs nearly buckled out from under him. So powerful was his sense of relief, it nearly brought him to his knees. Reaching out, he put his palm against the glass wall to steady himself. Janet came to his side. He took her in his arms for a moment, kissing her forehead.

The scientist gestured for Mark and Janet to sit at a workbench. They did so. Before seating herself, she removed her glasses, folded them and slipped them into a pocket of her lab coat.

Jensen cleared his throat. "And the smoke detector?"

A frown crossed Dr. Murphy's face. "Your daughter's insight is commendable," she said. "That device was *not* a smoke detector. It contained a vial of the Black Sunrise virus, with a solenoid-powered steel chisel to break the vial open and a fan connected to a digital timer. The vial was broken. The timing mechanism triggered at exactly 9:00 p.m. A CO_2 cartridge released, jetting the virus outward through the vents in the casing."

"And?" Janet prodded.

"We've analyzed the disposal bags. Not surprisingly, the inner plastic bag was contaminated." She stopped and sighed. "None of the outer twenty-nine bags were. The blood tests for everyone we've tested, including your daughter and her friend, came back clear." With a shrug, she added, "They were very lucky."

"We *all* were," Janet corrected.

The woman nodded sincerely. "That's true."

"When can we see her?" Jensen asked softly.

"Follow me." She guided them into the inner laboratory. Christie and Roady stood behind yet another glass wall. Christie had crossed her arms in front of her chest. A sad smile crossed her face when she saw him. Her brows rose, as if to acknowledge that bad news might be coming.

Jensen locked eyes with her and stabbed both thumbs into the air.

She dropped her arms, and her shoulders sagged with relief.

Kenehan mouthed the words "thank you" and embraced Christie tenderly from behind.

"Use the intercom, here," the woman said, pointing to a panel mounted in the glass.

Jensen pushed the button. "Christie? Can you hear me?"

"Yes, Daddy," the speaker clearly projected her voice.

"You saved a million lives tonight, Kissy," Jensen couldn't resist using his daughter's early childhood nickname, which arose from her earliest efforts to say her name. "From now on, whenever you look up at the night sky, I want you to think of each star you see as a person who is still alive because of you. Your mother and I are so proud." Jensen locked eyes with Kenehan. "Of both of you."

"Thank God this woman knows her way around a kitchen," Kenehan said.

Christie smiled. "And Daddy? Don't give me any more crap about reading the society pages."

• • •

"You think she knew all along?" Nathan Fitch asked.

"No," Brecht replied, shaking his head. "She would have said so earlier."

"Remarkable," Fitch mused. "She's what? Twenty-four? And she solved a code that had stymied the NSA."

"You've made up for that," Brecht said. "You found the last vial." Brecht was referring to the fact that the NSA had pieced together disparate fragments of physical evidence and electronic intelligence to discover Beeman's purchase of a plane ticket using a credit card he'd acquired under a false name.

"We're about to alert the FBI. They'll be waiting for Beeman when he comes for the last vial. We know what flight he'll be on, and we know when and where he'll show up. We'll have them there in time."

"So you folks are good for something after all."

Fitch looked down for a moment before speaking.

"Albert," he said at last, shaking his head slightly, "Once again, we owe you. But we can't allow this to go public. Even among our own intelligence agencies and the upper echelons of government, the details of Beeman's virus and North Korean spying, its invasion plans —and the rest of it—must never get out. The risk is too high—if these matters were to go public, the world outcry and political fallout would be globally destabilizing, damaging American interests at home and abroad." By "the rest of it," Fitch was alluding to the fact that they'd fed the press a story about the rescue raid on the Korean ship. It described Christie Jensen and Jackie Dawson as human-trafficking victims and the Asians on the boat as members of a South Korean organized crime syndicate.

"Your secrets are always safe with us, Nathan. But you're right— you do owe me. And that debt is about to grow."

"Oh, really?" Fitch raised his eyebrows. "Do tell, Albert."

"Nathan, you can't take Beeman into official custody. A trial would have to be public, and even if it were not, the media would eventually catch wind of it. Too many details are in the open; a persistent investigative reporter would piece them together. On the other hand, the legal consequences of his arrest on US soil would prevent imprisonment without a trial. Beeman is a US citizen. The government can't keep him indefinitely under the law of *habeas corpus.* He doesn't meet the legal definition of an enemy combatant. The military can't intervene under *posse comitatus.* The US simply can't risk skirting those laws in the aftermath of this situation. The public outcry for truthful disclosure would be like a tsunami. If you take Beeman in, the entire story *will* get out, and as you so aptly put it, the upset across the globe would have repercussions that would last for decades. The political pressure on the president would be just the beginning—it *could* spark a war with North Korea. That would draw the Chinese in, and everything will spin out of control from there. When Beeman goes for that last vial, the FBI *won't* be there and *won't* take him into custody." Brecht looked directly into the camera. "No one will be there."

Fitch's mouth slowly broke into a grim smile. "No one?"

"Nathan, Robert Sand once observed that you only see what you choose to see. Prove him right. Beeman will be permanently retired."

"No due process of law?"

"Nope." Brecht shook his head. "No process. Just due."

Chapter 57

Beeman gestured to the cab driver. "Pull into the parking lot of that motel. I'll be going across the street. I need you to wait for me right here. I won't be more than fifteen minutes."

The driver nodded as Beeman stepped from the cab. He'd promised a $300 tip on top of the fare for a round trip from the airport to his uncle's gas station and back. As he strolled across the two-lane highway, he spotted a sign hanging in the window: OPEN.

Though he'd never said it to the man, Beeman detested his uncle. Calvin Dougherty was his late mother's brother—a pompous Baptist zealot from Oklahoma City. After Beeman's mother was gone, Calvin had paid off Beeman's student loans and offered him affection—which meant nothing to Beeman. Calvin had also tried to control Beeman's career choices and infect him with the mental madness he'd called "Salvation by the Grace of Our Lord Jesus Christ."

Disgusting.

But Beeman had acted the role of the doting nephew for a time, as he knew Calvin had wanted, to perpetuate the façade. After all, he'd needed the money, and in those days direct confrontation hadn't been Beeman's style. He'd always preferred to do things in more indirect ways, setting forces in motion to bring about the results he desired.

A bell jingled over the door as Beeman pushed it open and stepped inside, expecting to find his uncle at the counter behind the cash register.

"Hello?" Beeman called out. "Anybody here? Calvin?"

Silence.

Beeman stepped outside and strolled around behind the station to find the garage door closed with no one there.

He went back inside and stepped behind the counter. The door to Calvin's office was open, but the room was deserted. Beeman looked through the papers on his desk, finding nothing but receipts and bills and a copy of an old magazine called *Your Daily Guide to Miracles*, published by the Oral Roberts Ministries. The magazine was open to a page with a Bible passage circled many times in red pen. Smirking, Beeman read the verse:

> *And in those days men will seek death and will not find it; they will long to die, and death shall fly from them.*

> —REVELATION 9:6

Beeman stared at the words for a long time. It seemed prophetic that this passage should appear before him now, as if Calvin knew of his frustration in the wake of recent failures. But, of course, it was mere coincidence. His failure tainted his perception of everything.

His dummy smoke detector had failed to release the virus; Kim must have revealed the location of the device before he died.

Antonio was dead; the girls were safe. He was a wanted man, dogged by the full force and might of the federal government and cooperating state agencies. He would lose his home, his work and the life he'd lived. All he had left was a bit of money, his encyclopedic scientific knowledge and—in a matter of a few more minutes—one vial of the deadliest biological weapon the world had ever known.

He pushed the desk forward several feet, moving it away from the hidden trapdoor that concealed a floor safe Calvin didn't even know was there. He dialed the combination from memory. The tumblers clicked, and he turned the handle, pulling the circular door upward, expecting to see the sealed polymer case containing his last vial of Black Sunrise and an envelope containing several thousand dollars in cash along with a fresh credit card.

When he bent over and looked into the safe, his blood ran cold.

The safe was empty.

Had Calvin found it and removed the contents? Not possible. Calvin could never open this safe without damaging it. Beeman tipped the door back to look carefully at the outer surface. There were no scratches or evidence of an attempt to force the safe door open.

He searched the office, looking in the drawers of Calvin's desk, on shelves, in a metal file cabinet, and in the medicine cabinet of Calvin's private bathroom. He found nothing of value.

Where was Calvin?

The front door had been unlocked. No one had turned the sign on the door to show the station was closed. Yet the garage door had remained closed; it was Calvin's habit to keep it up whenever the station was open for business.

Something was definitely very wrong.

Beeman knew he had to get out—immediately.

He stepped quickly out of the office and around the counter toward the door, stopping in his tracks when he gazed out through the glass window toward the motel across the street.

His taxi was gone. He hadn't paid the driver.

He thought of calling for another, but his instincts told him to get away on foot and out of sight as quickly as possible.

On the other hand, the sooner he had transportation, the faster he could put distance between himself and this place. Willing himself to be calm, he went back into Calvin's office and picked up the telephone.

It did not surprise him that the line was dead.

There was nothing left for him to do now but run—on foot.

He had the sudden, powerful sense that someone was watching him. He set the receiver on the desk and turned slowly to face the doorway. No one was there. He called out, yet no one replied.

He decided to walk back to town. If he were lucky, someone would give him a ride. After all, he didn't look dangerous—more like the professor he was.

He bent down to close the safe door.

As he did so, he felt something hard pressing into the back of his head.

He knew it was a pistol.

Beeman waited for his life to end, but it did not. Without turning, he asked his unseen assailant, "What do you want?" The steadiness of his own voice pleased him.

"I don't want anything."

Beeman recognized the voice. It was the long-haired man who had taken him from his home. The man who called himself Tomahawk.

"I honored our agreement," Beeman said. "You rescued the women."

"I know."

"So what's the problem?"

"There is no problem."

The deadly calm in the man's voice caused Beeman's pulse to escalate once again. He should have listened to his instincts and ran. If he'd sprinted suddenly from the building, he might have had a chance to get away.

"Do you intend to shoot me?" Beeman realized that if they found his body over an open safe door, they would likely write off the circumstances of his murder as an everyday armed robbery.

Would he enter eternal oblivion as nothing more than a crime statistic? How tawdry.

"Do you want to die?"

Beeman grunted. "No one will ever erase my existence."

"What makes you think that?"

"My work will continue."

"You mean your virus?"

"Yes. My virus will continue. It is a new life-form. I created it. And I will create others."

"I have some bad news for you."

Beeman sighed. He turned around to face Kenehan and took two steps backward.

"Yesterday the president signed an executive order directing the destruction of all existing specimens of the Black Sunrise virus, obliterating it from the face of the earth along with all records of its genetic structure and how to produce it."

Beeman shook his head slowly. "Did it occur to you that perhaps there are samples of live virus unaccounted for?"

"The smoke detector."

"You found that too, didn't you?"

The man gazed at him with those beautiful shark-death eyes.

"Kim told you where it was?" Beeman probed.

Kenehan chuckled. "Christie Jensen figured it out while reading a newspaper."

"I'm not surprised. She's a very unusual specimen."

"That she is," Kenehan said. "We found it about two minutes before it released your stuff."

"How were you able to contain it?"

Kenehan smiled. "Contrary to environmentalist claims, mankind's destiny was to find salvation in plastic garbage bags."

Beeman settled into the chair at Calvin's desk and then rocked back and put his feet up. The barrel of Kenehan's automatic tracked his movements.

Beeman closed his eyes. "Life is death is life," he intoned.

"Dr. Beeman, you've got the equation wrong," Kenehan corrected him. "Life is life. And death is death."

Those were the last words Beeman would ever hear.

He didn't even hear the sound of the pistol's sharp report; the portion of his brain responsible for processing sound sprayed across the wall behind him just as the sound waves reached his eardrums.

•   •   •

Kenehan pulled out of the parking lot of the gas station with the cell phone at his ear. "Have Jennifer call the sheriff now." He slipped the phone back into his pocket and checked his watch.

With any luck, he could reach Eloy before sunset.

Epilogue

So light was her grandfather, it barely took any effort for Christie to push his wheelchair. The old man sat up a little straighter as she rounded her way through the open doorway and onto the veranda of the nursing home. A canopy of palms overhead provided shade, and the afternoon was growing pleasantly cooler.

Albert Brecht sat at a wooden picnic table, dressed as always in a dark suit and striped tie.

The two old men gazed at each other in silence. Christie straightened the blanket on her grandfather's lap. "I tried to tell him what happened. I think he understands, but he comes and goes. If you need me, I'll be inside."

She left them alone.

"Conrad?" Brecht said tenderly, leaning forward on the bench. "Do you recognize me?"

The old man gave no reply but simply stared at him. Brecht wasn't sure his old friend could even see him, let alone recognize him. Too many years had passed.

The soft breeze played havoc with the unruly clouds of each man's fine white hair.

Brecht sighed. "They told me you might not remember, old friend."

Still the old man in the wheelchair said nothing.

Brecht sat quietly for a long while, feeling the weight of all of his years. At least he'd paid the debt—but it would have been sublime for Conrad to share the victory with Albert.

After a long while, Christie stepped back onto the veranda.

"How's it going?" she asked.

Brecht shook his head slowly.

"I'm so sorry," Christie said sadly. "You never know. Sometimes he comes out of it. I have my own car, so I'll head home now. Stay as long as you want. Let the nurse know when you're ready to leave, and she'll take Granddad back to his room." Christie kissed her grandfather on the forehead and then gave Brecht a quick hug and left.

Brecht reached into his pocket and withdrew two small objects. They were heavy in his twisted, age-spotted hand.

He gazed into the infinity of time, his mind lost in the past.

His life had been a good one.

He looked at the small pieces of lead, and sighed.

"Oh, well," he said, starting to rise.

The man in the wheelchair stirred.

"Is that what I think it is, Albert?" Dr. Conrad Jensen asked, his voice barely audible. "Are those the bullets from my brain and spleen? You kept them all this time?"

Brecht settled back onto the bench. Conrad was making eye contact now, and Brecht was gratified to see a flash of humor in his eyes. "Yes, Conrad. The bullets."

The ancient physician nodded, closing his parchment eyelids for a few seconds. "That was quite a night," he murmured. "Sometimes I remember it more clearly than what happened an hour ago. I'm getting old, you see." He opened his eyes and gazed at Brecht. "But then, you're no kid yourself."

"Conrad. You gave me a life, at the risk of your own."

"And it's weighed on you since that night. I've always known. But it shouldn't have, Albert. It was my privilege to serve. I was just a doctor. It was an *adventure*."

Brecht said nothing. The silence hung between the two old men the way a comfortable old robe hangs on its owner.

"Albert," Conrad Jensen said at last. "I know what you did."

"You do?"

"My son told me."

Brecht's steel eyes misted over.

"Those bullets are your debt, Albert."

The breeze caressed both men lovingly.

"Give them back to me now."

Brecht placed the deformed slugs into Conrad's palm, closing his equally deformed fingers around it.

"Thank you, my friend," Conrad whispered. "Go with God."

• • •

They found Brecht the next morning, slumped over the wheel of his car in the parking lot outside Conrad Jensen's nursing home.

His aging heart had finally given out.

They flew his body to Arlington National Cemetery. The president gave his eulogy. Two past presidents attended, as did the prime minister of Israel, the king of Jordan, the British prime minister and the past or present leaders of eleven other countries.

A few members of the FBI domestic counterterror operations unit known as the Skunk Team were also present.

Nathan Fitch sat without expression as the guns went off and the bugle played.

The Jensen family cried—even Mark.

Kenehan put his arm around Christie and pulled her close as she wept, glad that she could not see his own tears.

Jackie stared at the ground.

Robert Sand bowed his head and whispered, "Say hello to the Baron for me, old warrior. And keep a place for me."

• • •

When Brecht had climbed into his car, he'd been consciously aware of the moment his heart stopped beating. In his last seconds, knowing that the end had finally arrived, he'd given silent thanks. This was how he'd always wanted to go—with dignity, in triumph, his debt repaid.

The final sounds to echo through his mind were, strangely enough, those of Mark Jensen as he'd recited Christie's favorite poem. As a bright light and a feeling of great serenity forced the blackness aside, he heard the words.

They seemed so appropriate.

One grand, sweet song.

Author's Note

I hope you enjoyed *Black Sunrise*. If you did, please consider posting a favorable review—I would appreciate it so very much. Also, if you would like to reach out to me, my email address is :

Brett@BrettGodfrey.com.

I always love to hear from my readers!

Black Sunrise is a work of entertainment. It should be read as nothing more. All names, characters, places and events portrayed in the story are used fictitiously. Any resemblance to actual persons, living or dead, businesses, companies, incidents, or locations is purely coincidental. The ideas expressed in the story and in the commentary below are those of the author and do not necessarily represent those of the distributors or sellers of this book.

The Brecht Group does exist—but only in the imaginations of the author and the reader! You will learn more about the Brecht Group in *Convergence of Demons,* the upcoming second book in the Brecht Group series. Christie and Roady have great adventures in store!

Elite private security agencies do exist, and some of them have resources, networks and political connections that come close to those possessed by the Brecht Group. The author has had the privilege of working with some of them.

It is also true, in the author's opinion, that the leader of North

Korea has found himself in an unsolvable quandary. His nation simply cannot continue to sustain itself indefinitely without the infusion of massive resources; he and his paternal ancestors have dreamed of solving that problem by taking back the Republic of Korea—also known as South Korea—by force. The "Democratic Republic" of North Korea has no defensive justification for the size of its military or the obsessive zeal with which it chases the dream of nuclear parity. No one would invade North Korea for any reason other than the defense of the rest of the world from the whimsical impulses of a madman with an atom bomb. Some talk of the "reunification" of the Korean nations, but to the man who owns North Korea, invasion is the object of his longing and his perceived destiny. His recent actions and his professed desire to begin to re-enter the international community of civilized nations fits the pattern of similar false posturing by his father and his grandfather over a period of decades—none of which turned out to be sincere.

History teaches us to be suspicious on that front.

We live in an age of technology that is growing at an exponential rate. As with all of man's great discoveries, we will discover the full benefits—and dangers—of the scientific breakthroughs sitting just beyond the horizon through hard experience.

Most genies can't be put back in the bottle.

There are four new technologies that have long been the subject of science fiction which are on the verge of becoming real—nanotechnology, quantum computing, artificial intelligence and genetic engineering—which will inevitably combine to change the world in ways no living person can accurately predict. When they do emerge, they will converge, and produce a new era for mankind, for better or for worse.

Biological warfare is an even greater threat to mankind than nuclear weaponry. While the proliferation of nuclear weapons represents a grave threat, biological weapon research carries a deadlier potential, for nuclear inventions do not have the ability to reproduce and spread on their own, silently and without detection. Nuclear bombs are not contagious, they are much more difficult to transport, and emit radioactive signatures that can often be detected from space. There is no record kept each time viral particles reproduce to create more of themselves, which can happen in minutes, whereas a single nuclear warhead requires years to manufacture.

It is a cold, hard fact that, in this day and age, a single missing test-tube could end human life on this planet. Our ability to create designer superbugs grows with each passing month. In the author's opinion, the "genius" minds advancing biological weaponry are largely devoid of conscience and may be as motivated by death as Arthur Beeman.

The author knows that his sentiments on some subjects may meet with disagreement from those who enjoyed this book, but if you've come this far, perhaps you will consider whether the following notions carry any weight.

While the author favor gun control, the best approach begins is with the individual. Grip, stance, sight picture, responsible habits of gun ownership and respect for firearms would be sufficient—as they were when the country was young—but for the epidemic of violent crime, punctuated as it is by ever more frequent mass shootings. We must discover the root cause of this phenomenon. It is not the gun; it is something newer, something that has altered the psyche of thousands of people.

The great fictional character Robert Sand thinks that psychotropic medicines may play a role—the author agrees. Of course, Sand has seen the darkest side of the human psyche: for more on this, read the series *Black Samurai* from the 1970's. The author prides himself on the friendship he had with the Marc Olden, the writer of that series who authorized the continued life of his lead character in this book. Thank you, Marc. You will *never* be forgotten.

Human beings with guns do things that are terrible and things that are heroic. Some fear justice; others deliver it. Those among us who are most evil, most insane and most tyrannical must not be allowed to roam *armed* among a population that has been *disarmed* and thus unable to defend itself. Disarming the criminal elements in our society would indeed be the ideal solution if it were not completely impossible due to the hundreds of millions of untraceable firearms that have been scattered throughout this country during the past 100 years.

Some genies can't be put back in the bottle.

Defensive military forces are in scarce supply in movie theaters, classrooms, post offices and churches. The action of everyday citizens to fight back—with weapons—against evil is what is referred to as a "well-armed militia" in the second amendment. Nothing in the history of the Constitution suggests that only those in uniform are entitled to keep and bear arms. The phrase "shall not be infringed" means just exactly that. The second amendment states the reason, but no limitations whatsoever on the protection of that right are included, as none was intended. The words were not selected by happenstance, they were sculpted with great care and clarity. We were expected to read them with the same care and clarity.

This is not to say that we shouldn't try to disarm criminals (Roady Kenehan is particularly good at this), but reality and the basic right of armed self-defense, as guaranteed by the Constitution and natural law, must persevere until better solutions are found. Gun control *is* necessary—starting and ending with the criminal—but if we pretend that the Constitution says that which it clearly does not, no matter how artfully our judges may justify doing so, then our legal precedent will turn back on itself and undermine the core document upon which it is built and we risk the systematic dissolution of the rule of law in western civilization. Thus, gun control can only be achieved legally if the Constitutional right to keep and bear arms is amended for the sake legal consistency and intellectual honesty.

While this book—among many others—aggrandizes and romanticizes the exploits of Tier One special forces, the heroic accomplishments and sacrifices of ordinary troops go largely unacknowl-edged. Rarely are the members of our military shown the deep ap-preciation they deserve. We allow them to board flights first, and we say, "thank you for your service" with the same automaticity that way we say "gesundheit" when someone sneezes, but our treatment of veterans who are in need of medical, psychological and financial help is appalling. We can, and must, do better for those who are will-ing to sacrifice everything to keep us safe.

How do we protect ourselves from the risks that our technologies, including guns, atom bombs, deadly microbes, and the much more powerful threats we are just now perfecting in order to protect our-selves from our ever-growing capacity for inadvertent self-destruc-tion?

The sagacity to accomplish this task will come not from our scien-tists or industrialists, but from our courts, through reason enlight-ened by sophisticated advocacy.

This is why I made Mark Jensen a lawyer—and why I am a lawyer.

As we see in this book, private citizens, working with the right tools, can often accomplish what governmental agencies cannot. Many of our most powerful tech companies were started by individ-ual persons. This is why we must, at all costs, protect individual lib-erty and free enterprise. Just as we seek to build a compassionate so-ciety, we must protect freedom within society. We must always strive to be worthy of our inalienable rights. We must behave as an enlight-ened people, which means that as individuals, we must each behave in a way that reflects positively on our status as members of free na-tions. Those who read these words who are not citizens of free na-tions must, like Mark Jensen, find a way to persevere and protect that which is most sacred. We must root out of our souls the urge to de-value our fellow man. Treating our brothers and sisters as enemies because of their race, national origin, color, sexual preference or oth-er superficial considerations is evidence of nothing other than mind-less barbarity.

Protecting our borders is utterly essential due to the tide flowing into America of human traffickers, drug-dealers, criminal syndicates, enemy state-agents, terrorists and others who would destroy our way of life. That said, losing our humanity in the process makes the protection of our great nation's borders purposeless. We must earn the protections and freedoms that we demand. Many *native* Americans wish this land had been closed to outsiders two centuries ago; the ancestors of the rest of us entered into the land of liberty and made it what it is and what it yet could be, but in the process decimated cultures of no less intrinsic value than any other.

We are a species searching for a way out of darkness. We live in a world where the strong tend to prosper and the weak tend to perish. Idealism alone will not solve our problems, any more than will violence. We must learn to come together and work as one to build a society better than any that has come before. Or perish.

What we must have is not merely knowledge.

We require wisdom.

About the Author

Brett Godfrey is a trial lawyer who lives in Denver, Colorado. He is the founding partner of Godfrey | Johnson, P.C., a law firm that handles complex technological and scientific litigation throughout the US and eight other countries. Before becoming a lawyer, he was an Air Force officer, and before that, he was a practicing chemical engineer.

He is an experienced pilot, trained in several martial arts, skilled in defensive pistol tactics and gunsmithing, and was a competition skydiver for many years.

He is also a painter of western landscapes. His paintings are viewable at:

http://www.brettgodfrey.com.

He is currently working on his next two novels: *Convergence of Demons*, a story about Roady Kenehan and Christie Jensen, and *Kilik's Detour*, the first novel in a terrific new series about a great leader who traveled farther than any man in history and who shaped history in the process.

Made in the USA
Coppell, TX
25 November 2020

42083382R00247